MW00654591

Copyright © **2016** by **Amb**

Typewriter Pub, an imprint of Blvnp Incorporated
A Nevada Corporation
1887 Whitney Mesa DR #2002
Henderson, NV 89014
www.typewriterpub.com/info@typewriterpub.com

ISBN: 978-1-68030-737-5

DISCLAIMER
This book is a work of fiction. The characters, incidents, and dialogue are drawn from the author's imagination and are not to be construed as real. While references might be made to actual historical events or existing locations, the names, characters, places, and incidents are either products of the author's imagination or are used fictitiously, and any resemblance to actual persons living or dead, business establishments, events or locales is entirely coincidental.

THE RUN

AMBER LEE

I dedicate this book to those who I love and those who have loved me.

CHAPTER ONE

The recognizable smell of the lake fills her lungs. She can feel the water, lapping around her waist and cooling her overheated skin. It's such a warm day and after being outside for most of it, the family has decided to jump in; clothes on and all. She can hear her siblings giggling and laughing as splashing and half-hearted threats fill the air around her.

She spots a duck, one of the many who calls this lake their home. They often don't hang around when she and the family come to the lake, scared off by the threat that they presumably pose, but this duck has stayed. Its small black eyes, meeting her own gaze in near defiance. Then, it parts its bright colored beak and lets out a shrill loud noise.

She frowns, confusion setting in. That isn't the sound a duck makes, is it?

Again, it makes that offending noise. Then again and again and again.

Rae's fist hits the top of the alarm clock as she groans and rolls onto her back, staring up at the patchy white ceiling above. She contemplates how long she'll get away with just laying here this time. One mississippi. Two mississippi. When she reaches a new record of twenty-four mississippis, three knocks sound on the outside of her door. *Huh*, she thinks, it must be a slow morning for everyone.

Every damn morning is like clockwork.

1

"Rae, Cassidy won't let me in the bathroom." Her nine-year-old sister, Poppy, calls through her door. "Can I use yours?"

Not wanting to get up, Rae just yells back, "Did you bribe her?"

"Yes. She said she won't come out, and I really have to pee!"

"Did you ask Jace for help?" She calls back, referring to their sixteen-year-old brother.

"He said to ask you."

With a groan, Rae sits up and runs a hand through her chin-length blonde hair, getting her hands stuck in a knot. Sitting on the edge of her bed, she stretches her toes until they crack—a habit after years of ballet—and manages to find the will to get to the door. Opening the door, a blur of blonde hair and gray long Johns goes flying past her before her bathroom door is slammed shut behind it.

Well, Rae thinks with a yawn, *guess she really did have to pee.*

Heading for her dresser, Rae picks out her work clothes and throws them on her bed, waiting patiently for Poppy to finish. When she hears the toilet flush, she leans against the doorframe with a raised brow. Poppy reemerges from the bathroom looking a little embarrassed and a small smile in place.

"Good morning," Rae greets.

"Good morning. Sorry about that."

Rolling her eyes, Rae ruffles her sister's already rat nested hair. "No worries, kiddo. You sleep okay?"

Poppy grins and nods, making her glasses bounce a little. "Yup. I had a dream the moon was populated with unicorns that mined skittles with their horns."

"Sounds like an awesome dream."

"It was. Hey, Rae?"

"Yeah?"

"Can I have skittles for breakfast?"

"Not in your life. Now go get ready for school."

2

Poppy pouts at her. "Will you braid my hair?"

"Sure, but you're going to have to make it quick. I already told Cassidy last night I'd braid hers too."

"Okay!" she shouts before running out of the room and down the hallway towards her room.

Rae rolls her eyes and is about to shut her bedroom door so she can get dressed when she hears her sister shriek. This one is her seventeen-year-old sister, Cleo. Since hitting the teen years, Cleo has been a handful, but the older she gets, it seems to Rae that she only gets worse.

"Cassidy, get out of the bathroom now!"

Cassidy, their six-year-old sister, opens the door to yell back at Cleo, "No! Go away!"

Deciding to just let them deal with it, Rae shuts her door and locks it before heading back towards her bed. Stripping off her nightclothes, Rae replaces them with her cleanest pair of jean shorts and her white button up short-sleeved work shirt. The words 'Peter's Patties' is written on the back and left breast with red lettering.

Rae corrects her collar and straightens out the gold charm necklace around her neck. It was a gift from her mother on her fourteenth birthday, the year of Rae's first shift. Rae, like her father, is a werewolf and up to this point, the only one of her siblings able to shift. Her mother gifted her a gold moon charm to go along with the four-leaf clover she gave her on her birthday. Before she passed, she also added a heart to remind her of the love in her life.

Rae lets go of the necklace and gets back to getting ready, not wanting to dwell too much on thinking about her mom. It's been three years since the six Applebee siblings lost their mother to brain aneurysm and their father to grief, but none of them have been able to get over it. Losing your parents in a one-two punch is never easy, especially when the youngest is just three years old, and the oldest, Rae herself, was only sixteen.

Despite the hard times, Rae has pulled her family by bootstraps and made sure they stay together, no matter what. It is what Rae knows her mother would have wanted, and Rae plans to keep that promise she made on the day of the funeral. She would keep them together no matter what.

Parting her hair down the middle, Rae puts her pink-tipped hair in twin low pigtails and puts on her watch. Grabbing her fringed brown leather satchel and black beaten down converse, she goes through a mental checklist to make sure she's got everything. She's pretty sure she does, but her track record isn't so good.

"Rae, I'm ready!" Poppy yells through the door.

Unlocking the door, Rae opens the door to see both Cassidy and Poppy, this time ready to have their blonde tangles tamed. Poppy with her large blue eyes, glasses, and blonde hair looks a lot like their father while Cassidy, also blonde, has their dad's brown eyes. Whistling, Rae moves towards the stairs, grabbing the brush and hair ties in her hands as she passes the girls.

"So you girls excited? It's almost the fall equinox," Rae asks as she walks down the stairs.

"Fall what?" Cassidy asks, screwing up her face adorably.

"Equinox," Poppy tells her slowly. "It means that there will be equal parts of night and day from now on. Usually, the pack does the celebrations, you know the ones when we're stuck with Hudson for the night while they all go and party."

"We do not go out all night and party. We just do the rituals of the pack, Poppy, you know that," Rae corrects, but it falls on deaf ears.

"Hudson is so boring, though," Poppy whines. "He doesn't let us do anything!"

"That's not true," Hudson's voice objects from the bottom of the stairs. Hudson is the semi-middle child in the Applebee clan at the age of fourteen, and with his brown hair and brown eyes, looks the most like their father. "I let you watch those stupid *Twilight* movies."

"They're not stupid!" Cassidy yells. "Edward is my boyfriend!"

Rae winces at her volume, but it's Hudson who speaks up. "Cassidy, you're too little for boyfriends."

"I am not!"

"Jacob's my boyfriend, and I'm not too young," Poppy adds.

"Yes, you are," Hudson tells her. "No boys until you're both thirty."

"Rae!" Both girls shriek.

"What the hell is going in here?"

Rae slaps her hand over her face as her brother Jace gets into the mix. Jace got the quirky genes in the family, giving him red shaggy hair and freckles along with their mom's blue eyes. With the small black gages in his ear and lip ring, Rae can't help but think he looks adorable. He hates it when she says that, but she can't help herself. In her mind, he'll always be her baby brother.

"Hudson said we can't have a boyfriend until we're old and gross!" Poppy tells Jace.

Jace's eyebrows shoot up, and he gives Rae a "what the hell" look. Rae just shrugs and smiles at him. She really has no words to go into why two young girls shouldn't even be interested in boys, let alone a sparkly vegetarian and a giant whiny puppy. When she was Cassidy's age, all Rae liked was eating mud and throwing sticks at the ducks in the pond.

"I don't know why you'd want to like boys, anyway. They have gross germs."

"No, they don't," Poppy denies but sounds unsure.

"They do," Jace insists with a nod of his head. "Every boy who is related to you has these gross germs that can only affect you. They make you sick, make your stomach hurt, and can sometimes turn you into zombies."

"And that's where I'm going to stop you," Rae says, suddenly clapping her hands. "Come on girls, you gotta eat."

5

"I'm not hungry," Poppy says, holding her stomach.

"Me neither."

Rae gives Jace a dirty look which he only shrugs at. Rolling his eyes when she gives him a silent warning, he sighs. "I made chocolate chip pancakes."

"I call the big one!" Poppy yells before running for the kitchen, only to have Cassidy run after her.

With both the girls gone, Rae gives Jace a flat look. "Zombies? Really?"

"Hey, it'll keep them away from the boys," Jace states with a shrug.

"Keep who away from boys?"

Jace, Hudson, and Rae all look up to see Cleo walking down the stairs and grimace. Today, she's dressed in high-waisted red shorts too short to be legal, a white half shirt, and a leather jacket. Her shoes are black platforms, and she's wearing a daisy tattoo choker on her neck which Rae is pretty sure is attempting to hide a hickey.

Cleo has been dressing more and more provocatively lately, and from what Rae's been hearing, it's not going to waste. She's just happy they got Cleo on birth control at fifteen and had "the talk." At this point, Rae is pretty sure that's all she can do without making her run away again, claiming Rae is "stifling" her. Maybe she is, but Rae would rather stifle her sister than have her sister knocked up and running off with some jerk off boyfriend.

"Nothing," Rae dismisses, deliberately not reacting to her sister's behavior as usual. "Jace, do you need a ride today or are you good?"

"Actually, Shane and Connor are going to pick me up today."

"Hudson?"

"I'll take the ride."

Rae nods before turning to Cleo. "How about you?"

6

"Ride in the Scooby Doo van with you? No thank you." Cleo scoffs.

"Suit yourself." Rae sighs before waving the brush and hair ties in her hair. "Now, if you'll excuse me I have some hair to tie into submission."

She's about to move towards the kitchen when Jace grabs her arm and stops her. Speaking lowly, he tells her, "The alpha called this morning."

"What did he say?" Rae asks past her dry throat.

"Said he needs you to stop by before you go to work today."

"Did he say why?"

Jace shakes his head, "No, but with the equinox coming up . . . I'm sure you can guess."

"But . . . I can't do it this year."

"Rae, you're nineteen," Jace says sadly. "You were exempted last year due to our circumstances, but he's not going to let it slide this time. We all have to do it; it's just a rite of passage."

Rae hangs her head and grunts, "I don't want to."

"Oh, come on, it's not that bad," Jace says, hitting his shoulder with hers. "It's just a chance for people to find their mates, Rae. There's no guarantee you will so why not just go on with it, have some fun, and make the alpha a happy man. He'll be off your back, and you'll be off the hook another year. Besides, Phillip went last year, and he found his mate. She even accepted him, poor woman. So I'm sure your mate will look past your ugly face too."

Laughing a little, Rae punches his arm. "Ass."

"You love me."

"Like a rash I can't shake."

"Why would you shake a rash?" he asks, faking stupid.

Pushing his head, he chuckles as he goes towards the kitchen to eat with their other siblings. Rae pinches her lower lip between her fingers and thinks over everything Jace said. *He has a point,* she realizes. If she just goes to the damn Run this year, the alpha will let it go, and she can just go on with her life.

But what if she finds her mate? She thinks faintly.

"No," she mumbles out loud to herself. "That'll never happen."

Shaking her head, Rae heads into the kitchen, ready to start the beginning of what is sure to be a very long day.

CHAPTER TWO

Rae feels her nerves knotting her stomach as she pulls the van up outside the alpha's house. When she puts it into park, she winces as the clutch gives out. She hates driving stick, but this VW van is the only thing she could find on her limited budget that could fit everyone in it.

Angling the rearview mirror, Rae checks her hair. Usually, she couldn't care what she looks like but when faced with seeing the ultimate authority figure, she imagines looking presentable wouldn't hurt. So after smoothing down a few stray strands of hair and pinching her cheeks a little so she doesn't look so scared shitless, she sits back with a sigh.

Better get this done sooner or later.

Climbing out of the van, she shuts the door hard knowing that if she doesn't, it won't stay shut. That was how the van lost its radio the first time. Currently, it's on its third radio, and this one Rae isn't too keen on losing. Putting her satchel over her head, the strap cuts across her chest as she grips it for dear life while approaching the alpha house.

The house is unsurprisingly huge but also has a down home feel about it. It's not too stuffy or modern. In fact, it kind of reminds Rae of a plantation style home with the double porches, white columns, and orange trees planted outside with little flowers sprinkled here and there. It's the kind of home Rae wishes she could raise the kids in but knows it'll take a hell of a lot more money to achieve.

Her knuckles are about to hit the wood of the front door when it suddenly swings open to show the beaming alpha female. Alpha Julia looks as beautiful as ever with her long strawberry blonde hair in two braids, bright blue eyes, and creamy white skin. She's dressed in a flowing navy blue sundress with bare feet.

"Ah, Rae! Were we expecting you?"

Rae puts on a polite smile, "Yeah, Jace told me that the alpha wanted me to stop by."

Smacking her forehead with the palm of her hand, Alpha Julia rolls her eyes. "Of course! Kendrick told me, but I'm so hair-brained these days I completely forgot. Come in, come in!"

Walking in with a quick bow of her head, Rae stands in the colorful entry. "How is the little new addition?"

This is actually the first time Rae is actually speaking with the alpha female beyond pleasantries. Alpha Julia and Alpha Kendrick only found each other about five years ago, and Rae hasn't seen her since her mother's funeral three years before. So just to be safe, she's trying to be on her best behavior.

Alpha Julia grins at the mention of her new baby. "Great! I'm just glad he isn't having colic like Sadie did. I swear the first year of her life all she did was cry."

"I'll take your word for it." She smiles.

"Do you want some tea or anything while you wait? Kendrick had to run to the border quick to check with his Beta. I don't know why he didn't remind me you were coming before he left, though."

"Alphas have a lot on their mind. I'm sure he was just too concerned with other things to remember such a small detail as my visit."

Rae almost wants to gag as she says it but with alphas, it's better to just pretend you're less than them, or it could set off their wolf. Alpha wolves are terribly touchy about real or perceived

10

disrespect. They fought for their position, and the paranoia about having it taken away makes them edgy. It's one of the reason a lot of non-ranked wolves don't like having direct one-on-one conversations with them. It's like walking on egg shells the whole time.

"Oh, whatever," Alpha Julia says with a wave of her hand. "He's just as exhausted as I am with Noah. He probably was just lumbering around like some zombie and totally forgot."

Rae blinks. "I-If you say so, Alpha."

"Please, just call me Julia."

"Um . . ."

She smiles softly at her. "Or would you be more comfortable with Alpha Julia?"

Sighing gratefully Rae nods. "Yes, please."

"Oh, all right."

Suddenly, the front door bursts open, making both women jump. Julia purses her lips and rolls her eyes when she catches her mate's scent while Rae only goes stiff. Rae's wolf is restless too, just being in the room with an alpha, she's so used to the relaxed atmosphere of being with her family it's putting them both on edge.

Julia surprises Rae by patting her hand comfortingly. "Don't worry, sweetheart, he's like a teddy bear once you get to know him."

Alpha Kendrick is in his mid-thirties with short brown hair, gray eyes, and tanned skin. He's very handsome objectively but definitely not Rae's type. Actually, Rae's not sure she has a type. She hasn't dated since her freshman year in high school, so it's hard to say.

"Miss Applebee," Alpha Kendrick says with surprise. "Was I expecting you today?"

"Uh, my brother Jace said you called."

He frowns before realization comes over his face. "Oh! Right. Sorry about that. Do you mind coming up to my office?"

11

Hesitantly, Rae gets to her feet and nods. "Of course, Alpha."

Pointing for her to follow him, Rae does so with her head bowed. Of course, that doesn't stop her from curling her nose a bit at the smell of his BO. Just because he's an alpha doesn't mean he smells any better than anyone else. Though compared to Hudson, after he comes home from basketball practice, he might as well be a bouquet of roses to Rae.

"How are the Applebee's these days?" the alpha asks as they walk up the stairs.

"We're doing fine, Alpha."

"You still doing pack daycare, Rae?"

Rae nods then mentally smacks herself when she realizes his back is to her. "Yes, Alpha. I also work at the diner in town, Peter's Patties."

"Two jobs?" he asks, frowning at her over his shoulder. "How does that work?"

"I work at the diner during the week and then do pack daycare on the weekends and the occasional weeknight."

"Peter's Patties, you said? Is that Peter Falkner's place?"

"Yes, sir."

The alpha stops at a door and enters inside. Rae follows dutifully though still a bit wary of the reason behind this whole conversation. The alpha's office is surprisingly bright. It's all whites, silvers, and dark blues with the décor, reminding Rae of a naval theme. Gesturing towards the one chair in the room, the alpha sits behind the massive desk before her.

"What about a boyfriend?" he asks her suddenly. "Has anyone caught your eye?"

Rae frowns at the question, unsure where he's going with this. "N-No, Sir. I've been busy with work and the family."

"Then why are you so opposed to participating in the run? It's a way for young people, such as yourself, to find their other half."

Rae sighs and bows her head. "Can I be blunt, Alpha?"

"Please do."

"I don't want to participate because it seems a bit archaic, don't you think? I mean I'm only nineteen, and I have way too much on my plate to be even thinking of a forever relationship. Besides what if my mate expects me to come to his pack? I can't do that with my siblings being as young as they are. This pack is all they've known."

"You could leave them here," he suggests.

Rae's jaw clenches. "I'm not abandoning them."

"I hear you have an aunt and uncle within the pack boundaries, they even have a son that's a member of the pack. Why not send them to live with them?"

"Jojo and Everett are great people, but I can take care of them myself."

"That's a lot of responsibility for one so young," he observes.

Rae shrugs. "It's not as much of a burden as it would seem. I like the fact that I can keep my family together despite whatever happens. I take pride in that."

"As you should."

Rae stares at her fingers as silence comes over them. It seems they're at an impasse. Well, it seems that way until the alpha speaks again, and his tone tells her that it's a done deal.

"The Run will be next weekend. I expect to see you there, Miss Applebee."

Rae sighs and bows her head heavily. "Yes, Sir."

* * *

"Order up!"

Rae scowls at the newly placed plates on the ledge as she picks them up. Carrying them over to the table, she's practically stomping as she walks. She's just so pissed she barely knows what

13

to do with herself. Damn alphas, acting all high and mighty telling her what to do. Who do they think they are? Who appointed them anyway?

"Here," she grunts as she sets the plates on the table. Giving a plastic smile, she smiles at the young couple before her. "Enjoy."

Dropping the smile immediately, she turns to head back behind the counter when she rams right into a brick wall of body. Looking up, she makes a face while rolling her eyes. Just figures, he would show up when she's already in a shit mood.

"Hey, baby." Graham grins down at her.

"Not today, Graham."

He chuckles as she sidesteps him. Graham is the nephew of the Beta who thinks he's hot shit. He's cute, sure, but he's also obnoxious. He also likes to bother Rae more than anyone else just to get a rise out of her. It's almost a hobby for him, and though Rae has put her foot up his ass more than once, he can't take a hint. Still, she can't help but like having a friend, even if he is an annoying one.

"Bad day, sweetness?"

She grimaces at the pet name. "Can you just . . . not. I'm serious, Graham. Today is not the day to make my life harder than it has to be."

His smirk falls into a frown. "Are you okay? One of the kids?"

"No, thank god," she breathes with a shake of her head.

"Then what is it?"

Giving the place a quick one over, she dips her head to whisper, "The alpha is making me do the run this year. No excuses, no free passes, and no more ignoring my lack of attendance."

"Well, shit." Graham chuckles. "That's all? Here I thought you were about to go all John Green novel on me and die."

"You read his books?" she asks with an arched brow.

14

He shifts in his chair, looking embarrassed. "No. My sister, Violet, made me go see that movie with her."

"Really? Did you cry?"

"Damn it, Rae! I'm trying to be a nice guy here."

Rae laughs but puts her hands up in surrender. "Okay, okay. I'm sorry."

He nods, looking more comfortable.

"But seriously, did you cry?"

"Rae." He warns her flatly.

"Okay!" She laughs with a grin. "I'll stop now."

"Thank you," he grunts. "But seriously *that* has ruined your day? Most girls would die to be able to do that whole fairytale bullshit."

Rae rolls her brown eyes. "Yeah, well, I think we both know I'm not most girls."

Graham chuckles. "True. So, no out?"

"No out."

Leaning forward, he puts his hand on her shoulder. "Tough shit, kid. So I guess you only have this week to accept my offer of a date before some 'dreamy' guy comes to take you away from me."

Pushing his arm off, Rae gives him a flat look. "For the three-millionth time, no."

"But this could be our last chance!"

"Graham, there wasn't even a first chance."

He clutches his heart dramatically. "Baby don't go breaking my heart like that! You know you're the only one for me, and yet you reject me."

"I'm sure you'll survive."

"Of a broken heart? Never!"

Chuckling, she shakes her head before the bell dings again. "Order up!"

Sighing, she gets back to work. At least it'll help her get her mind off things for a while. If she can say anything about the diner, it's that it may be dull, but it keeps her busy.

Lord knows she needs it.

CHAPTER THREE

Drumming her fingers on the steering wheel, Rae bobs her head along with the music pouring from her speakers. It was a long day at the diner, but Graham was there to make sure she wasn't able to fall out of sorts for long. Since the town is fairly small and along with the population, all the schools are connected, making it easier for her to pick everyone up.

It's a relief most days especially after those days that just won't end, to have more stops before home. Letting the purposely soothing music flow over her, she closes her eyes and rolls her head side-to-side, hoping to crack her neck. She's so tense.

She really needs to let her wolf out, she realizes. With the equinox coming up and the run coming into play, she needs to let her out as often as possible. The full moons are always dreaded among the lycanthropes of the world. When a full moon comes into the play, especially the first one of the month, it makes for one miserable wolf. They're locked in the body, unable to come out during those times, totally enslaved to the human side.

It was one of the reasons the run was created. Not only is it a great way for mates to find each other but also for a wolf to relieve some of its frustration. For that, Rae gets it, but the rest of it? She'd rather do without.

"Rae!"

Snapping out of her thoughts, she turns to see her younger sisters crawling into the van. Poppy is wearing a huge grin on her face as she climbs in while Cassidy is wrestling with her backpack. Hudson comes up behind the youngest Applebee and helps her close her bag. He then helps Cassidy get into the van quickly before coming to sit in the front passenger with Rae.

"Cleo?" Rae asks.

Hudson just shakes his head as he puts on his seatbelt. Hudson has always been the quietest of her siblings. He's always ready to help when needed but mostly keeps to himself, enjoying reading in his room or wandering in the woods on his own. Rae has always felt a kinship with him since she's of similar temperament.

"Everyone buckled in?"

"Yes!" The girls yell in chorus, making Rae roll her eyes.

As she pulls away from the school, Rae spots Cleo in the parking lot with a boy, practically dry humping each other. Rae usually ignores the shit Cleo pulls knowing it's for a reaction, but this time, she's just trying to stop a niece or nephew in progress. Stopping the van near them, Rae pushes down on the horn until they separate from each other. Cleo looks around until her blue eyes land on the van and glare at Rae.

"What?" Cleo yells.

"Need a ride?" Rae asks innocently.

Her sister scowls at her. "No. I'm fine."

"You sure? I have plenty of room. What about you, handsome? Need a ride?"

The boy looks completely flustered. "Uh . . . no, I'm fine. I have my own car."

"That's great." Rae grins, before narrowing her eyes threateningly. "That better be all you'll be riding while around my sister."

"I . . . uh . . . well . . . I . . ."

"Rae!" Cleo shrieks.

Rae just blows her a kiss. "I'll see you at home, baby sis!"

Driving away, Rae smiles smugly to herself. Cleo hasn't always been this way, of course. She used to be a sweet girl, but after their mother's death and their father's disappearance, Cleo changed. Rae gets it; she really does, because she too has a hard time even three years later with it. Still, that doesn't give Cleo the license to act like such a bitch, especially to her family.

"She's going to be spitting fire when she gets home," Hudson comments as they pull off of school grounds.

Rae shrugs. "Then let her."

"You have to tell her."

Her hands tighten on the steering wheel. "It'll just upset her. You finding out wasn't even supposed to happen."

"Rae, it's her dad too, and you can't protect us from everything."

"I can try."

"If you try too much you're not only going to wear yourself out, but you'll fail. We're going to screw things up Rae. It's just how people are."

Sighing, Rae doesn't respond, though she knows he's right. After their mother died, their father suddenly disappeared. Most of the pack believed that he went into the woods and simply gave in to the grief. It was what Rae and the kids thought too, until about two years ago, Rae saw him.

He was in his wolf form, but it was definitely their dad. He was skinny, feral, and skittish, but she could pick out those brown eyes from anywhere. Ever since then, she's been feeding him, petting him when he allows her to, and talks to him about how the family's doing. She doesn't know if he really even recognizes her, but she likes to think that maybe he does.

It's most likely a lie she likes to tell herself.

She didn't tell her siblings, of course. She didn't want them to see their father like that instead of as the man he was. Rae can see it in his eyes when he looks at her, the lost look and wildness there. Their father isn't there anymore; the wolf has completely taken over so why let them suffer over it like she does?

19

Of course, Hudson, on one of his late night walks stumbled on them. He immediately started tearing up, but when he tried to reach out to their father, the wolf ran away. Hudson demanded to know everything, and Rae, trying to explain herself and calm him down, told him. Ever since then, he's been also coming in the meetings but not as often as at first. It's hard for him.

"Rae?" Cassidy calls from the back of the van.

Sitting up a little so can see her in the rearview, Rae responds, "Yeah?"

"Where's Jace?"

"Uh . . ." she trails off, looking over at Hudson.

"Friends," he grunts, not looking up from his cell phone.

Rae shrugs. "I guess he's with a friend, kiddo. Why?"

"I saw him kissing a girl! It's not fair! He said I couldn't have a boyfriend, but he can kiss girls? That's gross! I just want to hold hands with boys!"

"Well, I guess he'll turn into a gross zombie, won't he?"

Cassidy makes a face. "Will he still live with us?"

"Maybe. I think I have the antidote somewhere, but I'll have to look when we get home."

"Okay." Cassidy nods seriously. "But make sure you do it before dinner cause Jace said he'd make me a grilled cheese sandwich."

"I can make you one, Cass," Rae says, rolling her eyes.

"You don't make it like Jace does!"

"Alright!" Rae exclaims. "I will give him the antidote as soon as he comes home, okay?"

"Okay." Cassidy shrugs before going back to looking out the window.

Shaking her head, Rae looks back out the front window feeling exhausted. She needs a shower or maybe a swim in the lake. That always calms her down. Pushing a strand of hair behind her ear, she decides that's what she'll do once all the kids are down for the night.

20

"Who are you texting?" Rae asks Hudson.

"John."

"Who?" she asks with a frown.

"Just a guy I know." He shrugs.

"You didn't meet him on the Internet or something, did you?"

Hudson snorts. "No. He's from school. We're doing a project at school together."

"Oh? What project?"

"Rae." He sighs, putting his phone down. "You're my sister. I love you, and I get that you're trying to be involved, but you're annoying the crap out of me. It's an English project. He's my partner, and we're texting to get a schedule to figure out when to get together."

"I'm just asking," she says, putting her hands up in surrender.

He rolls his brown eyes. "Sure."

"By the way, I love you, too, kid." Rae smiles at him.

He doesn't respond, but she sees a smile on his face.

* * *

"This one!" Cassidy yells, grabbing the large book from the shelf.

Poppy groans from beside Rae. "Not again!"

"We've read this one a hundred times, Cassie. Are you sure?" Rae asks from her position on the large queen-sized bed the girl's share.

Cassidy nods, making her blonde hair flop all over the place. "I love this story. Please, Rae? I'll let everyone in the bathroom tomorrow, I promise!"

"What do you even do in there?" Rae asks, genuinely curious.

Cassidy's face is straight as she answers, "I get pretty for the day. Brush my teeth and my hair, make faces in the mirror, and make sure my armpits don't smell."

"Why would your armpits smell?"

"Because I run a lot in my dreams and if you run a lot, you smell."

Rae and Poppy give each other looks before Rae puts her hand out for the book. "Good point. Okay, crawl on it."

Handing her the book, Cassidy climbs into the bed to sit on the other side of Rae. Cracking open the book, Rae clears her throat.

She asked Cassidy once why she liked this book so much to which the six-year-old replied that it was just how it was. Cassidy was growing up to be a little odd, but Rae couldn't help but love it.

So without a second more of hesitation, she begins to read the story of a little girl called Alice who fell down a rabbit hole into a world called Wonderland.

"All in the golden afternoon full leisurely we glide,
For both our oars with little skill,
By little arms are plied,
While little hands make vain pretense
Our wanderings to guide.
Thus grew the tale of Wonderland."

About an hour later, Cassidy is asleep in Rae's lap, Poppy is yawning every five seconds. Slowly closing the book, Rae places it by her feet before gently maneuvering Cassidy off her lap. The little girl frowns and whines a little before going right back to sleep with small pouted lips and a scowl. Poppy is easier to move but since she's still half awake, it doesn't surprise Rae when she speaks up.

"Rae?"

"Yeah?"

"Do you think Jace will really turn into a zombie?"

Laughing a little, Rae shakes her head. "No, baby, I don't think he will."

"Good." She yawns. "Good night, Rae."

"Good night, Poppy."

Kissing her sister's forehead, she also slips off her glasses to place it on the side table. Moving a few strands of hair out of Cassidy's face, she also kisses her forehead before turning off the light. Shutting the door slowly, she sighs once it's closed all the way.

"Are they asleep?"

She turns around to see Cleo stumbling up the stairs. Her eyes are bloodshot, and her shoes are in her hands, dangling. Rae's tension comes back with a vengeance when she catches the smell of weed and alcohol on her—Vodka, to be more specific.

"Yeah, they are."

"They love you."

"And I love them."

Cleo smiles sloppily. "Do you love me?"

"Of course I love you."

"Then why can't you just let me be?"

Rae rolls her eyes and tries to move past her to head towards her room. Cleo reaches out though and grabs her by the arm making Rae growl at her. She doesn't like being grabbed, and she really doesn't like it when it's keeping her trapped.

Cleo giggles. "Oh my, did I wake the big bad wolf?"

"Fuck off, Cleo."

"I try to but then you just drag me back, don't you? Why can't I just go live with Aunt Jolene and Uncle Everett, Rae? Why won't you let me out of this fucking prison?"

"Because this isn't a prison." Rae hisses at her. "I have done everything I can to keep this family together with a roof over our heads, food in our stomachs, and clothes on our backs. And do you appreciate any of it? No!"

"How can I when all you do is dictate what I should or shouldn't do! I don't know if you forget this Rae, but you're not mom! She's dead, and she isn't coming back, but that doesn't mean you can play house with all of us!"

23

Rae's hands curl into fists. "Keep your voice down."

"Make me." She smirks at her. "Can you, Miss Self-control? Can you even let that wolf of yours slip out? I bet she doesn't even know what it's like to feel the wind through her fur anymore. You don't deserve a wolf."

"And you do?"

"At least I know how to live a life!"

Rae's about to speak but is cut off by the sound of a door cracking open. Turning towards it, Rae sees Poppy standing in the bedroom doorway, looking scared. Cleo immediately lets go of Rae's arm and takes a few steps back.

"What's wrong?" Poppy asks.

"Nothing," Rae says, not taking her eyes off Cleo. "Just go back to bed."

"Rae . . ."

"Poppy, go back to bed, please."

The door shuts and Rae takes a few steps coming towards Cleo with her eyes cold enough to make the younger girl flinch. "I have done nothing but try to keep this family together, Cleo. Do you think I don't want a life? A mate? Of course, I do, but I can't even imagine those things because you come first."

"So what . . ." Cleo says, struggling to not to lose her anger. "You want an award or something?"

Rae shakes her head with a sigh. "I'm done talking to you tonight. Go to bed and sleep it off. We'll talk in the morning."

Moving past her sister, Rae goes down the stairs. At the foot of which she finds Hudson and Jace giving her sad looks. Not wanting any pity from them, she doesn't say a word to them as she moves towards the front door. Opening it, she exits the house without looking back.

Once the coast is clear, tears begin falling down her face as she walks through the tall grass towards the lake. Her arms are crossed over her chest as she cries, trying to keep herself together but failing miserably. Does she want a mate? Yes, of course, she does. It's only out of fear of change and what could happen to her family that keeps her from participating in the run.

A fear of happiness for herself that keeps her running from a mate she hasn't even met.

Once the lake comes into view, Rae's bare feet step onto the wooden dock gingerly. She remembers playing in the lake with her parent's happily. She remembers what it was like splashing with Cleo and being able to hug her without her sister telling her she hated her. She remembers not having to force herself to smile and laughing without it sounding so rare. She remembers being happy.

Stripping out of her jean shorts and the plain blue t-shirt she changed into before dinner, she sits on the edge of the dock. Pulling her hair from her pigtails, she adds the ties to her pile and runs her hands through her stringy hair. Closing her eyes, she balances her arms on the edge of the dock and slides her body into the cool lake water.

The water laps at her hips as she moves her hands over the dark water. Angling her head up, she looks at the crescent moon in the sky with her cheeks wet and heart heavy. Walking further into the lake water, she holds her breath as it flows over her head. As she lets out a scream into the water, quiet and unheard, a quote from *Alice in Wonderland* floats through her head.

"I can't go back to yesterday because I was a different person then."

CHAPTER FOUR

The kitchen is silent in the morning when Rae walks in. The girls are sitting at the breakfast bar, while Jace is in his usual place behind the stove. Hudson is at the kitchen table with a book in his hand and a bagel frozen mid-bite in his grasp. Cleo is sitting on a windowsill with a cup of coffee in her hands and her eyes glued to whatever is outside.

Rae lifts a brow at everyone, and they quickly go back to eating, but none of it looks relaxed. The only one who seems unaffected is Cassidy, who is humming to herself while picking out the brown pieces from her *Lucky Charms*. Moving towards the fruit bowl on the counter, Rae kisses the top of Cassidy's head, making the little girl swat her away.

Smiling slightly, Rae takes a green apple from the bowl before leaning over to take a knife out of the stand. Jace's eyes watch her every move like a hawk, but Rae just gives him a dirty look. It's not like she'd stab Cleo for heaven's sake, and besides, she's not nearly awake enough to commit assaults just yet.

Sitting down at the kitchen table across from Hudson, Rae cuts into the apple before putting a slice to her mouth. She learned this little habit from her father. When she was in her teens, she had braces, and she couldn't really bite into things at first. So her dad taught her how to cut up an apple without losing a finger. The habit stuck with her even after her braces came off.

The silence continues until suddenly the front door slams open and a tornado comes in without hesitation. This tornado, though, is named Jolene or Jojo to those who know her best. Jolene is Rae's aunt on her father's side, and since the passing of their mother and disappearance of their father, has been a constant source of love for all of them.

"Jojo!" Cassidy and Poppy yell in unison before jumping off their stools.

Both girls nearly tackle the petite brunette, but she manages to stay upright. "Well, a mighty hello to you too, girls."

"Jojo, did you bring us any treats?" Cassidy asks, puppy dog look in place.

Jolene puts a finger on her chin in thought. "I may have, but that depends on if you've been good girls."

"We have!" They yell in unison again while jumping around.

Jolene's hazel eyes move over to Rae who just shrugs as she puts another slice of apple into her mouth. Rae hears a crinkle before the girls scream, making everyone but Rae, jump at the sound. She's so used to the screams of kids at this point she can just block it out.

The sounds of the girls running out of the room and most likely towards the living room to eat their treats leaves the kitchen quiet. Rae keeps her eyes on her knife as it slices into the crisp green skin of the apple, while she feels everyone's eyes moving between her and Cleo again. Finally, it's Jolene who breaks the silence.

"Well, can someone at least hug me for some reason other than candy?"

Rae smirks a little while Jace and Hudson chuckle. Cleo, being typical Cleo, just continues to look out the window in her own little world. Jace comes over to Jolene first with the spatula still in hand and sweeps her up in a hug. Hudson soon follows and kisses her cheek, making Jolene ruffle his hair. Cleo finally turns her head and smiles softly at Jolene as Rae's grip on the knife gets tighter.

She would pull that little innocent smile of hers out of her ass now, she thinks bitterly.

"Hey, Jojo," Cleo says daintily.

Jolene rolls her eyes, "You can pull that shit with other people, Cleo, but that doesn't work on me."

Cleo just shrugs while bringing her coffee cup to her lips. "Worth a shot."

"You—" Jolene exclaims, pointing a finger at Rae. "—are coming with me."

"For what?"

"Shopping."

Rae hums as she cuts another slice out of her apple. "Yeah, that's not happening."

Turning to Jace who has her tucked under his arm, Jolene says, "Did you hear your sister, Jace? She thinks she can tell me 'no'!"

"I did hear," he says before clicking his tongue. "Not a smart move."

"Traitor." Rae hisses, pointing the knife at him.

"Put the knife down, get your ass upstairs, and get dressed, Rae Marie," Jolene orders with a glare. "I am too old to be carrying you over my shoulder, kicking, and screaming."

"It's okay, Jojo. I'd be happy to help you." Jace grins.

Patting his cheek, Jolene coos at him. "You've always been one of my favorite nephews."

"Hey!" Hudson yells.

"I said one of my favorite nephews." She soothes him before turning her attention back to Rae. "Why are you still sitting there, girl? GO!"

With a sigh, Rae puts down the knife and the last bit of her apple on the table. Putting on her fakest smile, she approaches her brother and aunt before curling her fist. Ramming it into Jace's stomach, she ignores Jolene's scolding and Hudson's bouts of laughter. Though that doesn't stop her from grinning on her way up the stairs.

That'll show him.

* * *

"What about this one?"

Rae looks at the ugly monstrosity in her aunt's hand and gives her a dry look. Without a word, Rae moves past her towards the sunglasses rack to browse. She doesn't know why she's being dragged into this mess, especially on her day off. Though in truth, even Rae knows when Auntie Jojo tells you to do something, you do it.

"Rae, you can't turn down every dress." Jolene huffs.

"Yes, I can," Rae answers while putting on a pair of cat eye red shades.

Taking them off her face, Jolene gives her a no-nonsense look. "The run is in three days, and you need a dress."

"Why can't I just do it in jeans?" she whines.

"Because it's tradition for the females to wear a white dress to show their availability, while the mated women must wear red. Now since I don't see a mate anywhere in sight right now, it'll have to be white."

"But I hate wearing dresses."

"Honey, I hate to break it to you, but the run is not about what you like. Hell, it's not even about what your mate likes. We have rules and traditions for a reason, and as a member of the pack, you as well as I, have to obey them."

"You suck."

Jolene just pokes the tip of her nose, "Don't sass me, or I'll take you over my knee. I don't care how old you are."

29

With Jolene's arm over her shoulder, Rae chews on her lower lip debating on asking what she's about to ask. After her swim the other night and the constant battling between her and Cleo, Rae has come to a hard decision. Maybe it's time that Cleo did go to stay with Jolene and Everett for a little bit.

"Jo—"

"You know she's welcome anytime," Jolene says, squeezing Rae's shoulders. "I know it's hard. She's a teenager and with that comes rebellion, but she's suffering. Losing not only her parents and having you go from sister to parent . . . I can't imagine it's easy for her to take in."

Rae sighs, kneading her forehead. "I know. Believe me, I know. It's been hard on all the kids, but she's getting out of control. I have too much on my plate with work, the kids, and now the run coming up . . . it's just too much."

"She can stay with us until the run is over," Jolene decides. "I know you two can't stop being around each other longer than that. After that, I think she'll appreciate everything you do for her."

"Now, that is hopeful thinking." Rae snorts as she runs her fingers over the fabrics and making the hangers clack. "Thanks for this, Jojo. Really, it means a lot to me."

"Anything for my girls."

Rae is about to reply when she catches a whiff of something. Frowning, she turns to try to find the source, but instead sees nothing but people passing by the entrance of the shop. Shaking her head, she sees that Jolene has moved deeper into the store. Crossing her arms over her chest, she pauses as Jolene pulls out a dress from the rack.

It's beautiful in its floor length with a white form fitting slip underneath and a lace overlay. It has short sleeved with a scalloped neckline; nothing too showy or too modest. *Perfect,* she thinks, but with the gleam in Jolene's eyes, she refuses to admit it. She doesn't want to see her aunt's hideous "I told you so" dance.

"That's nice," she says impassively.

Jolene lifts a brow. "Nice? This is the one, Rae."

"How much is it?"

"Don't worry about it."

Rae sighs and runs her hand through her hair. "Jojo, you can't—"

"I can and I will," Jolene says shutting down the argument. Putting the dress over her arm, she smiles brightly. "Now, what about shoes?"

Rae points to the red converse on her feet. "Done."

"Sneakers?" Jolene asks.

"Did you expect me to run in heels?"

"Well, no, but—"

"If I have a mate, I don't want to make him just throw me over his shoulder five minutes in. He's going to have to earn the right to claim me. So I'm going to need shoes I can run in without breaking an ankle."

Jolene's eyes unexpectedly water before she brings her in for a hug. "Oh honey, your daddy would be so proud of you right now."

Rae hugs her back feeling tears build in her eyes. No, she scolds herself; you are not going to start crying at the mall of all places. Pulling back from her aunt, Rae rubs a hand down her face.

"Alright, well now that that's all settled," Jolene says, wiping her eyes and clearing her throat. "Let's go get some food, hmm?"

After everything is paid for, the two exit the store with a yellow-colored plastic bag dangling from Rae's hand. Rae catches that scent again and looks over her shoulder trying to spot what it is. It's an odd mixture of scents—something flowery, but also refreshing like rain. Her frown only grows deeper as her wolf lets out a low whine, making Rae clutch her chest.

"Rae? Honey, is something wrong?"

31

Taking a deep breath, Rae shakes her head, "No, I think I'm okay. Just a bit tired is all."

"You sure?"

"Yeah." Rae nods. "Let's go eat."

"We can go home . . ."

Rae forces a smile and shakes her head. "I'm okay, Jojo, let's just go."

"Okay," her aunt agrees slowly.

Rae turns her head one more time as her eyes scan the many people walking through the mall. Where is that scent coming from?

* * *

It's nearing eight at night when Jolene pulls her car up outside the house, and Rae practically jumps out when she hears screaming coming from inside. Running towards the house, she slams open the door to see Jace standing over a half-naked guy clutching his nose.

Taking in the scene with assessing eyes, she finds Hudson has Cassidy balancing on his hip, while Poppy is hugging his leg. Both girls are crying and are hiding their faces. Jace, on the other hand, just looks pissed. His blue eyes are slits of rage as he stares down at the boy groaning in the entryway.

Lastly, her eyes land on Cleo, who is also crying from her position on the nearby steps. Rae takes in her sister's messy blonde hair, missing shirt, and unbuttoned jean shorts only to feel her own rage built. She doesn't need to be a genius to realize what the fuck just happened.

Stalking towards Cleo, she grabs her upper arm making the girl cry out in pain. Rae doesn't care, though, she just wants this shit to stop. Walking her up a few steps, Rae practically shoves her sister the rest of the way until the first landing.

"What are you going to do, ground me?" Cleo asks, nose still red from crying. "Jace is the one who hit him for no reason!"

"Do yourself a big favor, Cleo, and shut the fuck up," Jace tells her lowly.

"Rae, I—"

"I don't want to hear it anymore!" Rae yells at her. "I don't want to hear the excuses, the nasty remarks, or the bullshit lies! Grab your shit, and get out of my house!"

"This isn't just your house!" Cleo yells back. "This house belongs to all of us!"

"What's—" Jolene stops short when she too takes in the scene. Lifting her eyes to take in Cleo's appearance, her eyes go flat. "Oh, Cleo."

"Jojo, please let me stay with you," Cleo pleads, her eyes getting glossy. "I can't take it here anymore."

"You're already going," Rae says lowly. "At least until the run is done and over with, you'll stay with Jojo and Everett so I can figure out what to do with you."

Cleo scoffs before stomping up the stairs to her room. Once the door slams shut, Rae slowly descends the stairs again towards the boy still on the floor, clutching his bloody nose. Realizing the boy is human, Rae drops the approach she was going to use and instead just motions for him to stand up.

"What's your name?" she asks as she realizes it's the same boy from the parking lot the day before.

He wipes his nose on his forearm before standing a bit straighter. "Kip."

"Kip," she repeats with a nod. "Well, Kip, I don't need to ask you what you were doing with my sister, it's pretty obvious. I can warn you though that if I ever catch you near her again, I will beat the shit out of you with your dismembered arms, we clear?"

He scoffs. "I'd like to see you try it."

Jace steps forward, fists clenched. "You better watch how you talk to my sister."

33

Rae steps between the two boys, making sure Kip's attention is solely on her. Her wolf gladly steps forward to flash golden eyes at the boy. It's a subtle warning, but from the widening of his eyes, she can tell he didn't miss the threat of something other.

"Now get the fuck off my property." Rae hisses.

Kip doesn't need a second order. Grabbing his things nearby, he bolts out the door. Once he's gone, the girls rush over to Rae to hug her. She pets both of their blonde heads as they snuggle into her, feeling the guilt of leaving them here begin to weigh her down. Going to her knees, she kneels before them and uses a hand to cup both of their faces.

"You guys okay?"

"We thought Jace was going to kill him." Poppy sniffles.

"I would have," Jace spits at no one in particular.

Rolling her eyes, Rae quickly soothes the girls. "Jace isn't going to kill anyone tonight, I promise. In fact, you guys are going to keep an eye on him for me."

"How?" Cassidy asks, wiping one brown eye.

"Make him read you a story and give you lots of hugs," she whispers. "Jace can't help but smile when he gets cuddles from his favorite girls."

"Really?" Cassidy sniffles, looking up at Jace.

Jace looks at Rae for a long time before sighing and turning to Cassidy. "Of course. You're my favorite girls in the world."

"You like us even more than that girl who turned you into a zombie?" Cassidy asks innocently.

"What?" Jace asks with a frown of confusion.

Shaking her head, Rae gets to her feet again. "Just take the girls up and get them ready for bed. I'll explain later."

With a hesitant nod, he leans down and grabs Cassidy into his arms before starting up the stairs. Poppy follows after them slowly, her glasses in her hand as her tiny bare feet climb the stairs.

Once Rae hears their bedroom door click, she cups her face in her hands, trying to keep the last strand of her sanity intact.

Jolene comes up and slowly lowers Rae's hands. Taking her face in her hands, Jolene kisses Rae's forehead. "You're made of strong stuff, kid."

Rae smiles a bit. "I learned from the best."

The sound of stomping footsteps has Rae closing her eyes in frustration. Jolene drops her hand and crosses her arms over her chest. With a cheerleading duffle bag from her middle school days, Cleo comes down the last section of stairs. Luckily, she's thought about putting on a shirt but put her hair in a ponytail and making sure all can see her hickeys.

"Where's Kip?"

"Left," Rae says simply, turning to face her sister. "Call me at least once while you're gone. I want to know you're doing okay."

Cleo looks a bit thrown by Rae's dull tone and frowns. "Yeah, sure."

Giving her a solitary nod, Rae moves her gaze to the staircase and moves to the side so she can pass. She does this quietly, and both Cleo and Jolene leave without another word. Once she hears the car start to pull away, Rae leans back her head, trying to not let the building tears fall. Well, she thinks dejectedly so much for keeping the family together.

"She'll be okay," Hudson says quietly.

Rae wipes her cheeks and laughs a little. "Oh, I know she will. Jolene will have her scrubbing floors if she even steps one toe out of line."

Hudson smiles slightly. "She needs that."

"I just wish mom was here sometimes," Rae admits in a near whisper.

"I know. Me too."

Both stand in silence for a few minutes before Rae lets out a few chuckles. Hudson frowns at her but smiles despite his confusion. "What?"

35

"That kid's face was priceless." Rae snorts.

She and Hudson begin laughing a little as they both remember the look on Kip's face when Jace stood over him, ready to rip his face off. Still chuckling, Rae moves towards the kitchen with Hudson following. Taking a newly added pizza box from the fridge, Rae raises an eyebrow at Hudson in question who only shrugs. Throwing it on the kitchen table, she grabs a grape soda from the fridge before sitting at the table.

"I think I'm going to head to my room," Hudson announces after grabbing a pop from the fridge as well.

With her mouth full of cold pizza, Rae nods. "Okay."

Making a disgusted face, Hudson exits quickly. Opening the can with a crisp crack, Rae takes a quick sip before sitting back in her chair. Closing her eyes, she pushes aside the guilt, the anger, and the resentment to the side, hoping to clear her mind. *Only three more days till the run,* she thinks.

She has never been less excited for anything in her life.

CHAPTER FIVE

Hearing the bell on the diner's door ding, Rae lifts her head with a smile plastered on her face, ready to greet. It falls quickly though when she sees it's just Graham strolling into the building, looking too mischievous to be up to any good. Continuing to wipe down the table of the family that just left, she tries to ignore him. Graham being Graham, though, won't let that happen without a fight.

"Hey, sweetie buns," he greets with a huge grin.

Rae gives him an unamused look, "Sweetie buns?"

"Don't like it?"

"Graham, I like zero of the ridiculous pet names you use on me. What made you think 'sweetie buns' was going to be a hit?"

He shrugs. "I'm just naturally optimistic I guess."

"And incredibly resilient," she adds with a little smile. "So what can I help you with? You look to be up to no good again."

"I'm just here to remind you we have the pack meeting tonight."

Rae lets out a groan as she grips the sides of the tub with dirty dishes. "Shit. When is it again?"

"In an hour. I came here to make sure you weren't late. Alpha Kendrick is short tempered these days."

"Yeah, Alpha Julie said that baby has colic." Graham gives her a blank look, making her elaborate. "He cries a lot."

Graham scoffs and waves a hand at her. "I knew that."

"Sure you did."

"I did!"

"Sure." She smiles. "So what else are you up to? The look on your face tells me you have something else up your sleeve."

"Me?" he asks, pointing to his overly innocent face. "I'm not sure I like you accusing me without evidence, Miss Applebee."

"Well, I don't like you putting me in the middle of your shenanigans. So spill the beans or leave me to work in peace, *Mr. Jones.*"

He gives me a huge white-toothed grin. "You know you love it but since I'm feeling nice today, I'll let you in on my little secret. I think I met my mate today."

Rae stops mid-glass lift to look at him in surprise. "You think?"

"Well . . . I mean, I think she's it."

"Your wolf didn't tell you?" she asks as her surprise fades into confusion.

Graham rubs the back of his neck. "Well . . ."

Rae brushes her hair behind her ears and straightens her body to sigh in his direction. "Graham, a wolf knows by their mate's scent, their looks and even the way they speak. Everything calls to you, and when you see your mate, your wolf will go crazy with wanting to be near them. That's how it works. Now, did you feel any of that with this girl?"

"No," he admits lowly before sighing heavily. "But she was so hot."

Rae rolls her eyes as she grabs the tub of dirty dishes in her hand. "Then that's your dick talking, not your wolf."

Following her into the back of the diner, she can feel his eyes on her ass but doesn't call him out on it. At this point, she's immune to him checking her out. She figures since he's kind of the only friend she has these days; she can cut him some slack. Besides, it's nice to know she can still turn a few heads.

38

Putting the dishes next to the sink, she pats Trevor, the dishwasher on the back. He just started at the diner two days ago, and she's been training him since no one else really has the time. He's a nice kid and reminds her of Hudson a little in his shy personality.

"This is the last of them," she tells him with a smile. "You did well today."

"Thanks, Rae. Is it always this busy?" he asks.

Rae nods as she reaches back to undo her apron. "Yeah, especially on the second Friday of the month. A lot of people on the edges on the county come into town around then."

"Why?"

Knowing he's human, she lets a lie spill out. "County meetings and stuff. Don't worry, the rest of the time it's more manageable. Do you need a ride home?"

Trevor shakes his shaggy blonde head. "Nope. My mom let me take the car into work today."

"Very nice." She nods appreciatively before tucking her hair behind her ear again. "I gotta head out, but I don't work again until Tuesday. Kent should be here for a bit longer so feel free to ask him any questions. Do you need anything else?"

"No, I think I got it. Thanks, Rae."

"No problem. Drive safe, Trevor, and have a good night."

"You too."

Heading into the back storage room, Rae grabs her gray zip up hoodie and purse from her bin in the back. Graham doesn't follow her into the back room, so she takes her time to collect herself. Her stomach is filled with her nerves, due to the fact that the pack meeting is most likely about the run which is tomorrow night. She's been avoiding thinking about it as much as she can, but tonight she knows that the pack's lands will be crawling with new people.

Taking a few steady breaths, she tells herself a bevy of reassuring things. Most of them are lies, and some of them are just

39

hopes. She tells herself that her mate is most likely not here. She tells herself that no matter what; she'll come out of this perfectly fine, and nothing will change. She tells herself these things, but she doesn't believe them. How can she when she knows that the odds are stacked against her?

Fifty new wolves are now in her pack's territory. Some of them female but most of them male, looking for their mates. They come every year waiting to see if the next crop of newly legal pack members could be their other half. All members with wolf blood participate in the run. Not just the ones that can shift, and Rae is dreading the day Cleo has to start joining in.

Quickly moving away from that thought, Rae runs a hand through her hair as she walks out of the storage room. Graham is chatting with Kent, one of the cooks who volunteered to close up tonight, when she emerges. A part of her wishes Graham is her mate. He already belongs to this pack and then she wouldn't have to consider moving her family. That, and it's not like he's hard on the eyes, not to mention that he can make her laugh.

Still, fate doesn't give her that option, so she shoots that idea down quickly.

"You ready?" Graham asks as she approaches the two men.

"Yup." She nods before turning to the older gentlemen. "You sure you're okay with closing up, Kent?"

He smiles kindly at her. "I'm a man of many talents. Closing this place down seems to be one of them. Enjoy your night. He seems like a nice guy."

"What? I'm not—"

"Come now, darling." Graham cuts in with a smirk. "Our reservation won't wait all evening for us to get there."

Glaring at him for a second, Rae suddenly smiles sweetly. "Of course, dear. Let's get going."

Graham wraps an arm around her shoulder and starts leading her towards the door leading to the main part of the restaurant. Just as he reaches out to push open the door for her, she

40

rams her elbow into his gut. Graham grunts at the impact, but Rae just smirks at him.

"Oops. You know how clumsy I am sweetheart. Can you ever forgive me?

"It'll be hard," he tells her in a choked voice. "But I think a quickie in the back of my car might fix me right up."

"Wow," she mutters while shaking her head. "And just when I thought you couldn't get any more pervy."

Graham grins at her as they exit the diner. "You know you love it, baby."

"Yeah . . . we'll go with that."

* * *

Rae stands at the back of the room with her arms crossed and her eyes averted. She doesn't like being around so many people, especially the ones that like to talk straight to her. Since her parents were such big fixtures in the pack, a lot of people like to ask her about her siblings and how they're "holding up." She knows they're just trying to show concern, but too many pitiful stares make Rae edgy.

"Stop acting so sketchy would you?" Graham complains from beside her. "People are going to start thinking you're going to rob them on the way out of here."

"Maybe I will." She shrugs.

"It's only as bad as you make it, Rae. Seriously, just relax."

Rae grumbles to herself but tries to stand up a bit straighter. When she does, she catches a powerful scent. It's the same one from the mall, but despite its potency she can tell it's a few hours old. Her eyes scan the room hoping that maybe she can pinpoint from where the scent leads, but she can't make heads or tails of it with so many other scents in the room.

"What?" Graham whispers.

41

Rae shakes her head but doesn't speak as she sees the alphas coming into the room. All conversations quickly go quiet as Alpha Kendrick and Alpha Julie make their appearance. Alpha Julie is smiling and nodding to people as they walk past them, while Alpha Kendrick just scans the room with impassive eyes.

When they reach the front of the room, Alpha Julie stands beside her mate as he crosses his arms over his wide chest. He looks a bit more rested, Rae notices with a tilt of her head. When the alpha's eyes meet hers, though, she quickly averts her eyes again, not wanting to be seen as disrespectful.

"Welcome," Alpha Kendrick's voice greets. "I hope to find all of you are well since our last meeting."

"Yes, Alpha." A series of voices assure him.

He nods before speaking again. "As I'm sure all of you are aware that our annual fall equinox run will be held tomorrow night. This is an exciting time for the pack. We hope to gain new members, but we will be sad to lose a few as well. I expect all eligible males and females to be wearing your ceremonial masks and abiding the dress code. The females will meet the alpha female at the alpha home, while the males will meet me at the training grounds."

"Alpha, will the ones from the other packs be meeting there as well or at the west woods?" A pack member asks from the crowd.

"All the females and males will enter the west woods together, no matter the pack affiliation," Alpha Kendrick answers. "Any other questions?"

Graham raises his hand, and Rae's eyes double in size as he speaks. "Alpha, what will happen if someone doesn't show up when they are eligible?"

The alpha's eyes flicker to Rae for a second before clearing his throat. "They will have to be punished."

"Yeah, but how?" Graham asks. "You know, just in case someone gets any ideas, Alpha."

"They will have to go into wolf form and be repeatedly challenged by me until they can prove to me they are worthy of being part of this pack. The run is a tradition of not only this pack but of our kind. Any kind of disregard of that will be treated with the same as a personal disrespect to me."

Rae swallows thickly. Shit.

"Thanks, Alpha. That'll be sure to keep them in line, well that, or make them shit their pants in fear."

The room erupts with laughter, and even Alpha Kendrick cracks a small smile. "Thank you, Graham, but watch the language, huh?"

"Yes, sir!"

Rae slaps her palm against her forehead at Graham's antics but can't stop the small curl of her lips. He's an idiot, but an idiot with a point. She can't skip out on this, and if she did, she'd just be putting her and the kids in jeopardy for nothing more than her pride. Sighing, she feels the nerves come back in full force.

No way out, she thinks.

Figures.

The announcements change course shortly after that, and Rae starts to zone out. It's not that she's not interested in the ways of the pack, she just doesn't want to hear about the patrol schedule. She's brought out of her thoughts though when Graham suddenly starts shaking her.

"What?" she asks, blinking rapidly.

"Meeting's over."

"Already?"

"Did you want to stay longer?" he asks with one arched brow.

Rae shoves him a little. "Smart ass. You giving me a ride back to the diner so I can get my van or what?"

"Sure." He shrugs before winking down at her, "Can't let you tire your legs out before the big day now, can I?"

43

Her expression falls into a scowl immediately. "You're an asshole, by the way."

"What?" He laughs when she shoves him again. "I just wanted to make sure everyone knew the consequences should they attempt to skip out."

"Yeah, real subtle, Graham."

He's about to speak again when another voice cuts in. "Hey, Graham."

Both of them turn their heads to see Veronica smiling at Graham seductively. Veronica is an ex-conquest of Graham's, and if the rumors are true, half the other males in the pack as well. Rae usually doesn't put much stock in rumors, but from what Graham has told her, she's not too sure she can disregard all the stories as lies.

"Oh, hey, Veronica," Graham mutters.

"I need a ride home. . . help, but I already said I'd bring Rae to the diner," he tells her, pointing a thumb in Rae's direction.

Veronica's blue eyes narrow at her. "Oh. Hi, Rae."

"Veronica." Rae nods.

"Still working at Peter's, I see," Veronica observes, while looking at the uniform Rae is still wearing, with disgust. "Don't you do the daycare?"

"I do both."

"Well, that's . . . something I guess."

Rae clears her throats but doesn't respond. She really doesn't have anything to say to Veronica, let alone find the patience for idle chitchat. Veronica is the same catty bitch she was in high school as she is now, and Rae just doesn't have the time for it.

"Well it was nice seeing you, but we gotta go," Rae says eventually.

"Of course." Veronica smiles, but it's tight.

Rae turns on a heel and walks out of the building quickly, knowing that Graham is following her after a quick farewell. Rae can feel a few drops fall from the sky and onto the skin of her arms

44

as she walks towards Graham's jeep, and can smell the rain in the air as well. Graham unlocks the doors quickly as the few drops turn into a heavy downpour.

"Holy shit," he yells after getting into the jeep. "That came on quickly, didn't it?"

"It's supposed to be good luck," she says, looking out the front window. "Some kind of sign of prosperity and fertility, I guess."

"Who told you that?"

"My mom."

Graham doesn't say anything in response, and she doesn't blame him. Reaching over, he turns on the heat when Rae shivers a bit from the rain seeping into her bones. After a few moments, Graham finally speaks again.

"Rae?"

"Yeah?"

"Do you know how much I love you?"

Rae rolls her eyes but answers. "I can't say I do, Graham."

"I love you so much I turned down getting laid. And let me tell you, Veronica is one wild beast in the sack. I mean she does this one thing where—"

Rae slaps his shoulder making him laugh. "You're gross."

"Made you laugh, though, didn't I?" He grins.

Rae crosses her arms over her chest but can't deny the smile on her face. Sinking back into her seat, she stares out the passenger side window and watches the rain slide across the glass. Just one more night until everything could change for the worse or improve for the better, she thinks.

One more night until Rae has to face her biggest fear.

CHAPTER SIX

Rae tugs on the shoulder of her dress as she stares at herself in the mirror. It was the day of the run, and she had barely gotten any sleep last night. Her eyes had bags under them, and she was struggling to not just go back to bed for just a few more hours of sleep.

Her night was filled with nightmares and dreams of what her mate would be like. Would he be a macho jerk who used his words like they were written in stone? Or would he be like her dad had been with her mom: sweet and understanding? What did she want her mate to be like? Rae had never really thought about it before.

She would want him to be understanding of her situation. She would want him to be supportive of her and good with her siblings. She would want him to be patient because adjusting to a mate being around would be a big adjustment. All in all, she just wants someone who gets her.

That's all she can hope for really; fate seems to take care of the rest.

Running her hand through her hair, Rae looks at her reflection one more time and shrugs. Well, it's too late to do much else. Grabbing her red converse off the bed, she touches her mom's charm necklace on her neck. Saying a silent prayer for luck to her mom, she kisses the heart charm before letting it fall back down on her chest.

Well, better get to it.

Opening the bedroom door, she hears the usual chatter of her family downstairs and smiles, wondering how they'll react to seeing her in a dress. She hasn't been dressed up since the homecoming dance in her sophomore year. Since then, wearing dresses has been impractical, especially when you have two brothers who think it's funny to lift them in public.

Walking down the stairs, she sees not only Graham here, but also her cousin Garrett. Garrett is her aunt Jolene and uncle Everett's only child. Garrett favors his father in the general looks department with his height, body type, and short black hair. He did get his mother's hazel eyes, though, but luckily got his father's laid back personality.

Grinning, Rae practically jumps on Garrett's back, making him stagger forward a bit before steadying her. Rae notices Jace look at her with a raised brow but says nothing about her behavior. She can't help herself though when it comes to Garrett. She's known him since they were both in diapers, and seeing him always brings out the playful person she used to be.

"Have you gained weight?" Garrett asks, faking strain.

Smacking him upside the head, Rae slips off his back. Turning around, Garrett grins at her before ruffling up her hair, making her scowl up at him. Slapping his hand away, she sticks her tongue out at him. He tries to grab it, but she slaps his hand away again which does nothing more than make him laugh.

"You know if you stick your tongue out, you'll lose it."

"I'd like to see you try."

"Don't tempt me."

"Hey, Rae, why can't you jump on me like that?" Graham asks, receiving two punches in each arm from both Jace and Garrett. "Dude! What the hell?"

"That's my sister."

"And my cousin."

"So watch your mouth," Jace warns him.

Graham rolls his eyes while rubbing his left arm. "Did you hear her complaining?"

"That's because I'm used to your pervy ways, Jones."

"Didn't say you didn't like it though, did you, sweet cheeks?" Graham smirks.

Rae turns away from the boys with a dejected sigh. She hears a few more smacks being delivered but ignores them in favor of seeing her little sisters. Heading into the living room, she watches her sisters as they sit a mere foot from the TV. Hudson is sitting on the couch, texting again while trying really hard to ignore the second *Twilight* movie playing.

Clearing her throat, she gets the attention of all three, but it's the girls who have the best reaction. Both gasp as they look at her before jumping to their feet and rushing over to her. Poppy starts jumping up and down, screeching all kinds of things Rae can't quite make out while Cassidy starts rubbing her face on the lace of her dress.

"Cassie, what are you doing?" Rae laughs.

"It feels funny on my face."

"… And you look like a princess!" Poppy yells suddenly.

Rae smiles softly at her little sister, "Well, aren't you all kinds of sweet today?"

Poppy beams up her happily while Cassidy continues to rub her cheek against the lace on her thigh. Hudson whistles lowly, getting her attention, and she smiles as he looks at her with wide brown eyes. He gets off the couch and nods appreciatively at her.

"You clean up nice."

"I try."

"Jojo had Garrett bring over your mask."

Rae raises her eyebrows in surprise. "Really? It's here?"

Hudson nods. "She hand-painted it herself. She just used her old one since she knew mom didn't have one you could use."

"Did you see it yet?"

He smiles teasingly at her. "I may have peeked."

"And?"

"It looks like you Rae, but then again, I think that's the point."

Feeling suddenly excited to see what it looks like, Rae grabs Poppy's hand in one hand, and Cassidy's in the other, leading them back towards the boys. When she spots them, Rae puts on her sweetest smile; the one Cleo learned from her, and Garrett immediately narrows his eyes.

"What do you want?"

"Where are they?"

His smile turns teasing. "I can't imagine what you're referring to."

"Gare-Bear, don't be a meanie and hand them over."

Poppy chimes in then. "Yeah, Garrett, be nice!"

"You don't even know what she wants," Garrett informs her with an eye roll.

"Garrett, my loving cousin, you're losing focus. I want to see them. Please?" Adding her most pathetic pout into the mix, Rae sees his resolve shaking.

Dropping his head, he groans loudly. "You're killing me with that look."

"That's what it's there for," Rae answers quickly, still making the face.

Turning around, Garrett takes a black box off a nearby table. Handing it to Rae, he gives her a dirty look. "You were supposed to wait till you got the alpha house."

"I'm impatient, you know that."

"I do, but I was hoping with age would come with maturity."

Rae snorts. "That, my dear cousin, was your first mistake."

Lifting the top box, Rae peers inside to find a black wolf mask with gold, green, and blue autumn leaves painted around the eyes, in the ears, and on the cheeks of it. It doesn't take a genius to know this is Garrett's mask since his black spiked hair and bright hazel eyes match it perfectly. Unable to help herself, though, Rae pets the long-nosed snout of the mask marveling at the softness of it.

"Wow," she whispers.

Garrett peeks into the box and smiles. "Oops. That's actually mine."

Taking the mask and handing her the second box, he grabs his own mask out of the box. Slipping it on, Rae can't help but smile at how bright his eyes look in it and notice how much it does resemble the features of his wolf.

"How do I look?" he asks, putting his arms out so she can get a full view of him.

"You look so cool, Garrett!" Poppy yells.

Cassidy runs over and starts to try to get to the mask by jumping on Garrett. He leans down and grabs her before balancing her on his hip. Cassidy immediately starts rubbing her hand over the soft suede of the mask with delicate fingers.

"Pretty," she whispers with awe.

"Rae?" Garrett asks. "What do you think?"

"I'm going to quote Hudson here and say it looks like you," Rae answers with a soft smile. "Your mate is going to be a lucky girl."

"Really?" Garrett asks before moving over to a mirror in the entryway to peer at himself. "Wow, Mom did a really good job with these," he says in awe before turning to Rae and gesturing to the black box in her hand. "Now try yours on."

Lifting the lid of the box, Rae lets out a small gasp. It's perfect. Much like Garrett's mask, it has the basic wolf head shape, but this time it bears the colors of Rae's wolf. It's mostly silver in color with a black colored nose, but the designs on it really take her breath away. White swirls frame the eyes and the rims of the ears and cheeks before coming down to an apex at the top of the black snout. Running her fingers gently over the patterns, Rae feels tears form in her eyes.

"Oh, don't cry now, sting ray." Garrett sighs, using his childhood nickname for her as he wraps an arm around her shoulders. "You'll ruin your looks for the run."

Laughing, Rae wipes her cheeks before rolling her eyes at him. "Don't be a jerk."

"Come on." He smiles as he puts Cassidy back down on the ground. Stepping forward, he pulls the mask from the box and tosses the box onto a nearby table. "Let's get your wolf on."

Rae laughs again and wipes a few more of her fallen tears. Garrett places the mask over her face with gentle fingers, and Rae closes her eyes at the feel of it on her face. Securing it tightly with the white ribbon and a clasp over her hair, Garrett comes to stand before her, grinning widely. "All done."

"How does it look?" she asks, opening her eyes to see everyone just staring at her with soft smiles. "Well?"

"You look beautiful!" Poppy yells before clapping her hands. "I can't wait till I can do the run! I want to pretty like you, Rae!"

Rae's mask hides her blush. She's pretty sure she hasn't received so many compliments in one day in a long time. Graham suddenly comes into the room with a sandwich in his hand and his mouth full. His eyes go wide, and his mouth pops open a little as he takes her in.

"Damn, sweet cheeks. Are you trying to get me to fall more in love with you?"

Jace smacks him upside the head before turning to Rae with a smile. "You look good, Rae. Your mate won't stand a chance."

"Hudson?" Rae asks, tears rimming her eyes again.

"It looks like you," he echoes, using his words from earlier. "It looks like the real you."

Walking over to the mirror herself, Rae grins at the sight of it. Her brown eyes really stand out under the contrast of the lighter colors of her mask. *Hudson's right though,* she thinks, she does look like herself, like the real her. Taking a deep breath, Rae opens her eyes and turns to her cousin feeling more confident about this than she has all week.

"I think I'm ready." She exhales.

* * *

Colton is incredibly annoyed.

He doesn't want to be doing this shit, and he especially wouldn't want to be doing this when he could have been helping his dad with the pack. He doesn't like mingling with people, or being forced to do things, and he really doesn't like the idea of having to chase down a girl. In general, he's just highly peeved to be here.

"Dude, will you chill?" His friend Andy says. "It's a run, not torture."

"Then why does it feel like it?" Colton grumbles, running his hand through his dark hair.

"Because you're a douche bag."

Colton scowls in his direction. "Like you're one to talk."

Andy shoves Colton's shoulder. "You're such a grumpy bitch, you know that?"

"Shut up."

"Whatever," Andy dismisses, rolling his eyes. "I don't know what you're so pissed about. We get to run in the woods and have fun without supervision. This should be the best night of our lives."

"I'd rather be home doing something that matters."

"Oh yeah? Like what? Buried in paperwork at your desk or doing course work instead of sleeping? Is that the kind of fun you were thinking of instead?"

"Yes."

Andy scoffs and shakes his cleanly shaven head. "You are quickly becoming a lost cause, my friend."

"Gentlemen, nightfall is fast approaching," the alpha informs them in a loud, commanding voice, getting all their attention immediately. "I suggest you put on your masks."

Reaching into a backpack, Andy quickly produces two masks: one for him and one for Colton. Earthy, direct to the point, and with great workmanship, his mask echoes his personality. The brown leather mask stops halfway down Colton's face leaving his mouth and chin exposed. Other than that, the only things distinguishable about him are his dark blue eyes.

Andy's mask is showier, much like the man himself. It's black with electric blue colored designs. One thick line with a circle on the forehead serves as the main eye catcher with matching blue framing lines under the eyes and down to the snout that ends over Andy's mouth. Colton smirks at that because if anybody knows how much Andy needs his mouth covered, it's Colton himself. All in all, though, he has to admit Andy's mask looks good.

"You're admiring my good looks aren't you?" Andy grins widely.

Rolling his eyes, Colton let a reluctant grin spread across his face. "You're not my type."

Andy scoffs while waving a hand dismissively at him. "Whatever, man. I am everybody's type. I mean, look at me."

Colton does, and he can't see the appeal. Sure, Andy's dark skin, happy dark eyes, and impressive height are attractive to some people Colton just doesn't see. Though he could probably chalk that up to not being interested in men.

"Yeah, still not my type."

"You'll come around." Andy grins with a wink. "They all do."

Shaking his head, Colton sticks the mask on and secures it around the back of his head. "Whatever, dude."

"The others are arriving," the alpha announces, again getting everyone's attention. Turning towards the newer arrivals, the alpha instructs, "Men come join us."

About twenty more guys come to join the already thirty waiting in the clearing, all wearing different custom masks. Tonight, their wolves must stay hidden, and they must hunt in their human skin due to the full moon—a time when werewolves are at their weakest. The ritual, as Colton's father had explained it to him, is to help ward off the depression and frustration. Well, that and helping them find mates.

"Whoa," one of the men behind Colton whispers, making him look up towards the direction that has everyone else so captivated.

It doesn't take him long to figure out why. The females have arrived. The alpha female is in the front, wearing a dress of red to symbolize her being mated as she guides the women to the clearing. The female alpha's mask is also red and made of leather like his. Behind her are about forty young women dressed in white, all in various design and lengths. All of their hairs are down with masks covering their faces.

"We come to join the run, wolf," the alpha female states in a strong projecting voice. "May we run with you?"

"All women of age who seek a completed soul may run under the moon this night," the alpha responds in the customary way. "Are there such women among your party?"

"There are," the group of women chorus, followed by giggles that have Colton rolling his eyes.

"Are there men who seek the same in your party, wolf?"

"There are," the men chorused before a few slapping sounds and chuckles follow it. Colton mutters his answer, getting a slap of his own from Andy.

"Then we shall run together," the alpha female answers. "Do you accept?"

"With you, my lady, I will run just about anywhere," the alpha says huskily before kissing the back of his mate's hand.

The alpha female giggles happily. "You big dope."

"Love you too," he murmurs before speaking louder for everyone to hear with his arm wrapped around his mate's waist. "Here are the rules of the run, everyone. If you injure another, you will be punished. If you touch another in a way they do not like, you will be punished severely. You must have your mate's consent to mark. If they do not give it and you do it anyway, you will be punished. Break my rules, and I break your neck. Understood?"

"Yes, Alpha," everyone agrees.

Nodding, the alpha male turns to his mate who grins back at him. Kissing her temple, the alpha turns to the face the groups and yells, "Girls get a head start. Boys . . . good luck."

"Let the run begin!" the alpha female yells before laughing.

The women all start running for the woods while the men watch their white fabric covered bodies escape deeper into the night. Colton can feel his wolf pacing in his head in anticipation for the chance to hunt, and find his mate among them. Colton, on the other hand, isn't so sure she's among these women. Still, he can't help but feel a bit excited to run free in the woods as he pleases.

"Men." The alpha grins. "Go fetch."

Colton smirks.

Time to run.

CHAPTER SEVEN

Rae can feel her sneakers sink into the mud of the forest floor, making her lift her skirt up to her knees as she attempts to keep moving. It's been about an hour since the beginning of the run, and she's been able to keep a pretty low profile, but this could slow her down. Using a nearby tree as leverage, she's able to pull her mud-coated sneaker out of the mess.

Deciding to just ditch the shoes, she bunches her dress around her knees and keeps the fabric in its place between her legs. Leaning down, she unties both her shoes and lets her now bare feet feel the dark earth under them. Letting her dress fall the rest of the way, she picks up her shoes by the laces and begins on her way again.

For half an hour, she just hide up in a tree. She's seen other girls being tracked down by their mates while moving through the woods. Veronica finds her mate pretty quickly and from all the moaning she heard a few minutes later, she's guessing Veronica accepted the bond.

It's nearing dusk, and the sky above is being painted in pinks and oranges. Rae feels something approaching her and turns to look over her shoulder to see another girl in white. This one has a purple mask with golden swirls on it. Rae can tell from her unfamiliar scent this girl is not from her pack, but she's curious to see what will happen.

Hiding behind a nearby tree, Rae watches a young man, not terribly tall but well-built with a golden mask on. His blonde hair is long and tied back from his face in a low ponytail at the nape of his neck. He's shirtless, of course, and dressed only in a pair of light colored jeans. As he approaches the girl, Rae sees him inhale the girl's scent deeply.

"Mine," he growls.

Rae's eyes move to the girl. She's a petite girl in every way and as she moves back against a large oak, Rae can see her shaking. Seemingly seeing it, the boy stands up straight and takes a different approach. Reaching behind his head, he removes the mask and smiles encouragingly at his mate.

"I didn't mean to scare you," he says sheepishly. "Are you okay?"

"Y-Yeah." She whimpers. "I . . . I . . ."

"Hey, it's okay," he soothes. "I'm Toby. What's your name?"

"T-Tara."

"Tara." He smiles. "It's a beautiful name."

"Thank you," she whispers, making Rae smile.

Tara dips her head, making her straight black hair fall over her mask a little while Toby drops his head too.

"I'm not going to hurt you."

"I don't want to . . . I don't want to be claimed yet," she admits quietly.

"That's fine," he tells her, slowly moving closer to the girl. "We can wait as long as you want. You look cold. Do you want to go back to the alpha house? We can get you warm, and we can talk."

Rae starts moving back from the scene with a smile on her face. Knowing that she probably stayed longer than she should have, she starts moving deeper into the woods. She shivers as the cold of the evening begins seeping into her exposed arms. The dress is pretty thin, and though werewolves have pretty good inner heating, she's not immune to the cold.

Deciding to warm herself a bit, Rae drops her shoes near a tree, mentally noting to come back for them and takes off running. Her bare feet beat against the hard forest floor as her breath comes out in a hard pant. She feels a genuine smile on her face at the feel of the air moving through her hair, and the freedom she feels as the sky begins to darken further around her.

Coming to a stop, her chest is rising rapidly as her breathing continues to be labored. Looking around for a direction to head to, she spots a large willow in the middle of a nearby clearing. Deciding to climb in there so she can get a little breather, she breaks into a sprint again in its direction.

Rae slows down a bit when she catches that same scent that's been taunting her the past few days. It isn't something familiar, but it was something that catches her attention. The scent in other times is a pleasant and clean signature, but doesn't carry the flowering scent from before. She frowns as she looks around but keeps walking towards her original destination instead of going to investigate. She doesn't want to accidently stumble on a mating in progress or something.

Rae's feet freeze in place though when a deep growl echoes in the woods. Turning towards the sound, she sees nothing but trees, making her frown. Where the hell did that come from? Shrugging it off as one of the other male wolves hunting their mate, Rae turns back toward the tree but stops mid-step again when a second growl sounds, though this time, unmistakably closer.

"Hello?" she calls into the darkness before wincing at how stupid that sounds.

"Mine."

Rae frowns deeply as she looks around. She still doesn't see anyone. She still doubts that whoever it is has that "mine" directed towards her. Wouldn't her wolf have told her already? Still, she can't help but be intrigued by the voice.

"Mine!"

Rae screams loudly as two arms wrap around her waist and lifts her clean off the ground. The scent is surrounding her as she tries to beat the arms off her. She doesn't know what the hell this guy thinks he's doing, but just grabbing someone is beyond rude.

"What the hell? Let me go!"

"No!" The voice snarls as the arms squeeze her tighter against them. "Mine!"

"What? Is that your one word? Put me down!"

She felt her captor freeze behind her before slowly lowering her down to the ground. Quickly turning around, she feels like she was just physically slapped. Her breathing gets caught in her throat as she comes face-to-face with a beautifully crafted brown leather wolf mask. That rich, indescribable scent is heavier in the air now, and she can finally hear her wolf's low growl in her mind.

Ours.

"Oh, dear god," she croaks, feeling panicked.

His visible full lips tip up into a smile. "I prefer to be called Colton but if that works for you . . ."

Rae feels her cheeks burn. "Uh . . . sorry. You just . . . startled me."

"It's fine." He smiles.

Rae doesn't have a response to that, so she just stands there awkwardly. The guy or Colton continues to just stare at her. The longer they stand there in silence, the bigger his smile seems to get. Rae tries to rack her brain for something to say, but after almost a full minute of coming up with nothing, she just blurts out the first thing she can.

"So . . . What do we do now?"

He laughs, making her gut tighten. Smiling still, he steps towards her as he shoves his hands in the front of his jeans. "Well, you could accept me as your mate."

Rae is momentarily too distracted by his bare chest, abs, and arms that she doesn't register his words. When she finally does,

59

she raises her in surprise at his boldness. Is he always going to be this cocky or is this just a byproduct of the awkwardness?

"I don't even know you."

"True." He nods. "But I'm not seeing any reason not to at least accept that we feel something, right?"

"Do you even want a mate?"

His smile falters a bit, and he lowers his head. Lifting it again after a few moments, he looks at her under his dark lashes. "Can I be honest?"

"Please do."

He sighs. "If I told you that I came here looking to find you, I'd be lying. I was just doing it to get my dad off my back. That being said, though, I am happy I found you. I didn't know it could be this . . ."

"Instant," she answers quietly.

He nods. "Exactly. So you feel it too?"

"Yes."

"So why not accept the bond and just see where this goes. If you realize I'm a giant dick who you can't see yourself spending a minute with, let alone a whole lifetime, you can walk away. I'm not going to make you do anything you're not comfortable with."

Letting out a sigh of relief, she feels herself smile. "You can't imagine how happy I am to hear you say that."

"What, that you can leave me whenever?" he asks, but she can tell he's teasing.

"No." She laughs, feeling herself blush. "I just . . . I didn't want to not have a choice."

"Hey," he says softly, taking a few steps towards her. "This may be a bit quick, but I promise that with me, you will always have a choice, okay?"

Biting her lower lip, she nods.

After silence falls again, she spots him smiling softly at her. "Are you going to do it anytime soon or . . ."

"Oh! Right!" she says while smacking her forehead. "Um, alright. I, Rae Applebee, accept you . . ."

"Colton Woodward," he supplies with a wider smirk.

"Right," she mutters before beginning again. "I, Rae Applebee, accept you Colton Woodward as my mate."

Rae feels something in her chest pull at her, pushing her towards this guy she just met. She feels an overwhelming need, even stronger than before, to be in his arms. She feels her fingers tingle with the urge to touch him but most of all, she wants him to take off the mask.

"And I, Colton Woodward, accept you, Rae Applebee, as my mate."

Now the pull is even greater. Her body is coiled tightly as she tries to fight the compulsive need to just jump up in his arms. A total one-eighty to how she was just a full ten minutes before, but it feels different now. He has a name, a voice, and a scent that seems to make her want to know everything about him. Not to mention, he just gave her the best gift one mate can give to another. He gave her a choice.

"Now what?" she asks, completely at a loss.

No one really told her what was going to happen when she met her mate. Mostly, she was just told vague comments and romantic ideas that didn't really prepare her for anything as awkward as this. Rae had kind of hoped her mate would know what to do when the time came, because she sure as hell doesn't.

Colton just smiles and shrugs. "I don't really know. I suppose you could take your mask off, and I could take off mine."

"We could." She nods before adding, "Just to warn you now, though, you already accepted, so no running in fright when you see my face."

"I doubt that's going to happen," he says with a laugh.

Rae shrugs but feels her lips pull up at the sound of his laugh. "If you say so."

"Rae?" he asks lowly, taking a step closer to her.

"Hmm?"

"Take off the mask."

"Right," she breathes. Swallowing thickly, she reaches behind her head to unclasp the tie in the back. Fumbling a bit, she swears lowly when she can't get it off. His scent fills her lungs as he comes to stand mere inches away from her. Lifting her eyes, she watches him reach around her to take over the task. Rae inhales shakily at the tingles she feels in her fingers when his brush them. Letting her hands fall to her sides, she closes her eyes, just enjoying the feel of him so close.

Colton easily releases the tie and places his hands on the sides of her mask before slowly pulling it off her face. Rae keeps her eyes closed until it's fully off. When it is, she slowly opens them to find him just staring at her with his intense dark blue eyes. He scans her face, almost like he's putting it to memory before a lopsided smile comes across his face.

"So this is Rae Applebee."

Rae can't hide her blush this time as she shrugs. "This is her. I guess the whole running for the hills things doesn't seem so silly now, does it?"

Colton chuckles before shaking his still mask-covered head. Lowering himself a little, she feels his lips brush her ear as he speaks lowly, "If anything, it only makes me want to stay more."

Rae shivers at the sound of his voice. Clearing her throat, she lifts her gaze to see him looking back at her with a dazed look in his eyes. "Well that's encouraging, but don't you think you should return the favor?"

"Already making demands?"

"Maybe," she whispers with a teasing smile of her own.

Reaching behind his head, he unties the knot on the back of his head. Rae doesn't move her eye from his face, afraid to even blink. When the brown leather wolf mask is lowered, she can feel her heart ready to beat straight out of her chest. His cheekbones are low set but sharp. His chocolate colored hair is fairly short with floppy fringe hanging over one of his intense blue eyes. Rae notices a small black plug in his left ear lobe before her attention falls to his full pink lower lip. She clenches her teeth as the image of herself biting it comes into her mind.

"Damn horny wolf," she grumbles to herself.

"So . . ." She trails before clearing her throat. "You're Colton Woodward."

He smiles a bit shyly at her recycled words. "Yeah, this is me."

She nods appreciatively. "Not bad."

He lets out a surprised laugh. "You're going to be trouble. I can tell that already."

"Already complaining?"

"Not in a million years."

A shiver wracks her body, this time from the sudden chill in the air. Wrapping her arms around her arms, she looks up at Colton already looking concerned. Putting his hands on each of her arms he starts moving them up and down, trying to warm her up. All it does, though, is make her shiver more at the pleasant little shocks that ignite over her already goosebump-riddled arms.

"Cold?"

"A little," she admits.

"Do you want to head back to the alpha house? I hear that's where the celebrations are going to be."

She nods. "Yeah, I know. This is my pack."

Colton's brows rise in surprise before he nods. "Okay then, can you lead the way? I have no idea how to get back. This forest is like a maze."

She tilts her head while her eyes turn assessing. "Couldn't you just follow your scent trail back?"

"I guess I could." He shrugs. "But what's the fun in that when I have such a beautiful tour guide to show me the way?"

Rolling her eyes, Rae grabs one of his hands with hers. "Are you ever not charming?"

"Only when I'm asleep." He winks at her.

The two begin walking back towards the alpha house with Rae leading the way. She doesn't doubt her palms are sweating as she continues to clasp his hand. Still, she can't stop the giddy smile on her face. She found her mate, and he wasn't anything like she feared he'd be! The relief makes her almost want to giggle stupidly, or smile like the cat that caught the canary.

Her smile drops a little though when she realizes that Jace will be at the celebrations along with Cleo. Gnawing on her lower lip, she lets out a low sigh as the tension slowly starts to come back. Well, she thinks wearily, he was bound to meet the family some time.

CHAPTER EIGHT

Colton can feel her nerves, making him frown in confusion. She hasn't said a word since they started heading this way, and it's starting to worry him. He's not sure if she's nervous because of him, or because of the celebrations they're heading to. Either way, he squeezes her hand a bit tighter as they walk through the woods.

Noticing her relax a little, he smiles to himself. He doesn't know it is going to be like this. He wasn't lying to her before when he said he didn't come here for a mate. He didn't even think fate would come up with a woman who would have the ability to put up with him. Seeing her though, it changed everything.

Despite the obvious reason being how beautiful she is, Colton finds himself drawn to her personality, at least what he's seen of it so far. Brave; that was the first characteristic he added to the list. Colton has taken part in the run the past two years and never has he seen a captured female actually try to fight her mate off. At first, his wolf thought it was exciting, but then she snapped at him. That was what brought him out of his hunting mode and back into himself.

The second characteristic he's been able to figure out is intelligence. She can verbally spar with him on a level that most people he's been around can't. She immediately calls him out on his shit about the acceptance. In all honesty, he just wants to claim her as soon as he has seen her, but the hesitance in her eyes tells him that the brute approach isn't the way to go. He needed to slowly build up to that, earn her trust, and eventually, the right to mark her.

The final characteristic he's been able to collect has been the one he finds he likes most about her. Rae Applebee is strong. He can see it in the way she carries herself, the way she speaks and even the weariness in her eyes. Colton has always tried to be an observant kind of guy and being in the position he's in, it's served him well. So as he's watched her, he can see it clear as day, his mate is as strong as they come.

The details are obviously lost to him. He doesn't know why she's had to be so strong. He doesn't know why she keeps sneaking looks at him like she's afraid he'll disappear. He also doesn't know why the closer they get to the clearing, her hands are shaking.

But he has every intention of finding out.

"Can we take a quick detour?" she asks without looking at him.

"Sure," Colton agrees with a frown.

Turning to the direction, she leads him towards the east. He catches the faded trail of her scent, and when they come up to a tree nearby, he can't stop himself from laughing. Rae crouches down next to a tree before picking up some mud-covered shoes in her hand. He doesn't have to ask to know those are hers, her blush says it all.

"Okay, we go now," she says quietly.

"Rae?"

"Yeah?"

"Is there something wrong?"

Her wide brown eyes move to meet his, making his heart speed up in his chest. He can feel it the most when she looks him in the eyes and the pull to her nearly overwhelming. Stepping towards her, he cups her cheek in his palm, letting his fingers embed themselves in her honey blonde hair. He watches her close her eyes

66

before leaning into his touch, making him smile softly at her. He likes this, he decides, and he likes that he can give her comfort.

"I . . ." she trails off before letting out a low breath. "I'm a little nervous. My family is going to be at the party and . . . They can be a bit much. I have a lot about me that may be a bit overwhelming actually, and I want to warn you, but at the same time, I want to keep you with me. I didn't think I would find you, let alone feel this strongly, and it's all just . . . I'm nervous."

Taking another step closer to her, he kisses the top of her head before wrapping his arms around her. She doesn't hug him back immediately, and if he's honest, he's surprised with himself. He's not a naturally affectionate person, but it seems so natural that he can't help himself. Slowly, she wraps her arms around him as well, and he shivers at the feel of her petite hands on his bare back.

"We're starting to get to know each other," he tells her simply when he's sure she's relaxed and listening. "I imagine you have a lot to tell me about yourself just like I have a lot to tell you. Either way, you don't have to worry about me ever leaving you unless you send me away. I accepted you as my mate, Rae, and that means there will never be anything that could tempt me away."

Laying her head against his chest, he feels her hair tickle his skin and her arms tighten around him. He lowers his head to inhale her addictive scent, apples oddly enough, that has his mouth watering and his wolf howling in his head. He presses his lips to her forehead as they stand holding each other. The full moon is the only thing giving any light in the woods now, and he smiles as he notices how bright her hair looks in its rays.

"Better?" he asks, reluctant to let go, but knowing they have to present themselves.

Rae nods her head before looking up at him. "Much better."

Taking her hand in his again, he lifts it to his mouth to kiss her knuckles. "I'm here and just so you remember that, I won't let go of your hand the whole time."

67

"Are you going to be this perfect the whole time?" She sighs with amusement in her dark eyes.

Colton laughs. "I don't know. Most people think I'm a complete dick, but I figure I need to pretty up my personality a bit for you."

"Don't," she says with a seriousness that surprises him. "I don't want you to pretend for me. Just be yourself, and I'll either love it, hate it, or like it enough to put aside all the bad parts just to have you stay."

He smiles softly down at her while brushing some of her hair behind her hair. "I think I can do that."

"I, on the other hand, can be a raging bitch from hell and you just have to deal with it with a smile on your face."

"Deal." He chuckles. "Now come on, beautiful, we have a celebration to get to."

She lets out a shaky exhale before nodding. "Okay, let's do this."

As Colton walks with Rae back toward the alpha house, he can't help but smile. He really is one lucky son of a bitch.

* * *

Rae bites her lower lip hard as she and Colton come into sight of the alpha house. The beautiful plantation styled home is decorated for the equinox. The tall white columns are wrapped in lights, along with the trees. Some of the younger pack members are carrying sparklers around, and she wonders if she should start letting Poppy and Cassidy come. Though when she sees a young couple practically dry humping, she shoots that down quickly.

Looking through the crowds, Rae spots her brother Jace's recognizable head of hair from across the yard. He's standing with a still solo Graham and Garrett, making her heart sink a little. She really wanted at least one of them to find their mate this year,

68

especially Graham. Maybe then he can stop hitting on her all the time.

When Jace's bright blue eyes land on her, she sees them widen. Her face is starting to feel hot, and she fights the urge to hide behind some bushes. This urge becomes even stronger when she sees Jace get Graham and Garrett's attention before pointing in her direction. She rolls her eyes though when she sees Graham choke on his drink, making Garrett pat on his back.

"Do you know them?" Colton asks.

Rae's head snaps up at the near growl in his tone. "Yes. See the redhead? That's my brother Jace. The tall brunette, that's my cousin Garrett."

"And the other male?"

"My friend, Graham."

"He's glaring at me."

Rae turns her head to see that Graham is, in fact, glaring at Colton. Taking a deep sigh, she runs the hand not holding his through her hair. "Full disclosure, though, Graham has asked me out on occasion and likes to hit on me. We're just friends, though. Not that I have to explain myself but . . . yeah."

Colton smiles down at her, looking amused. "You're cute when you're rambling."

Bumping his arm with hers, she gives him a dirty look. "Shut up."

"So . . . the redhead is your brother?"

"Yup." She nods before clearing her throat. "One of them."

"One of them?"

"I have another brother."

"Really? What's his name?"

She smiles at his interest. "Hudson. He's fourteen."

"And this brother's name is Jason?"

"Jace," she corrects. "He's sixteen."

69

Colton nods, seemingly processing that information. "So it's just the three of you then?"

"Not exactly," she admits with a wince. "I—"

"Rae!"

Rae looks towards the source of the voice to see Cleo walking over. She's dressed in a red bandage skirt and a threadbare Van Halen t-shirt. Cleo's long blonde hair is messy as it hangs loosely around her shoulders. Added to the fact that from the lazy smile on Cleo's face, Rae doesn't have to be Sherlock Holmes to know she's drunk.

"Cleo, what do you think you're doing?" Rae asks, feeling the tension come back so fast she can feel her knuckles crack as they ball into fists.

Cleo stumbles to a stop before her, before hugging Rae. Rae wrinkles her nose at the heavy scent of rum on her sister. "I missed you, Rae-Rae!"

"Cleo, you're drunk."

Cleo snorts. "Duh. I know. I was there." Taking a drink from her red solo cup, Cleo's gaze lands on Colton beside her. "Who is this?"

"This is my mate, Colton."

Cleo immediately spits out her drink and begins to laugh. She cups her mouth as she continues to giggle uncontrollably. "You? You're mated to my sister? Oh man! You must be in the need for a stick because Rae has one shoved *way* up her ass."

"Excuse me?" Colton asks, looking at Cleo with disgust.

"Cleo, please don't do this now," Rae begs.

Cleo narrows her eyes at Rae and points a finger at her. "Don't act like I'm the bad guy here, Rae. We both know what you were like when you were my age. Cody, let me tell you, she was a loose cannon. She used to smoke weed and party and kiss boys. She was a regular little rebel!"

"Cleo, stop."

"Then our parents up and died. Suddenly, Rae the rebel is Rae the controlling bitch from hell. Everything has to be her way or the high way. That's why she doesn't like me, you know. She's jealous that she has to take care of snot-nosed kids while I get to live a life. Hear that, Rae? You are peanut butter and jealous!"

Rae shuts her eyes and turns her head away from her sister. She feels her eyes brim with tears, but she doesn't let them fall. Since taking over the family, Rae has never let anyone see her cry. Her tears, her worries, and her pain, are her own cross to bear. That, of course, doesn't stop the urge as it slowly builds up inside her.

"Cleo, what the fuck do you think you're doing?" Jace snaps, suddenly by Rae's side.

"Oh look, her guard dog showed up just in time!"

Reaching over, Jace grabs Cleo's arm, making her nearly fall to the ground. Picking her up, Jace gets her back on her feet before grabbing the cup from her hands and tossing it. Cleo lets out a squawk of anger, but Jace doesn't even acknowledge it.

"Jace, wrangling her isn't your job." Rae sighs, removing her hand with effort from Colton's to help him with Cleo. "I can take her back home."

"I'm not going anywhere with you," Cleo spits.

Rae rolls her eyes. "Like you really have any choice right now."

"This is bullshit, Rae," Jace growls. "This is your night to be happy, and she isn't going to ruin this."

"She—"

"I'll take her home," Garrett volunteers. "Mom would love to hear about this."

"It's after the run, Garrett. Cleo isn't your mom's problem anymore."

"You still have tonight right? Let me take her back to my parent's place, and in the morning, she can be yours to deal with. Just enjoy tonight for once. Just do something for yourself."

"I . . ."

"Rae," Jace says quietly, putting his hand on her shoulder. "Let us handle this."

Taking a deep breath, Rae exhales with a nod. "Okay, okay, take her to Jojo's. But in the morning . . ."

"We'll deal with it then," Jace assures. "Go back to your mate. Something tells me he has a lot of questions."

Feeling dread settle in the pit of her stomach, Rae nods. "Yeah, I bet he does."

* * *

Colton watches Rae's brother tow away the drunken blonde from the yard and out of sight. He doesn't really know how to respond to anything that just happened. He doesn't know what to make of it. When he spots Rae walking back over towards him looking incredibly stressed, his first instinct is to comfort her.

Meeting her half way, he dips his head, trying to catch her eye. He wants to see her face; to know she's okay even if he knows deep down she isn't. When she doesn't look up at him willingly, he reaches under her chin and lifts her face. His heart breaks a little to see a glossiness to them she's trying desperately to not let go of.

"Hey, it's okay," he soothes, rubbing his thumb over her chin.

She shifts her eyes away. "No, it really isn't."

"Who was that?"

"My sister." Rae sighs, kneading her forehead with her fingers. "Cleo is my younger sister. She's seventeen and apparently, can't hold her liquor."

Colton smiles a little at her attempt at humor before asking, "Is she all you have for a sibling?"

Rae shakes her head. "No."

"How many more?"

"Two," she admits quietly. "Two more younger sisters."

72

"So . . . five siblings?"

"Yup." She nods before letting out a humorless laugh. "You know it sounds way more daunting when you say it out loud like that."

"How old are they?"

"Poppy is nine, and Cassidy is six."

"And how old are you?"

"Nineteen."

He frowns. "Then why didn't you run last year?"

He watches her bite into her lower lip. "I . . . I got a pass. My parents . . . I'm the one who takes care of them. Cassidy was barely over five years old, and I wasn't sure that my mate . . . or I guess you, wouldn't want me to leave them. I didn't want to leave her when she was so young, I still don't but the alpha . . ."

"Forced you," Colton finishes tightly.

"More like convinced me with a threat."

Colton's hands curl into fists at this new information. His wolf is snarling in his head at the idea that anyone would dare make his mate do anything. He's almost thankful for the full moon knowing that if it weren't hanging in the sky like a safety net, he'd be shifting and going for the alpha's throat. His blood-drenched thoughts are cut off though when he feels shocks run up the length of his arm.

Looking down, he sees Rae's hand on his forearm. Her brown eyes are concerned as she looks up at him. "Colton?"

"Sorry," he mutters, dipping his head. "I didn't scare you, did I?"

Shaking her head, she answers, "No. Why are you so upset? That's just how alphas work, Colton. They tell you what to do, and you do it, easy as that."

"Not all alphas," he grunts.

Rae lifts a brow at him before snorting. "Really? What kind of alphas are you hanging around?"

"My father."

73

Rae is about to retort when his words seem to sink in. Colton watches her face go from shock to horror to shock again and then finally a blank expression. Chuckling, he takes her hand off his forearm to bring it to his lips so he can kiss the knuckles of it. The jolt of his touch seems to bring her out of it as she gapes up at him like she just saw him for the first time.

"Your father is an alpha?" She squeaks out.

"Yes."

"So you . . ."

"Am his beta currently. I'll take over once he feels ready to accept my challenge."

"So you'll be alpha?" she asks, swallowing thickly.

"Yes." He nods stepping closer to her with a smile. "And you will be alpha female."

"Holy fuck sticks," she breathes.

Colton grins down at his mate. Yup, one *lucky* son of a bitch.

CHAPTER NINE

Rae is trying to process Colton's bombshell when she hears the alpha start calling for everyone's attention. It's a distant sound, something hard to hear through the blood rushing through her ears but still one her wolf answers to. Automatically, her body move towards the alpha's position, but her head is just in a daze of information.

Her mate is a beta. Her mate's father is an alpha. Her mate will become alpha male of his pack, and she will be his alpha female. They will run a whole pack together, side by side. Rae swallows thickly at the thought as panic starts to set in. She can't be an alpha! She can barely remember to brush her teeth in the morning!

"I'm right here," Colton whispers in her ear as his hand tightens around hers. "I'm right here, and I'm not going anywhere."

Her body relaxes automatically at his words as she squeezes his hand back. Forcing herself to focus on the alpha on the deck of the alpha house, she tries to put all her doubts to the side. She can let them drive her insane later, right now, she's got other things to worry about.

"Everyone, I want to start off by thanking you for coming to the fall equinox, and the council for allowing us to host it this year. The White Stone pack has never been more honored to host the run as a new generation of mates find each other yet again," Alpha Kendrick says with a huge grin. "Now with that being said, I would like to ask all our mated pairs to come up to the front so you may present yourselves to your fellow pack members."

"Ah, hell," Rae mutters.

Colton smiles down at her. "What? Afraid to show me off?"

"I just don't like being the center of attention, and they always catcall at these things. I don't know about you, but I really do not want to be yelled to 'get at it'."

Rae rolls her eyes as Colton starts laughing. She likes how big his smile is and when he smiles really widely, she can see dimples show up on his cheeks. His blue eyes crease a little at the ends with happiness, but she notices it looks a bit out of practice. It seems to her that he doesn't laugh as often as he should. The thought makes her sad to think about, but she quickly resolves to fix that. He's made her happier in the past two hours of being together than she's been in months.

It's only fair she tries to do the same for him.

"Come on," he says with a crooked smile. "Let's get this done and then we can get to know each other more."

"There really isn't much more to know about me, Colton. I'm pretty boring."

"Now, that, I doubt."

Gently pulling her through the crowd, Rae follows after him as she feels her heart picking up speed in her chest. She wasn't lying when she said she doesn't like being the center of attention. Hell, in second grade, she had to sing a solo for school choir and instead of singing, she ended up vomiting on the gym floor. She doesn't do well with eyes watching her like some kind of star attraction at the zoo.

Alpha Kendrick's eyes scan over the faces of the people coming up, but they stop at Rae's face for a second too long. She watches his eyes widen as they not only take in the fact she's mated, but they nearly bug out of his skull when they see who it is she's mated to. *Yeah,* she thinks with a sigh, that was a shocker for her too.

Beside her, she hears Colton let out a low growl, making her look at him in surprise. He's not looking at her though. His attention is on the alpha who quickly averts his own eyes to look at the rest of the mated pairs. When Rae feels the alpha's attention is off of her, she lets out a light exhale in relief. She's really going to need to work at that for the future, she realizes.

"You okay?" Colton asks.

Rae nods, chewing on her lower lip.

"How about after this bullshit is taken care of you show me around? Show me your favorite place in the whole territory, so we can unwind and talk."

"What about the celebrations?"

He arches a brow at her. "Do you really want to watch people get drunk, dance around like idiots and then pass out in their own sick?"

"Well, not when you put it that way."

"Though I am curious to see what you'd be like drunk," he says with mischief clear in his blue eyes.

Rae snorts. "Not as fun as you'd hope."

"Again, I doubt that."

"Who next has been blessed to find their other half?" Alpha Kendrick calls out.

"That'd be us." Colton smiles. "Deep steady breaths and when in doubt, just look at me."

Nodding her head, Rae closes her eyes and lets Colton lead them up the stairs of the porch. When she stumbles a bit, she hears a series of laughs from the crowd before Colton's growl shuts them all up. Watching her feet the rest of the way, she can feel her face heat as she turns towards the crowd. A series of whispers begin to sound in the crowd, but Rae keeps her eyes glued at the sky above them all.

Clearing his throat, Alpha Kendrick speaks, "Names?"

"Colton Woodward."

"And you, miss?" the alpha asks when she doesn't answer right away.

"Uh, Rae Applebee."

"And Miss Applebee, have you accepted your mate?"

"Y-Yes."

"And you, Mr. Woodward, have you accepted your mate?"

Colton straightens to his full height beside her before speaking in a loud, proud voice, "Yes."

A series of whooping and hollering starts among the men. Colton looks down at her and rolls his eyes, making her fight back a laugh. She likes how relaxed he is and in turn how relaxed it makes her. She thinks that maybe this can work, but she doesn't want to put all her eggs in one basket just yet. She needs to see how he'll act around the whole family, including Cleo. Rae sighs. How the hell is she going to deal with that tomorrow?

"I wish you two the best of blessings," Alpha Julie says, bringing Rae out of her own thoughts. Standing before them in her long red dress, the alpha smiles kindly at the pair. Placing a wreath of gooseberry veins on each of their heads, the alpha female gestures for them to get off the stage.

As they begin to move off the porch, Alpha Kendrick grabs Colton's shoulder before Rae sees him whisper in Colton's ear. Rae frowns at the scene, surprised she can't hear them despite how good her hearing really is. When Alpha Kendrick releases him, she notices how tense Colton is. His jaw is clenched, and his free hand is balled into a fist.

Despite that, though, Rae doesn't say anything. She doesn't want to discuss when there are too many people nearby to hear it. As soon as they dissolve into the crowd, Colton reaches up and takes the wreath off his head. Tossing it onto a nearby picnic table, he ruffles his hair, but he still has a few small leaves stuck in it.

"Here." Rae smiles, letting go of his hand as she reaches up. Plucking a few pieces of leaf out of his hair, she lets the feel of his thick brown hair linger on her palm. Realizing that she's practically petting him, she retracts her hand quickly with a blush on her face. "Sorry."

"Don't be." He smiles. "Should we go?"

"Yes, please."

* * *

Colton is trying really hard not to go back to the party and rip the alpha's throat out. The need is boiling under the surface of his skin, pushed by his wolf. The reason the alpha had pulled him aside was to tell him they needed to discuss Rae, *his* mate. Apparently, something about their pairing was rubbing the alpha the wrong way, but Colton couldn't give a fuck.

Rae is *his*. The primal need for all to know that seemed to only heighten in him after the alpha's words. No one is going to convince him anything other than the fact that Rae is perfect for him. Her family, her own doubts, and fear, or even the alpha of her pack, couldn't convince him otherwise. She's his, and some bullshit meeting with a nosey alpha isn't going to change his mind about that simple fact.

"Colton, are you okay?"

He gazes at his mate and feels his wolf howl in his head. With the dirty white dress, berry wreath on her head, and those large dark eyes, Colton can't think of a more beautiful sight. Colton stops walking and pulls Rae against him making her squeak in surprise and a smile to form on his face. Leaning down, he hears her breath catch before lays a soft loving kiss on her cheek.

Inhaling her scent deeply, he closes his eyes and lingers long enough to relish those shocks on his lips before pulling back. Her eyes are still closed, and her full bottom lip is a bit pouted, making him fight the urge to claim it with his own. He wants to kiss her. He wants it so much it's almost painful, but he doesn't do it.

He has made a promise to himself he's taking his time with her, and he will.

Even if it kills him to do so.

"I'm fine," he assures her.

Slowly opening her eyes, his mate gazes up at him with a little frown. "But the alpha—"

"Is nosey. I'll deal with him tomorrow morning."

"Does it concern me?"

Colton debates on lying to her but eventually sighs. "Yes."

"What about me?" She scowls, anger filtering into her gaze.

"He wants to discuss our mating, I suppose. It's nothing to worry about, though, because I'm going to set him straight."

Rae purses her lips, drawing his attention back to her lips. God, what he would give right now to just taste that mouth with his own? He fights back a groan when he sees her pink little tongue come out to lick her lower lip. This is going to be harder than he anticipated, he thinks with a growled agreement from his wolf.

"I want to come with you."

Colton's gaze moves up to meet hers with a frown. "Why?"

"Because if he's talking about me, then don't you think I should be present to at least defend myself?"

Running his fingers down the soft skin of her cheek, he asks quietly, "Will that make you happy?"

"Yes," she tells him a bit breathlessly.

His lips twitch up on one end. "Then you can come."

"Really?" she asks, looking genuinely surprised.

"Isn't that what you wanted?"

"Well yeah, but I didn't think you'd actually fold so fast."

He smiles crookedly at her. "You give me too much credit. From the minute you accepted me, I was wrapped around your little finger, Rae. I wouldn't doubt that there isn't anything I wouldn't do for you."

"But . . . You hardly know me. Shouldn't you at least get to know me before you start turning into a sonnet spouting Romeo?"

80

He makes a face. "Did you have to pick the wimpiest Shakespeare male? Couldn't I be Benedick to your Beatrice?"

"Hey, he got tricked into telling Beatrice he loved her," she tells him with a teasing smile. "Would you rather play the fool or the horny suicidal teenager?"

"I'll go with the fool." Colton smiles, genuinely pleased she got the reference. "He may have been tricked, but he got the girl at the end of the play."

Rae laughs before slapping her hand over her face. Parting her fingers, she peeks at him with humor clear in her eyes. Colton's smile turns into a full-blown grin at the sight of her so carefree. It's a total one-eighty from how she was with her sister only a half hour ago. He likes that he can do this for her; to make her happy.

"You are so beautiful," he whispers, making her slowly drop her hand with a bashful look on her face.

"Already composing love sonnets, huh?" she asks awkwardly.

Colton grins while shaking his head. "Nope. I've never been very good with rhyme."

"Never?" she asks with that teasing smile back on her face. "Even that one time?"

"Clever." He smirks. "So where is your favorite place?"

"That's a bit tricky, actually."

"How so?"

"My favorite place is by my house. It's a lake my family owns."

"And that's tricky why?"

"Well . . . because of earlier. It might be awkward."

"It's almost one in the morning, Rae," he tells her flatly. "I doubt they'll be much of a bother."

She blushes and dips her head. "Good point."

Lifting her head by her chin, he gives her a reassuring smile. "And even if they were, I wouldn't mind meeting them.

81

Other than that sister of yours, they all seem really loving towards you."

"You only met Jace." She grumbles.

"And I'm sure eventually I'll meet the rest, right?"

"Yes."

"Then don't worry about it. I come from a pack where thirty people a day barge into my office and demand my attention. A few kids won't be much of a challenge."

Rae scoffs. "That's because you haven't met Cassidy yet."

"Cassidy is the youngest, right?" he asks, before grabbing her hand.

"Yup. She's six. Loud and weird as hell but that's what I like about her. Like the other day, she asked me if the reason people get old is because they drool when they sleep and if that was why people get all wrinkled. Apparently, what all older people need is a good watering."

Colton laughs with a shake of his head. "I guess that makes sense. What about your other sister?"

"Poppy?" she asks. At his nod, he watches a fond smile come across her face. "Poppy is a miniature of our mom. She even has the same sense of humor and sometimes says things that my mom would have said in the given situation. Sometimes it's hard being around her some days. It just reminds me of what we lost."

"If you don't mind me asking . . ."

"Brain aneurysm," Rae tells him in a dull voice. "It came on so sudden I don't even think she knew what hit her. She was human, my dad and her went to school together, and one day he just walked into class and knew."

"No chasing involved, huh?" Colton asks, trying to get her to smile.

He's washed with relief when it works. "Yeah, she saved him a lot of leg work."

"Can anyone else shift in your family or is it just you?"

"Just me for now. Hudson, Poppy, and Cassidy could have it, but you never know."

"What about Hudson, tell me about him."

"Hudson is just . . . Hudson. He's got this quiet way about him and this old wise man kind of temperament. I swear I think he should be petting a long thick beard while talking sometimes."

Colton smiles adoringly down at her when the smell of lake water hits his senses. He doesn't realize how much time as passed while they've been talking that they could have made it to her house already. Colton lets her take her hand out of his as she walks ahead of him towards the large football-field length lake.

Rae lifts her dress a little as he sees her bare feet step onto the worn down wood of the dock. She seems to realize he's not following and turns around to look at him over her shoulder. The innocent look on her face makes his wolf go silent, and his mind to go blank at the image she presents. A small smile spreads across her face as she looks at his dumbstruck face.

"Are you coming?" she asks.

Anywhere, he thinks, feeling winded. He'd follow her anywhere.

CHAPTER TEN

Rae closes her eyes and listens to the sounds of the lake. Crickets, the gentle lapping of the water against the shore, and the wanderings of the wildlife. This is her haven; her place away from it all and as Colton asked, and her favorite place in the territory. Hearing the dock creak under his approaching footsteps, Rae turns her head a little to see him watching her.

"Are you going to stand there all night or . . ."

Colton's mouth immediately twitches up. "Does me standing make you nervous?"

"Yes," she admits with hesitation. "I don't like not being able to see what you're doing back there."

He lowers himself down on the dock to sit next to her with a smirk on his face. Once he's settled down beside her, Rae uncrosses her legs and sticks her dirty feet into the water. She bunches her dress in her lap before finally turning to Colton who is too busy looking out at the lake with a clenched jaw.

"Are you okay?" she asks with a frown.

"Perfectly," he says quickly before putting an obviously forced smile on his face. "So you own this?"

Still a little bemused by his behavior, she answers, "Technically, it belongs to all of us kids, I just took over the responsibility when I turned eighteen."

"When did your parents . . ."

"Three years ago. I was sixteen and had no idea what I was doing. My aunt and uncle helped out a lot that first year, teaching me how to run everything and get me my jobs. It was tough, but once you get into the swing of things, it gets a bit easier."

"I'm sorry, did you say 'jobs' as in plural?"

Rae nods with a sigh. "Yup. I work at a diner in town, and I also do some of the pack daycare. If I hadn't been participating in the run tonight, I would have been armpit deep in kids right now."

"And you take care of all your siblings?" he asks slowly.

She hums in agreement before adding, "It sounds like a lot but I think I've got it all balanced out. Besides, it's not like I don't have help. Jace and Hudson are great with the girls, and even Cleo sometimes helps with the daycare on occasion."

"She helps with daycare?" Colton asks doubtfully.

Rae laughs a little at his incredulousness. "Yeah, but I have to pay her for her time."

"So it's not really helping out of the goodness of her heart."

"Look, Cleo is a teenage girl. I expect her to be difficult. Hell, you heard her say I was no better when I was her age. She's not all bad. Cleo took our parents' absence the hardest out of all of us because she was the closest to them. She and our mom were thick as thieves, and maybe that's caused me to be a bit lax with her but . . . I guess I just understand where she's coming from."

Colton doesn't say anything, and Rae knows there isn't really much to say in regards to this. She's so lost in her own thoughts she jumps a little when she feels him wrap his arm around her shoulders before pulling her into his side. She smiles at how natural it feels to be there, inhaling his scent and feeling the shocks of their bond moving across her skin.

"So . . ." She trails, deciding to get the subject away from herself for once. "What about you?"

"What about me?"

She rolls her eyes. "Your family. What are they like?"

"Oh. Well, my father is alpha, so he's often busy. We usually don't have much contact outside of the beta-alpha relationship due to his responsibilities. My mother . . ." Rae sees an adoring smile come over his face. "Well, my mom is one of those doting moms."

"No siblings?" Rae asks with a smile echoing his.

"An older brother, but he didn't get the shifting gene. He decided to take up the more business side of the pack by running the construction business. He still lives on the pack land though, with his wife."

"One sibling." Rae sighs dreamily. "Must be nice."

"Not when you're the youngest." Colton huffs.

Rae laughs loudly before turning around, so she's laying on her back on the dock. Her head is in his lap as she looks up at him with a comfortable sigh. She feels her body relax into the position when his fingers start brushing through her hair. Closing her eyes at the blissful sensation, she tries to come up with another question. When a thought occurs to her, though, she frowns.

"Colton?"

"Yes?"

"Where are you staying?"

"At the alpha's house, unfortunately." He grumbles, his fingers still moving through her hair absently.

Rae nods while biting her lower lip. She's considering offering to let him stay at her house. That way her siblings can get to know him, and he can get to know her in her own space. She doesn't want to come off as clingy or demanding of his time, though. He could have things he has to do back at the alpha house, and she also knows that she has Cleo to deal with in the morning. Still, she feels her wolf stirring restlessly in her mind at the idea of having him so far away from them.

"Colton?"

He laughs a little before grinning down at her. "Yes?"

"Do you want to stay at my house tonight?"

86

Colton's smile falls, and he begins scrutinizing her face. Silence fills the already quiet darkness around them, and Rae starts to fear she may have overstepped her bounds. She opens her mouth, about to retract her question when he speaks up.

"I don't want to pressure you into anything, Rae."

Rae frowns. "What do you mean?"

Exhaling steady, he runs a hand through his own hair while looking out at the lake. "I don't want you to feel that just because I'm your mate and you accepted me that you have to do anything . . . intimate with me."

"Intimate?"

"Yeah . . . you know . . ."

Rae grins up at him and lets out an uncharacteristic giggle. "Oh, I know what you mean, Colton. I just wanted to see you get uncomfortable."

He gives her a dirty look. "Yeah, well I hope you enjoyed the show."

Lightly hitting his chest, she gives him a scolding glare. "Lighten up. I was just trying to have a little fun, party pooper. I know you wouldn't force me to do anything, and I don't feel forced to do anything. I just know both of our wolves are going to be whining all night if we separate now."

"Good point."

"Those are the only kind of points I have," she quips back with a smirk.

"Clever."

"Always," she teases before sitting up, so she's face to face with him. Looking into his eyes, she can feel her heart speed up in her chest. "I don't want you to leave me just yet."

Reaching up, he brushes some of her hair off her face and behind her ear. "And I don't want to leave."

"Then it's settled." She smiles with a nod. "I get to hit you over the head with my club and drag you back to the cave."

Colton laughs before leaning forward to kiss the tip of her nose. "I promise I won't be complaining when you do."

* * *

Colton looks around the house as Rae leads him inside. He's trying not to laugh out loud at how adorable she looks, tip-toeing around like a burglar in her own house. Her sneakers are still in one hand as the other is entwined in his, a feeling he's not sure he'll ever get used to.

He watches her shoulders droop with a sigh. "I think everyone is asleep."

"I'd be worried about your family's sleeping patterns if they weren't," he whispers in her ear, smirking smugly when he sees her shiver.

Slapping his shoulder, she gives him a weak disproving look before starting to pull him towards the staircase. She stops on the fifth step up and tenses when a creak from the wood sounds in the quiet house. When she doesn't hear a stir, she continues leading him up the stairs. Colton is pretty sure he's never been so amused. He feels like the bad boy that the good girl is sneaking into her house under the nose of parents.

Only it's children that Rae is in fear of explaining things to.

The house is pretty and simply decorated with white walls with framed children's drawing on the walls and family photos scattered here and there. He smiles widely when he spots a school picture of Rae on the wall wearing braces, skinny as a twig with huge glasses on her face, and low pigtails of blonde hair falling on either side of the neck. She can't be more than ten in the picture, and he can't help but like this version of her too.

When they reach the third and final level of the house, he sees only three doors, but her scent trail leads to the one at the end of the hallway. He notices her tip-toeing again as they walk past the other doors but doesn't follow her lead. He has nothing to hide, and when it comes to introducing himself to people, Colton isn't a fan of the subtle approach.

"I should call you pink panther," he whispers in her ear as she grabs the doorknob of her door.

Rae rolls her eyes at him but doesn't say anything as she leads him into her room. Now this is the place that really interests Colton. You can tell a lot about a person by their room and Rae's speaks volumes. Everything is bright, understated, and practical. Still, he has to admit she obviously wasn't expecting company. He watches her with amusement as she suddenly smacks her forehead before trying to straighten up.

"I'm sorry," she whispers as she kicks her scattered clothes into a pile. "I didn't really think I'd need to clean today."

"It's fine," he assures in a low but normally toned voice. "It's nice."

"It's a mess."

He smirks at her. "Well, that too."

Smiling a little, she drops her mud-encrusted shoes on the hardwood and puts her hands on her hips, looking around. Moving some of her hair out of her face again, she bites on her lower lip, making his gaze move there. She's trying to kill him as he thinks in dejection; she has to be. It was the same back at the lake with that sight of her legs when she lifted her dress. All he could think about was how they would feel wrapped around him and his wolf's lustful growls in his head, echoing his sentiments.

"Do you need to use the bathroom?" she asks, bringing him out of his thoughts.

Shaking his head, he forces an assuring smile. "No, I'm fine."

"Okay," she mutters quietly before grabbing some clothes off a nearby chair. "I'm going to go change, and then I'll be back. Um . . . There's some men's sweatpants in the bottom drawer of the dresser. I think they might fit."

He narrows his eyes but answers, "Thank you."

Nodding awkwardly, she scurries off the connected bathroom and gently shuts the door behind her. He moves towards the dresser and opens the lower drawer to spot a pair of gray sweatpants. He doesn't like to think these are leftovers from another guy, but his possessive wolf keeps pushing the idea. Bringing the pants to his nose, he sniffs them and is relieved to only smell Rae on them. Though she could have washed them, making any trace of a male unnoticeable.

Colton shakes the thought off before it has a chance to anchor itself in his mind. She's made it pretty clear she hasn't had much of a life outside of the family these past few years. Also, he doesn't want to assume anything about her like that. Rationally, he also knows that he can't really blame her for dating someone else before she even knew of his existence. Irrationally, the thought of anyone else touching her makes him want to rip the hypothetical man to shreds.

He's brought off his homicidal thoughts when he hears the door click open. Turning around, his breath catches in his throat at the sight of her. To most, she wouldn't look like anything more than a girl ready for bed, but to him, she looks like the most beautiful creature ever set on earth. Her legs are on display with a pair of white cotton shorts, but the shorts are barely visible under the hem of her oversized tie-dye shirt.

Swallowing thickly, he tightens his grip on the sweatpants in his hand. Yup, she is definitely trying to kill him. At the sight of her red cheeks, though, he quickly looks away while clearing his throat. He doesn't want to make her uncomfortable or make her think he just wants her physically. He promised himself he'd do this right, and he will.

She just needs to stop being so damn tempting.

"You didn't change," she observes with a frown.

When she talks, he notices a hint of silver across her teeth. Tilting his head, he asks, "Is that a retainer?"

Her face goes red, and she cups her mouth with her hand before scowling at him. "So what? I have to wear it at night, okay?"

"I'm not saying anything," he defends, putting his hands up in surrender. "It looks cute."

Rolling her eyes, she gives him a dry look. "Oh yes, I'm the next Miss Universe over here."

Smiling adoringly at her, he makes his way towards the bathroom. Caressing her cheek as he passes, he hears her heart pick up speed, making his smile only widen. Deciding to get her heart really racing, he dips his head to lay a barely there kiss on the corner of her mouth. Pulling back, he sees her eyes closed and her mouth slightly open.

"I'm going to get changed now." He smirks.

Opening her eyes, she answers a little hoarsely, "Okay."

So tempting.

* * *

Rae stays perfectly still until she hears the bathroom door close behind him. Without hesitation, she throws her arms in the air and does a ridiculous happy dance. Covering her mouth with her hands, she tries her best to quiet the squeal she lets out as she jumps around. Once she's pretty sure she's got that out of her system, she's still grinning as she moves towards her bed.

Pulling back her comforter, she jumps into her bed and lands with a little bounce. Letting out one more squeal into her hands, she pushes her hair off her face and tries her best to calm down. Rae would be mortified if he saw how she's acting but she can't stop herself. This is so much better than she thought it would be.

He is so much better than she thought he'd be.

Pulling the comforter over her lap, she tries to pull on her poker face, but the need to keep giggling keeps rising in her. Closing her eyes, she sweeps her hands out in front of her, trying to find her Zen. It fails. She's back to pumping her arms in the air in celebration again before she can help herself. When the bathroom door opens again, she drops her arms and turns bright red. He looks incredibly amused, but she doesn't call him on it, hoping that it doesn't have anything to do with her little display.

"Better?" she asks, trying not to sound breathless and busted.

His face splits with a huge grin. "Definitely."

"So, um, do you have a side preference or . . ."

He shrugs. "I don't care either way."

"Right," she says, before clearing her throat awkwardly. "So are you going to get in or . . ."

His blue eyes light up with mischief. "Just can't wait to get me in bed, can you?"

She reaches over the lamp on her side table as she mutters, "Shut up."

Laughing quietly to himself, Rae feels her heart going crazy in her chest as he comes towards the bed. He crawls onto the bed and comes to lay behind her with his back against the wall. Curling up behind her, he pulls the comforter over himself as Rae turns her back to him stiffly. They lie like that for a few minutes, not touching and silent. Finally, she hears him let out a low exhale before he wraps an arm around her waist.

Pulling her against his chest, her whole back comes alive with shocks as her neck tingles with the feel of his warm breath on her skin. Closing her eyes, she tries to keep her breathing even and not like she's having a panic attack. Rae freezes though when he kisses her cheek before whispering in her ear.

"Good night, Rae."

Rae smiles a little and relaxes into him. "Good night."

Surprisingly it doesn't take long for her to fall asleep and it's one of the best in a long time.

* * *

Colton wakes up to the sound of little whispers nearby. His arms tighten around Rae as he nuzzles his face into her neck. He inhales her scent to remind himself she's still here and sighs happily, knowing she didn't remove herself from him in the night. The whispers get more high pitched when he does this though, and it makes him frown. What the hell is making that noise?

Opening one eye, he peers over a still sleeping Rae's shoulder to see two little girls. Both have blonde rat nests on the top of their heads but different colored eyes as they stare at him wide-eyed. One has blue eyes with a pair of large brown glasses while the other just stares blankly at him with eyes very similar to his Rae's. When they both see he's awake, they both stand perfectly still.

It's a stand-off of staring before the littler one of the two speaks up in a small whisper, "Are you a robber?"

Well, good morning to you too.

CHAPTER ELEVEN

Rae comes into consciousness to the sensation of something tickling her arm and a light humming noise. Opening her eyes, she sees a small figure sitting on the edge of her bed, drawing on her arm. Using her free hand, she wipes the sleep from her eyes before turning back to the small figure.

Poppy looks up at her over the top of her glasses and gives Rae a quick smile before going back to her doodle. Glancing down at her arm, Rae notices purple-marker drawn flowers going up her forearm. Rae watches Poppy for a few minutes, not wanting to ruin her masterpiece and wonders where the hell Colton is.

Something akin to him either being chased out of the house with pitchforks or being tied up and gagged in the basement come to mind, but she quickly disregards them. Jace and Hudson are simply too lazy to put that much effort into anything that elaborate. The next thought is of him going to see Alpha Kendrick by himself, but she tries not to jump to conclusions. No matter how easy it is to assume, she doesn't want to make it a habit in her relationship with him. It usually only leads to trouble.

"Okay, all done," Poppy says simply as she puts the cap back on her marker.

Inspecting it, Rae asks, "What inspired the drawing session today?"

Poppy shrugs. "I saw some pretty flowers outside my window today."

"Ah." Rae nods before frowning. "Where's Cassidy?"

"Eating breakfast."

Rae nods, still wondering where the hell Colton is.

"Your boyfriend is making her breakfast," Poppy adds after a second.

"My b-boyfriend?"

Poppy pushes up her glasses before nodding. "Yup. He's really nice. He said he would make her breakfast if she didn't wake you up. Cassidy wasn't too sure about him at first, but I told her he didn't look like a robber. He looked more like a teddy bear because you were cuddling up with him like one."

Rae feels her face get hot at the cuddling bit but quickly sat up. She scurried out of bed and was about to rush out of her room when she realized she should probably freshen up a bit. Running into her bathroom quickly, she brushes her teeth and washes her face before running a brush through her hair. It's all hopefully subtle things, but as soon as she's finished, she realizes how unprepared she feels for the inevitable meeting.

Inside, she's really just forcing her impending panic attack to the side. She doesn't have time to have a heart attack right now. For all she knows, he's down there alone with Cassidy who more than likely is digging in his mouth to see how big his teeth are. Rae knows how she is mostly due to the fact she pulled a similar expedition earlier this week.

"Come on, let's go see what the teddy bear is doing down there," Rae says as she offers Poppy's hand.

"I told you, Rae, he's making breakfast."

Rae rolls her eyes. "Well, let's make sure he's not burning the place down."

Poppy takes her hand with a sigh, and they both leave her room. As soon as they start descending the stairs, Rae hears Cassidy laughing. This is coupled with the smells of eggs, cinnamon, and bread, along with Colton's own personal scent. Rae feels a bit of relief knowing that he's still here as she moves down the last few remaining steps.

Poppy lets go of Rae's hand and runs ahead into the kitchen as Rae starts playing with the hem of her t-shirt. There's a fear lingering in her head that maybe this nice guy act was just until he got her acceptance. Maybe now, in the morning light, he'll decide she doesn't need to come to the alpha's house or choose how to continue this mating.

A larger part of her knows that that isn't what'll happen, but she can't help that long-held fear in her heart. She doesn't want it to be an act or a way for him to just sweeten her up before showing his real personality. With all these doubts swirling in her head, she doesn't hear anyone approaching her until a warm hand lands on her shoulder. Letting out a squeak, she jumps nearly out of her skin.

"Calm down!" Jace chuckles, with his hands up in surrender. "I didn't mean to scare you, but I did assume you were going to hear me. You are the one with the heightened senses."

Unsurprisingly, Jace is shirtless with nothing more than plaid pants on. His shaggy red hair is a mess on the top of his head as he grins at her. He looks a bit tired, and she doesn't need to guess why. Underage or not, the kids always drink at the equinox parties and Jace now being sixteen is no different.

Giving him a quick dry look, she runs a hand down her face with a groan. "Sorry, I was deep in thought."

"I could see that. What about?"

"Do it again!" Cassidy shrieks from the kitchen making both of them turn towards the room.

Jace frowns at the kitchen door. "Who is she in there with?"

"Colton."

"Your mate, Colton?" Jace asks in surprise.

Rae nods while chewing her lower lip. "Apparently, Cassidy blackmailed him into making her breakfast."

"Ow, I feel so replaced."

Rae smiles at her brother's wounded look. "Don't worry, you'll always be her favorite chef."

"Until she finds a mate."

"Even then, I'm sure she'll always ask you to make her grilled cheese. Apparently, no one else makes it like you do."

Jace snorts. "Damn right, no one else does. So, how did it go last night?"

"Good," she admits with a goofy smile. "He's really nice."

"Does he know about our situation?"

"Of course. It's not like I can hide you guys from him. Besides, I wouldn't want to. He's going to be part of this family too, Jace. I want him to love you guys as much as I do."

Jace makes a face. "Don't you think that's a little much to ask from him?"

"I'm not asking him to love you guys. I'm just hoping. Can't I just be optimistic?"

"Sure, you can." Jace nods. "I just don't think it's healthy."

Rolling her eyes, Rae decides to change the subject. "Did Cleo get back okay?"

"Back in one piece but she'll be feeling like hell today," Jace says with an overly pleased expression. "She was pushing the limit with me last night, Rae. I can't imagine how pissed you must be at her."

"I'm not really," Rae says quietly.

"What? How are you not pissed as hell at her?"

"She's having a hard time, Jace. I can't just—"

"She's having a hard time?" He repeats like the words are dirty. "News flash Rae, We're all having a hard time! None of us are okay and guess what, we're never going to be okay but that doesn't give her a pass to act the way she does."

"I know that but—"

"No 'buts' Rae. She needs to have some damn sense knocked into her and if you keep letting her do this shit, then so do you!"

"Is there a problem?"

Both Jace and Rae turn at the sound of the curt voice. Rae's wolf howls in her head as she takes in Colton outside the kitchen. He's still shirtless with his arms crossed over his bare chest as he glares at her younger brother. His eyes aren't blue right now though, they're the yellow of his wolf telling Rae he's not happy about Jace's tone.

"This really isn't any of your business," Jace tells him flatly.

Rae winces at his choice of words before shifting her gaze to Colton again. Colton runs his tongue over his teeth before a cold smirk comes across his face. Dropping his crossed arms to his side, she sees them still locked into fists as he approaches the two of them. Her body reacts immediately to his proximity, but she tries to keep herself from focusing on the incoming disaster and not on her hormones.

"It becomes my business when you start threatening my mate."

Jace frowns. "Threatening?"

"Uh, Jace, why don't you go check on the girls in the kitchen," Rae suggests, putting her hands on Colton's chest when he takes a step forward. When Jace hesitates, she adds a quick, "Now."

Jace narrows his eyes at Colton before moving past them to enter the kitchen. Once the door swings closed behind him, Rae drops her hands off his chest to smush her face with the palm of her hand with a groan. She feels shocks go up her arm when Colton grabs her wrist and lowers her hand so he can look at her. Scanning over her face, he frowns at her.

"You're upset."

"Well, you kind of did just have a standoff with my brother," she tells him dryly.

98

Colton drops his head and sighs deeply. "I'm sorry. I don't know why I acted that way. I forget how it can be between siblings sometimes."

"Your wolf was just trying to protect me, I get that."

"You're very understanding," he tells her with a small smile.

Rae scoffs. "I have to raise five siblings, I kind of have to be."

Taking her hand in his, he lifts her arm and uses his fingers to trace one of the flowers on her arm. "Nice artwork."

"Poppy is the artistic one in the family."

"I tried to get her to come down here with me, but she promised she'd behave so I let her be." Colton says as his fingers dance up her arm, making goosebumps rise on her skin. "She didn't wake you, did she?"

Rae shakes her head as her breathing speeds up. "No. I think I just noticed you were gone."

"Miss me, did you?" He smiles looking pleased.

Despite her red cheeks, she sticks her tongue out at him before muttering, "Arrogant ass."

His grin only widens. "I'm sorry, what was that? I didn't hear you."

"You are an arrogant ass," she says slowly.

Rae lets out a shriek that turns into laughter as he suddenly throws her over his shoulder. A smack on her butt has her shrieking again before she starts pounding her fists on his back. He doesn't let her down though. Instead, he just moves towards the kitchen with what she assumes to be a triumphant smile on his face.

"Colt, why do you have Rae on your back?" She hears Cassidy ask with what sounds like a full mouth.

"Because he's an arrogant ass," Rae mutters, knowing that no one but Colton can hear her.

Colton chuckles, before smacking her butt again, making her cry out. His voice turns sugary sweet as he answers Cassidy

99

though, "Well, honey, Rae was saying naughty words out there, and naughty words are never okay."

"Is butt a naughty word?" Cassidy asks after a second.

"No," Colton answers with laughter in his voice.

"What about poop?"

"Nope."

"What about freak?"

"Depends on the context," Colton answers after a second of thought.

Cassidy is silent for a second before asking, "What about fuck?"

"Cassidy Lenore Applebee!" Rae gasps as her stomach starts to churn at being upside down so long. It's only made worse by the fact that Colton's body is shaking with laughter. Rae hits his back with a loud smack of her hand. "Tell her it's a bad word Colton, or I swear to god—"

"Sorry, honey, that is a very bad word."

"Well, then why does everyone keep saying it?" Cassidy asks innocently.

"Because they're older," Poppy replies smartly.

"So when I'm older I can say it?"

Jace steps in then. "Maybe."

"Jace!" Rae yells.

"Or maybe not," Jace corrects.

Rae smacks Colton's back again. "Okay, now you need to put me down."

"But I like the view."

"You won't for much longer if I puke down your back."

Still laughing, Colton slowly lets Rae back onto her bare feet. She stumbles a bit as her blood starts returning to the rest of her body in a rush and Colton steadies her. Smiling down at her adoringly, Colton brushes some of her hair out of her face. All her earlier annoyance drains out of her body, making her annoyed all over again. It's not fair that she can't stay mad at him or even remember why she was mad in the first place.

"Better?" he asks.

"Much." She sighs before looking over her shoulder at what everyone's eating. "Is that French toast?"

"Special recipe that one," Colton tells her as he pulls her by her waist against him. "Maybe if you're nice, I'll tell you what's in it."

"Well, if you did tell me it'd be a waste. I can barely boil water in a pot. Jace is the real chef in this house."

Colton looks over at her brother inspecting one of the pieces of French toast with a keen eye before smirking at her. "Well that's interesting."

"I guess," she agrees with a confused look, having no idea where he's going with this. "Anyway, thanks for making the girls' breakfast."

"My pleasure."

"Can you guys move this little love fest into the hallway?" Jace asks with a dull look. "You're going to make me hurl."

"Shut up, pipsqueak," Rae says quickly, not taking her eyes off Colton who looks amused, then she frowns and turns her head. "Where's Hudson?"

Jace shrugs as he brings his glass of orange juice to his mouth, "I don't know. I'm pretty sure I was told, not even five seconds ago, to shut up."

"Jace, don't make me three name you. Where's your brother?"

"Where he always is," Jace tells her with an eye roll. "He's out running."

"Again?"

"Basketball training, I guess." He shrugs, again.

"Huh," she grunts before turning back to Colton. "Are we still going to see the alpha this morning?"

"You sure you still want to come?"

"Yes."

Colton nods. "Then yes. We'll leave in about a half an hour. Will you ready by then?

Rae rolls her eyes. "Thanks for the question, but it only takes me fifteen minutes to get ready."

"See?" he says with a wink. "I knew you were a keeper."

"Gag," Jace drawls from behind her.

"Is that a bad word?" Cassidy asks.

Rae drops her head on Colton's chest. Well, it could have gone worse.

CHAPTER TWELVE

When Colton woke up that morning to the faces of two little girls, he was more than a little caught off guard. He realized that Rae was still asleep and seeing her so relaxed, decided not to wake her. So he beckoned the girls forward, and so began one of the strangest conversations he has been involved in.

"Are you a robber?" the younger girl asks again.

Colton frowns but shakes his head as he whispers back. "No. Why would you think that?"

"Because you broke into our house, but on TV they steal stuff. Did you steal anything?"

"Uh, no. I can't say I did."

"Poppy," the younger girl whispers to the older one. "I don't think he's a robber."

The older girl or Poppy, he supposes, rolls her big blue eyes behind her glasses. "Of course he's not a robber. Maybe he's a teddy bear."

"He doesn't look like a teddy bear," the younger one says, giving him an uncomfortably intense stare. Reaching out, she pokes his bare arm. "He's not furry like one."

"I'm not a teddy bear," Colton says, wondering if he should just come out and say it. "Do you girls know what a mate is?"

Both of them shake their heads and Colton sighs before ruffling a hand through his hair. This just got harder to explain. Biting his lower lip, he looks over at the still sleeping Rae and decides to just bite the bullet. They

103

haven't discussed what they are on a more conventional level, but he knows what he's going to ask her to be.

"Well, I'm not a teddy bear, but I'm your sister's boyfriend."

"How did you know we were her sisters?" Poppy asks with her hands on her hips.

Taking in their blonde hair, attitudes, and matching noses, Colton arches an eyebrow. It's pretty obvious these girls are related to his Rae. Besides, what other kids would be hanging out in her house this early in the morning?

"Maybe he's magic!" the younger girl, who he's guessing to be Cassidy, squeals.

Rae starts to stir in the bed beside him, making both him and Poppy shush Cassidy. She crosses her little arms over her chest and huffs, but Colton's eyes are already back on Rae. When she pouts her lower lip and nuzzles her face more into her pillow, he relaxes knowing she's still asleep.

"I'm not magic, but you do look a lot like your sister," Colton whispers.

Poppy scoffs before pushing up her glasses. "Tell us something we don't know."

"Do you have a name?" Cassidy asks.

"Colton."

"I'm Cassidy," she says before putting her hand out for him to shake. Colton grins as he reaches out to shake it a few times. He can see what Rae meant by saying the littler one was a bit strange. "This is my sister, Poppy."

"Hello," Poppy says with a wave.

"Do you girls usually come up here to wake her up?"

Both of them nod and Colton frowns. Well, first thing he can do is at least let her sleep in a bit. He promised her he'd let her go with him to the alpha's today and as much as he doesn't want to do that, he won't go back on his word. He also wants a little time to get to know his soon-to-be little sisters. Motioning for them to back up a little, Colton tries to not jostle Rae as he crawls out of bed. When both of his feet hit the hardwood floor, he lets out a little sigh.

Turning his attention to the girls, he smiles at them. "You girls hungry?"

"I'm hungry!" Cassidy says with her hand in the air.

"What are you making?" Poppy asks.

"Um . . . French toast?"

Poppy narrows her eyes at him. "Is it any good?"

Colton shrugs with a little laugh. "I can't really say. I don't really cook much, but I'd be happy to try."

"I'm hungry!" Cassidy says again, but this time jumping around a bit.

"Okay, can you show me the kitchen?"

Cassidy nods her head excitedly before grabbing his hand in her much smaller one. He stumbles forward a bit in surprise with how strong she is as she pulls him towards the bedroom door. Noticing Poppy isn't following, he hangs onto the door frame while frowning at her.

"Are you coming?"

Poppy shakes her head with a little smile. "I'm not hungry."

"You sure?"

She nods before asking, "Colton, are you really my sister's boyfriend?"

"Yup."

"Do you like her?"

Colton smiles. "I like her a lot."

"So you won't hurt her?"

"I'll try my best not to."

"Okay." Poppy nods as she sits on the end of the bed by Rae's feet. "Colton?"

He steps back into the room while Cassidy continues to try to pull him towards the stairs. "Yeah?"

"Don't let Cassidy touch the stove. She likes to see how big she can get the flames on it, and Rae gets mad when we burn pots."

Colton laughs a little at the troublemaker still tugging on him. Winking at Poppy, he grins. "Will do."

Colton comes back into the present as Rae's figure disappears from the kitchen to go get ready for the meeting with the alpha. He can feel his wolf's disappointment not to have her

105

near anymore and lets out a sigh. He can't help but dislike having her out of his arms too.

"You always so whipped?" Jace asks from behind him.

Narrowing his eyes, Colton turns to face him. "Are you always this irritating?"

"No, not always. You just caught me on one of my good days." He smirks.

Colton runs his tongue over his teeth before turning to the more adorable company sitting at the counter. "How's the grub?"

Poppy looks up with cheeks full of food to give him two thumbs up while Cassidy just grunts as she stuffs a huge piece in her mouth. Smiling at the sight, Colton sits on one of the stools at the counter beside Cassidy. He's found a soft spot for the little girl since their cooking adventure earlier.

She especially liked when he flipped the french toast in the air, he recalls.

"So what's this meeting about the alpha?" Jace asks, his tone oddly serious.

Colton shrugs. "I can't really say. All I know is he pulled me aside and said he wanted to talk to me."

"About Rae?"

"I got that feeling."

Jace shakes his head before bringing his glass of orange juice up to his mouth. "He'll probably try to warn you off. He likes Rae, I'm pretty sure he has a lot of respect for her even, but he's not going to be fond of her finding an alpha heir as a mate."

"And why would that be?"

"First of all you're going to want her to come with you, and if you take her, you're going to need to take us, too. She won't leave us behind, and I know you aren't going to leave her behind."

"True, but why would that upset that alpha? Should he be happy she found someone who can help her?"

"Are you going to help her?" Jace asks tightly. "Or is this nice guy act going to go to the wayside when she lets you mark her?"

"Look," Colton says with some force as he narrows his eyes. "I care about your sister, a lot. She is the other half of my soul and the one my wolf has been going crazy for since he first saw her. I would never let anything hurt her, and that includes me. That's what mates do. They watch out for each other's needs and no matter how much I want to mark her, I will wait until she's ready. Call it whipped, call it being her bitch, but if that's what I have to do to keep Rae by my side happily, I'll do it."

Jace stares at Colton blankly for a few minutes before a huge grin spreads across his face. Holding up his glass of orange juice towards Colton, Jace winks at him. "Well then, I guess there is hope for you yet."

Colton picks up his own glass and clinks it against Jace's glass, "Let's hope you're right."

Because he really, really likes Rae.

* * *

Rae uses her towel to dry her wet hair as she steps out of the shower. Grabbing some of her hair in her fingers, she inspects the pink tips at the ends and notices they're fading out. Blowing a raspberry with her lips, she drops the piece of hair and shrugs. No time to do it now.

After slipping on her underwear, she grabs the pair of light colored skinny jeans and a white V-neck t-shirt off the sink and slips them on. Wrapping the towel around her head, she continues her after shower routine as her mind begins to wander. At the thought of Colton, a huge smile comes across her face, and some toothpaste drips out of her mouth.

She feels so comfortable with him. Their little display in the kitchen just made her realize how comfortable she really is. She's dated some guys in the past, no one really to write home about but generally nice guys all the same. Still, she never did much PDA with them, let alone in front of her family. Even when her parents were alive, it was just something she never liked doing. With Colton though, it just feels natural to be that way.

She hopes that's just not the mating bond.

Her shoulder tingles a little and her stomach clenches at the thought of being marked by him. When she thinks about marking him herself, her gums tingle, and her wolf growls lustfully in her head. Her wolf is just as desperate to mark him as she is, but they don't want to rush anything. Rae asked him to hold off on doing that until she could figure out a solution to her situation, so it would be silly of her to go back on that now.

Right?

Rinsing out her mouth, she puts her toothbrush back in the nearby holder before standing up straight again. At the sight of her reflection, she tilts her head as she realizes how different she looks. All glowing and well rested. Continuing to inspect her face, she decides to just go all natural for the day. She simply doesn't have the willpower for anything else.

Exiting the bathroom, she realizes her sneakers are still mud-caked, so she grabs her nude ballet flats. As she slips them on, she hangs onto her dresser, and for fun, slides her feet and free arm into third position. Feeling muscles stretch that she doesn't even realize she used in her many years of ballet, she grunts a little.

"Do you miss it?"

Looking over her shoulder, Rae sees Cleo watching her from the doorway. Dropping her hand, she turns her feet forward and shrugs. "Sometimes."

"Mom always liked when you danced."

Rae smiles a little before shaking her head, "No, mom always liked it when *we* danced. Something about building the bonds of sisterhood or some *Oprah* type shit."

Cleo laughs a little and Rae turns to face her. Cleo is in a pair of cut-off shorts and a tight pink shirt that shows off most of her stomach. Her long blonde hair is in a messy bun on the top of her head, and her face is clean of any makeup. Rae smiles at the sight, this is the Cleo she remembers, the Cleo she misses.

"Listen, about last night," Cleo begins with a heavy sigh. "I didn't mean to say all the stuff to you. I . . . I'm a little jealous. I always wanted a wolf and a mate, but I don't have either, and you have both now. I'm sorry for telling him all that stuff about you, about us, I was a little drunk."

Rae plays with the hem of her shirt as a goofy smile comes across her face. "I know that. Despite what you may think, Cleo, I don't hate you. You're my sister and despite how annoying or downright nasty you can be, especially drunk, I still love you."

"I know that," Cleo says quietly. "I know you love me, and I love you too. Despite what a controlling and embarrassing sister you can be sometimes."

"Well . . ." Rae trails off with a little laugh. "We can't all be perfect."

"But we get pretty close."

"We do."

Cleo smiles a bit shyly before pushing herself off the doorframe. "So where is your knight in shining armor?"

"Downstairs with Jace, Cassidy, and Poppy."

"And you just left him down there?"

Rae shrugs. "Well I needed a shower, and I couldn't exactly let him watch."

"Why not?"

Rae rolls her eyes before taking the towel off her head to throw it at Cleo. The tan towel lands on Cleo's face, making her shriek before throwing it off and onto the ground. Giving Rae a dirty look, Cleo flips her sister off, making Rae laugh before stepping forward to wrap an arm around her younger sister's shoulders.

"Don't be such a spoil sport."

"You threw your dirty towel at me! It touched your ass, and now it was on my face! I probably have pink eye now!" Cleo yells as she tries to get out of Rae's hold, but Rae only tightens it.

"Don't be so dramatic," Rae tells her with an eye roll.

"Whatever," Cleo dismisses flippantly. "Let's go save your boyfriend from our family."

As they walk down the steps together, Rae can hear Cassidy and Poppy running around downstairs, apparently no longer in the kitchen. She hears their footsteps lead to the living room, and the TV turn on before the *SpongeBob* theme comes on. She really needs to get them outside more, she tells herself.

"What's that smell?" Cleo asks "Is Jace making french toast?"

"Nope. Colton did."

"Colton is your mate, right?"

Rae nods. "Yup. Apparently, this is his mother's secret recipe version of French toast."

Cleo raises an eyebrow. "Isn't that just bread, eggs, and cinnamon?"

"Yes," Rae agrees with a little laugh. "Part of me was hoping he put some vodka in it or something."

Cleo groans and holds her forehead. "More liquor is something I so do not need right now."

"Noted."

When they reach the bottom step, Rae kisses Cleo's temple, prompting her to make a face. Rae doesn't care if she doesn't like it, though. Rae's holding out hope that this apology for last night is just the beginning to a whole new Cleo. Maybe things will go for the better, she hopes. Maybe they can be like they used to be before their parent's died.

Cleo heads for the kitchen, but Rae doesn't follow. Instead, she just sits on the third to the bottom step on the stairwell and runs her hand through her hair. Cleo's earlier question pops into her mind, *does she miss dancing?* Yes, part of her misses it, but she had to stop soon after their mom died.

She simply couldn't pay for it anymore and though Cleo was more than welcome to continue, she too soon quit. It was something they used to do for their mom, an avid lover of ballet. They used to put on these little productions in the living room for their parents and when Jace was born they even had him join in, much to his strong dislike.

Rae cuts off the thought immediately. She can feel the tears coming, and she really doesn't want to be a blubbering mess in front of Colton. He has years of finding out what an emotional mess she can be, best not to lay it all on him at once. Running her hands down her face, she lifts her gaze to the deer antler chandelier hanging above the entry. Why her dad thought that was a nice decorative choice is beyond her.

"Are you ready to go?"

Rae turns her head so fast her neck cracks, making her wince. Colton looks like he took a shower and from the scent mixed with his, she's guessing he borrowed some of Jace's clothes. Well, that and she does most of the laundry in the house, and she'd recognize that *Black Veil Brides* shirt from anywhere. His brown hair is a bit damp and in the light filtering in from some of the windows, the ends look almost golden, making her sigh. Like it or not, she can't help but enjoy the way he looks.

Hell, his jaw line is more structured than her life.

"Huh?" she asks after a second.

Colton smiles smugly at her. "I asked if you were ready to go."

"Yup. Are we walking there or . . ."

"Actually, I thought we'd go in wolf form."

Rae drops her head and whines, "Oh, come on, man! I just got dressed!"

Colton laughs before walking over to kneel before her. Brushing some of her hair behind her ear, he smiles when she

111

shivers as his fingers trail down her cheek. "I know, but I want to see your wolf. If your mask is any kind of hint, I think she'll be beautiful."

"You're trying to be charming." She observes begrudgingly. "And it's working."

"I try my best."

"Fine." She sighs. "Let's do it then. She's dying to get out, anyway."

Colton stands up straight as Rae gets off the steps. Taking her hand in his, he leads her towards the front door. It's only a short walk, and when they reach the woods, they separate. Rae strips back out of her clothes and folds them into a pile. Getting down on her knees she feels the heat of the shift come over her body. She barely feels the bones cracking, her skin turning into fur or her body contorting into a new shape, anymore.

It wasn't so easy the first time. At first, she didn't know what the hell was happening. She was restless weeks before it happened, irritable, and closed off from everyone. She thought maybe her period was just coming up, but when this red hot pain shot through her body one night, she knew she was wrong. Her dad had come bursting into her room when he heard her scream and when he saw her condition, rushed her outside. It took hours the first time and hurt like hell, but once it was over, she never felt more whole.

Shaking her body, Rae, now in wolf form, moves over to the clothes pile and scoops it up in her mouth. No way is she wasting this understated but cute outfit today. Still, she tries really hard not to drool on it, nothing is worse than having to wear slobbered on clothes. It's not only gross, but it's also wet.

Rae moves out of her section of the brush and comes out into the open to see Colton already waiting for her. She'd love to say she's surprised by how handsome his wolf is, but she isn't. His wolf looks like him—thick, chocolate-colored fur, and blue eyes, but with a splash of gold around the iris with a proud air in his posture. Yeah, she thinks with a mental eye roll, that looks like her Colton.

They communicate through the mind, like they aren't fully mated, and he isn't in her pack. Pride, pure as day, comes across his face as he takes in her gray and white wolf. She's a bit smaller than him, sleeker, and built more for speed than brawn, but she's been known to pin a wolf or two when needed. When his eyes drop to the clothes in her mouth, though, he tilts his head curiously.

Rae just rolls her eyes. She can't and doesn't want to explain, so to get things moving, she decides to just bolt. The wind moving through her fur, and the feel of the ground yielding under her feet have her struggling to keep her clothes in her mouth. She really wants to open her mouth and stick her tongue out to taste the air. Her wolf is enjoying it too. Rae doesn't get many opportunities to let her out so when she does, both of them don't take it for granted.

Colton comes into her peripheral vision, weaving through the trees and Rae works her legs faster. She knows he's not as fast as her, and she likes having a leg up on the competition. Pushing herself harder, she can feel him dropping back behind her as the alpha house comes into view and she feels the presence of other pack mates near.

That you, Applebee? one of the sentries, asks through the mind link.

Yes, Sir. Me and my mate, Colton Woodward.

I heard about that, congratulations.

Thanks, Bobby.

Not hearing a response, Rae starts to slow down a bit when the alpha house is only a mile away. She needs to get dressed again, and Colton, who didn't bring clothes, needs to find some fig leaves or something. Softening her run into a light jog, she heads towards a nearby utility shed on the property. There's no sentry over there to accidentally see her, and due to years of group pack runs, she can get dressed pretty quick.

Feeling the air caress her now bare and very human skin, Rae shivers at the coverage change. Slipping on her bra and underwear quickly, she's about to clasp the button on her jeans when she feels eyes on her. Lifting her gaze, she sees Colton dressed in jeans and an ill-fitting t-shirt. She freezes. She doesn't have her shirt on yet, so she's just in jeans and her black sheer bra.

Squeaking a little, she crosses her arms over her chest while her face turns bright red. He just had to walk in now, didn't he? She hears him approach but refuses to look up at him. She's embarrassed but also a little nervous about what he'll do. Male werewolves aren't exactly known to be the most patient when it comes to finishing mating. A nice guy or not, Colton is a male wolf.

That's probably why she's so surprised when she feels the cotton of her t-shirt being pulled over her head. Glancing up, she sees Colton's eyes are bright yellow with his wolf at the surface, but his hands are gentle as he pries her arms off her chest to help her slip them into the sleeves. She shivers a bit when his knuckles rub down the flesh of her stomach as he continues to pull the shirt down. Once she's covered, she clears her throat, trying to think of something, anything really to say.

"Thank you," she whispers.

Colton grips her chin in his fingers, making her look up at him, "No rush, no pressure, and never in a place anyone can walk in."

Her cheeks start to burn again, and he smiles adoringly down at her. Lowering his head a little, he lays a kiss on each of her cheeks before leaning back. His eyes are half lidded as he gazes down at her and she watches the blue slowly begin to take over the gold there.

"I love it when you blush, you know that?"

"Uh . . . no."

"Well, I do."

Rae fights to not blush again. He seems to notice and smirks at her before grabbing her hand in his again. Lifting their entwined hands, he kisses the back of hers with his eyes never breaking contact with her own wide ones.

"Let's go talk to the alpha," he murmurs.

Nodding, her tone is almost breathless. "Okay."

As he pulls her towards the alpha house, Rae feels her palm begin to sweat. She doesn't see this ending well, or even starting well, but if the alpha wants to discuss her, she'll be there. She never backs down from a challenge, not even from the alpha himself.

CHAPTER THIRTEEN

Rae is going to vomit. At least that's what feels like. With every step closer to the front door of the alpha house, she's fighting the urge to bolt. It's odd because it's not like the alphas are particularly mean or strict, they just scare the crap out of her. It's like you breaking something and your parents finding out. You know they're going to be pissed, but you're not sure at what level of pissed off they're going to be.

"Rae, it's going to fine," Colton tells her with a heavy sigh.

"I know," she says quickly. "But it doesn't mean I can't be nervous."

"But why are you nervous?"

"I don't know! It's like going to the principal's office or something."

Colton chuckles. "I promise you won't get detention. I have connections."

Rae slaps his arm and gives him a weak glare. "Don't be cute. I'm trying to have a panic attack here."

"Well, stop."

"Yes, sir. Will do, sir."

Colton rolls his eyes. "Sarcasm is the lowest form of wit."

"Yeah, but at least I'm still witty. Now knock on the damn door so we can get this over with."

He lifts a brow at her before shaking his head. "And people call me bossy."

"Shut up."

Colton smirks before knocking on the door of the alpha house. Rae tries to keep still, but the urge to start rocking on her heels or drums her hands on her legs is getting worse the longer they wait. She wants to know what the alpha wants to say to Colton, but on the other hand, she doesn't want to know. You can't forget something once you've heard someone say it.

Rae's about to drop off her facade of control when the door opens. She's unsurprised to see Alpha Julie answer the door again but this time she has a little girl balanced on her hip. The little girl, Sadie, is adorable. With her light brown hair in high set pigtails that curl at the ends and bright blue eyes, Rae feels her heart melt at the sight of her. She's always been a sucker for little girls, especially the cute ones. It's probably why Poppy and Cassidy are as adored as they are.

"Rae!" Alpha Julie says with clear surprise before she turns her eyes towards Colton. Inclining her head a bit in respect, Alpha Julie smiles tightly. "Were we expecting you both today?"

"Your alpha told me last night he wanted to speak with me," Colton tells her simply.

"Just you?" she asks, giving Rae a quick glance.

Colton narrows his eyes, and Rae can feel the tension practically rolling off him. Squeezing his hand tightly, Rae steps in. "Is the alpha here by chance?"

"Yes," Alpha Julie replies with her still plastered on smile. "Please, come in."

Alpha Julie steps out of the way and lets both of them inside the house. Nothing's changed since her last visit, but Rae is still blown away by the house. It makes her admittedly run-down house look even more like a crap shack. Following the alpha female into the living room, she suddenly turns and faces them.

"I was just going to put Sadie down for a nap," she informs them. "Rae, would you like to help?"

117

Rae opens her mouth to respond, but Colton's cold voice cuts in, "That won't be necessary, Alpha. Rae wishes to come into the meeting between the alpha and myself."

"Well, that's boring," the alpha dismisses. "Why don't you come help me? I can show you the baby's room."

"I think I'd rather sit in on the meeting, Alpha," Rae says quietly with an apologetic smile.

Alpha Julie purses her lip for a second before sighing heavily, "Fine. Kendrick is up in his office. I assume you know the way, Rae?"

Rae doesn't miss her friendly tone disappear and feels her nerves peak. "Yes, Alpha."

"Well, head up then. You know how he hates waiting."

Rae begins dragging Colton towards the stairs with sweaty palms and a churning stomach. She doesn't know exactly what this meeting is about, but if Alpha Julie's behavior is anything to go on, it can't be good. Deciding to at least not act as freaked out as she is, she stands up a bit straighter and wipes all expression from her face. She needs to just buck up and face this, Alpha or not, she's not just going to sit by and let him talk to her mate without her.

It's just not happening.

"You good?" Colton asks lowly in her ear as they reach the top of the staircase.

Rae nods with a steady exhale. "Yup."

Colton nods reluctantly before grabbing the doorknob. Rae initially is shocked. No knock, no greeting, nothing. He just walks into the room like he owns the damn place. Rae's jaw unlatches, and she gapes at him, but he doesn't see it. His eyes are already narrowed and cold as they zero in on the alpha behind his desk.

"I see . . ." Alpha Kendrick says into the phone pressed to his ear. His eyes lift up to take in both Colton and herself with slight surprise before they wash off all emotion. Sitting back in his chair, the alpha's gaze never leaves them as he continues to talk on the phone. "And you spoke to Vince? Okay, okay. Well, keep looking. I don't want him losing the trail. Alright."

Alpha Kendrick puts down the phone without so much as a "goodbye" and leans forward in his chair. Entwining his hands before him on his desk, the alpha's eyes take in their clasped hand with narrow eyes. Rae stumbles a bit, too interested in what the alpha is doing and doesn't notice the chair right in front of her. Rubbing her thigh, she blushes red and quickly moves to sit in the chair.

"Well, this is a surprise," Alpha Kendrick says finally, once they're both settled before him. "I didn't expect to be seeing you, Rae."

"I-I wanted to come with."

"Didn't I make it clear I just wanted to speak to you, Colton?"

Colton's anger is immediately visible from his seat beside her. His arms flex and his hands curl into fists on the armrests. Rae isn't touching him anymore so she can't really soothe him. Instead, she just watches as he coldly smirks at the alpha who looks highly annoyed by her presence.

"What you want and what's happening are two very different things, Kendrick."

The alpha narrows his eyes. "Call me Alpha, Colton. I've earned it."

"Then call me Beta. I earned my position just as rightfully as you won yours."

Alpha Kendrick huffs a laugh before sitting back in his chair, "Alright then, *Beta*. Did I not make it clear that this was a private meeting?"

"A meeting about what exactly?" Colton asks directly. "Maybe if you told me what exactly it is you want to discuss; I can judge how private it needs to be."

The alpha's eyes move to Rae for a split second. "I think you know exactly the subject of our talk, Beta."

"Then she has every right to be here, don't you think?"

"This is a delicate matter," he answers through gritted teeth.

Colton smirks at his agitation. "I'm sure she can handle it."

Rae watches the exchange between the two men with wide eyes. She could never even dream of speaking to an alpha like that, let alone an agitated one. Her dad was an enforcer, a protector of the alpha family, and he always told her that disrespect leads to punishment. It's engrained in her like the "A, B, C's" or talking. You just don't mess with the alpha, but that's exactly what Colton's doing.

"Fine," the alpha replies tersely. "I wish to discuss the compatibility of your mating."

"What about it?" Colton asks coldly.

"I don't think this would be a smart undertaking for either one of you."

Colton's knuckles are white as his fists tighten on the chair armrest. "I assume you have a good reason to suggest such a disrespectful thing."

"I do. Besides the fact of you being next in line for an alpha and Rae's status as a lower rank member of the pack, it seems inappropriate. Also, there is the fact of her family situation. She has five siblings, all under legal age who would have to be taken on by your pack and in turn, a burden on your resources. Lastly, I would also point out the fact that Rae, though highly skilled in many things, would not be fitting to run a pack your size."

Rae hears Colton's bones begin to crack as the alpha speaks. At first, she can't help but think that her alpha is not only an asshole but a snobby asshole. His points are kind of valid, she can admit that. She doesn't know how to run a pack. She does have a large family that needs to be taken care of. Also, it is true that she is of lower rank than Colton. All of that is true, but you don't fucking say that!

120

"I warned you to keep her out of here," the alpha continues before turning to Rae herself. "It's not that I don't think you're a good girl, Rae. You've been dealt a hard deck of cards in life, and you've coped beautifully with it, but I don't think this is a right fitting for you. My concern is heartfelt on this matter. Both of you will only suffer with difficulties if you continue on the course to a full mating."

Rae's mouth is dry as she asks, "So what? You expect us to just break the bond and forget about each other?"

"It's for the best in the long run," he replies sympathetically.

"No," Colton growls.

"Colton—" Rae starts, but Colton's bright yellow eyes meet hers, abruptly making her close her mouth. Colton isn't home right now, she realizes, and from the look on his face, his wolf isn't taking any messages.

Colton stands up from his chair, and she hears his bones breaking and some beginning to jut out from under his skin. His wants out, wants to shift, and most likely wants to taste Alpha Kendrick's innards. Leaning on his fists on the edge of the desk, Colton's lips curl back from his teeth to show already sharp fangs. The alpha looks unaffected on the surface, but she can see the caution in his eyes. He's just as scared shitless as she is right now.

"She is *mine!*" Colton snarls.

"Stand down," the alpha orders using his command voice, but Colton doesn't yield.

Colton growls and leans more into the alpha's face. "She is mine! She will be my alpha female. She will bare my young, and she will stand by my side! She is mine!"

The alpha gets out of his chair and goes head to head with the seething Colton. "Stand down!"

"Mine!"

The alpha snaps, glares at Rae, "Get out of here, now!"

"B-But—"

121

"Now!" he orders, cutting her off.

Seeing the yellow of his own wolf begin to filter into his eyes, Rae wordlessly nods and backs away from the two men before heading for the door. She knows that if she gets in arms reach of Colton right now, his wolf will mark her. It's not that she doesn't want that, but not like this. He'll regret it, and she doesn't want him to regret anything as important as that.

Opening the door, she slips out of the room with her heart nearly beating right out of her chest. Once she closes the door, she hears some snarls, glass breaking, and furniture tossing, making her jump. Without a second thought, she runs for the stairs and takes them down, two at a time. When she reaches the ground level, she hears the alpha female's voice speak from behind her.

"I warned you not to interfere."

Rae turns on her with a disgusted look. "You knew, huh? What he was going to say to me? Do you agree? Think I'm not worthy of my own mate?"

"Worthy isn't the question here, Rae," she says simply as she crosses her arms over her chest. "The question is what is good for not only Colton's pack but also for the good of our pack. We can't lose six members of our pack, Rae. We don't have the numbers to not feel the absence."

"So this is about White Stone is it?" Rae sneers. "Figures that whole 'good for the both of you' shit was just that, shit."

Alpha Julie narrows her eyes. "You forget your place, Rae."

"And where is my place? With my face pressed in the mud so you can walk all over my back? I don't think so."

"I am alpha here!"

"Well, I'll be alpha there!" Rae yells back before narrowing her own eyes. "So maybe it's you who needs to learn your place, *Julie.*"

The office door slams open, and Rae looks up in time to see a sweaty and bleeding Colton coming down the stairs. His eyes are blue again, but he looks no less enraged. Blood is trickling down his nose, and she can see four claw marks going through the left shoulder of his shirt. When he spots her, he narrows his eyes again and stalks over to her.

"Come on, we're leaving," he grunts before grabbing her upper arm. Looking over his shoulder, he sneers at the alpha female. "Your mate is upstairs in wolf form. Apparently, he's not as in control as he thought he was."

"What did you do to him?" she spits.

"Nothing he didn't deserve," he spits right back at her. Turning to Rae, he grabs her chin and looks down at her fiercely. "You need to let your siblings know that we're taking them back to my pack, a place they can be free to do as they choose."

Alpha Julie scoffs before smirking at him. "Good luck moving them off the property, Colton. She won't leave *anyone* behind, including the feral and mentally unsound."

Rae feels her stomach drop. "How did you—"

"Kendrick is the best tracker in North America, Rae. Did you really think that he wouldn't have caught a trail as familiar as your father's? Do you really have such little faith in your alpha?"

"He's not her alpha," Colton snaps. "Not anymore."

"We'll see." Alpha Julie shrugs before turning her gaze to Rae, "Wolves value loyalty but it's truly only the weak who don't cut off a dying limb."

"Fuck you!" Rae growls as she takes a step towards her.

Colton grabs her around the waist and starts dragging her towards the door. Putting his lips to her ear, he starts whispering calming words, but they don't work. It's not only Rae but her wolf that wants to rip the alpha apart now. She wants to shift and see just how "low rank" she'll think Rae is with her throat in Rae's jaws. That's when she knows it's over here for her.

Her loyalty is dead for this woman and her husband.

They don't deserve it. Not after this.

Once they're out on the porch, Colton spins her around, so she's facing his chest, but she's still struggling to get out of his hold.

She wants to shift, she wants to run and rip apart something, but him restraining her is putting a pin in those plans. Trying to push him away harder, it only annoys her more when he doesn't even seem affected by her smacks and punches to his torso. Instead, he just takes it while looking at her like she's most likely a crazy person. Of course, she doesn't know for sure, but she can guess that's how he's looking at her.

"Rae, come on, baby, calm down."

"Don't!" she yells, feeling wetness slide down her cheek as her vision blurs. She punches his chest more, still trying to get him to release her but still it gets her nowhere. "Don't act like I'm being irrational. You have no idea what it felt like to hear yourself talked about like that! And my dad? She had no right bringing him into this! No right at all!"

"But is it true?"

She begins struggling again. "Let me go!"

"Rae," he calls softly. "Is it true? Is he still alive?"

She stops moving and lets out a sob. She hasn't seen her dad in weeks, three to be exact, and last time she did she could tell he wasn't doing well. He was skinny, and he seemed a bit mentally lost. She didn't doubt he was sick and still doesn't, but she knew it was going to come to this, anyway. He isn't her dad anymore; just another wolf, but she still loves him.

She still wants to help him.

"Yes," she says quietly before sniffling. "Yes, he's still alive."

"Why didn't you say anything?"

"Because he's not right in the head, Colton. He's more wolf than anything."

"When did he disappear?"

"Right after she died. That very night, he just went out into the woods and never came back. We just assumed he died, despite not finding a body. We'd heard that could happen, the surviving wolf mate dying of grief. It didn't seem impossible."

124

"But he didn't die."

Rae shakes her head and wipes her cheeks with the sides of her hands. "No, he didn't die. He had just slipped into his wolf and let the wolf keep them alive. Dad didn't want to live anymore, and the wolf did so he took control."

"Are you sure he can't shift back?" Colton asks, gently.

"Yes. He's not mentally there enough to come back."

Colton closes his eyes looking just as pained as she feels. Laying his forehead against hers, he holds her closely to him. "I'm so sorry, Rae."

"Don't be," she says thickly. "That's just how things are."

"Not anymore."

Blinking through her tears, she frowns up at him, "What do you mean?"

"You're coming to my pack," he tells her before looking past her to give a scathing look to the alpha's front door. "They don't deserve to even be breathing the same air as you after this stunt."

"But my family — "

"Will come too," he answers, cutting her off. "My mom will love having little ones around again to spoil."

"I can't just move them without talking to them, Colton. That isn't fair to them. They deserve a choice."

Colton nods. "I know. We'll discuss it with them."

Rae nods and lets out a shaky exhale. "I'm not ready for this conversation."

Colton grabs her hand and kisses her knuckles one at a time, softly. When he's done, he looks at her over the tops of them. "I know, but I'll be there every step of the way."

As they begin walking off the porch and back towards the house, they don't say much else. She doesn't know what he's thinking about, but from the little smiles on his lips, she knows it's happier than her own thoughts. Rae isn't thinking about anything happy at the moment. She's just thinking about what they'll say

125

when they find out their dad is alive. She's thinking about how much they're going to hate her.

And she won't blame them for it.

Not one bit.

CHAPTER FOURTEEN

As Rae and Colton walk home back from the alpha house, they are quiet. Colton is watching her. She can feel his eyes on her, checking to see if she's okay but they both know she isn't. She doesn't need to tell him that fact as it's written on her plain as day. So he doesn't ask, and she doesn't say, because what we would be the point?

Eventually, Rae slips into memories. Colton's grip on her hand seems to fade away into the background and with it, the sensation of the mating bond. Her mind decides to make her relive probably the most defining moment of her life. It was the day of her mother's funeral and two days after her father's disappearance. After that day, things changed for everyone in that house, and it was a decision that Rae has never been sure she was right to make.

Rae closes the bedroom door slowly, wanting to make the image of her sister curled up together last as long as she can. Cassidy doesn't know what's really happening. She's only three years old and Rae, at only sixteen, doesn't really know what to tell her. Every time Cassidy asks for their mom or dad, Rae just leaves the room. She can't tell her; she doesn't have the strength to do it.

Poppy understands better than Rae thought she would. She's an intelligent six-year-old and seems to have put it all together. On the night they had gotten the news that their mother was dead, Poppy had found Rae on the front porch crying. Poppy doesn't say a word; she just hugs her older sister as hard as she could. Explanation in a family as close as theirs doesn't seem needed.

Once the girl's door is closed, Rae moves down the hallway in a daze. She knows she should get back down to the wake. She knows that her other three siblings are down there in as much of a fog as she is. Hudson hasn't spoken a word since it happened, often just going into the woods by himself to think. Jace just sits in his room all the time in the dark, watching TV. He doesn't come out much, and when he does, he doesn't even so much as look at anyone. Cleo has taken it the hardest as she was the one who found their mom that afternoon.

Cleo had come into the house after school. Hudson and Jace both had after school activities, so they were at the school still. Cleo told Rae she thought it was weird when their mom hadn't picked her up from school but had walked home, anyway. Cleo walked into the house and heard Cassidy screaming from her playpen in the living room. She was calming Cassidy down when Poppy came into the room and told her that something was wrong with Mama.

Rae closes her eyes tightly from the image that brings into her mind. At the time Cleo told Rae about what happened that day, Rae sat quietly and listened. Part of her wanted to know and wanted to be the good sister she hadn't been in the past few months. Ever since getting her wolf, Rae had become distant from her family, trying to adjust to the new changes. Cleo had told her everything and afterward, Rae felt regret for asking to know. Now it was what all her nightmares were about.

Rae looks across the hallway and sees that her parent's bedroom door is cracked open. Moving towards the door, she puts her hand on the doorknob and stands there, doorknob gripped so hard her knuckles are white. She can feel tears slide down her cheeks as she stands there, tortured with the day's old scents of her parents leading into the room. Opening her eyes, she lets in hitching bits of air into her lungs, trying to not slip into full blown sobs as she opens the door a bit more.

The heels of her boots click against the hardwood floor of her parent's room as she enters. It still smells so strongly of them, and when she inhales the scents, she can hear the still bizarre sound of her wolf whining in her head. Moving towards the bed, it's unsurprisingly made as she moves her hand gently

128

across the quilted fabric of the bedspread. A few more tears fall from her eyes, and she wipes them away with the sleeve of her black sweater.

"I'm sorry," she whispers into the empty room. "I'm so sorry. I didn't know this would happen. I didn't know. I should have treated you better. I should have—" She's cut off by her own choked sob and clasps her hand over her mouth. "Mom, please just . . . come back. I can't do this without you, mom. Please, I'll do anything. I'll do anything if you just promise to come back. Please."

As she speaks, she continues to cry and soon, all she can do is fall to her knees next to the bed as she continues to plead for the impossible. When she had first heard about it, she didn't believe it. Her mom was a superwoman. She couldn't die! It wasn't even possible. Then it set in a bit, and she was just so angry. How could she dare leave them! She was their mother, and Cassidy and Poppy were so young! They needed her, Rae still needed her and yet she left them!

It wasn't fair, none of it was fair, but it was happening all the same.

Leaning her head against the edge of the mattress, Rae falls apart while trying to think of what to do next. Her mom was the one who knew what to do in these situations, and with her gone . . . she was so lost. Rae refuses to think of her father at the moment. She's still angry at him. She doesn't want to even say his name, or even acknowledge his smell in the room, mixed with her mother's. What kind of man leaves his kids?

In the back of her mind, she knows this is the same question she asked about her mother when she died. Still, she can't move past the anger with her dad. She can't move past the fact that he just left them. She can't make herself understanding enough to just let that anger go, because she knows that it may be the only thing keeping her sane at the moment. It's the only thing keeping her from slipping into a darker place that she's afraid she'll never come out of.

Distantly, Rae hears the bedroom door creak open and catches the scent of her aunt wafting into the room. Rae relaxes, knowing it's not one of her siblings and continues to let the tears fall without control. Jojo comes beside Rae and sweeps her up in her arms as she holds Rae against her chest. Rae wraps

129

her hands around her and continues to cry so hard she's having trouble breathing at this point.

"Shh," Aunt Jolene soothes as she rocks Rae back and forth in her arms. "Shh, sweetheart. I know it hurts."

Rae just cries until she is reduced to nothing more than a tear-streaked mess. When she's doing nothing more than hiccupping, Jolene leans back and sadly smiles down at her. Moving a few strands of loose hair from Rae's face, Jolene leans forward and kisses Rae's forehead softly. Rae closes her eyes and absorbs the loving gesture like a suit of armor, hoping it will give her strength for the days ahead.

"I talked to Everett," Jolene begins softly. "We think that it would be best if we take the little ones with us. The rest of you can decide what you want to do."

"Can we stay in the house?" Rae asks hoarsely.

"I can speak with the alpha if that's what you want, but you know if you stay in the house, Cleo and Jace will want to stay too. They're only fourteen and thirteen though Rae, you can't expect them to know how to help with these things. Maybe it's best you all just come live with me."

"But this is our home."

Jolene sighs. "I know it is, honey, but this is too big of a responsibility for you. Just come with us until you're a bit older and then you can come back and live in the house."

"We both know that's not true, Jojo," Rae says softly. "If we leave this house, the alpha will just claim it's not being used, bulldoze the house and take over the land."

"Thank God, Kendrick is taking over next year," Jolene says with a sigh. "Maybe things will be a bit more democratic around here."

Rae snorts. "I doubt it."

Both are silent for a bit before Jolene asks, "Are you sure about this?"

"I want to keep us together. Mom would want that."

"But what do you want, Rae? You're only sixteen, something like this can be overwhelming for even the most mature people. You'll have to become the bad guy in a lot of situations. You'll be the one your brothers and sisters *look to for guidance, for comfort, and for their needs. I don't think this is a good idea."*

"Jojo, please just give me a chance," Rae begs. "Give me six months. Six months to see if I can do this on my own. If you think in six months I'm screwing it up, then we'll come move in with you, but I want to try to do this."

Jolene's hazel eyes scan Rae's face before she sighs heavily. "Fine, but I refuse to let you suffer through this. Your mother had been putting together trusts for you. Yours has about twenty thousand in it. When you need it, you let me know."

"I'm sure Pete will let me pick up more shifts at the diner."

"If he doesn't, he'll have to deal with me."

Rae gives a brief smile, but the sound of Cleo calling her name from the stairs has it falling right off her face. She needs to get back down to the wake. No more hiding from her family anymore. She has to be strong just like mom would want. She has to keep them together no matter what, because Rae knows that this is all she has left.

She can't lose anyone else.

Never again.

"Rae?"

Colton's voice brings her back to the present, and she blinks up at him in confusion. Has he been here the whole time? Frowning, she looks around and realizes that the house is in view. Her hold on Colton's hand tightens as she realizes the conversation she's about to have.

"Colton, this is going to be a hard conversation to hear for you," she tells him as they continue to walk. "They're going to say things to me you're not going to like, but I need you to keep yourself in control. They don't mean it, and if they do, I don't blame them for feeling that way. I probably made a mistake not telling them about dad, but it's something I can't take back. You standing up for me will only make the situation worse. It may even make you into a scapegoat. So do us both a favor and just . . . blend into the wall."

"Do you really think they'll be that upset?"

"I don't know about the boys. I mean, Hudson already knows but Jace . . . I don't know. Cleo will most likely hate me. To be honest, I'm not sure she'll want to leave the pack, this is her home, and she's very attached to the house."

"What about Cassidy and Poppy?"

"They hardly knew dad, let alone remember him. I don't think it'll affect them all that much, but like most times, I could be wrong." Rae says before pinching the bridge of her nose tightly. "I've been wrong about so many things when it came to them. I've made so many mistakes. I don't want to make another one, Colton."

"So why not just let them decide what to do?" he suggests softly. "Just let them choose where they want to go."

"I don't want us to be separated. It's the thing I've been avoiding since mom died. I didn't want to lose the only thing I have left."

Colton raises their conjoined hands. "They aren't all you have left anymore. I'm not going anywhere."

"You can't be my everything, Colton."

Pulling to a stop, his face is sincere as he speaks, "I'm not asking to be your everything, Rae. I'm telling you that I want to be a big part of your everything. I don't expect you to throw all your family ties for me, I'm not that big of an asshole. What I'm saying is that you aren't alone with this anymore. You've been living without support for too long, and now I'm going to help you."

"My aunt and uncle helped." She grumbles lamely.

He smiles a little. "I do not doubt they did, but mostly it's been you on your own because you're too stubborn to accept anything from anyone else."

She scoffs. "I'm not stubborn."

He only lifts a brow at her. Rolling her eyes, she starts walking towards the house again. Okay. Maybe she's a *little* stubborn. Not that she'll admit it. Okay. Maybe she's more than a little stubborn. Still, she won't admit it.

Opening the front door, she hears the TV going in the living room, clicking from a phone keyboard and Jace talking to Cleo. Rae leads Colton down the hallway, past the kitchen, and towards the living room, feeling her nerves build with every step. It's pretty early in the day still, and absently, she wonders where the girls are.

Entering the room, all eyes land on her, and Rae almost flinches back at the concern she sees in them. She's never been blessed with the ability to bounce back quickly from a good crying session. She always ends up with bloodshot eyes and a red nose every time, making it pretty easy to tell when she's upset.

"Where are the girls?"

"Jojo took them out for ice cream," Hudson enlightens her, his eyes still on his cell phone.

Suddenly, Jace's cold voice cuts through the room. "What happened?"

"Jace," Rae sighs.

"What did you do?" Jace demands of Colton before getting off the couch and to his feet.

Rae lets go of Colton's hand and stops Jace by placing both her hands on his chest. "Stop. He didn't do anything."

"Then why were you crying? Was it the alpha? What did he say?"

Rae lowers her head trying not to feel affected by the alpha's words. "Nothing I really want to repeat."

"Rae, what did he say? Is he making you move to Colton's pack?" Cleo asks as she comes to stand beside Jace.

Rae shakes her head, "No. He's not making me leave. He . . . he actually wants me to . . . reject Colton."

Colton growls behind her at her words. She knows how angry his wolf must be. Her wolf isn't fairing any better with her alpha's words. Rae's wolf has mostly been a follower to the alphas

133

in most things, but she's not on this one. Her wolf is demanding the alpha female's blood on her fur. Rae's a little surprised by the sudden hatred her wolf has towards the alpha couple but doesn't blame her. She's not too happy with them either at the moment.

"Why the fuck would they ask you to do that?" Jace yells, his face pinched in rage. "Don't they know what would happen to you, both of you, if you did that? Don't they care about that?"

"Not really. They think that with Colton and me mated, we'll be leaving the pack. They're worried about their numbers. The pack is very highly populated considering our territory size, and they don't want to lose pack members no matter if they can shift or not."

"Selfish pricks," Jace mutters.

"Considering how Kendrick's father was, I can't say I'm surprised."

"Wait, why would they think we're leaving?" Cleo asks pointedly while crossing her arms over her chest.

"Come on, Cleo. Did you not just hear what they asked her to do?" Jace says, looking completely fed up.

"Rae?" Cleo asks, ignoring Jace. "Why do they think we're leaving?"

"Colton is the Beta of his pack," Rae admits quietly. "When his father is ready, Colton will challenge him for the right to be alpha."

"Holy shit." Hudson laughs from his position still sitting in a recliner. "Oh, that is just perfect. Our big sis is going to be alpha female!"

"Oh, shut it." Rae grumbles.

Hudson doesn't say anything but continues to laugh quietly. Jace is grinning happily at her, looking incredibly proud, but Cleo's face is nothing but angry. Her eyes are narrowed, and her mouth is pursed unattractively as her face keeps getting redder the longer she stays quiet.

"So what? That's it? You're just going to ditch us here?" Cleo finally spits at her.

Rae scowls at her. "No. I want to ask you guys to come with me. I want you guys to be among a real pack with real alphas who really give a shit about us. This is a real chance for us to start fresh and get away from the bad things that have happened to us here."

"You want us to forget about mom and dad, is that it?"

Rae sighs deeply and prays for patience. "I would never ask you to do that, Cleo. I'm just saying it could be a great opportunity for us."

"There's something else," Hudson says after a minute of silence. Rae averts her eyes at the question, affirming his suspicion. For a fourteen-year-old, he's too perceptive, and Rae has never disliked it more than now. "What is it?"

"There's something I haven't told you guys, something that makes the alphas so sure I'm not going to leave."

Hudson's brown eyes grow wide as she speaks, but Jace and Cleo just look more confused. Finally, it's Jace who asks, "What?"

"Dad."

Jace only frowns deeper. "What about Dad?"

"He's . . . He's not dead."

"What?" Cleo whispers.

Rae runs a hand down her face and keeps her eyes focused on a homemade vase on a faraway table. She can't look at them knowing that betrayal, hurt, and anger will be written right there for her to see. She feels Colton's presence behind her and knows he's trying to give her strength; something she needs right now. All she wants to do is run away and hide instead of having this conversation, but after dropping that bombshell, she doesn't think she'll get out of this easy.

"What do you mean he's alive?" Jace snaps.

"He's not even that, really. He's more animal than man now. His wolf has taken over, and I think if there is anything left of dad inside there. He isn't coming out anytime soon," Rae admits quietly, looking up at him through blurry eyes. "He's not right in the head, Jace."

"How long?" Cleo whispers, tears falling down her face.

"Since the day of the funeral, I'm guessing. He was so heartbroken he—"

"No, Rae, how long have you known?" Cleo demands.

"Two years."

"Oh, for fuck's sake," Jace mutters as he runs a hand through his auburn shag.

"Are you fucking kidding me!" Cleo screams.

Rae jumps at her volume but keeps her voice even. "I was trying to protect you, Cleo. I didn't want you to see him like that. He wasn't himself when I first saw him. He was wild and feral. Hell, he almost bit me the first time he saw me because he didn't recognize me. I didn't want you to see him all broken down like that. *He* wouldn't want you to see him like that."

"You know after last night, I had a chat with Jojo," Cleo says as she stares at Rae with hatred. "She told me that I was being unreasonable for holding a grudge against you. She said you were doing your best to keep our heads above water and that I should appreciate you more. I thought she was right, but now I see the truth. "

"You didn't know mom and dad like you think you did. You kept pushing them away towards the end, acting like you were suddenly too good for us now that you had a wolf. You must feel like shit every day knowing you never treated mom the way you should have and now, look at you? All you do is try to take her place. Well, guess what? You never will because you could never earn even a fraction of my respect. You are just as selfish and self-serving as ever."

The words hit Rae in the core of her being because she knows how true some of them are. She didn't know her parents as well in the last year of their lives in this house. She was too busy getting lost in her own problems to even think that they could be taken from them, let alone as quickly as they were. She blames herself every day for that, but she can't take it back. What's done is done, and in the end, she has to live with the mistakes she's made.

Every last one of them.

"Watch how you speak to my mate," Colton says lowly as he comes to stand right behind Rae.

Cleo scoffs and crosses her arms over her chest. "Oh, mister bodyguard comes to the rescue yet again! Gonna go all wolfie on me too, stud?"

"Colton, it's okay, I deserve this," Rae says quietly.

"Enough!" Hudson yells, surprising everyone. Getting out of the chair, he comes over to stand by Rae and glares at his sister and brother. "You guys don't seem to realize how much this has hurt her. Do you think she didn't want to tell you? Do you think she didn't want to give some of this burden to someone else? She's been out there taking care of dad. She gives him food when he's starving and comfort when he allows it. Do you people even think about anyone but yourselves?"

"You knew, didn't you?" Cleo says with narrow eyes before laughing bitterly. "Of course, you did. You're like her fucking lap dog."

"Screw you, Cleo," Hudson snaps.

"Rae?" Jace calls, his blue eyes intense as they level her with a glare.

"Yes?" she whispers, feeling the worse she's ever felt.

"I want to see him."

Rae feels her jaw unlatch and her mouth gape. "I-I don't know where he is."

He narrows his eyes further before turning to Hudson, "Do you know?"

Hudson looks over at Rae, unsure for a moment, before he nods, "Yes. I know where he is."

"I want to see him," Jace repeats before moving towards the door. "Now."

Cleo follows after Jace with a few stomping steps of her own until Rae hears the front door slam shut behind them. Rae closes her eyes and hangs her head, feeling like she's never been more tired in her life. Colton hugs her from behind and repeatedly kisses her hair while she melts back into him.

"Rae, I'm sorry," Hudson says quietly.

Opening her eyes, she smiles sadly at him. "Don't be. You have nothing to be sorry for. I should be the one who should be sorry. I never should have put any of this burden on you. I'm so sorry."

"Hudson!" Jace yells from outside the screen door.

"Are you going to come?" Hudson asks after a step towards leaving.

Rae sighs heavily before nodding. "Yeah. Let's go see dad."

CHAPTER FIFTEEN

Colton can feel the tension between the siblings as easily as he feels the air. It's thick as all four of Applebee's continue to walk in a loaded silence. A broken stick or a cough could break out into a huge fight, and he knows that. So instead of trying to mediate, he stays just as quiet.

His eyes shift to Rae, and he feels a heaviness enter his heart. She looks so alone and scared that his hands itch to comfort in some way, but he keeps his distance. As soon as they left the house, she's been this way, walking in front of him with her arms crossed around her middle. He wants to hold her, touch her, or even just hear her speak but he has to keep his distance. This is something she obviously wants to deal with on her own.

Colton catches a scent suddenly that has his wolf as confused as he is. It's an odd scent. Usually, shifts can tell the difference between another wild wolf or a shifter, but this one is muddy and unclear. It has the dirty almost damp scent of a wolf but also the undertone of a more human fragrance, but one he still can't decipher.

"To the north," Colton says, moving already in that direction.

Rae frowns at him over her shoulder and sniffs the air. "You sure? I don't have his scent yet."

"I'm sure," he says without hesitation before pushing a branch out of his way as he tracks the scent trail. He knows the others are following him, and he can hear their footsteps and the beats of their heart as well as their breathing. Colton, being of alpha blood, has very good senses, and it's one of the reasons he's such a good tracker. It's also why he makes such a good beta.

He's trained his whole life to lead a pack.

"Usually he's more south," Hudson says quietly, but the question is clear in his voice.

"It makes sense he would trail north with the game as it is lately," Rae says, but her voice is raw as she speaks. "He usually follows the game."

"How the fuck have you been able to keep this hidden from us so long, both of you." Jace hisses, making Colton send him a low warning growl. He really doesn't like how they speak to Rae.

Colton hears Rae sigh heavily. "We don't see him often. It was an accident that even Hudson found out. He doesn't come as often as much anymore, though."

"Why not?" Cleo demands, "Ashamed of seeing behind our back?"

"No. I just don't want to see him like he is." Hudson snaps at her with what Colton guesses is a glare. "He's not healthy, Cleo."

"Well, maybe if you guys told us sooner, we could have gotten him some help," Cleo counters with venom.

"He's beyond help," Rae says in a pained whisper.

Colton hears some rustling and catches a newer wave of the scent. He snaps his head in the direction he's caught it from and feels his wolf push to the forefront of his mind. As much as Colton likes tracking, his wolf fucking loves it. No matter the prey, his wolf always loves them, so Colton lets him take more control in his human body. Colton's now golden eyes scan the area before they land on a patch of dark colored patch of fur in the distance.

"There," he says quietly as he nods in its direction.

Rae comes to stand beside him and narrows her eyes as she too lets her wolf use her eyes. Colton can't help but notice how beautiful her wolf's bright eyes look on Rae's face. It makes her look even more spectacular, and he shoves his hands in his pocket to stop himself from reaching out to her. This isn't the time to try to make out with her. He has all the time in the world for that later.

"It's him," Rae confirms with a sigh as she runs a hand through her hair. "That's him."

Cleo comes running up beside Rae. She freezes when her eyes land on the worn down looking brown wolf curled up beside the base of a tree. He doesn't seem to notice them at first, a first sign of his dulling senses and the complete takeover of his wolf.

Colton has only ever seen a shifter like this once before, and eventually, they had to take her down because she was too crazed. She had become confused and had attacked her own children, nearly killing one of them. The woman's mate had died six months before, and she had tried to take her own life, but her wolf fought for survival. It was then that it took over, as often is the case. Colton never wanted to see another like that again, but here he is looking at just that.

"Jesus," Jace breathes as he too comes to stand beside Rae. His blue eyes are wide as he takes in the skinny body and snarled fur of his father's wolf form. You could count the ribs poking out of the side of the wolf's form, but Colton knows it's not from starvation, it's the mental illness.

Hudson doesn't come up to look at their father, and Colton looks over at the younger boy to see him staring at the ground instead. His fists are clenched, and a few tears are trailing down his face. Colton can feel the boy's pain just looking at him, and he knows that this is what Rae was trying to stop them from feeling. The pain of seeing what their father had become. Not an easy burden to bear, but one she did without hesitation.

Colton and his wolf are filled with pride for their mate at the realization.

She is so strong.

"I . . . I need to touch him," Cleo says quietly, tears rolling down her own cheeks.

141

Rae wipes her eyes before shaking her head. "He's too dangerous. You saw him, and now you see how sick he is."

"Isn't that more of a reason to help him?" Cleo snaps, rage clear in her eyes.

"You don't understand. He—"

Cleo scoffs. "I don't understand because you didn't tell me. How could you let me believe my own dad was dead, Rae? How could you live with yourself knowing you lied to us every day?"

"She was trying to protect you," Colton growls, sick of them ganging up on Rae. Their blindness feeds his rage. Can't they see the pain and wear that is clearly on her face? He recognized it the minute he saw her, how can her own family not be able to see it?

"Stay out of this," Cleo spits. "This isn't your family."

"It is now," he says fiercely, making her eyes widen and take a step back from him.

Cleo seems to collect herself quickly, though, and glares at him. "I will never be your family."

"Cleo!" Rae gasps, looking horrified.

"Don't even look at me like that," Cleo sneers. "You have no right to look at me like that ever again after this."

Rae's eyes well with tears. "Can't you see I was just trying to protect you? I didn't want you to see him like this! He isn't right in the head. Wouldn't you want to remember him how he was?"

"I want my dad back!" Cleo yells.

"We all want our dad back!" Rae yells back, stepping towards her sister who is a few inches taller than her. "You are not the only one hurting. You are not the only one who doesn't want to feel anymore. You are not the only who hates me every minute of every day! Do you think I want to be like this? Do you think I want to play mom to my own siblings? No! I don't!"

Cleo is silent, and Rae runs her hands roughly through her hair like claws as more tears trail down her face. She looks up at Cleo with wide brown eyes that are rimmed in red and hold so

142

much grief in them that Colton's heart aches. Still, he keeps his distance, not wanting to end this outpouring too soon.

"I want to be nineteen," Rae says thickly. "I want to be with my mate without hesitation, and I want to be able to be the kind of sister you would all be proud of, but I can't. I can't be, because he . . ." she says, pointing at the wolf in the distance. ". . . wasn't strong enough to stay. I have to be the strong one, and I have to be the one you all hate because that's what being me means. It means I have to take it all on my shoulders."

"No one asked you to," Cleo says quietly.

"I'm the older sister!" Rae screams, making Cleo step back. "I am made to protect you. My very heart, bones, and soul are made to carry your burdens! I am destined to be your keeper!"

"Rae . . ." Jace trails off, trying to come towards her, but she steps back with a shake of her head.

"No." She sobs. "No, don't come near me. You all act like it's so easy. You all like to pretend that I don't suffer as much as you do. You think I wanted mom to die? Do you think I wanted to take her place? I just wanted to keep us together, I wanted you to be happy. I didn't want to lose any of you, and if that makes me selfish then fine, I'm selfish. I'll take that title, but don't you dare act like I don't do it out of love."

"Rae," Colton calls as he comes near her as he can't take it anymore. His wolf is whining in his head, begging him to soothe her, make her happy again, but Colton doesn't think it'll be that easy. He doesn't really know what to do to make her happy like she wants to be. Being there for her is all he can think of, and for now, that's all he can do.

Rae turns toward him, making his heart clench with so much sadness. "I just want to be with you like I was meant to be. I used to dream about what you would be like when I was little. Is it sappy to say you turned out to be everything I wanted you to be? Is it sad that none of it matters now?"

"What do you mean?" Colton asks, his wolf on high alert at her phrasing.

"I'm not an alpha female," She tells him with her chin wobbling as more tears fall. "I can't be what you need."

"You are," he insists, coming a few steps closer to her and encouraging her when she doesn't step back from him. "You're exactly what I need, and you'll be an amazing alpha female. You've already raised your own pack."

She looks away and drops her head into her hands as she starts to sob. It's not even conventional sobs; they are heart breaking whole body sobs that are nearly paralyzing in their power. Falling to her knees, she continues to let out the years of grief he has no doubt she's been holding in. She's letting in big gasps of air as she falls apart on the ground before him, and this time, he doesn't hold himself back. Getting on his knees in front of her, he grabs her in his arms and holds her against his chest.

His hands caress her back, and he whispers in her ear. "Shh. It's okay, baby. I'm here, and I'm not going anywhere. I'm not leaving you behind, and I'm not letting you leave me. We're going to get through this, okay? I promise I'm going to make you so happy."

She doesn't answer, but she does wrap his hands around his neck. They're so wrapped up in each other that they don't realize that the wolf has begun approaching the group. None of the others sense him either, too caught up in the emotional moment. None of them see it coming until Cleo screams.

* * *

Rae lifts her head immediately at the sound of Cleo's scream. She sees their father on top of Cleo and biting into her forearm. Blood spills from her sister's flesh and onto Cleo's face as Cleo tries to keep their father from biting down on her neck. His eyes are wild and not focused as he continues to attack. Jace, who is

144

closest, tries to get him off first, but their father stops biting Cleo long enough to slash his claw across Jace's chest.

"Jace!" Rae screams as she scrambles away from Colton. "Colton, help them!"

She doesn't even bother removing her clothes before she shifts into her much smaller gray wolf. Despite their father's health, he is still a large wolf. But with his disjointed thoughts, she can't image he'll be able to use it to his advantage. Snarling at him to get his attention, Rae jumps at him and gets him off Cleo before he can attack again.

Both wolves slide down the small hill and tumble to the ground a few meters down. Rae lets out a high-pitched yelp when she hits her back against a tree, but she recovers quickly enough to dodge an attack. She can hear Cleo screaming her name, but she shuts it out. She can't pay attention to them right now when she has much more pressing matters like a snarling crazed wolf to worry about.

He drops his head and curls his lips back from his teeth as he snarls at her, spit dripping off his teeth as he does. Rae slowly begins to circle, and her father begins to follow her lead by also circling. Rae isn't snarling back. She's just watching his every move as he continues to try to intimidate her. It's not working, if there's anything her father taught her when he was still himself, it was to never be intimidated by your opponent.

He makes a move towards her, and she dodges the swipe of his already bloody claws. She instead takes the opportunity to wrap her jaws around his hind leg and bite at the tendon there. He howls in pain but quickly counterattacks by slicing his claws across her side. She uses her body weight to push him, making him stagger a bit, but it's not enough to push him over. Letting go of his hind leg, she uses more of her weight and manages to push his already frail body over to his side.

He yelps, but she barely acknowledges it in favor of getting on top of him. She bares her teeth at him and snarls right in his face as she lets her wolf fully out of her cage in her head. Her father bats at her face with his claws, cutting open her flesh along her muzzle but she doesn't get off him like he wants. Instead, she buries her teeth into his neck, making him whine. She doesn't clamp her teeth, she doesn't want to kill him, but she doesn't want him to stand down. When he struggles a bit, she tightens her jaws, and he whines loudly, but she stands her ground.

"Release him," a voice demands, making her lift her eyes, but not remove her jaws from his neck, to see Alpha Kendrick running towards him.

Rae snarls at him as some of her father's blood spills onto her fur and inside her mouth. She doesn't answer to him anymore, she tells herself. This isn't even his problem, so why is he here?

Kendrick's eyes narrow. "Release him now."

She unclenches her jaw but only to lift her head and snarl more loudly at him. Her wolf feels no loyalty to this man who calls himself Alpha. She feels nothing but disdain and disrespect at the tone of his voice. He is nothing to her now, and he will learn his place just as his wife suggested she learn hers.

"Rae!" Cleo's voice screams, getting her attention.

Rae sees the pack doctor with Jace, who looks to be in great pain at the top of the hill. Cleo is holding a piece of Rae's shirt to her wound while Hudson tries to keep Cleo from coming down the hill. Colton is already running down the hill and towards her, looking frantic. A clearing of a throat closer to her position gets her attention again, and she sees Kendrick glaring at her.

"I am your alpha, get off him now."

"You are not her alpha." Colton snarls as he comes to stand near her. "She is my mate and soon to be your equal, Kendrick. I suggest you don't forget who you call when you need help next time you speak to her like that."

Kendrick sneers. "I call your father, boy. I wonder how happy he'll be with your choice of mate."

146

"Probably as happy as your father was with yours," Colton says coldly.

Kendrick's body is riddled with tension as he turns back to Rae and growls out the command again. "Release him now!"

"*Rae.*"

Rae looks down at the wolf beneath her and feels her eyes widen at the clarity she sees in its eyes. Brown eyes, so familiar, look up at her with undeniable grief, sadness, and shame, she feels the urge to cry. He closes his eyes slowly and open them again but only half way as she hears the voice again in her head.

"*Rae, I love you.*"

Then she watches in horror as all clarity evaporates, and the madness clouds them over. He snarls at her again, and she's so caught up in her own emotions she doesn't see it coming. His claws come slamming into her side, making her yelp loudly as they slice between the ribs. Blood pours out of her side as he retracts his claws from her body and she collapses into her side. Screams and yelling seem very distant as she lies on the ground. Her vision becomes blurry the more blood pours out of her, but before losing all consciousness, she hears Colton's voice in her ear.

"Stay with me," he begs. "Stay with me."

CHAPTER SIXTEEN

Colton runs a hand down his tired face as he sits beside Rae's bed. She's alive, thank god, but she's not in the best of shape. The wound was deep enough to cause some major damage, and healing for a shifter is never as easy as it looks. Pain is just as expected in the healing as is it in the injury, and Rae's injuries aren't going to be a cake walk.

Her right cheek is cut open with three long claw marks which are stitched up but expected to heal with minimal scarring. Her leg thigh, where more claw marks were made, are also stitched up and expected to heal fine. It's the injury on her side that has him watching her every minute for the past three days.

It was deep enough to cause some serious internal damage, and after some miracle working done by the pack doctor here, she's been stabilized. Still, the healing has her sweating, crying out in pain, and vomiting. Her wolf is trying to push out any infections as well, trying to get her body back to perfect condition. Colton has never felt as useless in his life as he does now.

The past few days have nearly driven him mad. He doesn't feel the need to eat, he barely sleeps, and leaving her side seems like an impossible task. He's been doing his best to keep his head on straight for the rest of the family.

The girls often lay in the bed with her during the day, cuddling with her and talking to her. Cleo occasionally sits with him or sleeps with her at night, lending Rae her warmth while Colton sleeps in the recliner in the corner. Hudson often comes in and cleans up while also taking Rae's vital signs often, just to reassure himself. Jace doesn't say anything and refuses to enter the room, but he does leave a tray of food outside for Colton every morning, afternoon, and evening. Colton barely touches it, but the thought is appreciated.

Three knocks on the door has Colton sitting up straighter in his chair before the door cracks open to show his father in the doorway. Colton's eyes widen as he stands up quickly from the chair, wobbling on his feet a little from the weakness of his body. Colton's father, Dalton, puts up a hand and gestures for him to sit as he wordlessly comes farther into the room.

"How—"

"Your mother told me," Dalton says gruffly. "I don't know why you didn't call me yourself."

"I didn't want to disturb you."

Dalton gives him a dry look. "You're my son first and my beta second, Colton. This isn't something I want to hear second hand."

Colton lets out a shaky sigh and runs a hand through his hair. "I'm sorry. I've just been . . . overwhelmed."

"Understandable." Dalton nods before moving to the chair Cleo usually sits in. Sitting down, Dalton looks over his son's state and puts a hand on his shoulder. "How is she?"

"Stable and healing."

"So you thought you should have her chew your ass out once she's awake by turning yourself into the walking dead?"

Colton smiles a bit, the first time in days that wasn't forced and shrugs. "Seems only fair."

"Eat something," Dalton commands before taking his hand off his shoulder. "You'll be better for it."

"Okay."

Silence settles between the men, twenty-seven years apart in age but still so similar. Colton has his mother's brown hair, but

149

his features, body language, and temperament are more akin to his father. Both share the same determined blue eyes, height, and even now, are sitting the same way in their respective chairs. If his mother were here, Colton knows she'd comment on it.

A habit that drives both Colton and his father insane.

"I spoke to Kendrick," Dalton says suddenly, making Colton tense. "He's not too pleased with either one of you."

"Like I give a shit."

"He's given you two days to leave the territory."

"I'm not going anywhere," Colton growls, his eyes never leaving Rae's pale face.

"I don't see what other options we have, son," his father says as he sits back in his chair. "Kendrick wants you both off his land and as much as I'm against doing anything that prick says, I have to agree that staying here isn't safe for any of you."

"I can't just take her to our pack without talking to her. I told her I would never take that choice away from her."

"I understand that," Dalton says with a sigh. "But we don't really have the time to fight it. I can't afford a war right now, and you can't afford to put her family in danger like that. I know Kendrick, and I know his family. Staying here for any longer will cause him to act, and he doesn't play clean."

"He won't survive a direct challenge from me."

Dalton grins and pats his son's back. "I don't doubt that son, but your girl here isn't going to be too keen on you getting into a fight over her."

"You haven't even met her."

"I know you enough to know that any girl that has you in knots is a girl worth her salt. She won't want you fighting over nothing."

"This isn't 'nothing.'"

"It is in the grand scheme of things, Colton. Kendrick may be more looks than brains, but he's not afraid to go for the throat."

Colton hangs his head and thinks it over before speaking again, "Her siblings won't be pleased."

"I've already spoken to them. They've already agreed to come with."

"Even Cleo?"

"Which one is that one?"

"The blonde."

Dalton lifts a brow at his son. "I repeat, which one?"

"The older one."

"Ah! The one who looked ready to cry at the drop of a feather. Yes, she agreed. Is she always like that?"

Colton shakes his head. "No. To be honest, before this, she was a complete spoiled brat. I wouldn't have been broken up over it if she had decided to stay."

"She seems concerned about her sister."

"Yeah, after she protected her and nearly died," Colton says bitterly.

"That ought to do it," Dalton says with a little laugh. "Listen, sometimes you have to make decisions for your mate when she can't make them. Of course, you better be ready to take the consequences, but she seems like a smart girl, and she'll understand that you did this for her."

"What about her father?"

"The wolf that attacked?" At Colton's nod, Dalton shakes his head sadly. "Kendrick said he died overnight in the cells."

"How convenient," Colton mutters.

"In the end, it's for the best, really."

"Maybe, but Rae will be devastated."

"She has you now to help her through it," Dalton tells him lowly. "With you by her side, she'll be able to get through anything and vice versa. You both have to be each other's strength now, that's what being a mate is."

Colton feels his eyes blur with tears and he runs his hands over them, trying to wipe them away before they fall. "Yeah, yeah, you're right."

"She'll be okay."

"I know," Colton says, almost more to himself. "I know."

"Your mother will love to meet her. She's been going on and on about her ever since she received her call. She keeps screwing up her name, though. What is it?"

"Rae."

"Ah. Spelled the man's version or . . ."

"No, R-A-E."

Dalton nods, looking slightly impressed. "Unique."

"All of their names are. Cleo, Jace, Hudson, Poppy, and Cassidy. Their parents seemed the more unique names."

"Applebee, right? I think I heard of the father before. Enforcer, right? Good fighter?"

"Now you understand why I've been so scared shitless. She could have been injured even worse than she was," Colton says quietly, watching Rae's chest move up and down with every steady breath. "God, she was fast, though."

"Father must've trained her well."

"I wouldn't doubt it. If he was as good as they said he was, it wouldn't surprise me that he'd at least show his kids a thing or two."

"He did," a new voice says from the doorway. "He showed us everything he knew."

Both Woodward men turn their attention to the door to see Cleo standing there. Her face is ashen as her blue eyes stay trained on Rae's sleeping form. Colton notices that Cleo looks as tired as he himself feels. Dark circles are under her eyes, and her long blonde hair is greasy and messily tied in a knot on top of her head. She's also been wearing the same baggy pullover sweatshirt and jean shorts for two days now.

"Do you want to come in?" Dalton asks, getting the young woman's attention.

"Are you an alpha?"

"Yes."

"Can't you command her to wake up?"

Dalton gives her a sad smile. "I'm sorry, son, but that's not how it works."

"Then what good is an alpha command if you can't even use it for shit like this?" Cleo asks and Colton tries to keep himself from growling at her. This man is not only his father but also his alpha. Both Colton or his wolf does not look on disrespect towards him fondly.

"She isn't in my pack," Dalton informs her calmly. "I have no sway over her wolf."

"But your son does. Can't you make him do it?"

"If that would have worked don't you think I would have tried?" Colton snaps.

"All I see you doing is sitting there and waiting for her to wake up! We can't just sit here and do nothing!"

"I am doing everything I can!" Colton yells back, getting out of his chair so fast it falls to the ground behind him. His hands are fists at his sides as he stares at the young woman who needs more of an exorcism than a grounding.

"Well, it's not enough." She hisses.

"S-Stop." Rae moans, getting all of their attention.

Colton rushes to her side and takes her damp face in his hands. His eyes look over her face frantically as he hopes that she'll stay awake this time. He's had a few false alarms like this where she's opened her eyes for a few seconds, but she always falls back asleep. This time, though, she's spoken, and Colton is brimming with hope that this means she's taken a turn for the best.

"Rae, baby, can you hear me?"

"Stop . . . fighting," she croaks at him.

Colton grins in complete relief. "Anything you want."

153

"Rae?" Cleo sobs. "Can you hear me?"

"I'm . . . not . . . deaf."

Cleo laughs and wipes her cheeks as a grin comes across her face. She, without warning, pushes Colton aside so she can sit on the edge of the bed. Cleo takes Rae's hand in hers and puts it against her face while more tears come down her face. At this point, Colton's surprised she can even produce any more tears.

"I'm so sorry, Rae. I am so sorry. I didn't understand because you never talk to us. You never tell us anything, and I didn't understand, but now I do. I get it, and I am so sorry for how I treated you. I'm going to try to be better. We're going to get a fresh start at Colton's pack, and we'll be a family again just like you wanted, okay?"

"Who . . . are . . . you?"

Cleo frowns at her. "Huh? I'm your sister."

"You're . . . too . . . nice."

Both Cleo and Colton giggle in relief when they hear those words. Rae smiles a little and begins closing her eyes again. Colton thinks she's fallen asleep again when she opens them again to zero on Colton's dad sitting at the end of her bed. Rae squints her eyes and licks her chapped lips a few times before speaking again.

"A-Alpha."

He smiles kindly at her. "I prefer to be called Dalton."

"This is my dad, Rae," Colton tells her before taking her hand to squeeze in his. "He's talked to Kendrick, they want us out in two days."

"The . . . house."

"Jolene will look after it," Cleo assures her. "We've talked about it, and we're going to come with you. If we like it, maybe we'll sell the house, but until then, Jojo said she'd look after it."

"Everyone?" Rae asks hoarsely.

Cleo nods with a smile. "All of us."

"W-What . . . about . . . dad?"

"He . . ." Colton trails off, swallowing thickly.

154

"Jolene will look after him too," Cleo says, quickly cutting him off. At Colton's surprised look, she gives him a glare. "He doesn't have long to live, and he should be okay just where he is."

"Okay." Rae nods stiffly before laying back. Her eyes drift close, and Colton sees her breathing start to even out again. "Okay."

Once he's sure she's out again, he turns to Cleo. "What the hell was that?"

"She doesn't need to know he's dead yet. Let her think he's alive until she's better. Once she's up and awake full time, then feel free to be the bearer of bad news, but until then, let it be."

"A little hypocritical of you, don't you think?" Colton asks with a sneer.

Cleo only smirks at him. "Welcome to the family."

CHAPTER SEVENTEEN

Rae feels like hell warmed over. Still, she wishes she could at least help with the chaos that is going on around her. The entire Applebee family is on the move along with Jolene, Garrett, Everett, and even Graham going in and out of the house. Colton, of course, is right there among them, carrying boxes to put in the back of the moving truck.

Colton's father isn't here. He left that morning in wolf form to head back to his territory. Rae's taken an immediate liking to him in the little slots of time she's had to converse with him. He's got the seriousness in an alpha she can respect with the touch of empathy that any good leader should have. Doesn't hurt that he's incredibly handsome for an older man with a quick wit. In fact, he reminds her of her own father.

Rae shuts out the thought immediately, feeling her wounds ache a little at the reminder. Shifting in her seat, she tries to keep the urge to cry bottled up. She doesn't want anyone misinterpreting them as her being in pain.

The whole lot of them seem to consider themselves nurses now that she's awake, checking on her even if she just sighs heavily. It's proving to be as amusing as it is annoying to seem them all catering to her like this. The evil side of her is half tempted to milk it for all its worth. Luckily for them, though, she's stubborn enough to just whine about it.

"How you feeling, honey?" Jolene asks as she comes to sit beside her on the porch swing.

"Sick of that question."

Jolene laughs before wrapping an arm around her shoulder. "Give us a break. You've only been out and about a day on your feet. We're bound to be worried about you."

"I'm perfectly fine," Rae grumbles with a pout. "I should be up and helping."

"Bored?"

"Incredibly."

Jolene laughs again and moves over so Rae can lay her head on Jolene's shoulder. Rae watches as Garrett hands Colton a box to put into the back of the truck. Rae's eyes drift from his hands on the box, up his muscular arms, and across the sweaty white fabric of his t-shirt before landing on his grinning face as he catches her staring. Rae averts her gaze quickly, suddenly very interested in a tree branch across the yard.

"No shame in checking out what's yours, darling," Jolene whispers in Rae's ear, making Rae go beet red.

"I wasn't."

"You forget who you're talking to, Rae. I know you like the back of my hand. I can tell when you're lying, when you're sad, and when you're checking out your mate."

Rae groans and hides her face in Jolene's shoulder. "Stop talking, please."

"Oh, come on Rae, there's no shame in it. Everett and I were the exact same way. Of course, I didn't have a wolf, so it wasn't as intense, but I know how hard it is to keep your hands off each other."

"Okay, now you *really* need to stop talking."

"Newly mated couples can be more like rabbits than wolves . . ."

"Jolene, I'm going to hurl."

". . . and that's why you need to be careful. You don't want children this early in a relationship. Best to wait when you guys know each other better." Rae relaxes a little, more comfortable with this route in conversation. Then Jolene keeps talking, "That's why I slipped a box of condoms in one of your bedroom boxes."

"Oh my god," Rae mutters, covering her red face with her hand.

"Ain't any shame in it, darling. Everyone uses them."

Rae grits her teeth, highly aware she can't physically escape this conversation. "I'm aware of what they do and how they're used, Jojo."

"Well, I wasn't sure you had . . . that talk."

"When I was thirteen," Rae says, blushing even more when she remembers how awkward that conversation was. "Mom explained all about the mechanics of it all and dad pretty much said it didn't matter because I was never going to do it anyway."

"Sounds like him," Jolene says with a small smile.

Rae takes Jolene's hand in hers before staring into her hazel eyes. "You will take care of him, won't you?"

Jolene closes her eyes for a second before opening them with tears rimming the edges. Rae notices how forced the smile is, but doesn't understand the real reason why. She figured it may have to be with how Jolene herself didn't know about her dad being alive. She thought he was dead just like everyone else. Rae wonders if Jolene's upset with her as well or if she'll be her normally understanding self.

"Are you mad at me?"

Jolene frowns a bit, "Mad? Why would I be mad, honey?"

"Because I didn't tell you."

"No," Jolene says after a few seconds of silence. "I'm not mad. I know how hard it must have been to keep that to yourself. I also know you did it out of love for the rest of us. You've been burdened with so much, Rae. I just wish I was able to help you more than I have."

"You've helped us more than you know," Rae tells her truthfully. "You've always been here for us and given us more than we can ever pay you back for."

Jolene brushes some of Rae's hair behind her ear. "Ain't nothing to be payback, sweetheart. We're family. We look after our own."

"I'm going to miss you," Rae whispers, tears threatening to spill over.

Jolene kisses her forehead. "Not as much as I'll miss you."

"What about me?" a small voice asks.

Both women turn their heads to see Cassidy standing in front of them with her plush white rabbit in her arms and a curious look in her brown eyes. Her blonde hair is thrown up in a messy bun on the top of her head that Cleo did earlier that morning and is dressed in a yellow sundress. She's barefoot, as usual, and as Rae takes in her littlest sister, she frowns when she sees a toothbrush in her hand.

"What's with the toothbrush?" Rae asks.

Cassidy looks at the pink toothbrush in her hand. "I was brushing Mr. White foot's teeth. I want him to look extra pretty when we go to the new house."

"Did you brush your teeth?" Rae asks.

Cleo comes out of the house with a box and says, "Yup. I got her all ready this morning, now stop fussing."

Cleo walks off the porch and heads for the truck. Colton takes the box from her, and Rae doesn't miss the little glare he sends her sister's back. Rae herself isn't too sure what to make of the new helpful Cleo. She wants to believe that the incident maybe helped her realize that Rae has done everything she's done for the family. She can never be sure with Cleo though. One minute she can be like she used to be, the next minute a raging little bitch. Rae sighs, time will tell she supposes.

"Cassidy, can you help Poppy?" Cleo asks as she passes them again on her way back into the house. "You need to go through your books to see what you want to bring."

"Do we have to move, Rae?" Cassidy asks, ignoring Cleo.

Rae doesn't really know what to say to that. She's still struggling for words when Colton's voice cuts in, "Hey, Cassidy?"

"Yeah?"

"Do you like horses?"

Cassidy nods her head as she clutches her bunny tighter. Colton jumps off the back of the truck and walks over to the porch with a smile on his face. Coming to stand by the porch, he leans his arms on it as he continues to talk to Cassidy.

"Well, you see, my mom has pretty horses that she just doesn't have time for. We were wondering if you and Poppy could help."

"Help?"

"You know, keep them company, brush them, and maybe even ride them once you learn how to. They look mighty lonely without little girls to talk to them."

"Are they nice horses?" Cassidy asks, still unsure.

Colton nods solemnly. "The nicest horses."

"Do you have wolves like they do here?"

"Yup, lots of those."

"Are they nice, too?"

"The nicest," Colton assures her with a grin.

"Rae, I wanna go!" Cassidy says, jumping around, "Can we go now?"

"That's why we're packing you ding-dong," Cleo says with an eye roll.

Jace hits Cleo upside the head as he passes with a box. "Don't be a brat."

"Hey, that hurt!"

"Get over it!" he calls as he continues to walk towards the truck.

"Where's Hudson?" Rae asks, looking around.

"Inside with Poppy, I'm assuming. We should ring a bell on him." Cleo says before entering the house while rubbing the back of her head.

"I'm going to tell Poppy about the horses!" Cassidy shrieks before running into the house.

Rae watches her run inside before turning to Colton with a dry look. "Horses? Please tell me you really have them."

"We do. Of course no one but my mom and some of the other human mates can go near them. They can sense the animal in us, makes them get spooked."

Rae makes a face. "I don't know why I can't imagine horse meat would taste any good."

"They just sense the danger." He shrugs before giving her a less than subtle once over. "How you feeling?"

"Perfectly fine. A bit useless, but fine."

"Take the break while you can, Rae," Jace says while passing them to reenter the house. "We aren't going to be putting this shit away by ourselves."

"That doesn't surprise me," Rae tells him with an eye roll. "Say, have you seen Hudson?"

"Isn't he inside the house?" Jace asks with a frown.

"I don't know. I haven't seen him in an hour."

Jace's frown only gets deeper. Gripping the door frame, he pokes his head into the doorway and yells, "Hudson! Where the hell are you?"

"Jace Caleb Applebee, you better knock the swearing nonsense off right now!" Jolene scolds him from beside Rae.

Jace gives her an annoyed look before yelling into the house again, "Hey! Hudson!"

"Y-Yeah?"

Rae feels her body relax a bit at the sound of Hudson's voice. She was worried he was off in the woods. Dalton gave her a warning about Kendrick before he left and told her not to let any of

161

her siblings out of sight, just in case. His face was serious and the threat to her family seemed a little too real at that moment to really disregard. Of course, the relief is quickly changed into concern when she sees Hudson's tear streaked face.

"Are you crying?" Jace asks.

"Jace, go pack," Rae dismisses him immediately.

Jace gives her a quick scowl before heading into the house. Colton gives her a quick kiss on the forehead before leaving the porch to head back to the truck. Jolene also mumbles about needing to pack some glassware before heading into the house herself. Everyone else is kindly keeping their distance as Rae gestures for Hudson to come sit beside her on the swing. Wiping his face, he does just that.

Rae doesn't say anything, just watches him, hoping that just by looking at him she can figure out what's wrong. Instead, all she sees is an upset little brother who probably won't tell her a damn thing. Sighing, Rae sits back into the porch swing while looking up at the tops of the nearby trees. This is something she'll miss about this house, the false silence of nature. Everything feels so serene and still but in truth, there are little things happening everywhere, concentrated chaos under the facade of peacefulness.

Rae opens her eyes, a bit surprised at herself. When did she get so deep?

"So . . . Are you going to tell me or do I have to guess?" Rae asks after a while.

Hudson balances his elbow on his knees and shrugs. "Nothing to tell."

"Hudson, I know you. You don't cry without reason. So what's up?"

"Rae, just let it go."

"Is it about dad?"

"No."

"Moving?"

"No."

"Is it about—"

"It's nothing you can guess, Rae, so just drop it."

"Come on, Hudson. I'm just here to help."

"I don't want help," he snaps, shooting her a glare. "There's nothing wrong with me."

Rae frowns, surprised by the venom in his voice. "I didn't say there was."

"I don't have to tell you everything, Rae."

"You don't tell me anything, Hudson, and usually I let that go, but if you're this upset . . ."

"Just drop it."

"No."

Hudson squeezes his eyes shut, and she sees a tear fall from his eyes. Rae moves closer to him on the swing and places a hand on his back as he begins to cry into his hands. She didn't want to upset him like this, she just wants to find out what was wrong so maybe she could help him figure out a solution. His reaction though has her worried that maybe this is something big, bigger than what she could have even dreamed.

"Hey, Hudson, whatever it is, honey, I won't judge you," Rae whispers into his ear as she rubs his back, hoping to calm him. "I just want to know what's bothering you so we can figure it out together."

"I know," he mumbles before lifting his head and wiping his cheeks. "I just don't want you to hate me or be disgusted."

Rae frowns at him in confusion. "Disgusted? Hudson, what the hell are you talking about? I would never be disgusted or hate you. You're my blood, my little brother, nothing you could say would change that."

"I'm . . . I'm . . ."

Rae watches him struggle and feels tears coming to her own eyes. Hudson's always been the kid to have all the answers, and now . . . He looks totally lost. She hugs him tighter, trying to give her silent support, knowing that speaking will only make this

163

harder for him. She hears the silence of the others around them, some of them unable to hear, others just waiting with anticipation for what it could be.

"I . . . I like a guy."

Rae blinks at his words before asking, "Just guys or . . ."

"Just guys as far as I know," he says, careful not to meet her eyes. "I like a guy here, and I had to break it off."

"Because of the move?"

"Yeah, but that doesn't mean I don't want to move. I like Colton, and this pack isn't our place anymore. Besides, it wasn't serious or anything."

"Is it that guy from school? The one you were doing the project with?"

Hudson laughs a little and shakes his head. "No, no. John is just a partner for school."

"So, you're . . . gay."

"Yeah."

"Oh."

"Yeah."

Rae looks over her brother's profile as he stares off into the distance. She can tell how uncomfortable and tense he is telling her this. He thinks she's going to push him away, but he is sorely mistaken. Instead of doing what he expects, she puts her head on his shoulder, making him jump. His shoulder relaxes under her head slowly, and she waits until he's completely relaxed before speaking again.

"You know, I have an idea you were."

"Bullshit," he says with disbelief.

She angles her head so she can smirk at him. "You think you're so smart, trying to hide your texts from me and being all sneaky. You've underestimated my detective skills, dear brother."

"So you knew?"

Rae shrugs. "I had an idea, but I wanted you to tell me when you were ready. As I said before, Hudson, I love you, and

164

you're my brother. Who you love or want to date will never get in the way of that."

"Do you . . . Do you think everyone else will feel the same?"

"If they don't, then they're not really friends or family, are they?"

Hudson wraps an arm around her shoulders and hugs her to his chest. "I love you, Rae."

"I love you too, Hudson." She grins before kissing his cheek. "My cutie bootie little baby brother who I love oh so much."

Hudson pushes her off and wipes his cheek, making her laugh. Hudson gives her a weak glare. "You're annoying."

"And you're gay."

His mouth drops open while Rae tries really hard not to laugh at his expression. After a minute, he clears his throat and nods. "Yes, yes I am."

"Ugh." She groans after a second of silence. "More boys to worry about."

"What are you worried about? You have a mate."

"True." She nods before giving him a wicked smile. "But someone's gotta keep your virtue safe from all those dirty little boys who come by trying to steal it."

"You're creepy," Hudson says with a weird look.

"I think it's the painkillers," Colton says, suddenly rejoining them. He turns to Hudson and smiles encouragingly. "Just so you know, we have a few pack members like you, even some mated pairs."

"Really?" Hudson asks, his eyes lighting up.

Rae watches them chat with a smile spreading across her face. This will be a fresh start for them, all of them. A new page in the book that, before now, was reading more like a tragedy than anything else. Sitting back into the porch swing, she feels so relaxed and happy.

But then again it could just be the painkillers.

CHAPTER EIGHTEEN

Rae grips the banister at the top of the stairs as she tries to catch her breath. She snuck away when the others weren't watching and made it up the stairs unnoticed. Well, most likely not unnoticed, but definitely left alone. Once she's caught enough of breath to not think she's dying, she heads for her bedroom and pushes open the door.

It's practically empty already, she notices as she looks around. There are a few odds in ends here and there, left to be taken out like her record player and a few wrapped but unpacked knickknacks. Gripping her side, she moves toward her bed and sits on the bare mattress. Looking around a bit more, she can't help but feel like a stranger in her own room now.

Everything is just . . . gone.

A few knocks on her door has her turning to see Graham in her doorway. She wipes her face as quickly as she can before forcing a smile. He doesn't answer it, though, and instead just walks deeper into her room. Rae stares down at the weave of her jeans while Graham comes to sit beside her on the bed. Wrapping an arm around her shoulders, he looks around the room himself.

"I think you need to redecorate in here."

Rae lets out a reluctant chuckle before wiping a few more tears away. "God, I feel like all I do these days is cry."

"It's a lot of big changes."

166

"It is, but hell, shouldn't I be excited? I'm getting everything I wanted. I get my mate, a new pack, my family finally getting back together, and some help with everything. Yet here I am crying, again, over a room."

"Well, think about it," Graham starts giving her a sympathetic glance. "We're expected to meet our soul mate, accept them without knowing them, and then drop everything to be with them. It's more than a little fucked up."

Rae laughs a little. "That's true."

"It can be overwhelming, even for me. Shit, Rae, who am I going to hit on now?"

"Anyone else."

"Yeah, but they're no fun. You're the only one who doesn't fall at my feet."

"You're such a cocky douche bag."

"That's *incredibly handsome* cocky douche bag to you, miss."

Rae rolls her eyes. "Sure, Graham, whatever you say."

Graham doesn't say anything for a few minutes before he reaches over and takes her hand in his. Entwining their fingers, he stares down at their hands. Rae does the same, but all she feels is flesh on flesh, nothing close to what she feels with Colton. Secretly, she's pleased with that. It reminds her that he really is her soul mate and that no matter what, that won't change.

"I'm going to miss you."

Rae comes out of her thoughts and smiles at Graham. "I'll miss you too."

"If he messes up, you know who to call, right?"

She puts a finger on her chin in fake thought. "Somebody who won't get their ass kicked?"

"Ha ha. You're hilarious."

"I know, it's one of my finer points."

"Seriously, though, Rae, call me. If you need anything at all, I'll be there."

She bumps her shoulder against his. "I know."

"Can I tell you something?" he asks quietly.

"Can I stop you?"

He rolls his brown eyes at her. "I'm being serious."

"Okay, okay, sorry, continue."

"Before the run . . . I thought, hoped actually, that maybe you were . . . my mate."

Rae blinks at his words before dropping her gaze to their hands. Untangling their hands, she wraps them around her waist. She had known that there may have been more to his flirting all the time, but she hoped it wasn't true. Graham lowers his head and whispers in her ear, making her shrink back from him a little.

"Because if you were my mate, I would get to annoy you to death without interruption."

Peeking over at him, she sees amusement clear in his eyes without a hint of anything else. No pain, no longing, no sadness, just plain old Graham being his normally dick-ish self. Narrowing her eyes at him, she punches him in the arm, making him laugh loudly and falling over on the bed. He grips his arm and grins over at her as she continues to glare at him.

"That was mean." She pouts.

"Oh, come on, Rae! What kind of friend would I be if I didn't ruffle your feathers a bit before you left me?"

"One I would miss," she grumbles.

He wraps his arms around her shoulders, hugging her tightly from the side. "Oh, love muffin, don't get all sad because I didn't admit my unrequited love. You know you'll always have my heart."

"Do you accept returns?"

"No receipt, no returns. You know the rules."

Rae snaps her fingers. "Just the luck."

Graham laughs, but it's cut off by the low growl from behind them. Graham immediately lets go of her, and Rae turns her head to see a pissed looking Colton in the doorway. His hands are curled into fists, and his muscles are tight with tension as he glances at Rae before snarling at Graham. He takes a step towards the pair and Rae springs to her feet. Her side pulls at the sudden movement, and she inhales sharply while gripping the footboard of her bed.

"Shit," Colton mutters before coming to steady her. "Goddamn it, Rae, you shouldn't be moving around like that."

"Well, I wouldn't have to if you didn't look like you were going to decapitate Graham," she snaps while holding her side with her other hand.

"I don't like how he was touching you."

"Well, get over it."

Graham decides to chime in then. "Colton, I meant no disrespect. I should have kept my distance."

"What?" Rae gapes at him, "No, no, Graham, you didn't—"

"Rae, it's not a big deal." Graham grins. "I get it. I'd be the same way with my mate."

"Well, then you're both idiots."

"Oh really? You'd be okay with some girl being all over Colton?" Graham asks with an arched brow.

Rae's mind conjures up the image of some girl plastered on her mate, and the reaction is immediate. Her hands ball up into fists, her teeth begin to grind, and rage starts to build in her chest. Her wolf, of course, is practically pushing for killing the imagined girl as well as pushing to be freed. Rae's wolf is not even having a hypothetical woman's hands on their territory.

"See?" Graham says, looking smug. "Not so crazy now, is it?"

"Shut up," she mutters.

Grinning widely, Graham ruffles her hair as he passes by. "I'll see you guys later."

No one says anything, and even once he leaves, the silence is still not broken. Slowly, Rae settles back down on her mattress, but feels Colton's hands hovering close by, just in case. Once she settles, she feels his hands grip her thighs and lifts her gaze to see

169

him kneeling in front of her. He removes a hand to cup the side of her face and runs his thumb across her lower lip making her breathing stutter.

"I'm sorry," he says quietly. "I didn't really think. I just reacted."

"No, Graham is right, I should have thought about your point of view. I would have ripped any girl's arms off that even brushed by you."

Colton smirks at her. "Ripped her arms off, huh?"

"Well, that's what I'd start with."

Colton chuckles lightly before leaning forward and kissing the apples of each of her cheeks with a lingering touch. Rae closes her eyes at the shocks that begin to dance across her skin at the contact. When he leans back again, she doesn't open her eyes right away, wanting to savor the feeling. Opening her eyes, she stares into his deep blue orbs as a question builds on her tongue.

"Colton, why haven't you kissed me yet?"

Colton's neck starts to turn red, and he averts his gaze. "I . . ."

"I mean, I'm not trying to pressure you or anything, I just want to understand."

"It's not that I don't want to, Rae. In fact, that's all I think about most of the time we're together," he adds, looking at her lips before smiling at her blush. "You know, when you blush it just makes your scent stronger."

"No, I did not," she mumbles, her cheeks getting redder. "Seems a bit unfair since you don't blush."

He lifts a brow, "I'm not really the blushing type."

Both are quiet for a minute, and Colton goes back to caressing her face with his fingers. Rae feels the need to tell him everything, her fears, her doubts, and even her excitement, but she can't get them past her lips. She's been bottling everything up so long that sharing her inner thoughts is becoming a chore. She wants to, though, god does she want to.

170

"You've been crying," Colton says suddenly. "Why?"

"I-I don't know."

"Do you not want to move in with me?"

"I do want to, Colton. It's not that."

"Then what is it?"

"It's all so . . . overwhelming. Do you understand? I mean, one minute I'm trying to keep my head above water and the next I'm getting everything I ever wanted. It's hard for me to process, I guess."

"I know this is hard. I know that this isn't anything close to what you expected to happen. Hell, I wouldn't have thought I would have found you when I came here, but I want you with me. Every minute you're out of my sight I feel your absence in my very bones."

Rae smiles softly at his words and lifts her hand to cup his face. "That is so cheesy."

"I'm being serious," he grumbles.

"I know." She grins before leaning forward to place her forehead against his, "And if you promise not to tell anyone, I'll admit that I feel it too."

He smiles a little. "Only if I don't tell anyone, though."

"Yes. I can't have the whole neighborhood knowing that I miss my *boyfriend* when he's gone."

"Boyfriend?" he asks, his eyes flickering up to meet hers.

She smirks at him. "Do you really think the girls wouldn't have told me? Cassidy was afraid I'd turn into a zombie. She wants to make sure I don't spread your 'cooties' to the rest of the family. You're contagious you know."

He clicks his tongue. "I should have bribed them to not to say anything."

"Oh yeah, why is that?"

"Because I wanted to ask you properly."

Rae leans closer, so their lips are millimeters apart. "I don't need all the pomp, Colton. I just need you."

171

Colton doesn't have a chance to respond. Rae leans forward the rest of the way and lays her lips against his. He doesn't respond, but Rae doesn't care at the moment. All she can feel is the shock that is tingling across her lips, along her jaw, and down her throat. Her heart is pounding in her chest, and she can't hear anything but the rhythm it's setting under the flesh there. She opens her eyes for a second to see his eyes closed, but he's still not kissing her back.

Rae starts to lean back, a little embarrassed, but Colton doesn't let her. He grabs the back of her neck and brings her lips crashing back down to his. He tilts his head and parts her lips with his tongue before deepening the kiss. Rae groans against his mouth and locks her arms around his neck as his other hand settles on her hip. Rae's hands dig into the thick brown locks of his hair, and she grips them in between her fingers, keeping him right where he is.

It's intense, all-consuming, and everything she wanted her first kiss with her mate to be. His hand moves around her hip to her lower back. When his fingers slide under her shirt and touch her skin, she arches into him making his chest collide with hers. He removes his lips from hers and Rae takes in a sharp gasp of air. Her shortness of breath isn't helped much when he starts kissing along her right shoulder before sucking on the curve of her neck.

Her hands tighten in his hair, and her wolf is practically whining with want in her head. Her wolf wants him to mark her, make them his forever, but Rae isn't too sure this is the time for it. She doesn't want anyone to walk in on them when they finally do the marking, and here everyone is walking into something. Still, she can't get herself to tell him to stop, especially when it feels this good.

When his teeth drag across her skin, though, she realizes how far they've pushed it. She becomes immobile against him, and luckily he notices it. He pulls back from her neck and comes back into her view. Rae mentally groans at how tempting he looks at the moment. His lips are swollen and parted as he tries to catch his
172

own breath. His hair is a mess on the top of his head from her hands still clinging to the stands, and his eyes are glazed with desire.

She wants to say to hell with it and kiss him again. She wants to, but she doesn't. Instead, she just lowers her forehead against his again and closes her eyes in hopes of calming herself down. Too much, she thinks, this is just too much.

"You make it so hard to keep my hands to myself," he says thickly before grabbing her chin and making her open her eyes. His lips curve into a smirk. "Now, I don't think I won't be able to stop myself from doing that all the time."

"Me neither," she admits in a whisper.

He smiles before leaning down to kiss her chastely but hard enough to send a message. "Yeah, I can see this is going to become a problem."

"A problem for who exactly?" She smirks.

"Tease."

"Don't see me denying it."

He pushes some of her hair back from her face. "We're going to need to leave soon. Do you have everything?"

"Just about."

Colton looks around and spots the few unpacked things. "I could have Jolene send anything else you think of on the way."

"Colton?" she asks nervously.

"Yeah?"

"Do you think your pack . . . Do you think they'll like me?"

His smile is small but adoring. "Of course they will. I like you, and my dad already threatened to break my legs if I messed this up. So yeah, I think the pack will like you. Besides, I hate to break it to you, but you're terribly hard not to like, Rae."

"You're biased."

"Maybe." He shrugs. "But it doesn't matter. In the end, you have your family, and I have you. There is nothing else that matters to me than that. Other people's opinions . . . are useless."

"You're being charming again."

173

"Should I not be?" he asks, leaning towards her again.

Rae smiles and is about to kiss him again when she hears a few knocks on the door. Snapping her head in that direction, her cheek turns bright red when she sees a very unimpressed-looking Jace and a shocked-looking Poppy. Poppy grabs Jace's hand and shields her own eyes, making Rae roll her own.

"What?" she snaps, still feeling heat in her cheeks.

"The trucks all loaded up." Jace tells her with a smirk. "Would you to like to join us or would you like a little more *alone* time?"

"Colton?"

"Yes?"

"Kill him for me, would you?"

Colton stands up and cracks his knuckles. "Gladly."

Jace's eyes widen, and as soon as Colton steps forward, he bolts for the stairs. Colton goes after him, and Rae hears Jace grunt as Colton tackles him in the front entry. She looks over at Poppy who is looking down at the boys down at the bottom level.

"Did he get him?" Rae asks.

"Yup. He's pinning him so he can't move. I think Jace is crying."

Rae laughs lightly. "Serves him right."

"Rae?"

"Yes, baby?"

"Boys are weird, aren't they?"

"The weirdest."

174

CHAPTER NINETEEN

Colton looks over at Rae and feels a smile spread across his face as she traces the veins on the back of his hand. At first, he thought that was a little odd, but that quickly faded once he realized how relaxing it was. Colton needs relaxation right now. He's not concerned about his pack's reaction to Rae, he wouldn't allow anything less than a welcoming one, but he is worried about slipping back into reality. Once they pass that territorial line, he won't be just Colton anymore, he'll be beta of the High Ridge pack.

The idea of it has him tensing. It's not that he doesn't like his pack, he loves them, but with Rae in the picture, they've become less important to him. His father warned him about this, that his priorities may slip, and he never believed it. Looking over at Rae again, he knows how true those words are now. He'll never value anything more than he values her.

"How many pack members do you have?" Cleo asks, getting his attention.

"One hundred and seventy-eight."

"That's a lot," Rae breathes, her nerves clearly written on her face.

Colton squeezes her hand. "They'll love you."

Cleo speaks up again, making Colton grimace. "Is the pack house big enough to house all of us?"

"Yes. All of you will have your own rooms on one of the upper levels. Well, other than the girls, they get to share," he says, smiling at the girls in the back of the van.

"Is your pack strict or are they lax?"

"You mean are they like your last pack who let the un-shifting members run around without supervision?" Colton asks tightly.

Cleo scowls at him. "I'm not a child. I can make my own choices, and that includes my own mistakes."

"Not in my pack, you can't."

"Okay," Rae says before clapping her hands and getting both of their attention. "Well, this has been a very interesting conversation, but I think it's one left for a better time. Like when we're not all packed in an enclosed space, maybe."

"Fine." Cleo shrugs before sitting back in her seat. "Just know I put up with Rae telling me what to do because she's my sister, but you're nothing to me beta boy so keep your commands to yourself."

"Cleo, please," Rae begs.

Cleo puts her hands up. "Just saying."

Rae glances over at Colton in the driver's seat and gives him an apologetic look. "Sorry, she's a bit edgy."

"It's fine," he tells her with a smile. "My mom will love having another teenager to take down a peg. I think she's starting to get bored with all the behaving kids. She's used to cracking the whip."

Rae's eyes light up at the mention of his mom. "What's she like? Your mom, I mean."

A fond smile comes across his face as he thinks about his mom. "She's . . . energetic."

"Energetic?"

"She's always doing something. She takes being alpha female really seriously. She likes to put her fingerprints on everything. She cooks, she watches the kids and takes over some of the issues most would bring to me or my father. She's superwoman."

"Must be where you get the work ethic." Rae grins.

Colton shrugs a shoulder. "My dad is the one who's more into duty. Mom is more into having fun. I'm still learning to balance it all. I've only been a beta about two years, but I like it. It means I can help the pack."

Rae squeezes his hand. "Well then, I'll do my best to charm them. I'd hate for them to clog up your day with complaints about their new Beta female."

"Like I'd let them." Colton snorts.

Rae's scent becomes thicker in the car, and he glances over to see her blushing again. Lifting their entwined hands, he kisses the back of hers, pleased to see her cheeks only get redder. Turning his attention back to the road, he glances into the rearview mirror and sees the moving truck following close behind.

Jace and Hudson are in that one with Jace driving, much to Jace's happiness. Colton snorts as he remembers the kid's reaction. His face lit up so much you'd think Christmas came early this year. Of course, Rae wasn't too sure about the driving thing, but she was already a mess from having to say goodbye to Jolene, Garrett, Graham, and her uncle Everett.

Everett was an interesting man, Colton thinks, as he looks out at the road. He was always in the background and the complete opposite of Jolene who seemed to fill every room she was in with her presence. He looked identical to Rae's cousin, his son, but he had a certain serenity in his face that the younger man was lacking. Colton stuck by him most of the day, his presence being oddly soothing in the chaos going on all around him.

He's taken out of his thoughts though when he hears Rae hiss in pain. Glancing over, he sees her clutching her head, and that's when he feels it. The boundary line of his pack's territory. His wolf is getting antsy, excited to be back on home turf where he

177

could keep their mate safe. Colton is half tempted to roll his eyes at his own wolf, like he would really let anything happen to her.

"Ow," Rae cries, making him tighten his hold on her other hand. She squeezes back and feels his wolf growl at the obvious distress in their mate. Colton knows it's just her pack mind-link and ties breaking, but it doesn't mean he has to like it. "Shit."

"It'll be over soon."

"What's happening?" Cleo asks, coming to get closer to Rae.

"She's relinquished her position in the pack. Her mind link to White Stone is being broken."

Cleo clicks her tongue before sitting back in her seat. "Shit deal."

Colton glares at her through the rearview mirror before taking turns between watching the road and Rae. The closer they get to the pack house, the more she seems to be getting uncomfortable. Tears stream down her cheeks, and Colton feels guilt rise up in him. He should have been paying attention so he could warn her. It doesn't change the pain of the process, but at least she would have been prepared.

She lets out a quieter sob before her whole body relaxes. Dropping her hand from her head, she blinks her watery dark eyes open. Her lashes are wet, and her cheeks look damp from her tears. Colton has to remind himself he's driving, so he doesn't reach out and wipe them away. He really hates it when she cries.

"Rae?"

"I'm okay," she says thickly before nodding. "Yeah, I'm okay. Shit, that hurt."

"I don't doubt that," he agrees with a sad smile.

Rae removes her hand from his and wipes her face. "I didn't even think I could cry anymore."

Colton doesn't answer. His wolf is too busy forcing him to look over every inch of her. His wolf needs to be assured she's not in pain anymore. When he's satisfied, he fades into the back of

Colton's mind again but clearly is on alert, just in case. Running a hand down his face, Colton tries to give her time to collect herself. He knows how much she likes to bottle it all up and deal with it later, this is just the first time he's letting her do it.

"Wow," Cleo breathes from behind them. "Girls, come look!"

Colton can see how the pack house could be impressive. It's five floors, not including the basement, and contains about thirty rooms with fifteen bathrooms. He supposes that would also sound impressive but considering the amount of people living in the house, it can get a bit cramped. It's why some pack members have their own houses away from the main one. Unlike at White Stone, though, the alphas don't have their own house, just their own section.

Glancing over at Rae, he's pleased to see her awed face as she takes in the house. It's a cottage style in design with a dark brown siding and black framing. It blends into the surroundings perfectly, and it's both an aesthetic choice as well as a tactical one. Keeping their activities hidden from anyone not within their world is key to keeping their people safe. It's a lesson Dalton taught him early in life, and one Colton has taken to heart over his course as second in command.

Colton's thoughts are invaded again as Cassidy yells, "It's a castle!"

"It's not a castle," Poppy tells her simply. "There isn't a moat. It can't be a castle without a moat."

"Yes, it can," Cassidy argues before she pokes Colton's cheek, getting his attention. "Colton is this a castle?"

"I can't be sure. We don't have any princesses in it so . . ."

"I'm a princess!" Cassidy yells, making him flinch with a smile.

"I'm a princess too!" Poppy yells.

"You have to say it's a castle if you want to be a princess." Cassidy says in the same tone as Poppy used earlier.

"Fine." Poppy sighs, making Colton smile at how much like Rae she sounds. "It's a castle."

"Yay! Now we can be princesses together!"

"Can I be a princess?" Cleo asks.

There's silence for a few seconds before Cassidy says, "I guess . . ."

"What about me?" Rae asks.

"You can't be a princess," Poppy says matter-of-factly. "You're too old."

"Old?" Rae scoffs. "I'm nineteen, not ninety."

"You look ninety." Poppy grins.

Rae glares at her mini-me before sticking her tongue out at her. "Meanie."

"Oldie."

"You know what? Just for that, I won't read to you tonight."

Cassidy and Poppy gasp in unison before Cassidy demands, "Say you're sorry Poppy!"

"But she *is* old!"

"Say you're sorry!" Cassidy yells, and Colton's pretty sure he even heard a foot stomp. "I want Rae to read to me!"

"I'll read to you," Poppy argues.

"I don't want you! I want Rae!"

"Girls," Rae sighs, but they don't listen.

"I can read too, you know," Cleo mutters from her seat.

"You don't do it right!" Cassidy argues but with who, Colton isn't too sure. "You don't make the noises and faces like Rae does."

"You make faces?" Colton asks Rae, making her face go red again.

Rae shrugs a shoulder while avoiding his searching look. "That's how mom used to do it."

"Don't get embarrassed, it's cute," he teases with a smirk.

180

She narrows her eyes at him. "You know what, I'm not reading to you tonight either."

"Like any of us believe that *that* is what you'll be doing tonight." Cleo snorts.

Rae crosses her arms over her chest. "It's official. I'm going to grow a beard and run away so I can join the circus."

"Awe," Cleo coos as she hugs Rae from behind. "But we'd miss you. Who else would keep the munchkins happy?"

"You."

"Uh . . . No, they hate me."

"They don't—"

"Horses!" Cassidy squeals. "Look, Rae, horses!"

Rae bumps her shoulder against Colton's. "Good to see you're not a dirty liar."

"What kind of knight would I be to lie to a princess?"

"Not a very good one I'd imagine." She grins.

As the van pulls up to the house, Colton feels Rae tense beside him. In turn, Colton relaxes at the sight before them. His mom, his dad, and his brother, Sawyer along with Sawyer's wife, Vivienne. When he spots a few nosey pack members peeking through the windows from inside the house, he knows that his mother ordered them to keep their distance, so they're not overwhelmed.

That's the last thing they need to be at this point.

Glancing over at Rae, Colton fights the urge to laugh. "Uh, Rae, what are you doing?"

Rae slouches more in her chair. "Don't talk to me. I'm invisible right now."

"Rae." He laughs. "It's fine. You're fine. My family will love you. The pack will love you. Everything is going to be perfectly fine."

She scowls at him. "I don't like that word anymore. You're now officially banned from using the word 'fine' around me."

"What if he asks for a fine point pen?" Cleo asks with a laugh.

"Not helping," Rae grumbles.

"Whatever," Cleo says with an eye roll. "Stop being such a chicken and get the hell out of the car, Rae. This is going to be your pack soon and acting like a scared baby deer isn't going to give a good first impression."

"Oh, and you know so much about that, don't you?"

Cleo shrugs. "I don't have to give good impressions, and you do. Now, are you going to be the hard-ass of a sister I know and love or not?"

"Awe, you love me?" Rae grins at her.

Cleo glares. "Get out of the car, Rae."

Colton watches Cleo open up the sliding side door of the van before climbing out. Cassidy and Poppy follow suit and Colton takes this as his chance to get Rae out of the car too. Unbuckling his seatbelt, he leans over and takes Rae's face in his hands. Looking her right in the eyes, he tries to give her as much strength through their still fairly fragile bond as he can before speaking.

"You're my mate, Rae, and as such I expect you to hold your head high."

Rae lifts a brow, clearly unimpressed by his word choice. "Expect?"

"And I expect you to do that because you have no reason not to," he continues, hiding his amusement. "Your beta female, soon to be alpha female. You have no reason to ever feel less than anyone else. My parents, my brother, his wife, and everyone else in his pack included."

"But—"

"This isn't like it was back at White Stone, Rae. There is no walking on eggshells here. You have no one to look down on you here."

Rae stares at him a long minute with wide eyes before she suddenly leans forward and kisses him. Colton takes a few seconds

182

to get over his surprise before he cups the side of her face and deepens the kiss. He doesn't give a flying fuck that his parents are probably watching. He doesn't care that most of the pack is most likely watching as well. All he cares about is making sure his mate is happy, comfortable, and safe.

Everything else is nothing but background noise.

"We should stop." Rae gasps as she pulls back.

"Why?" he breathes, not taking his eyes off her swollen lips.

"Because your mom is doing a really weird happy dance right now."

Colton shifts his eyes out the front window to see his mom doing just that. She's got her hands up in the air as she's jumping around like someone is throwing firecrackers at her feet. He raises an eyebrow at the sight before letting out a dejected sigh. Well, at least she didn't call him— "Pooky bear, come out of the car! I want to meet my new daughter-in-law!"

Rae, to her credit, tries really hard not to laugh. "Pooky bear?"

Colton drops his head onto the steering wheel.

He can only imagine how this will be used against him.

CHAPTER TWENTY

Exiting the van, Rae tugs on her shirt and tucks her hair behind her ears nervously. She's trying to find the inner strength to not make a run for it. It's tempting, oh so tempting, but she needs to get this done. Of course, she knew that meeting Colton's family would be a given, but actually meeting them in the flesh is incredibly daunting.

Sure she's met his dad, but he wasn't in alpha mode then. What if, after some consideration, he's come to the same conclusion as Alpha Kendrick? What if he thinks she's not good enough for his son either?

Colton grabs her sweaty hand, and she can feel the shocks move up her arm, soothing her. Glancing up at him, she sees it all in his eyes. He wants her to calm down, he's right there with her and it'll be fine. Yeah, she thinks with a mental snort, he says that now but what happens if they hate her? Will he be so calm then?

Rae is taken out of her thoughts as she's suddenly grabbed by the shoulders and brought into a tight hug. She squeaks as the hold around her tightens, and she swears she can feel her spine cracking in half. Still, she feels the need to give something back, so she awkwardly pats the woman's back a few times.

"Oh, I'm so happy!" the alpha female cries in her ear before pulling back to examine Rae. "And you're so pretty!"

"Uh, thank you."

Colton's mom is a beautiful woman herself. With thick caramel colored hair, dark brown eyes, and a light tan to her skin, she looks so warm. She's a few inches shorter than Rae herself, but from her build, Rae can tell the woman can beat some ass if needed. Still, her eyes are soft as she smiles at her, making Rae relax just a little. Maybe this won't be so bad?

"Mom, can you give her a minute to breathe?" Colton says from behind her. "She's had tough couple days already without you squeezing the life out of her."

"Fuss, fuss, fuss, that's all you men do," his mom grumbles back before winking at Rae. "Sometimes, they need a reminder we're stronger than they think we are."

Rae laughs, making his mother's smile only widen. "My name's Jessica by the way. No alpha female shit around me. The whole pack calls me by the name on my birth certificate, and that's how I like it!"

"Okay." Rae grins. "I'm Rae."

"Believe me, honey, I know." Jessica giggles. "My husband and my baby just won't shut up about you!"

"Other just-as-starved-for-love son over here mom," a man who Rae assumes is Colton's brother says pointing to himself. He obviously favors his mother in his looks. His features are a bit softer, but his hair is the same dark black as Dalton's with his mother's warm brown eyes that settle on Rae.

"I'm Sawyer. Colton's older and better-looking brother."

"Hi." Rae smiles with a little wave.

"And this is my best girl, Vivienne," Sawyer says, squeezing the tiny woman's shoulders standing beside him.

Rae watches the tiny little redhead's blue eyes roll as she puts a hand out towards her. "Welcome to the family and don't worry, they may seem weird, but they're good people."

"I didn't doubt it for a second." Rae smiles at her while taking her hand to shake.

A throat clearing behind her has Rae turning to see her siblings all standing by the van, looking uncomfortable. Well, the other three do, Cassidy and Poppy just look about ready to burst out of their skin with excitement. Waving them over, Rae bends down and picks up Cassidy when she comes over before settling her on her hip. Turning back to her mate's wide-eyed family, she smiles.

"These are my siblings," Rae says with a sheepish smile. "This is Cleo."

"Hi," Cleo says with a little wave although her arms begin crossed on her chest.

Rae rolls her eyes before moving to the next sibling. "This is Jace."

"Hey," he grunts before asking. "What's your kitchen like?"

Jessica frowns a little but keeps her smile in place. "It's a chef's kitchen so . . . "

"Really? Nice," Jace says, nodding appreciatively.

"Anyway," Rae continues. "This is Hudson."

Hudson inclines his head towards the Alpha couple making them chuckle. "Hello."

"Hello." The alpha couple return before Dalton speaks up, "I talked over what we discussed with the sentry. They agree with opening the south trail up again. It's a good running spot, I think you'll like it."

"Thank you, Alpha." Hudson grins.

"Dalton, please."

"Right," Hudson says with a happy nod. "Thanks Dalton, Alpha, sir."

Everyone chuckles a little as Hudson's neck and the tips of his ear go red in a blush. Rae pets Poppy's hair as she hugs Rae's leg. "This is Poppy."

"Hi," Poppy says with a shy smile.

"So precious," Jessica practically squeals.

186

"And this one is Cassidy." Rae grins, bouncing her a bit on her hip.

"Hello!" Cassidy yells. "I'm Cassidy, and I'm six! Do you have horses? Colton said you had horses, and he doesn't lie, does he? Rae says lying is bad. Is it bad because if it is and Colton lied you should put him in time out! Do I get my own room because I want to be with Poppy. Wow, you're pretty! Do you—"

"Okay!" Rae says loudly as she covers Cassidy's mouth. "Let's give them a little time to process, shall we?"

Cassidy mumbles against her hand with a scowl, but Rae just gives her a look. Though the look is weakened with the smile threatening to come across her face. She can't stay stern with Cassidy to save her life. How can she? She's just too damn cute!

"Well, that sure is a caravan you've got," Sawyer drawls, making Vivienne smack his arm. "What? That's a lot of kids!"

"Maybe I should cover your mouth," Vivienne grumbles, making everyone laugh.

"Well, Cassidy," Jessica begins as she steps closer to address her directly. "I do have horses, but they only let special people touch them. Colton said you and Poppy were very special little girls so maybe they'll let you come near them. Would you like to see them after dinner?"

"Yes!" Cassidy agrees with a very energetic nod before reaching down to tap on the top of Poppy's head. "Did you hear that, Pop?"

"Yes." Poppy hisses up at her before turning to Jessica. "Thank you, Alpha."

"Jessica, sweetheart, you can call me Jessica."

"Thank you, Jessica."

Jessica taps Poppy under the chin, "No problem, sweetheart." Jessica claps her hands and looks over all the Applebee siblings. "You guys must be so exhausted! Would you like to see your rooms?"

187

All she gets is silent nods from all of them. Hesitating a little, Jessica points to Dalton. "This is my husband, who I'm guessing you've already met." More silent nods. "And this is my older son, Sawyer, with his wife, Vivienne."

"You can call me Viv or Vivi," the redhead corrects.

"Hi," they all say in unison before Cassidy adds. "Your hair is so bright! You look like Merida."

"Who?"

"From *Brave*," Rae tells her before kissing the side of Cassidy's head. "So, shall we go in? I'm a bit curious to see the inside."

"Of course!" Jessica grins before reaching out for Cassidy. "May I?"

Cassidy goes for her without hesitation, making Rae smile. Rae takes Poppy's hand and starts following the rest of the Woodwards' into the house. Turning her head, she sees Colton walking beside her with a smile on his face. Rae straightens up a bit, knowing that she maybe passed some kind of secret test.

"Holy shit," Cleo breathes from behind her as they enter the house.

She's echoing Rae's thoughts perfectly. Entering the front doors, Rae's jaw drops at the sight of the house. Two steps lead you out of the entry and into a huge living room with three brown leather couches with two matching love seats, a brick fireplace with a flat screen TV hanging above it, built-in bookshelves on either side of the fireplace, and a circular glass coffee table in the middle of it all. Letting her eyes drift upward, Rae also spots a beautiful chandelier hanging above.

"Wow," she breathes, feeling overwhelmed.

"You like it?" Colton asks.

Snapping her head in his direction, her eyes are wide. "Like it? Are you kidding me? This is like a palace."

"How sweet of you to say!" Jessica grins before coming over to cup Rae's face. "I'm hoping you guys will be happy here."

Cleo snorts as she looks around the room. "If the rest of the house is like this, I don't see that being a problem."

Sawyer buries his face in Vivienne's face as she laughs openly. Colton raises an eyebrow, and everyone else in the family just rolls their eyes. They're used to Cleo's missing filter and abrasive ways. Rae doesn't want to offend anyone, though. They just got here, Cleo could at least wait a few days before making enemies.

"Cleo." Rae hisses, but Jessica puts a hand up, stopping her from continuing.

"It's alright," Jessica tells Rae before turning to Cleo. "I understand you like to dance and listen to music?"

"Yeah, I guess, but who doesn't," Cleo says as she shifts on her feet.

"Well, we have a dance studio in the backhouse with an amazing sound system."

"That's true," Sawyer chimes in. "I installed it myself."

"A lot of the kids dance around here," Vivienne adds, "Everything under the sun, really. Jazz, tap, ballet, hip-hop, interpretive, everything. I actually teach some of the classes."

"You dance?" Cleo asks, giving Vivienne's petite body a once over.

"Yup. I can show you the studio if you want."

"Maybe we should see our rooms first," Rae suggests, already feeling like she's imposing.

Jessica shakes her head as she adjusts Cassidy on her hip. "It's perfectly fine. Vivienne, you can show her room when you're done right?"

"Sure." She nods.

Rae is about to say something when she turns to already see Cleo on the move with Vivienne.

Cleo waves a hand over her hand before calling. "Don't worry, Rae! I'll be sure not to lure any cute boys away!"

189

"Cleo!" Rae groans, only to hear Cleo's laughter as she escapes from her sight. Turning to Dalton and Jessica, she gives an apologetic smile. "Sorry. She can be a bit much."

"No need to explain," Dalton says as he wraps an arm around Jessica. "I've had my fair share of dealing with teenage girls. Just be lucky she doesn't have a wolf. Hormonal girls with restless animals in their head is never a pretty sight."

"I can agree with that." Jace scoffs as he hooks a thumb in Rae's direction. "She was a downright bitch."

"Jace!"

"What?" He shrugs. "You were."

Colton's hands come around Rae's waist as she's about to respond. "Perhaps you can refrain from calling my mate names before I make you cry again."

Jace's eyes narrow at the very polite threat before he points at Colton. "You caught me by surprise."

"Really?" Colton asks doubtfully, before grinning menacingly at her brother. "Want to try again and see?"

"Uh, rooms?" Rae suggests nervously.

"Good idea," Jessica agrees quickly, her own eyes darting between the two men. As Rae comes to walk beside Jessica towards the stairway, Jessica whispers, "Are they always like that?"

"Well, I've only seen them together for about . . . Wow. Three days, but yeah, they're always this intense."

"Colton pinned Jace down and made him cry," Poppy whispers from beside Rae.

"Really?" Jessica asks with a smile in her direction. "How did he do that?"

"I don't know." Poppy shrugs. "But it hurt."

"Colton bent his arm back," Rae tells the alpha female.

Jessica makes a face. "Learned that one from Sawyer, I'm afraid. Maybe it's a territorial thing. Has Jace shifted?"

Rae shakes her head. "No. I've been keeping an eye on him, and I haven't seen any signs."

190

"What about Hudson? He's coming to that age."

"I don't know." Rae shrugs with a sigh. "Hudson keeps to himself a lot."

"Was your mother a shifter?"

"No," Rae says sadly with a shake of her head. "My dad was."

Jessica puts an arm around Rae. "Colton told me everything, and I have to tell you, honey, you've done a beautiful job with these kids. I wish I could say my monsters are as well behaved but I never could discipline them well. Just too cute."

Rae laughs before motioning to Poppy and Cassidy. "I have the same problem with these munchkins."

"I like you, Rae," Jessica says with a soft smile. "I like you for my son. He needs someone like you."

"I need someone like him too," Rae admits as her cheeks heat.

"That's what mates are, sweetheart. They are everything we need and want."

"That's a little . . . too much, isn't it? To expect from someone?"

Jessica thinks on it a moment before shrugging. "Maybe, but you have all the time in the world to figure it out."

Rae nods as they continue to climb the never-ending stairs.

All the time in the world, she thinks. Well, that's a start.

CHAPTER TWENTY ONE

Rae readjusts the bobby pin in her hair before reaching into the box placed on Colton's desk in his room. No, scratch that, she thinks, *their* room. Jessica directed her in here about two hours ago to unpack everything while she showed the girls the horses. They were supposed to wait until after dinner, but if there's anything Rae has learned in her short time here, Poppy and Cassidy are in for some serious spoiling. Jessica just seems like that kind of woman.

Rae is about to finish unpacking by now. She only has a few knickknacks to find places for and books to relocate to their new shelves. Rae was shocked initially when she came into the room and saw how bare it was. Then she remembers who Colton is. From what she remembers from her dad's dinner table gossip, betas tended to do all the heavy lifting of the pack.

Considering what she knows about Colton so far, that doesn't really surprise her at all. She hasn't known him long, sure, but he's a serious kind of guy. She figures a stranger could do that much from just being in his presence. A smile comes across her face though when she also notes how much he isn't like that around her. She feels a little giddy knowing that she can bring out another side of him.

She groans a little and drops her head when she lets that thought sink in. *My, my, how the mighty have fallen,* she thinks. One minute she's swearing mates aren't for her, and yet here she is, practically doing a happy dance 'cause she can make him smile. Pathetic? Maybe. Unable to be helped? Absolutely.

"What's wrong?"

Rae jumps at the sound of Colton's voice and puts a hand over her heart. "Where the hell did you come from?"

He lifts a brow. "From a different part of the house."

Rolling her eyes, she lets her shoulders drop. "Smart ass."

"Seriously, though, what's wrong?"

She frowns at him over her shoulder as she goes back to unpacking her boxes. "What makes you think there's anything wrong?"

"You were smiling then you groaned and looked annoyed."

Rae's cheeks go red. "You were watching me?"

"Yes."

"That's so creepy."

He shrugs and gives her a small smirk. Walking towards her, his smell fills her lungs. It's the same indescribable smell she caught out in the woods, the one that's tainted everything for the past few days and the one at the . . . wait a minute. Turning around, she narrows her eyes at him.

"You were at the mall."

He steps back with a frown. "Huh?"

"The mall. I caught your scent at the mall before the run. That was you. It had to be. I also caught another scent, a flowery one mixed with it. Who was that?"

With every one of her statements, his eyes go wide. Suddenly his neck and the tips of his ears go red, making her give him a weird look. Colton doesn't blush, at least in the time she's known him, and there's been plenty of opportunities. Putting her hands on her hips though, she doesn't back down.

"Well?"

He narrows his eyes at her. "Really? You're going to pull this card?"

"What card?"

193

"The pushing me into a corner until I tell you everything card."

Rae drops her hands from her hips. "Uh . . . apparently?"

He chuckles briefly before running a hand through his hair. His scent is thrown more into the air from the sweat on his skin, and her wolf growls in her mind. Her wolf enjoys his scent as much as Rae does, but instead of being soothing, her wolf just thinks of it as a huge turn on. Pushing away her wolf's more salacious thoughts, she crosses her arms over her chest as she waits impatiently for an explanation.

"I don't really know where to begin."

"How about with the beginning," she suggests with narrowed eyes.

"Well, before you jump to conclusions, I can tell you that I did not go to the mall with a female."

"But the scent—"

"Was floral based, yes. Andy has a really . . . interesting scent."

"Andy?"

"My friend. He's a member of this pack. I can go get him now, and you can smell him for yourself. Damn kid smells more like a *Bath & Bodyworks* than a wolf."

Rae drops her hands feeling suddenly deflated. "I don't think that'll be necessary."

"You sure? Because I can get him," Colton insists, pointing at the bedroom door.

She shakes her head as she backs up until her knees hit the edge of the bed. Sitting on the edge of the large king sized bed, she feels the urge to laugh. What was she thinking? Oh right, she wasn't thinking! She was so wrapped up in what Colton could have done she didn't think about who he's proven himself to be. He doesn't seem like the kind of guy who would do something like that, in fact, she's pretty sure he's still a virgin.

Rae lets out a little laugh at the thought. Once she starts laughing, she can't stop, and soon she's practically howling with laughter. It doesn't make a lick of sense to be laughing this hard about something like this, but she can't help it. It's just so stupid and ridiculous that she even thought he would be cheating on her when he didn't even know she existed! Rae drops her face into her hands and cuts off her own laughing with a groan.

She's just too high strung for this crap today.

"So, you believe me?"

"Yeah." She sighs, wiping the tears of laughter from her eyes. "I actually feel silly for even thinking that."

"It's fine," he assures her with a grin. "I would probably have reacted way worse."

Rae makes a face. "Poor Graham. I thought he'd shit his pants."

"I was kind of hoping he would."

Slapping his arm, Rae lays her head on his shoulder as he comes to sit beside her on the edge of the bed. His whole body relaxes against hers, and she smiles at the observation. She really likes the effect she has on him. Lifting her head a bit, she balances her chin on the edge of his shoulder while looking at his profile. She can see a small bump on the bridge of his nose, and she's half tempted to run her finger over it. Would that be weird, she wonders, or would that be within her right as his mate? Tough question.

"What are you thinking about?"

Her cheeks go pink as she looks up to see him already staring at her curiously. "I don't think you really want to know."

Colton's dark blue eyes shift down to her lips. "You have no idea how hard it is to keep my distance when you blush, do you?"

On cue, her cheeks darken. "Uh . . . no?"

He smirks, but his eyes don't deviate from their target. "And here I thought I was being obvious about it."

195

"Well, you're kind of hard to read sometimes."

His eyes lift up to hers for a second before going back to her mouth. "I try to be really careful. I don't like being out of control, but I knew with you, it would be different. I've been told since I first shifted how intense this would all be, but I didn't realize how . . ."

"Intense? Overwhelming? Distracting?"

"Yes." He smiles. "All those things and more."

"I get it," she breathes before mumbling to herself. "Boy, do I get it."

He takes hold of her chin and makes her look up at him. "Rae?"

"Uh . . . yeah?" she asks, her mouth going dry.

Colton shakes his head with a small smile. "Nothing."

Rae closes her eyes as his lips press against hers. Her hands immediately bury themselves in his hair as she suddenly finds herself in his lap. With her legs on each side of his, she pushes herself forward until their chests are pressed against each other. She doesn't mind that he's sweaty or that his hair is a bit damp or that he probably hasn't brushed his teeth today. She hardly has half the mind to notice it. Instead, she just feels the shocks floating across her skin and the mind numbing feel of his hands on her lower back.

He groans against her lips when she moves her hips a little against him, and his hands slide down to cup her ass. Colton presses her closer to him until there's a snowball's chance in hell of finding space between them. Rae lets out a little moan when he squeezes her jean-clad ass in his hands and in return, she moves her hips against him again.

The kiss is broken when Colton suddenly throws her down on the bed, and she lets out a squeal in surprise. She barely has time to breathe before he's back to kissing her. One of his hand grabs her leg and hitches it around his waist as his tongue invades her mouth. Rae groans at the taste of him against her tongue. It's just like his scent, indescribable, and utterly Colton.

He removes his mouth from hers, and she takes in a sharp inhale of air as he begins kissing along her jawline. Arching her neck, she grabs a handful of his shirt when he scrapes his teeth against her skin. Goosebump rise along her heated skin, and she fights to keep her mind clear, but it's a useless task. How can she even remember her name when he's doing *this*? And why would she want to?

That moment of carelessness is quickly brought to the forefront when Colton suddenly stops kissing her and buries his head in her neck. Confused, Rae turns her head, but Colton doesn't respond. He only nuzzles her neck more, making her think he needs comfort. Okay, she thinks with a frown, this is weird.

"Uh . . . Colton. What—"

"I can't," he tells her hoarsely, still not looking at her. "I can't continue, or I'm going to mark you."

"Oh."

Colton lets out a shaky exhale as he lifts his upper body and puts his weight on his hands. His face is serious as he gazes down at her, and Rae feels her wolf stirring uncomfortably in her mind. What's wrong now?

"Rae, I don't know how long I can hold back. I want to mark you. I want to mark you so much it's invading my dreams now. My wolf wants to see our mark on your skin, and we both want to see your mark on ours. I know it's been three days and we hardly know each other but . . . I just needed you to know."

"To know what?" she questions, feeling winded by this impromptu confession.

"How much I . . . want you."

Rae doesn't hesitate. Grabbing the back of his neck, she lifts her head to meet him half way as she crashes her lips to his. Rae isn't a virgin. She lost that first experience when she was fifteen to some asshole human at her high school. She didn't know she was a wolf, she didn't know that she could even have a mate, and if she did, she certainly didn't think he would be like Colton. Still, she

197

knows that this is a first and only she can give it to him. Marking her can be his first, last, and only with her.

And this she knows she won't regret.

"Colton," she breathes as she looks him in the eyes. "I want you to mark me."

"Now?"

"Yes."

"But—"

"Colton, I don't need more time to think it over. I accepted this bond, I've met your family, and I've moved to your pack. You've accepted my family, my situation, and me without complaint, and I couldn't ask for anything more. I know it's too soon for love so I won't say it, but I do know I care a lot about you. I care about you more than I've ever cared for anyone else, so yes, I want you to mark me. You, only you."

Colton stares down at her wide-eyed for a few minutes before he blinks. "Jesus, Rae . . . you put my little speeches to shame."

Rae smiles widely up at him. "Well, we can't all be as brilliant as me, I suppose."

Colton chuckles as he brushes back some of her hair from her face. Ducking down, he rubs the tip of his nose against hers. "I'll be the looks, and you be the brains in the relationship. Deal?"

"Hell yes." She grins. "That means I can go all natural. No more shaving my unibrows or my legs and proper pants? Might as well kiss that goodbye. From now on it's sweats or nothing, baby."

"Good to know." He chuckles before leveling her with a serious look. "Are you sure about this? You can't take it back once it's done."

"I wouldn't want to, Colton."

He lets out a slow exhale. "Okay. Oh, and Rae?"

"Yeah?"

"I like you too."

Rae rolls her eyes. "Well, I'd certainly hope so."

Laughing, he lowers his lips to hers again. Rae wraps her hands around his neck and tilts her head so they can deepen the kiss. They only break apart once they're both in need of air and Colton moves to kiss her neck again. Rae tries to keep her body relaxed, but it's hard when she knows the pain coming her way. No matter what anyone else tells her, Rae knows that being bitten, mate or not, is bound to hurt like hell.

She's a bit distracted though when Colton latches onto the skin on her neck. He sucks on the point over her rapid pulse, coloring it most likely in an unattractive purple. She's normally annoyed by that if her quick healing didn't make it halfway impossible for any sort of hickey to stay.

"Colton." She groans as her body arches off the bed. "Now."

Colton lets a growl vibrate against her neck before he pulls his head back and slams his teeth into her shoulder. Rae bites her lower lip, so she doesn't cry out. It hurts, fuck does it hurt, but she refuses to let him know that. She can feel some of her blood roll back from the wound and drip onto the comforter below her as his teeth stay embedded in her skin.

She's about to lose her resolve to stay quiet when a faint, warm feeling starts trickling its way through her veins. The pain in her shoulder becomes a distant feeling, and she releases her teeth from her lower lip to let in a sharp inhale. Her hands which she didn't even realize were gripping the back of his shirt so hard go limp and slide off him to land on the bed. Everything feels limp actually and maybe even a bit . . . dazed.

Actually, it kind of feels like being high. She just feels so relaxed.

She can vaguely feel Colton licking and cleaning her wound, but that's just a passing observation. When he finally lifts his head to look down at her, he tilts his head to the side, simply watching her. Annoyed that her buzz is being interrupted, she scowls back up at him, but it's a weak one.

199

"What?"

"You look really tired."

"I feel really tired. Aren't you tired?"

He shakes his head. "Quite the opposite actually."

"Yeah, well, I guess you did take a chunk out of me. I have every right to be exhausted."

Colton smirks down at her. "There's my girl."

Rae gives him a sloppy grin. "Officially."

"Officially," he agrees with a silly smile of his own. "Do you need anything?"

"Yes." She nods as her eyes start to drift close. "I need you to cuddle with me."

"I can do that."

"Then why aren't you doing it?"

Colton laughs as he rolls off her to lay beside her. Rae rolls onto her side, and Colton pulls her up towards the top of the bed where his pillows are. Pulling the comforter around them, he turns on his side as well and wraps his arms around her. Rae lets out a sigh as the tingly feeling of the contact moves through her body. Now, this she could get used to.

"Rae?"

"Hmm?"

"Did it hurt?"

Rae just grunts in response.

"I'm sorry if it hurt."

"Colton?" She sighs.

"Yeah?"

"Shh. It's quiet time. We need to be quiet now."

Colton laughs in her ear, making her frown before he kisses behind her ear. "Whatever you say."

Yup, she thinks before falling to sleep, she could definitely get used to this.

CHAPTER TWENTY-TWO

Cleo walks out the back of the dance studio and pushes some of her hair back behind her ears irritably. Sure, the place is nice, but she hates the looks she's been getting since she got here. Cleo doesn't like to be looked at like she's some kind of freak show attraction, and that's exactly the kind of glances she's been getting. *Well, fuck them,* she thinks as she pulls a cigarette pack from her back skirt pocket.

Placing it between her lips, she pulls out a pack of matches out too and strikes the tip against the back. Watching the flame ignite, she lights the end of the cigarette before waving the matchstick in the air. Exhaling the nearly invisible gray smoke past her lips, she glares into the endless tree-filled landscape.

Great. Stuck in the middle of nowhere with no escape. Fucking perfect.

Taking another drag off her cigarette, she nearly chokes when a voice comes seemingly out of nowhere. Quickly throwing her cigarette to the ground, she puts it out with the bottom of her sneaker and tries to stop coughing. Gasping for air, she turns around with a scowl to yell at whoever it is when her gaze becomes locked with a pair of dark brown eyes.

Her stomach churns and her heart rate picks up as she takes in the rest of the intruder. He's tall, really tall, and for a tall girl like Cleo, that's saying something. His skin is dark chocolate color and looks smooth to the touch, making her hand twitch toward him. His hair is shaved pretty close to the scalp, but it only seems to enhance his high cheekbones and full lips. Full lips that are pulling back into a huge smile that shows straight white teeth.

Realizing she's been staring, Cleo drops her gaze to the space behind his left shoulder. Rubbing her sweaty palms on the sides of her jean skirt, she clears her sore throat before speaking, "What?"

"I said, you shouldn't be smoking back here."

Cleo shivers at the sound of his low deep voice. "I'll remember that for next time."

Stepping around him, she tries to go back into the studio, but he catches her wrist, making shocks move up her arm. Cleo takes back her hand quickly and clutches it against her chest with a frown. That's never happened before. Yeah, she's pretty sure she's never felt anything like that before in her life. She decides to ignore it. Reading too much into shit has gotten her too much trouble in the past.

Then again, not reading into anything has lead to even more trouble.

Cleo scoffs at the thought. She's screwed no matter what she does.

"What's your name?" he asks, a charming smile on his face.

Scowling at him, she crosses her arms over her chest protectively. "What's it to you?"

"Just wondering if your name is as beautiful as you are."

Cleo scoffs. "Sure you were."

Turning on a heel, she says, "Screw it to the studio."

She has unpacking to do, anyway. She's pretty sure she remembers the way back to the pack house. It can't be that hard, right? Just left at the tree. Looking around, she frowns. Which tree was it again? Was it the oak with the knot on it or the one with the toppled over branch?

"Shit." She groans. She really should have paid more attention to Vivienne.

202

She likes Vivienne. She's spunky and obviously loves dancing. How could she not like her? She's practically what Cleo wants to be when she grows up. Secure, happy, and loved. What else could anyone ask for?

With a moment of hesitation, Cleo heads right at a turned over log, that looks oddly familiar. Her arm is still tingling from where that guy touched her and Cleo shakes out the limb, trying to get it to stop. Maybe she's having a heart attack. Isn't that how they start?

Cleo scoffs out loud at that. She would have a heart attack in the middle of nowhere. Fucking typical of her situation these days.

Don't get her wrong; she's happy for Rae really, she is. She's been quietly hoping that Rae would find someone to help her, but Cleo is also honest enough with herself to know she's also jealous. As the younger sister, she's always been jealous of Rae since she popped out of the womb. She's always felt inferior to Rae.

Rae has gotten her wolf. She was loved by their parents and was an obvious favorite of their dad. She is strong, beautiful, and caring for the most part. Sure, they had a few years in there when Rae was a straight up bitch, but Cleo didn't take it personally. She herself is known for her own bitchy behavior so who is she to judge?

But that isn't all of it.

Rae is also a reminder of how much things have changed. Cleo has tried to be helpful, pull weight along with Rae, but Rae didn't want her help. She wanted Cleo to be a kid, to be without the burden, but Cleo didn't see it that way at the time. Cleo thought Rae was pushing her way into replacing their mom. She thought Rae was just trying to make them forget about their parents by trying to take over as the parent in the house. It was complete bullshit to Cleo, and over time, she couldn't help but become resentful.

Justifiable or not, it's how she feels, and Cleo won't apologize for it.

"Shit," she realizes as she looks around her. Is she lost?

Looking around, she recognizes she is most definitely lost. Well, isn't this just fantastic! Muttering a flurry of swears under her breath, Cleo turns on a heel again and tries to retrace her trail back to the studio. Okay, maybe she shouldn't have brushed off the guy. He could have helped her back, no matter how much his presence unsettles her.

"Lost?"

Cleo lets out a scream as she jumps at the voice right by her ear. Covering her mouth with her own hand, she turns around to see the laughing face of the overly friendly guy. Scowling at him, she fights the urge to punch him for scaring the shit out of her like that. Instead, she just yells at him.

"What the hell!"

He chuckles as he puts his hands up in surrender. "Sorry, I just couldn't help myself. I tried to get your attention a while ago, but you must not have heard me."

"Obviously not," she snaps.

He doesn't seem bothered by her hostile behavior as he shrugs. "You must have been deep in thought then."

Shifting her eyes around, she shifts her weight from foot to foot. "S-So, you know how to get back?"

"I do."

"Well?" she asks irritably as he continues to just smile at her. "What are you waiting for?"

"You to tell me your name."

She snorts. "Well, you'll be waiting all night then."

"Why?" he asks, his full lips pulling up at the ends. "Afraid I'll tell everyone else? I promise your secret will be safe with me."

"Whatever." She sighs, with a roll of her blue eyes. "Let's just get back before my sister starts to worry."

Cleo starts walking in a vague direction, and he starts to follow after her. She keeps her back straight, and her arms crossed, so she doesn't give off any welcoming vibes. She doesn't know this guy, and since she's trying to turn her act around with this new pack, she's not interested in getting to know him. He practically reeks of trouble enough as it is.

"A sister? Is she as beautiful as you?" he asks but doesn't let her answer as he continues with the golden line of. "Nah, that's impossible. No one could be as beautiful as you."

"Good to know I'm not physically repulsive," she quips.

He laughs. "Good to know I could soothe any of your doubts."

"Listen . . ."

"Andy," he supplies. "Or Andrew. Whatever you prefer."

"Okay . . . well listen, Andy." She sighs as she stops walking to face him. "I don't know you and you flirting with me isn't exactly something I'm interested in listening to tonight. I got too much shit on my mind and going on in my life to be fighting off some charming one-night stand, okay?"

"What makes you think I want a one-night stand?"

She lets out a bitter laugh. "Honey, that's all guys want."

"I don't."

"I don't believe you."

He steps towards her with an unsettlingly determined expression. She backs up until her back is pressed up against a nearby tree. He doesn't stop walking until he's only six, maybe seven inches away from her. His dark eyes flicker down to her lips, and her breathing picks up at the look in them. She's never been looked at like that, and the fact that she's being looked at like that now is making her uneasy.

And uneasy is not a thing Cleo feels very often.

"You don't have to believe me right now," he says, his eyes finally lifting to meet hers. "But from the scents swirling around you, I'm guessing you're my new beta female's sister. That means you'll be sticking around and that also means I have time."

"T-Time?" she stutters, completely thrown off by his approach.

He nods with a small smile on his lips. Reaching out, he brushes back a stray lock of her bright blonde hair behind her ear. "Yeah, time. You're right that you don't know me, but I know you. I know you're scared, I know that you try to push away people so they can't hurt you, and I know that you're trying to hide."

"You can't possibly—"

"And I know that," he continues, cutting her off. "Because despite the walls you try putting up, it's all right there in your eyes."

Cleo stares at him blankly for a few minutes before smirking coldly. "Wow, you must be a real hit with the ladies, Andy. Seriously, I have to applaud you because that was some straight up *Dr. Phil* type shit right there. I mean, I've heard it all. Pickup lines by the boat load, but this has been a first for me. I've never been psychoanalyzed into someone's bed before. Really, Andy, color me impressed."

"See, that's where you're wrong," he says lowly, making her shiver as his breath tickles the curve of her neck. "If I just wanted you in my bed, you'd be there already, but I don't want that. I want something different, something more substantial, and though you may not be ready for it now, you will be."

"Don't you think you're coming off a little too strong?"

He smirks. "No, I just go for what I want until it has no choice but to give in."

"And who says I'll give in?"

"You will. I have no doubt about that."

"A little cocky, aren't we?" she asks with a raised eyebrow.

"I prefer the term confident."

"Prefer it all you want, that doesn't make it true."

He smiles and dips his head down, making her stop breathing. Cleo closes her eyes while his warmth seems to seep into her very bones. She flinches when she feels the softest pressure on her left cheek. It's soft, warm, and makes her stomach ache with butterflies. When the pressure is removed, she slowly opens her eyes to see an Andy smiling softly down at her. It's not a predatory look, or even an alluring one, it's actually more... adoring.

Almost like she's . . . special.

"It's getting dark," he says quietly. "We should probably head back now."

Cleo swallows thickly before nodding. "Yeah, you're probably right."

Stepping back, he lets her have some room to collect herself. Straightening her back, she steps around him again to start walking. Her left cheek is still tingling, and when she's sure she's ahead enough of him not to see her, she lifts her hand to touch the area he kissed.

God, when did she get all giddy over kindergarten shit like that?

Since now, apparently.

They walk in silence for the most part. Andy calling out directions when he needs to, and wordlessly, she follows them. She has so many things she wants to ask him. Why would he want to pursue her? What's his game? What's his malfunction? Okay, so maybe most of them are directed at his sanity, but can she be blamed for that? Who the hell just sees a person and just decides they want something more with them?

Unless . . .

"There," he calls from behind her, cutting off the thought.

She turns around with a frown. "Huh?"

He smiles at her, his hands pushed into his front jean pockets as he nods in front of her. "The pack house. Just keep walking straight, and you won't be able to miss it."

"Where are you going?"

He dips his head and shrugs. "I have to do some things."

207

"Okay . . ." she drawls with a frown. "Well, thanks, I guess."

"No problem," he answers, his troubled look fading into his apparently signature smile. "If you need a tour guide, just ask Colton about where I am, and I'd be happy to do it again."

"I'll remember that."

"Good."

Cleo hesitates for a second before turning back around and starting to walk in the direction he told her to. Once she gets about ten steps ahead, she stops and spins back around to see him just standing there, watching her. With an almost pained expression, she speaks.

"Cleo," she tells him reluctantly. "My name . . . it's Cleo."

Andy smiles widely and drops his head before looking up her under his lashes. "I know. I just wanted to hear you say it."

"But . . ."

"I'll see you around." He winks, before turning around and running in the opposite direction.

Cleo's jaw drops as she sees him shift into a large black wolf mid-air. His fur is short, more matted to his body, and his face longer, but his wolf form is still the most beautiful animal she's ever seen. Shaking her head and trying to dislodge the thought, she smacks her palm against her forehead.

"Come on," she scolds herself. "Don't be an idiot."

Still, she can't stop the smile that spreads across her face at the thought of Andy actually chasing her.

So screwed, she thinks with a sigh, like always.

CHAPTER TWENTY-THREE

Rae wakes up to the heat of the sun on her face. With a groan, she rolls her body away from the light and buries her face into the nearest pillow. Inhaling deeply, she savors Colton's scent as it clings to the pillowcase before conscious thought starts to seep in.

Shit, she thinks, how long has she been asleep?

She narrows her eyes as she rolls onto her back again and looks around the room. No Colton in sight, but from the distant sound of a shower going, she doesn't need to be *Nancy Drew* to figure out where he is. Pulling back the covers, she realizes she's still in her clothes from last night and feels oddly gross. She needs a shower and some clean clothes. Her stomach growls, making her look down at it. Oh, and maybe some food would be good too.

Pulling back the comforter from her body, Rae sits up and stretches her arms over her head. How long had it been since she slept that deeply and for that long? She doesn't know, and she doesn't have the mind power at the moment to try to figure it out. Dropping her arms, she stands on her feet with a groan.

The shower is still going, and Rae decides that if he's not going to leave her any hot water, she might as well get changed. She heads towards the large oak carved dresser and pulls out the middle drawer before peering in while humming. She pulls out a pair of jean shorts and puts on the top of the dresser when she catches her reflection in the above mirror.

Pulling on the blood-stained collar of her t-shirt, she sees the perfectly healed bite mark on her shoulder. Smiling a little, she reaches up and touches the tender piece of skin and feels her knees weaken at the contact. Laughing breathlessly, she hangs onto the edge of the dresser to steady herself. Okay, so apparently that is still really sensitive.

Lifting her head, Rae notices a brown leather wallet on the top of the dresser, beside her shorts and reaches for it. Looking over her shoulder towards the bathroom, she still hears the shower going and figures the coast is clear. Opening the wallet, she covers her mouth to stop her laugh when she sees Colton's driver's license photo.

Now, Rae can't really judge, her license picture is also an abomination, but this is just . . . priceless. His hair is longer, covering his eyes most of the way, and his face reads the utmost annoyance. A small smile spreads across her face as she takes in his image for a few more seconds before moving over to his stats. Her eyes widen when she sees his birthdate.

"You know if you wanted my library card you could have just asked."

Rae spins around and drops the wallet at the familiar voice. Caught red-handed, she blushes as she tries to come up with an explanation. Come on, she yells at her brain, think of something, anything! Colton's smirking face follows the path of the dropped wallet before crossing his arms over his bare chest. Wait, bare?

Rae's face only gets redder as she realizes he's shirtless and only in a pair of jeans. Sure, she's seen him shirtless before but never when he's fresh out of the shower and what a sight it is. His brown hair is darker from the water, his cheeks a bit pink from the heat, and the overwhelming scent of him practically wafting in the air.

"This is just so unfair." She mentally whines while she continues to look him over.

His smirk only pulls wider as he casually comes towards her, throwing his towel on the bed as he approaches and then crouches before her. Picking up the wallet from the ground, he stands up tall before her, making her really take in his scent. Holding up the wallet, he lifts a brow at her, making her remember that she's most likely in trouble right now.

"Looking for something in particular?" he teases.

Rae scowls, though the stupid blush is still on her face. "No."

"Really? So you just snoop through people's wallets for fun?"

"Maybe I do."

"Maybe," he says, tilting his head to the side in consideration before smiling down at her. "But I doubt it."

"Okay, fine!" she yells, completely fed up with this game. "So I peeked into your wallet! I was curious, okay? And maybe a little bit nosey, but I won't apologize for it! Who says I can't look anyway? You're my mate, I should be able to look anywhere I want and not feel guilty about it."

"I agree."

"And even if—wait, what?"

Colton grins down at her. "I said, I agree. I'm not mad or even annoyed that you looked. It's just a wallet."

He shrugs and tosses it to her, which she catches while she stares after him wide-eyed. Turning away from her, he heads for the closet, and she watches him in complete confusion. That's it? Rae remembers when her mom once tried to peek in her dad's work files and got a whole lecture about privacy. That's what she was expecting, and yet, all she got was a few teasing remarks.

"You look confused," Colton observes, stepping towards her with a white t-shirt now covering his torso.

"I am confused," she admits with a frown. "Most guys would be pissed I went snooping around. I'd be getting some 'don't

211

you trust me' speech." He just stares at her patiently. "This seriously doesn't bother you?"

"No." He shrugs. "Are you hungry?"

"Uh . . ."

"You look hungry." He smiles as he takes her chin in his grip.

His attention moves to her shoulder, and he gently reaches over to move her shirt collar away. He smoothes the pad of his thumb over the mark, making her knees give way at the feel again, but he quickly steadies her. Rae's eyes close as the more intense shocks of the bond move through her body.

"Whoa," she breathes.

Colton chuckles and brings her to him. Lifting her face, Colton kisses her forehead, making her whole body become wracked with shivers. *Holy shit*, she thinks, as if she needed any of this to be any more intense. Opening her eyes, she gazes up at him and says the first thing that comes to mind.

"You're old."

"What?" He laughs. "I'm not old. I'm twenty-three."

"That's old."

"Compared to who?" he asks with an amused look.

"Uh . . . other people who are younger?"

Colton rolls his dark blue eyes at her. "Well, with that kind of argument, who am I to deny you the privilege of being right?"

"See? You even sound old." She frowns.

Colton kisses her forehead again before sighing. "Well if I remember correctly, Poppy also thinks you're old. So I guess we can be old together."

"I guess," she grumbles, putting her head against his chest. He's so warm and comfortable. She could fall asleep again.

His fingers move through her hair for a few minutes before he asks, "Does it really bother you?"

"What?"

"The age difference."

212

She snorts, her eyes closed while she holds him tighter. "Hell no. I just like giving people shit. Graham is twenty-two, and my cousin Garrett, he's twenty-five, and I still hang around those old stooges."

"Yeah, but they're not your mate," he mumbles.

"Oh, for the love of . . ." Rae lifts her head to scowl at him. "It doesn't bother me. I was giving you shit. I like that you can rent a car or buy me liquor. In fact, I now count it as one of your many good qualities. There, feel better?"

"Maybe if you said it like you meant it."

She cuddles into his chest again. "It's too early for this."

"It's nearly noon."

"Too early."

"My mother has a barbecue waiting for you."

Rae lifts her head with a panicked look on her face. "Right now?"

"Well, it's being prepared now, but in another hour, yes."

Pushing him away, Rae nearly sprints for the bathroom. Looking at her mascara-smeared eyes, and the sleep lines on her face, she grimaces. Running her hands through her hair, she's relieved to notice it's not as greasy as she feared. Maybe she can do something with it. Oh god, what is she going to wear?

"You're cute when you panic," Colton observes from the bathroom's doorway.

The bathroom is huge. It has a tile shower with three showerheads and a bench in it. Rae thinks it's a bit much for a single couple to have in their bathroom but that doesn't mean she's not going to enjoy it. Well, if she can figure out how everything works in there. The damn thing has more gauges on it then her broken down van has on the dashboard.

"Why didn't you wake me up sooner?" she asks as she wipes her water-washed face off with a hand towel.

She sees him shrug. "Thought I'd let you sleep in."

213

"I slept for like . . . fourteen hours, or something equally ridiculous."

Colton sighs and comes over to her, wrapping his arms around her waist. She can see him standing behind her, his eyes on hers in the mirror. "You're getting worked up over nothing. The barbecue is just a simple get together. It's not really for you, specifically. We do it every Sunday."

"Then why did you say it was for me?" she asks him pointedly.

"Because you're the guest of honor."

She drops her head with a sigh. "Then . . . you . . . ugh . . ."

"It's not a big deal," he insists, making her glare at him. He smiles at her and kisses her cheek. "My parents already love you. My brother thinks you're great. Everything will be fine."

"I want to be accepted into this pack," she says quietly. "I want them to know that I'm in this for the right reasons, and I'll be a good leader. They've known you since you were in diapers, but they don't know me. You see what I mean? I have to make a good impression."

"Just be yourself and you will."

"You're biased."

"I'm honest."

"Same difference."

Colton rolls his eyes and sighs. "Okay, how can I help?"

She turns around in his arms and gives him a pouty face. "Tell me what to wear."

He just laughs.

But he helps.

* * *

Colton sits on his bed, looking through one of Rae's newly added books to his library and waits patiently for her to come out. She's been in the walk-in closet, changing in and out of clothes for

214

the past half hour. He wishes she'd just relax but doesn't push the issue. If he's learned anything over the years of watching his parents and brother's marriages, don't ever tell a woman to calm down.

Not more than once anyway.

Colton hears a thump and then her low string of swears and smiles. Since he doesn't smell any blood, and through their bond, knows she just stubbed her toe, he doesn't get up. Since marking her and making his side of the bond stronger, he has a better understanding of her, and it's a relief.

She doesn't like being coddled, but she also likes to feel cared for. She likes being near him, but she doesn't want to be clingy. She likes the way he looks but also the way he talks and moves. Most of these are just observations while some are coming straight from the woman herself. He can't read her mind, not in the traditional sense. He can catch her emotions, and if she's projecting enough fragments of her thoughts, but it's nothing really solid. It won't be until she's marked him.

Which he hopes is soon.

"Twenty minutes!" he calls as he flips another page in the book.

"Shit." He hears her groan making him smile.

"You know, I've never understood how a character's eyes can sparkle with mischief," he calls, knowing exactly what he's doing. "And a rich baritone voice that can make you think dirty thoughts. Is that even possible? The man only just introduced himself."

"Oh my god!" she yells, coming out of the closet to run at him. Colton laughs as she jumps on him and holds the book above her head so she can't reach it. "Colton, give it back!"

"*The Gentlewoman's Stable Boy?*" he asks, reading the title of the romance novel. "I pegged you as more of a biography reader than smut."

"It's not smut." She huffs, crossing her arms over her chest. She's straddling him, and Colton's body acts accordingly to

215

the position. He tries to distract himself by taking in what she's wearing, but it only makes it worse. She's dressed in a pale yellow sundress, ending mid-thigh, and strapless. Her cleavage is on display as her arms unknowingly pushes them up. "It is a story of forbidden love in a very restricted time in history."

"Yeah, smut."

"You're a dick."

"Maybe." He smiles, tossing the book on the other side of the bed. "But you still like me."

"True." She sniffs haughtily before squealing when he rolls her onto her back. "Colton what—"

"I like the dress," he tells her, running his nose up the column of her neck.

"T-Thanks," she stutters when he nuzzles her mark. "It's actually Cleo's."

"I like it better on you."

"But you haven't seen it on her."

"I don't need to."

"You're very . . . um, friendly today."

He smiles against her neck before tracing the mark with light kisses. "Am I?"

"Mhmm." She hums, her fingers burying themselves into his hair.

"I guess I haven't noticed," he teases before asking. "When are you going to mark me?"

"Uh . . . later."

"When is later?" he asks, pressing his body closer to hers. He grabs both of her legs and wraps them around his waist as he continues to kiss her mark. Rae's reply is breathy and disoriented, just like he wanted. "Later . . . tonight?"

"Promise?" he breathes against her neck, one of his hands moves up her leg to grab her thigh under her dress. She arches her chest into him and moans some kind of response, but he can't really make much sense of it. "Rae, promise."

216

"I p-promise."

"Good." he growls before kissing her.

The moment is ruined by his mother's muffled voice coming through the door, though. "Pooky Bear, is she ready yet? We have the whole pack simply dying to meet her! Oh and of course, those adorable little girls just keep asking for her. Rae, darling, your sister would like to speak to you, Cleo, I think. Also, have you two seen Hudson? I think Jace said he was in his room but I can't find him. Colton, your dad also needs some help with getting the grill going. The man can run a pack but can't get a grill going for the life of him."

Rae laughs as Colton drops his head onto her chest. Moving her head closer, she gets Colton's attention immediately when her lips caress his ear. Of course, any excitement he may have had about what she was going to say dies when she does speak.

"Yeah, come on, Pooky Bear. Mommy needs your help."

Damn it.

CHAPTER TWENTY-FOUR

Rae grips Colton's hand so tight she's pretty sure she could break the bones in it if she really wanted to. Despite things now being night and day compared to the pairing presentation at the run, Rae still doesn't like being the center of attention. She's not too sure anything can really ever change that. God forbid she ever has to make a speech.

Oh god, will she have to make a speech?

"Deep breaths," Colton whispers in her ear as they descend the steps towards the more populated first level of the pack house. Rae doesn't miss the hidden laughter in his voice and glances up to see it clear as day on his face.

"You're loving this, aren't you?" she accuses with narrowed eyes.

He shrugs with a grin. "As I said before, you're cute when you panic."

"Okay, you know what? Your pet name is now Pooky Bear for the rest of our lives. I will call you that every chance I get and you will have to just nod and love it." She hisses at him and watches with satisfaction as his face pales. Grinning at him, she adds, "Not so cute now, am I?"

"If I take it back, will you promise never to call me Pooky Bear again?"

"Depends on if you're going to tell me where it came from."

He sighs heavily and hangs his head before he mumbles, "It's from *Garfield*."

"*Garfield?* The fat orange cat?"

"Yeah," he admits with a wince. "The teddy bear that he cuddles with is named Pooky Bear. My mom calls me Pooky Bear because she said my dad is usually grumpy like Garfield until he's around me. Around me, apparently, he's a big softie. I don't know how the hell she comes up with this shit but yeah . . . that's where it came from."

"That's . . . actually really cute."

Colton makes a face. "It most certainly is not cute. It's embarrassing."

"I don't think so," Rae disagrees with a small smile. "My mom used to call me bumblebee."

"Really?"

Rae nods as she stares at her feet. "She never really told me why, she just did. We all had our nicknames when it came to my mom. Dad hated them, said it made us look like babies as we got older but she never stopped calling us by them."

"Do you look like her?"

"Who? My mom?" Rae asks before sighing heavily. "Kind of. Poppy looks the most like her actually, well, her and Cleo. Jojo says I have her heart. I don't know what that means, but that's what she says."

Colton squeezes her hand. "I would have loved to have met her."

"She would have liked you, I think," Rae says while bumping her shoulder against his. "She was a big romantic. She used to read 'smut' too, just so you know."

"Hey, can you really blame me for giving you a hard time? I mean, how would you feel if you found a stack of Playboys under my mattress?"

Rae thinks about it for a second before shrugging. "That you were holding out on me and that you're rude for not sharing."

"Wha—"

"Rae!" Jessica coos as she comes to the foot of the stairs to grab Rae into a hug. Rae inhales her vanilla tinted scent while her wolf commits it to their memory. Pulling back, Jessica gives Rae a once over before grinning. "Oh honey, you look beautiful!"

"Thank you," Rae says shyly before taking in the alpha female's own white sundress. It falls above Jessica's sun tanned knees, and the sleeves end just at her elbows. Jessica's caramel colored hair is thrown up in a high ponytail, and her makeup simple, making her simply glow. Rae can only help she looks this radiant when she's this woman's age. "You look beautiful, too."

"I know. Believe me, Dalton never lets me forget it."

Rae laughs at the woman's much-deserved confidence before she feels Colton's hand curl around her waist. "Mother."

"So formal," Jessica chides before whispering to Rae. "He's always such a stick in the mud. I'm hoping you can help loosen him up a bit."

"Uh . . . I'll try my best," Rae says awkwardly before deciding to change the subject. "Where are my siblings?"

"Oh yes! Of course, you'd be wondering! This whole thing has me losing my damn mind," Jessica says with an eye roll before clapping her hands. "Okay, well, Jace is actually helping Dalton with the grill, so Colton, can you help Sawyer with getting the stage all set up?"

"S-Stage?" Rae echoes, freaked out by how big of a deal this sounds like it really is.

"Just for some of the more musically gifted pack members to play. Jimmy Coulter and his boys are such great musicians. I'll have to introduce you to them." Jessica soothes while laying an arm on Rae's bare shoulder before turning to Colton. "So, Pooky, if you can be a dear and go help your brother."

"Yes, Ma'am."

"Ma'am? Who the hell is that?" Jessica asks with an innocently confused look that has Rae fighting back laughter again.

"Fine." Colton sighs with an eye roll. "Yes, mother dear."

"Better." Jessica nods before turning back to Rae. "I'll take you to the girls."

Colton pulls Rae towards him quickly by their still joined hands and kisses her forehead as he inhales her scent. "I'll see you in a bit. Stay out of trouble."

"Me?" she asks with dramatically wide eyes. "Trouble? Why, I've never."

He just smirks at her before lightly pushing her in the opposite direction. Rae lets out a little giggle as she watches him walk away. She's not being very discreet about checking out Colton's butt, but Jolene said she didn't have to be anymore. Besides, it is his mark she's wearing on her neck. Her wolf growls in her head at the knowledge that very soon, he'll be wearing hers too.

She can hardly wait.

"Come on, love bird." Jessica laughs as she grabs Rae around the shoulder to guide her towards the opposite direction. "We don't want you ruining your pretty dress with your drool."

Rae blushes and Jessica just winks at her. Rae takes in all the new scents of the pack as Jessica walks her through the people. She keeps her eyes ahead of her, not wanting to accidentally disrespect anyone or anything. She's made that mistake before at her old pack when another Alpha was visiting two summers before. Alpha Kendrick had the order sent down for her to do sentential duty and perimeter checks for two weeks. Not fun by any stretch of the imagination.

"Rae!"

Rae comes out of her thoughts at the sound of Poppy's shout before something nearly knocks her over. Jessica steadies her with a laugh as Poppy practically plasters herself to Rae's legs. Rae pets Poppy's loose and darkening dirty blonde hair before crouching a little to kiss the top of her head. She missed her so much.

"Rae, we saw horses!" Poppy tells her with a grin.

221

"Really?" Rae asks. "Did you like them?"

"They were really pretty, but they were big. Maybe next time, though. Cassidy says it was pretty high up there."

"That's so cool," Rae says with a doting smile before looking around. "Where is Cassidy?"

Poppy lets go of Rae and looks around. "I think she went with Hudson."

"And where did they go?"

Poppy shrugs. "I don't know."

"Okay, well, let's go find them," Rae decides as she takes Poppy's hand in hers. Turning to look at Jessica over her shoulder, she adds, "Should only take a few minutes."

"No rush, dear. Just don't run off on me! Colton is a fantastic tracker, and those boys just love a good chase."

Rae's face heats up. Oh, she knows all about how much Colton likes to chase. That's how they met for heaven's sake! Still, she just gives a nervous smile to Jessica before turning away to try to find her other siblings. Okay, she thinks, Jace is with the alpha; he'll be fine. Poppy is with her, so she'll be fine too. Now she needs to find Hudson and Cassidy. Shit. She also needs to find Cleo. Where the hell is she? Maybe she's with Virginia? Wasn't that Sawyer's wife's name? No, something more French sounding. Ugh, she's shit with names.

"Rae!"

Rae spins around and sees Cleo sneaking towards her, looking nervous. Rae takes in her sister's outfit with a degree of surprise. She looks very . . . unlike her. She's in a soft pink maxi dress with braided halter straps, and her hair is tied up in a messy bun on the top of her head. Cleo also seems to have skipped the makeup routine, and Rae notices a light coating of freckles across the bridge of her nose. She hasn't seen those in years! In summary, Cleo looks beautiful, and Rae opens her mouth to tell her so, but Cleo cuts her off.

"Can I talk to you?"

"Of course," Rae agrees, frowning at the edgy behavior of her sister. "What's wrong?"

"Nothing," Cleo snaps before sighing. "Sorry. I just didn't sleep well. Are you busy?"

Rae shakes her head. "No, it's okay. We're just looking around for Hudson and Cassidy. Have you seen them?"

"No, but I'll help you look."

"Cleo, you look pretty."

Cleo smiles down at Poppy. "You're looking very pretty yourself, honey. I like that color of blue on you."

Poppy blushes and moves closer to Rae. "Thank you."

Rae rubs Poppy's back and grins at Cleo. "So, what's on your mind?"

"Let's walk and talk," Cleo suggests with a nervous glance over her shoulder towards the party.

Rae frowns and looks towards the party but can't see any reason why Cleo is acting like this. Still, she likes that Cleo is coming to her with a problem and doesn't want to pass this opportunity up to get closer to her sister. So they start walking towards where Rae catches a whiff of Hudson's scent.

"So?"

"Rae, what is it like when you find your mate?"

Rae stops walking for a second before starting again. "Uh, well, it'll be different for you because you don't have a wolf, but there are a few basic things. You'll feel a strong attraction, everything about them is fascinating."

"Okay," Cleo says faintly before clearing her throat. "What else?"

"Well, you feel comfortable in their presence but at the same time, terribly nervous. It's so confusing because you feel so at peace but also like you should run in the opposite direction. When I first set eyes on Colton, I was divided between kissing him or vomiting on his feet."

Cleo laughs a little before smiling at Rae. "Yeah, that sounds like you. So, is that it?"

"No," Rae says with a shake of her head. "You'll also feel this tingle, that's what mom called it when they touch you. For me, it feels more like shocks of electricity traveling all over my skin, but for you, it'll feel more subdued. Still, mom said it nearly gave her a heart attack the first time dad touched her."

"Ew," Cleo says while scrunching up her nose. "I don't want to hear about mom and dad touching."

"Well, the werewolf stork didn't just drop us off, Cleo," Rae drawls with a dry look at her sister.

"How are babies made?" Poppy asks.

Cleo and Rae give their little sister wide-eyed looks before looking at each other with panic. How could she have forgotten Poppy was still here! Internally smacking herself, Rae stutters out a response.

"Uh . . . W-We'll talk about that later, honey."

"Yeah," Cleo agrees. "In like, ten years."

"But I'll be old in ten years. I want to know now."

"Okay, how about in seven years?" Rae bargains, just wanting this conversation to end.

"Two," Poppy counters.

"Six."

"Four and a half."

"Five. Final offer."

Poppy crosses her arms over her chest. "Fine, but I want details."

Cleo pats Poppy's head with a pitying look. "Believe me, kid. You won't."

"Anyway," Rae says with some pressure in her tone. "What's brought on all these questions?"

Cleo shrugs and looks anywhere but her. "Well, I mean I am almost eighteen. I'll be joining the run next year. This is probably something I should know, right?"

"But didn't mom talk to you about it? Or at least, Jojo."

Cleo shakes her head and shrugs again. "I don't think so. If mom did, then I don't remember and I usually just tune Jojo out when she's giving one of her speeches. She can go on for hours about nothing."

Rae laughs a little at that. "That's true."

"Rae . . . I just wanted to say that I'm not mad anymore. About dad, I mean. I get why you did it. You've always done your best to protect us, but I was always kind of annoyed that . . . you would just take it all on yourself. We all want to help you, but you have to let us. We're not kids anymore, and we can take the burden. Jace, too, but I'm talking more about me. I want to help out, so I've decided to be better. No more acting out, no more drinking, and no more guys."

"What about the smoking?"

Cleo makes a face. "I'm working on it."

"Okay." Rae nods before grinning at Cleo and wrapping an arm around her shoulder. "I love you, Cleo."

"Yeah, yeah, I know."

"Say it."

"No."

"Say it," Rae sings with a grin. "Come on. You know you want to."

"No, I don't."

"You do. Deep, deep, deep, at the bottom of your heart you are dying to say it," Rae says while poking Cleo in the chest with every word.

Cleo pushes Rae hands away and covers her chest with her hands. "Get your hands off me, you perv!"

"It's not pervy if it's me! You're wearing my bra, anyway. It's like touching myself."

"That's sick," Cleo says with a raised brow. "Does Colton know what a whack job you are?"

"If he doesn't, he'll find out soon."

"Will I be this weird when I'm older?" Poppy asks, more to herself.

Rae looks down at her next youngest sister and winks. "With any luck, yes."

"Gross."

"Hey, guys, shut up a minute," Cleo says, jogging ahead a little. "Do you hear that?"

Rae tunes into the world around her, her wolf stepping into the forefront of her mind as she tries to hear anything. When she does, she feels her heart drop to her toes. Dropping Poppy's hand and reaching up to pull the bobby pins out of her hair as she mentally prepares herself to shift.

"Rae?"

"Cleo, take Poppy back to the party and get Colton."

Cleo takes Poppy's hand and steps back. "Rae, what's happening? Was that crying I heard?"

"It's Hudson," Rae says as she unzips the back of her dress.

"What's wrong? Is he okay?"

"I don't know yet. Just get Colton. He'll be able to find me."

Rae doesn't say anything else before she bursts out of her human skin and into wolf form. As soon as her paws hit the ground, she takes off down the path of Hudson's scent trail and the sounds of his pain. It doesn't take her long to track him down, and when she does, she skids to a stop at the scene before her.

Cassidy is crying and hidden behind a tree with her hands over her ears. Her light pink dress is covered in dirt, and her braided pigtails are a mess around her face. Cassidy's eyes are closed as she cries, and Rae takes a step towards her, but Hudson's guttural scream has her pausing.

Hudson is lying in the middle of the forest floor on his back. His body is contorting in pain and Rae sees his skin move as his bones crack and shift. Rae lets out a whine at the sight of her

226

brother's pain but knows there isn't much she can really do. Not yet anyway.

Rae knows that at the end of the day, a person's first shift is always just a waiting game.

CHAPTER TWENTY-FIVE

It all starts with a pain at the base of his spine. That's the first thing Hudson feels when he wakes up that morning. He figures he just slept on it strange, he did have a new bed with a new mattress to get used to, and it made sense. So he ignores it and goes on with his routine.

A run along the paths Alpha Dalton had cleared for him: a light breakfast and a shower. In the shower though was when the pain became more intense. Now the pain is from the base of the spine all the way up to his mid-back and reaching around to make breathing a little more difficult. He doesn't understand the feeling, but keeps on ignoring it. Maybe he pulled a muscle or something.

Cassidy comes into his room while he was getting dressed and tells him about the barbecue. He's interested to see how Rae will do with this, since he's positive she'll be the special guest of the event. Personally, he has a hard time even believing that his big sister would really be an alpha female.

Hudson has grown to respect and trust Rae completely since their parents died. At first, he thought they were all doomed. Rae was going to take care of them. He remembers thinking that the girl who was more hungover than conscious was going to kill them all within months. He didn't even like Rae. In fact, he felt the same about Rae then as he feels about Cleo now—Indifferent.

He was sure that it would take a few weeks before they'd be living with their aunt Jolene and being miserable in peace. He was wrong. He was really wrong, and slowly, Rae began to show him that she wasn't what he thought she was. As the months dragged into years, he saw the strain it had on her. He would see her cry when she thought she was alone and the sadness that lingered in her eyes.

It actually hurt him to see her like that, so he decided to do something about it.

He started helping out with the younger girls, Cassidy especially. He likes hanging around Cassidy and hearing her babble on about the things she comes up with. It's always entertaining, and with her, he never felt different. He felt like maybe he was the normal one in the room.

Hudson shakes his head at the thought and continues to button up his white dress shirt. Figures that he would need to be hanging around a six-year-old to feel normal. Still, he has to admit after telling Rae about his . . . preference, he feels better. Lighter almost, like he's free. Though he hasn't told Jace or Cleo yet, he doesn't feel as daunted by it now that he has Rae's acceptance.

Maybe everything will be okay.

"Hudson, come on!" Cassidy yells, getting his attention and out of his thoughts.

Hudson smiles softly at his littlest sister. She looks adorable in her braided pigtails, light pink sundress, and white sweater. In fact, she kind of looks like a mini-Rae with her dark brown eyes wide with excitement.

"Piggyback ride?" he asks, hoping maybe she'll crack it with her weight.

"Yeah!"

"Okay," he agrees with a nod before picking her up, so she's standing on his bed. Giving her his back, he looks at her over his shoulder. "Climb on, monkey girl."

She predictably narrows her eyes at him. "I'm not a monkey. I'm a princess. Colton said so."

229

"Sorry, my bad. Well, beautiful princess Cassidy, how will your subjects look upon you if you don't get downstairs?"

"I could walk."

"True," he agrees, shaking some of his brown shag out of his eyes. "But every princess needs a carriage."

"You can't be my carriage, Hudson, you're my brother."

Hudson snickers before running a hand down his face. "Well, let's pretend that for today I've been turned magically into a trusty steed that only serves to carry princesses."

She eyes him shrewdly before nodding. "Okay, but your name isn't Hudson anymore while you play more horsey."

Climbing onto his back, Cassidy wraps her legs around his waist and her arms around his neck. Steadying her with his hands, he makes sure she's secure on his back before beginning to walk towards the door. His back feels a little better, but he still feels like there is a weight on his chest. Maybe a glass of water will help.

"What's my name then?" he asks as a way of distracting himself.

"Um . . . Kevin."

Hudson gives her a weird look over his shoulder. "Kevin?"

"Yup," she says with a heavy nod. "Kevin is a pretty name."

"Alright . . ."

"Don't you think so?"

"If you say so, princess."

"I rode a real pony yesterday. Jessica took me."

"Alpha Jessica?" Hudson asks as they start going down the stairs.

Cassidy shakes her head. "No, Jessica. Colton's mommy."

Not wanting to correct her, Hudson just lets it go. "Did you like it?"

"Yeah! The horses were so pretty and big! They could gallop like all those ones on TV, but they smelled really bad. One even pooped right in the middle of the field! It was so gross!"

Hudson laughs but gets distracted by a smell. It's faint, but it's really . . . intoxicating. Frowning, he tunes Cassidy out as she keeps talking and takes in a deep heavy breath. What the hell is that? He does it again and thinks he can identify it as something almost sugary. What is that?

"Hudson, look!"

Cassidy's scream in his ear brings him back into the task at hand. Her outstretched hand is pointing at a large cotton candy machine being wheeled out to the front yard. Hudson disregards the sugary scent, figuring that's what it must have been. Smiling at Cassidy over his shoulder, he sees her face lighting up with the idea of all the sugar she's about to get.

She kind of looks a little deranged actually.

"Hudson!"

He turns his head to see the alpha female, Jessica, jogging towards him. It's a little awkward of a motion since she's in strappy white heels, but she manages to make it charming in its own way. Hudson likes Jessica for the most part. She's nice and seems welcoming to Rae, but he's not exactly a fan of nosey people.

"Oh honey, where have you been? I've been looking for you all morning!"

"Why? Is something wrong?"

She frowns at him. "What? Oh heavens, no! I was just hoping you could maybe keep track of the little ones. I'll be really busy today, and I want Rae to feel relaxed with no stress. It's enough she'll be meeting the pack. Ugh, I remember when I first met them, I actually ran out of the house screaming."

He stares at blankly for a second before clinking. "Seriously?"

"Oh yeah!" she says with a wave of her hand. "Poor Dalton had to chase me down. I was so nervous. Found me all dressed up, bent over a tree, and vomiting up my breakfast. I come from a family of weak stomachs. Nerves and a full belly do not mix."

231

Hudson blows a steady breath at a complete loss at what to say.

"But that's not important," Jessica says, dismissing the whole subject. "What's important is making Rae feel comfortable. Do you have any tips?"

"Uh . . . well, don't make her get on stage or do any speeches."

"What about a simple 'I do.' Do you think she can handle that?"

Hudson's brows fall into a frown. "Why would she need to say that?"

"For the acceptance ceremony. You know, to welcome you all into our pack."

"Oh," he breathes, instantly relieved. He doesn't think Rae is ready for marriage right now. She's only nineteen for shit's sake. "Yeah, I think she can handle that."

"Good, good." Jessica nods with a bright smile before something catches her eyes over his shoulder. "Rodney, don't you dare leave that cooler there! People will trip over it!"

"Sorry, Miss Jessica!"

Turning back to Hudson, she brushes her bangs back from her face. "I feel like such a bad hostess for not talking to you more, but this party is turning into my own personal hell."

Hudson smirks and shakes his head. "No, it's okay. I'll watch the girls."

"You're a lifesaver!" she coos before leaning forward and kissing his cheek. Hudson flinches back, completely stunned by the action, and Jessica pulls back. She frowns at him and tilts her head like she's studying him. "That's odd."

"What?" he asks, his body feeling really warm all of a sudden.

Jessica opens her mouth but is cut off by someone yelling her name. Putting a hand on his shoulder, she gives him an apologetic look. "We'll talk later, dear. Cassidy, my darling, you look beautiful."

"I'm a princess, and this is my horsey, Kevin," Cassidy informs her cheerfully.

"Kevin?" Jessica asks with a smile in Hudson direction.

Hudson shrugs. "I live to serve."

"So it would seem." Jessica giggles. "Well, you two have fun."

"Sure. Thank you, Alpha."

"Jessica, Hudson, call me Jessica."

Hudson hesitates. "Uh . . . yeah, right, Jessica."

She winks at Cassidy over his shoulder. "Be good."

"Bye, Jessica!"

Hudson closes his eyes and feels his head begin to pound. He needs some fresh air, that's what he needs. Adjusting Cassidy on his back, he walks out of the house and feels the pain in his back intensify while his chest becomes even more weighted down. He's practically jogging by the time he's out of the house. With a wince of pain, he gently reaches behind him to remove Cassidy from his back. She lands with a little hop before running ahead into the yard.

Seeing her talking to Poppy and an older girl, Hudson walks stiffly around the house out of sight. Bending over, he grips his stomach while sweat starts to come over the skin of his forehead. Keeping one hand on his knee and the other around his midsection, he tries to catch his breath, but every intake of air is painful.

Is he dying? It feels like he could.

Knowing Cassidy is okay and most likely being watched for the time being, he hobbles towards the forest. He needs some air, some space, at least that's what his head is telling him. His body just wants to collapse onto the ground and just let whatever's happening to happen so it can stop all the sooner.

Hudson doesn't know how far into the woods he is by the time he collapses. He does know that he's never felt such unbearable physical pain in his life. Emotional pain, maybe. When his mom died that pain was indescribable but this . . . this is almost worse.

His skull feels like it's going to split in two, and his bones feel like they're ready to snap as he stares unseeing at the blue sky above. God, why won't it stop? When will it end? How long has it been since it began? He tries to keep his pain inside himself, not wanting to scream and draw attention but soon it proves to be too much. When a rib bone cracks in his chest, he arches his back and cries out.

Why can't he just die?

Why can't this just be over?

"Hudson?"

For fuck's sake, he thinks at the sound of Cassidy's voice.

Don't come here, Cass. Please just go back.

"Hudson? Where are you?" she calls.

He clenches his teeth and grabs the ground beneath him in his fists. Another bone cracks in his spine, and he feels his body fling itself onto his side. Curling into a ball, he lets out wheezing pants.

"Hudson, I'm scared. I don't like this game."

He opens his mouth to tell her to go back, but all he does is let out an agonized scream. Flinging himself back onto his back, his back arches again as three more of his rib bones shift and crack under his skin. That's when it suddenly hits him. He isn't dying. He's shifting for the first time. If he weren't in so much pain right now, he would laugh at the obviousness of it all.

How could he have not seen this coming?

"Hudson!" Cassidy screams, running towards him.

He doesn't know if it's him or his emerging wolf that does it, but Hudson snaps his jaws at her. She lets out a scream and falls back on her butt with tears coming down her eyes. He can see the tears so clearly, and he can smell the salty tang in the air as it's shed. She scurries back, dirtying her dress, hides, and curls up by a tree.

234

He wanted her to leave, but the distance will just have to do. Closing his eyes, he focuses all of his attention on his changing anatomy and tries to keep himself in check. He doesn't want to get out of control.

He doesn't want to be like his dad.

The sound of racing footsteps reaches his twitching ears, and he sniffs the air quickly. It's a crisp scent, like . . . apples. Rae, his mind supplies him. That must be Rae's scent. Turning his head towards it, he can fuzzily make out the image of a gray wolf coming to a stop in the distance. A part of Hudson's mind relaxes knowing that she'll be able to calm Cassidy down.

He really does feel bad about scaring her.

Hudson . . .

He flinches at the sound of Rae's voice in his head.

Hudson, I know it hurts, but you have to relax. Relax your body and just . . . let go.

Hudson presses his lips shut and closes his eyes as he tries to imagine he's back home at the lake. He used to just float on his back, stare at the clouds, and go with the motions of the water guiding him. That was when he was most relaxed in his element and at peace. Hudson feels his body go limp and though the sounds of his cracking and shifting bones are still audible, they seem distant.

Good, Rae's voice praises. *Now, open your mind. Try to clear it of everything and let your wolf in. He'll know what to do.*

Hudson does as she asks. He trusts her completely, especially right now. What other choice does he have, but to trust her? She's his only tie to the real world and his sanity.

Hudson's consciousness fades as something stronger, more dominant, pushes itself forward. The last thing Hudson can really feel is warmth that washes over him and the comfort of finally feeling like he's in the right skin. Like he's been hiding behind a mask, and he can finally breathe now that it's removed.

Hudson, in this moment, feels like him.

CHAPTER TWENTY-SIX

Rae pops her wolf head up as Hudson's cries suddenly cut off. She knows that Colton and everyone else will be coming soon, but she's more interested in what Hudson will do. Rae can remember what it was like for her the first time she switched forms, not exactly the most comforting feeling in the world.

"Rae, is he going to die?" Cassidy whispers into her fur.

Rae looks over her still upset sister and nuzzles her into her neck. Cassidy giggles and pushes Rae away, but she can still see the panic in the little girl's eyes. Catching Cassidy's gaze with her own, she slowly shakes her head as a way of answering the question.

Cassidy sighs before turning her and gasping. "Oh Rae, look! He's so pretty!"

Rae follows her sister's gaze to see a very handsome wolf indeed. Hudson is a beautiful light brown wolf with white fur on his two front paws like socks. His light brown eyes are wide as he looks around and flips his new body onto its belly. He tries to rise to his feet but his new legs shake under the unfamiliar weight, and he collapses back down on his belly.

Hudson, Rae calls through their blood tied mind link. *Stay calm. I'm going to approach you now.*

Rae rises to her feet slowly, not wanting to put Hudson's still wild wolf on guard. In wolf years, his wolf is still young. It'll take a few months for both Hudson and his wolf to get used to this arrangement. Rae doesn't fell envy for the poor kid at all. The first months are always the worst.

Moving towards Hudson's wolf, Rae keeps her eyes locked on his. When Hudson's wolf lets out a whine, she stops and decides to take a less direct approach. Dropping down onto her belly, she starts to shuffle towards him with body language as neutral as she can manage. When she's about two feet away from him, she realizes that they're not alone anymore.

In fact, they have a very captive audience made up of the alpha family and a hand full of pack members.

Hudson's wolf whines again at the sudden influx of people. Obviously, a very tentative wolf Rae decides to take action. Barking at him, she gets his attention back on her, and she again uses the mind link to try to soothe him.

Don't look at them, look at me, she orders, putting as much authority in her tone as she can. When his eyes are back on her, she shuffles forward a little more. *You know I won't hurt you, don't you? You know that you're safe with me?*

Rae?

Rae mentally sighs in relief to hear her brother's voice. *Yeah, kiddo?*

What the hell is happening? he asks, getting shakily back on his feet.

You shifted. Good thing too. I was beginning to get lonely being the only slobbering mutt in the family.

Hudson lets out a series of odd sounding barks that tell her he's trying to laugh. He stumbles back a little at the sound of himself and stares wide-eyed at his own white furred paws. *Oh my god. I really am a wolf.*

In the flesh, kid, she tells him with laughter clear in her voice. *Do you want to shift back?*

Uh . . . I don't know, but for future reference, what do I do?

237

Imagine yourself in your human body. Push your wolf's presence back, visualize a nice comfy kennel to go into if that helps, and let yourself take control again. Relax your body and just let it happen.

You make it sound really easy.

After the first time, it always gets easier.

That's what he said.

Rae rolls her eyes and shakes her head at him. *Okay, smart guy, let's see how smart you are when I kick your ass in a race.*

Hudson steps back a little in surprise. *Race?*

Yup, to the large rock formation up the way. We got to get you into the swing of things. Nothing will make you feel more in tune with your wolf than a run.

What about everyone else? he asks, his eyes flickering over to their company.

Don't worry about them. Just focus on yourself and your wolf.

Rae, I can barely stand up straight, he snaps, making Rae growl at him.

Watch your tone with me, Hudson. I may be more understanding in human form but when I'm a wolf you either fall behind me, or you don't follow at all. Am I understood?

Both of their eyes widen at her words. The most shocking thing for Rae is that those are *her* words, not her wolf's, though her wolf is in agreement. Rae dips her head and takes a deep breath of fresh forest air. She needs to calm down and find her patience, though the need in her to assert her dominance is still lurking in her mind. She'll have to ask Jessica about that later.

Sorry, she mutters to him.

I-It's okay.

Nodding her head once, she looks him in the eyes again. "*You ready?*"

Uh, sure.

Alright. Just remember to let go. That's all you have to do.

Okay.

Rae gives him a quick wolfie grin before suddenly taking off. She knows how competitive Hudson is, and a race is just what he needs to kick him into gear. Weaving her sleek gray wolf form through the trees, she looks over her shoulder to see Hudson's brown wolf coming up fast behind her. Turning forward ahead again, she pushes her wolf harder and tries to keep her lead, but Hudson is surprisingly quick for a new wolf.

He passes her quickly, and Rae has never felt so proud.

When they spot the rock formation sticking out of the side of a grassy hill, Hudson practically does a flip off it. Rae stops running and just watches him as he jumps up on some of the rocks and starts climbing the formation. He looks so much like their dad in wolf form, it's uncanny. Rae pushes the thought away quickly but makes a mental note to call Jolene to see how he's doing.

He must not have much longer to live, she thinks sadly.

I won! Hudson cheers down the mind link as he jumps down in front of her again.

Rae wags her tail at him and bows her upper half down in a crouch. *You did. Now let's try something else.*

Without warning, Rae tackles Hudson down to the ground, and Hudson lets out a yip in surprise. Rae begins to push him down with her front paws every time he tries to roll back onto his stomach, and it quickly starts to frustrate him. It's a good first lesson though in always being ready to be pounced on. It may seem like it'd be too early to teach him that already, but Rae's father's voice comes into her mind from when she first shifted.

It's never too early to start training.

Actually, Hudson is getting it easy from Rae. When Rae first shifted, she was barely on her feet for two minutes before her dad had her pinned. He taught her how to defend herself in human form, but in wolf form, he was even more strict. He would often bite her neck when she wasn't paying attention or if she wasn't doing something right. He often said he wanted her ready for what

239

she didn't know, but whatever it was, he wanted her ready for it as of yesterday.

Clive Applebee simply didn't play games when it came to that.

"Rae?"

Rae turns her head, still pinning Hudson to see Colton looking at her with surprise. In his hand is her yellow dress and some clean underwear. If she were in her human form right now, she'd be blushing. Did he seriously go through her underwear drawer?

"Uh, what are you doing?"

Rae sighs heavily and backs off of Hudson. Her brother quickly flips onto his stomach and narrow his eyes at her, clearly annoyed. She doesn't like doing this to him, but she doesn't know any other way to bring him into this world. This is the only way she knows.

Hudson barks at Colton, apparently trying to explain before making a face.

Remember, Kiddo, focus.

He gives her another dirty look before closing his eyes. His body begins to shake and shiver, and Rae looks away knowing that in a few seconds, he'll be naked. She may be immune to most people being naked, but her brother is not one of them. Actually, neither is her mate. Though she'd actually *want* to see Colton naked, so the need to gag is much less powerful.

"What the hell, Rae? Why would you tackle me down like that? Have you lost your mind or something?" Hudson yells, making her flinch but not look at him. "Why won't she look at me?"

"Because you're naked, man."

Hudson groans, seemingly having just realized this. "Please tell me you brought me clothes."

"Nope, just Rae's dress. Don't think it's your size, though . . ."

240

"Come on, man!"

Colton chuckles before Rae hears some fabric being thrown. "I'm a dick, but not that much of a dick."

"Good thing too," Hudson mumbles before announcing. "Okay, I'm decent now."

Rae turns towards him, still in wolf form and sees him in a pair of baggy sweatpants and an oversized *Hooters* t-shirt. The irony of which is not lost on her. She has to admit, though, he looks brighter almost glowing from his shift. She didn't realize how stressed and tired he's been looking lately until she sees him as he is now. How could she have been so stupid not to see this coming?

"Well?" Hudson demands, making her come out of her thoughts.

Rae whines and dips her head knowing why he's pissed. Still, it's not like she can really respond to him right now. He's in human form, and she's still a wolf. They can't use the mind link like this. Only mates can do that, so she turns her attention to Colton with begging brown eyes.

He holds up her clothes with a smirk. "Need these?"

She barks, making him laugh. Shaking his head, Colton walks over to her and points to a nearby tree which is large enough for her to hide behind. She follows him behind the tree and flinches back when he suddenly kneels before her. Running his long fingers through her hair, Rae closes her eyes at the shocks that move down her spine. It feels fantastic.

"Next time you decide to go for a run," he whispers in her twitching ears. "I'm coming along."

Rae shivers at the sound of his voice in her ear and peeks up at him to see him smirking smugly. Placing her clothes on a low hanging branch, he kisses the top of her head before walking out of sight. Rae closes her eyes and focuses on her human form last time she saw it this morning. It doesn't take very long to shift back, second really, and the pain of it hardly even noticeable anymore.

A cool breeze makes her shiver as it hits her naked skin. She quickly grabs her underwear and strapless white bra from the tree branch and quickly puts them on. Glancing down, she realizes she put her underwear on inside out, but she really doesn't have the time to fix it. Pulling on her dress, she clumsily pulls up the zip on the back as she comes out from behind the tree. She's still working on it when shocks move across the bare skin of her back.

"I got it," Colton says lowly behind her, making her shiver again. Her skin is always so sensitive after a shift that him touching her feels much more powerful than usual. Glancing at him over her shoulder, she sees that smirk on his face and realizes he knows exactly what he's doing. "There you go."

"Thanks . . ." she trails off in suspicion, and his smirk only becomes more pronounced.

"Are you two done now?" Hudson snaps, apparently still angry. "Rae, what the hell was that? Why would you attack me?"

"I didn't—"

"You did," Hudson tells her flatly. "Now do you mind telling me why?"

"You have to be ready for attacks Hudson," she says with a sigh. "I was actually using kid gloves on you compared to how dad used to do it."

Hudson and Colton frown at her but Colton's the one who speaks up. "What do you mean?"

Rae shrugs, not understanding why they look so concerned. "Dad was just really into training. Every evening after dinner, he takes me out in the woods and we'd train."

"Wait, is that why you kept coming back all bloody? Dad said it was because you were hunting." Hudson says, horror coloring his features.

She frowns. "Did he? No, we didn't do a lot of hunting. Mostly we'd do something called direct challenge. He was trying to build up my pain tolerance, so he'd tackle me down until sometimes my bones would break. They healed fast, it hurt, but it healed fast. He was just trying to prepare me."

"For what?" Colton asks slowly.

"I don't know," Rae says quietly. "He never really said."

"Rae . . . that's not normal," Hudson says like he's telling her something that should be obvious. "Dad shouldn't have been doing that. Right, Colton?"

Colton walks over to Rae and cups her face in his hand while looking her right in the eyes. "What else did he do?"

"I don't know . . . he said that I'd have to be strong for my mate. He said that my life with him would be tough, and I'd have to ready for that. I didn't really believe him, but I didn't question it. Whatever dad said kind of just went. We didn't question him, not even our mom, really."

Colton narrows his eyes at her. "What else did he say about this mate?"

"He was just talking, Colton. It doesn't mean anything."

"Just answer the question."

Rae frowns at the order in his tone. He's never talked to her like this, and she really doesn't like it. Stepping out of his grasp, she crosses her arms over her chest while staring him down. His hands drop to his side and curl into white-knuckled fists at the sight of her retreat.

"Why does it matter, Colton? What are you not telling me?"

"It's nothing," he says tightly. "Just something Kendrick said to me."

"What did he say?"

"It doesn't matter, right?" he asks coldly. "He was just talking."

"What the hell is the matter with you?" she yells at him. "Why are you acting like this?"

"Guys," Hudson calls.

They ignore him.

243

"You're withholding information." Colton grits out.

"So are you!"

"My information doesn't put you in danger!" he yells, his eyes coloring gold as his wolf pushes forward.

Rae's anger fades into confusion. "Danger? What are you talking about?"

"Uh, guys?"

"What?" Both Colton and Rae yell at Hudson, making him jump.

Hudson sniffs the air a little more. "Do you smell that?"

Rae runs a hand through her hair before sighing. "Smell what?"

"I smelled it before, in the house, it smells . . . like sugar?"

"Sugar?" Colton echoes, giving Rae a sideways glance. He inhales deeply, and his expression does a total turn around. "Oh. Well, Hudson, I think you should track it down."

"What? He shouldn't—"

Colton cuts her off with a raised hand and a grin. Turning to Hudson, he nods in the apparent direction of the scent. "Go."

Hudson's brown eyes flicker over to Rae. "You sure?"

Rae looks over at Colton's relaxed body language and grin. Sure, they're in the middle of a fight right now, but she knows Colton would never hurt Hudson. So with a heavy sigh, she forces a smile on her face.

"Go check it out."

Hudson gives them both doubtful looks before hesitantly stepping away. Rae makes sure to give him an encouraging nod, and he gives her a weird look before completely turning to leave. Rae watches Hudson sniffing the air as he walks away in silence though she's very aware of Colton's eyes on her. She's still pissed he won't tell her what the hell is going on, but she won't demand answers until Hudson's out of hearing range.

"He's too distracted to listen to us right now," Colton tells her.

Rae snaps her head in his direction with narrowed eyes. "Good. I'd hate for him to listen to your screams for mercy."

He gives her a flat look. "You're being dramatic."

"If whatever Kendrick said was so important why didn't you tell me before? In fact, why won't you tell me now?"

"Because whatever your dad said to you may have a direct bearing on what Kendrick said. I thought he was just talking out of his ass, trying to rile me up. But if your dad was getting at what I think he was, I'm going to kill Kendrick myself."

Rae shifts on her bare feet as her mind races with possibilities. She clears her throat and asks in a strong voice, "What did he say?"

Colton runs a hand through his hair and sighs. "He said that you didn't belong to me. He said that fate had other plans for you."

"Meaning?" she asks with an arched brow.

"I don't know," he says quietly. "That's why what your dad told you is so vital."

Rae stares at one of the large paw prints on the ground below and takes a deep breath before closing her eyes. "He said . . . he said that I would have to be strong. He said that my mate would ask a lot of me and I'd have to be able to take it. He said that I may not like my mate, that he may be harsh with me but I had to be prepared to fight for my position. He said that when the time came, I would have to leave him. I thought it was all just overprotective dad talk. I didn't think anything of it."

"Is that why you didn't do the run?"

She bites her lower lip and mumbles, "One of the reasons, yes. So what do you think Kendrick meant?"

"I don't know for sure, but I have an idea."

"Which is . . ." she leads, sick of the side stepping.

Colton levels her with an intense stare. "I think there is a reason he didn't want you to leave. I think there is a reason he didn't approve of our pairing and I think there is a reason he wanted to find your dad so badly. Rae, I think he arranged an alternative mate for you, someone other than me. Something to keep the wolves at bay, so to speak."

"Why would he . . ."

"White Stone has been plagued with rogue attacks for the past few years. It's a reason why their numbers have been dwindling. People have been leaving because they don't feel safe. It was one of the reasons I specifically came to the run this year, to talk to Kendrick about better security details. He kept pushing off the meeting, and I wasn't sure why, but he said he had it all taken care of. He said within the year, things we would be settled."

"And you think that has something to do with me?" Rae asks thinly.

Colton's eyes go soft. "I think that whatever he had planned was massively disrupted by our mating. I think a desperate man will do desperate things when zero hour is approaching."

Rae is getting an idea what he means, but she wants to hear him say it. She wants to be wrong. She doesn't want to believe her father would do that. She doesn't want to believe her pack would think that was a good idea, if they even knew. She doesn't want to believe that an alpha would stoop so low.

"Colton . . ."

"Rae, I think you were meant to be a peace offering. I think you were going to be given to the descending rogues so they would retreat off White Stone territory. Rae, I think that you were never meant to find me that night in the woods. I think you were meant to be taken."

The words hit home because deep down, she thinks she already knew.

CHAPTER TWENTY-SEVEN

As Hudson walks away from his sister, he feels his concern start to be overtaken with confusion. What the hell is that smell? At first, he thought it was sugar, but it wasn't that. He's actually pretty sure sugar doesn't smell at all, but it's definitely something sweet and mouthwatering.

Inhaling deeply, he feels his wolf perk up in his mind at the scent. It's an odd feeling, having someone else suddenly in your head with you, something other than yourself. When he hears a laugh, his head snaps up, and his eyes scan the woods around him. Where did that come from? Frowning, he moves towards the location of the laugh and realizes that it isn't actually a close sound but a farther away one.

Wow, he thinks in shock, Rae was not kidding about those heightened senses.

Shaking his head, he tries to focus on finding the source of that smell. He'll never be able to stop thinking about it if he doesn't find it. It's how Hudson has always been. Sometimes he can't even sleep unless he has the answer to a question or hasn't completed all of his homework. He just needs to know everything is put away and finished before he can relax. A personality quirk, he supposes.

When he hears the laughing and talking more clearly, he realizes it's a group of people around his age and walks towards the group. When he sees them from about ten feet away, he hides behind a tree and watches them. He doesn't want to look crazy, just barging into their circle and demanding who smells so sweet. He may turn into a giant wolf, but he wants to at least keep a facade of normalcy while he can.

"I mean who is she other than the beta's mate? I just don't get why she gets a whole party just because Colton is screwing her," A brunette with a black lace dress and a leather jacket says with a snort.

Hudson's wolf growls in his head as he realizes the girl is talking about Rae. He's half tempted to barge into the group now. He doesn't want to hit a girl, but he will if she keeps disrespecting his sister. Hudson can admit he's a bit shorter than Jace but with his first shift under his belt, he figures he won't be taken down so easily.

He's taken out of his thoughts by someone else's scoff. "You're just jealous that he didn't screw you when you offered, Melanie."

Hudson's eyes move towards a guy across the circle from the girl. He's about two inches taller than Hudson with a slimmer build. His face is only in profile, but that's all Hudson needs. His hair is tousled and a dark brown color. His nose is a bit upturned at the end, and he has fuller lips with a cigarette dangling out of them. The guy is dressed in black jeans, black converse, and untucked white button-up shirt. Hudson takes in a deep inhale again, focusing on this guy's scent and feels his wolf growling in his head.

Mine.

Hudson's eyes widen at the meaning behind that word. He can't find his mate now! He's fourteen, and he's never gotten farther than kissing someone. Besides, he's still getting comfortable with the fact that he is in fact, gay. Shit, he only just had the epiphany six months ago.

Hudson had just turned fourteen, literally two days before, and he was just sitting in his room. He couldn't sleep. He didn't know why, but he just couldn't, so he decided to just watch mind-numbing TV until he bored himself to sleep. He was flipping through the channels when he settled on some movie that looked stupid enough to do the trick.

It wasn't until about a half hour in did he realize that this movie wasn't the typical thing. His first big clue being that two guys were kissing. They were just having a normal conversation, nothing special, when suddenly, one of the guys leaned over and kissed his friend. What really surprised Hudson was that the friend was into it. He was pretty sure it wasn't porn, the movie actually had a story line, but he was still getting . . . excited.

After realizing his own reaction, he shut off the TV and sat in the dark in a daze. Was he gay? The longer he thought about it, the more it made sense. Whenever he was at school, he would check out the guys and not the girls. When he did watch straight porn, he was more interested in the guy than the girl fake moaning her way through the act. It was so obvious he wanted to smack himself.

Of course, he was gay!

Wasn't he?

Still, he didn't tell anyone of his suspicions. He ended up dating a guy from another school. Noah was a little older but at least knew what he was doing and could help Hudson figure himself out. Hudson didn't love the guy. Sure, he liked Noah, but he didn't *love* him. Most of their afternoons together ended up just being make out sessions, and that was it. Nothing even close to love but it was something Hudson felt he needed to experience. He needed confirmation that he really was gay.

Turns out he really likes men and nothing else.

Go figure.

Of course, the move to this pack spurred him into telling Rae, but the others don't know. Hudson figures they don't need to know just yet, but this new development is proving that won't be unavoidable for long. Why does he need to tell them, anyway? People don't come out as straight so why does he have to come out? Can't he just bring a guy home and let it be that?

249

Hudson runs a hand through his hair and sighs heavily. If only that was how the world worked. He doesn't realize how loud his sigh was until he feels eyes on him. Not just any eyes, mind you, *his* eyes. The guy who is supposed to be the other half of his soul. His mate.

Hudson finds breathing difficult as a pair of bright hazel eyes meet his. His wolf is practically whining in his head at the idea of getting closer to those eyes. He wants to touch his mate's smooth tanned skin and inhale the sweet scent directly from the source. The images his wolf is pushing into his head are downright graphic, and its beginning to overwhelm Hudson.

Dropping his gaze, Hudson takes in a few deep breaths and clenches his fists at his sides. He needs to leave. With the shit day he's been having, he can't face the possibility of rejection. He can't deal with it. So while still keeping his eyes on the ground, he turns on his heel and begins walking away.

The sound of hurried steps coming after him has him squeezing his eyes tightly closed. The sweet scent wraps around Hudson like a blanket, and he doesn't need any more of a hint about who it is. When a hand touches his shoulder and stops him from walking, Hudson's wolf is practically beating on the walls of his mind. He wants out, he wants his mate, he wants Hudson to at least look at their mate, but he can't. He doesn't want to look him in the eyes as he rejects him.

He's heard about rejection, and he is not into it one bit.

"Hey! Where are you going?"

Hudson's heart picks up at the sound of his voice. God, he just cannot catch a break, can he? Does his mate have to have one of the sexiest voices ever? It's not fair, it simply isn't fair. Of course, the shocks shooting down the left side of his body make resisting him seem even more impossible.

Trying to keep his distance, Hudson keeps his back to him and keeps his posture from tensing. "I . . . I didn't mean to intrude."

250

"You didn't," his mate says with a smile in his voice. "It was mostly just a shit talking session. Melanie is really jealous of your sister. She's had her eyes on Colton for years."

Hudson turns his head and looks at him wide eyed. "You know who I am?"

He shrugs. "I know who you are in relation to our beta, but other than that . . ."

"I'm Hudson."

"Hudson," he repeats with a small smile and a nod. "I'm Joseph."

"Joseph," Hudson whispers to himself before realizing how stupid he sounds. "S-So, you're a pack member?"

"Yeah, I don't shift but my mom can, so technically I'm just guilty by association."

"Well, that's—"

"I know who you are," Joseph says quietly as he steps closer to him. "What you are to me. I knew it as soon as I saw you."

Hudson feels his panic rise. Shit, he knows now, what is he going to do about it? Reject him? Maybe. A string of curses goes off in Hudson's head at the thought. This is exactly what he was trying to avoid.

"I don't—"

Joseph bites his lower lip and smirks a little. "You're shy, I get it. You also can't be older than what? Thirteen?"

"F-Fourteen."

"Right." Joseph grins and licks his lower lip, making Hudson's eyes follow the movement. "Well I'm sixteen, and I know that this is . . . overwhelming, but I don't . . . I don't want you to make any rash decisions."

"Meaning?" Hudson asks, his voice a bit gruff.

"We don't know each other, but I don't think you should rush into rejecting me."

"R-Rejecting you?"

251

"I don't know what kind of pack you came from before, but here, people are more accepting. They won't look at us like we're freaks and the age difference won't matter as much. I don't want you to immediately shoot down the idea, okay? Sleep on it, maybe?"

"I don't need to sleep on it," Hudson tells him with a scowl.

Honestly, he can't believe that his mate would even say this to him. Of course, he's not going to reject him. Why would he? Rejection is not only discouraged by their whole society, but it can actually get you kicked out of a pack. Trying to break up or steal mates is even worse, it's actually punishable by death.

Of course, Alpha Kendrick didn't seem to get that memo, he thinks scornfully.

"Okay," Joseph says quietly, his hazel eyes turning pained. "Just make it quick, okay? I don't want you to drag it out."

Hudson nods his head and takes a deep breath before walking closer to him and grabbing the back of Joseph's head. Pressing his lips against his mate's is nothing he's even felt before. It's better than running in wolf form or human form. It's even more addicting, and Hudson can finally understand what all the fuss is about.

Joseph grunts in surprise against his lips but kisses him back after the shock wears off. Hudson tilts his head and deepens the kiss which Joseph also allows him to do while also running his hands through Hudson's hair. When they both begin running out air, Hudson pulls back and brings their foreheads together.

"I'm not rejecting you," Hudson rasps out while staring into those hazel eyes.

Joseph smiles widely. "Yeah, I got that."

"Do you . . . accept me?"

Joseph doesn't say anything. He just kisses Hudson again. Hudson smiles through the kiss. He's pretty sure he hasn't been this happy in a long time.

And that's okay with him.

* * *

Cleo shakily brings a cigarette to her lips as she sits on the unpopulated side of the yard. Her back is up against the side of the pack house, and her legs splayed out in front of her. Poppy is with Jessica now, and she's pretty sure she's not welcome with Jace. He's still pissed about the Kip incident. She doesn't blame him for being pissed. It was a stupid thing to do.

"You know you shouldn't be smoking."

Cleo lifts her gaze to see Andy standing before her with his eyes narrowed at her. Her body comes to attention at how close he is to her, but she feigns aloofness. She doesn't need to have him thinking she's interested. Now isn't a good time for whatever bullshit he's trying to pull. She's already on enough thin ice with her family. Besides, she's a bit paranoid, he might know she dreamed about him last night.

It's an irrational fear of course. He can't know what's in her head and that he was the only thing in it literally. In every dream she had last night, he would show up. Either in peripheral or as the subject, he was there. Haunting her night now as much as her thoughts during the day.

"Cleo, are you okay?"

Clearing her throat, Cleo nods. "Yeah, I'm fine."

"No, you're not." Andy sighs before crouching in front of her. "What's wrong?"

"Nothing's wrong. I just didn't sleep well last night, and this whole get together is a little overwhelming."

"I'd call bullshit on that, but you look like you've had a rough day."

"I'd say," she mutters before putting her cigarette out on the grass beside her. "Andy, can I ask you something?"

"Anything."

253

Her lips twitch up at his immediate answer. "What's the first shift like?"

"Which one was it?"

Cleo flicks her gaze up to meet his dark brown gaze. "What?"

"Which brother was it? The redhead or the brunette?"

"How did—"

Andy taps his temple with a smirk. "It is all over the pack link."

"Oh. Well? What's it like?"

"The first shift?" he asks before sighing. "Well, it isn't easy. It hurts, and it's confusing as hell, but once it's over, it gets better. I did not realize how dirty that sounded until I said that out loud."

Cleo laughs, unable to help herself. "Yeah, it kind of does."

"You have a beautiful smile."

Cleo rolls her eyes, but her smile doesn't fade. "Okay, prince charming, what other compliments have you been practicing?"

"My material is endless."

"So, you're a player, huh?"

Dipping his head, he looks up at her with sincere brown eyes. "Not anymore."

"And why is that? Sudden change of heart?"

"You could say that."

"I could say that, but what would *you* say?" she counters.

He laughs, showing his bright white teeth. "No getting anything past you, huh?"

"Guess not."

"Well . . ." he begins with a sigh as he adjusts himself, so he's sitting on his undeniably nice ass in front of her. Cleo's eyes take in his gray t-shirt and his perfectly tailored jeans with assessing eyes. "I met someone."

Cleo feels a pang in her chest but ignores it. "Oh yeah? And she's worth giving up all your fun for?"

254

"She's worth a lot more than that, but yeah."

Cleo feels a sadness come over her at those words. She's pretty sure she'll never have anyone think of her like that. In fact, it's what she's been avoiding up to this point. She didn't want anyone to treat her like she was special because she didn't think she was. She still doesn't. Why would she when she's done everything in her power to be as worthless in everyone's eyes as she feels she already is.

"Lucky girl," she mutters.

"You got a guy?"

She lifts a brow at him but shakes her head. "Not really."

Cleo sees his hands tighten around some blades of grass and his jaw clench. "Not a definite no."

"Well, I don't really date," she answers, curious about his reaction. "I haven't met anyone willing to stay along long enough to want to date me."

"What do you mean?" He frowns, his full lips thinning in distaste.

She sighs sharply and sits back against the house. "What do you think I mean? You were a player before this girl, right? Well, so was I. I didn't need a guy for anything more than a distraction. Call me a whore or whatever, but it's how I am. I'm trying to change for my family, but it's hard. It's actually much easier being a train wreck."

Andy nods, looking to be in deep thought before speaking, "Changing yourself takes a lot of strength."

Cleo's voice is small as she speaks, "Especially alone."

A moment of silence falls over them, and Cleo fights the urge to cry. She's jealous of Andy's girl if she's honest with herself. To have someone who cares about you unconditionally and take you as you are, warts and all. That's special, something she'll probably never have but something she'll never stop wanting. Why should we be expected to give up our dreams just because we've grown up? Why can't she dream of a happier ending no matter how little she may deserve it?

Cleo jumps when she feels fingers under her chin. Tingles move down her throat and across her jaw before tickling her bottom lip. Tingles? Isn't that what Rae said was a sign of mates? Cleo tries to push that idea away, knowing that that is impossible. She can't have a mate, at least that's what she tells herself.

"Why do you have to be alone?"

Andy moves forward and presses his lips against hers. Cleo's toes curl, and her whole body feels light as a feather at the light kiss. It's not like any kiss she's ever had. It's sweet and makes her long to have more kisses like it. Still, she can't allow this.

Pushing him back, Cleo looks into his eyes, panting. "What are you doing?"

"It's you," he tells her quietly. "I have no doubt now."

"What do you mean it's me?"

"You're my mate."

Her eyes widen, and she shakes her head. "I-I can't be."

"You are. I know it now."

He leans forward to kiss her again, but she puts her hands on his chest, stopping him. She can feel his heart beating rapidly against her palm, and she can feel hers doing the same. She has to question his sanity, though. She can't be his mate. He's too good for her, and despite that happy part of her jumping for joy, she has to be sure he knows what he's getting himself into.

"Andy, I'm not . . . I mean . . . I'm not good. I do bad things. My family hates me. My parents would be disgusted to see me like I am if they were alive. You can't want me for a mate."

"I do," he insists, his fingers caressing her jaw line before his thumb caresses her lower lip. "You said you don't want to do this alone, and I want to be with you no matter what you think about yourself. You were meant for me, and I was meant for you. I don't know you, and you don't know me, that's true, but we have time to figure it out, right? All you need to do is give me a chance."

"A chance?"

"That's all I'm asking for," he assures her.

Nodding, she brings him closer to her and kisses his lips softly. "Okay. I can do that."

CHAPTER TWENTY-EIGHT

Rae wraps her arms around herself and tries to not panic. It all falls into place as Colton's suspicions all fall into place. The alpha was so pushy about her joining the run. Usually, it wasn't a big deal if a member of the pack wanted to hold out, wait until they were ready, but he was so insistent he practically made it an order.

She frowns at the thought. Didn't the alpha think she would find her mate? The possibility was high that she would, so why would he push it? That's when she remembers the growls from the night Colton found her. At the time she thought it was Colton growling, but there had been a secondary scent in the area.

It is less noticeable than Colton's overwhelming scent, but it is there. It smells more earthy like wet soil and pine, but at the time, she just thinks that it's the natural scent of the area. She doesn't think anything of it, apparently a habit of hers. Why doesn't she think anything of it? She should have. She definitely should have, but she doesn't. Rae feels the need to smack herself. She's been so stupid.

"Rae, say something," Colton pleads, dipping his head in hopes of catching her eye. "Anything, please."

Rae hesitates to ask the question, but she has to. Just to be sure. Taking a deep breath, she wets her lips and prepares herself for Colton's reaction. Lifting her gaze, she looks into his eyes and sees his search her face with concern.

"Colton . . . am I really your mate?"

His flinches back in surprise. "What?"

"You said Kendrick said I had a different destiny. Do you think that maybe we have it wrong? That maybe we're reading the signs wrong?"

Colton scoffs in anger and steps back from her. Turning his back to her, he puts his hands on his hips, and she sees him shake his head. She expected this but why isn't he answering her? Is he doubting it too now? It's not a question she wanted to ask but one she felt like she needed to ask. What if this rogue her father had been preparing her for and her alpha was going to give her up to has been her fate since the beginning?

"Don't," Colton suddenly snaps while turning to face her with anger written all over his face. "Don't even fucking think that, Rae."

"What am I supposed to think?" she asks, knowing that their bond has clued him into her more unfavorable theories. "My dad was primping me to be some rogue's war prize, Colton! He was apparently okay with enough to actually think ahead in training me. He knew I was going to be treated like dirt and yet he agreed to this fucked up deal! I think I'm allowed to question everything!"

"Not this," Colton snaps while gesturing between them. "Never doubt this. You *are* my mate, Rae. If you weren't, then that mark on your shoulder would never have healed and scarred. It would have been bleeding, infected, and you would have been sicker than hell. Your wolf would have fought me every bit of the way as I took you away from your home. You wouldn't feel the way you do about me if you didn't belong to me and I didn't belong to you."

Rae looks at the ground and shifts her weight from foot to foot. She can feel the tears prick her eyes as his words hit home, more than his theory about her alpha's intentions. He is her mate. She knows this, but part of her— a small part—mind you, wants to believe her dad wouldn't have just given her up for no reason.

Of course, there's a reason, she thinks bitterly. Rae may have loved her father, but he wasn't the kindest or loving man. He had always put his position as a pack enforcer above everything else. He would often put patrol or meeting with the previous alpha before the family. She has no doubt that in one of those meetings, the alpha with his lap dog of a son in the room, planned this. Her father had loved her, sure, but he never would have ignored or disregarded an order. He was a follower through and through.

What the alpha says is law, as he always used to say.

"Rae," Colton calls softly as he steps closer to her.

Rae steps back from him as she wipes a stray tear from her cheek. "I'm sorry. This is a lot to take in."

"I know," he whispers, taking another step towards her. "I know it is, but I'm not going to let anything happen to you. You're mine, and I'm yours. No one is taking you from me."

Rae lifts her head and nods. "You're right. No one is going to take me away."

Colton nods, seemingly relieved she's not on the 'you're not my destiny' route of thought. "No, because this pack will protect you with everything they have."

"I don't need a pack to protect me, Colton," she says honestly. "My dad may have been an asshole, but he trained me to fight. I won't be some princess in an ivory tower waiting for someone to rescue me. If this comes to a head, if Kendrick tries to mess with my family or us, I won't need a pack to help me. I'll rip his throat out myself."

Rae practically growls the last word, her wolf pushing to the surface in her own rage at the betrayal. Her wolf was just as attached to Rae's father and his wolf as much as Rae herself was. It's common for wolves to grow attachments to the human sides, or just humans in general in the family unit. Rae's wolf has grown to think of their family as a pack and Rae's dad as a sort of alpha of it. This sudden disregard of their loyalty has her wolf all kinds of pissed and Rae is right there with her.

Colton grins adoringly at her before coming close enough that only a few inches separate them. "You're going to make an amazing alpha female."

"I mean it, Colton," she tells him. "If this comes down to war, I won't be screwing around here. I'll kill him."

"And I'll be there watching with nothing less than pride as you do."

Rae smiles a little as she reaches up to wrap her arms around his neck. Affirming shocks run up both arms as she does, letting her know that Colton is indeed hers and meant to be hers.

"Tonight, I'm marking you," she says against his lips.

A shiver goes through Colton's body, and he nearly groans out his response. "Can we just do it now?"

"No." She laughs, caressing her lips against his. "We have a party to get to, and I need to check on Cassidy. She was really scared that Hudson was dying or something. She doesn't understand what being a wolf shifter means."

Colton frowns as he wraps his own arms around her waist. "You haven't told her yet?"

"I was always busy. I mean Cleo, Hudson, and Jace know because they were older when our parents died. They remember my first shift and they had seen pack members shift before, but Cassidy and Poppy haven't been exposed to it as much. I've tried hard to keep them part of the pack but separate for so long."

"Why? The pack could have helped."

"I didn't want their help, not the kind they were offering. They wanted to separate us. Make us live with Jolene or someone even suggested Cassidy and Poppy be sent to our mom's parents across the country. It was a whole mess of a pack meeting that night. I had to put my foot down after our mom's funeral because I wasn't going to lose them. I didn't care what I had to do."

"I repeat; you're going to make an amazing alpha female."

Rae smiles and goes up on the tips of her toes to give him a quick but meaningful kiss. "Thank you."

261

"For what?" Colton asks with a dazed look in his eyes.

"I don't know." She shrugs. "Being you, I guess."

"Well, then you are very welcome."

"Come on," she tells him with an eye roll. "Let's get heading back. I'm sure your mother is wondering what the hell is going on."

"Knowing her, she's already figured it out or is digging up information as we speak."

"I like her," Rae says with a laugh. "You know she called you a stick in the mud."

Colton rolls his eyes. "She thinks I'm too serious for my age. She looks at Sawyer and sees him being his normally immature and annoying self and thinks that's how I should be."

"But you're not."

"How can I be?" he asks with a tired sigh. "I'm the alpha heir. I am the first pick to challenge my father for his title as alpha when the time comes. I have responsibilities."

"Do you not want to be?"

Colton thinks about it for a second before dropping his forehead against hers. "I want to be alpha. This pack means a lot to me. This is my family, and I want to be sure that they're protected. Leading this pack . . . well, I can't think of a higher honor. Sometimes though I wish that I could just relax into my position."

"I'm sorry," Rae says sadly.

"Don't be," he tells her with a small smile. "It's getting easier already. With you being here at my side, it doesn't seem like such a burden."

"Well, that's good."

Colton chuckles and kisses her forehead. "You have no idea."

"So." She sighs regretfully. "Party?"

"You know, for someone who doesn't really want to go, you sure are pushing for it."

Rae shrugs. "I'm a single example from the bizarre species known as women. I don't have to explain myself."

Colton laughs again and kisses her temple while he inhales her scent. "Certainly not."

Stepping back from him, she grabs one of his hands and starts leading him back towards the house. It's about a mile and a half walk back to the pack house and the party, and most of the walk is silent. Both of them lost in their own thoughts.

Rae's are mostly preoccupied with what to do next. She has family and friends at White Stone. Would Dalton and Jessica be okay with her asking Jolene, Everett, and Garrett to come here? Would Graham come too? No, probably not. He has his sister Violet and his parents there. Besides, he's related to the Beta, so it's not like he can really leave without a really good reason.

Sighing in dejection, Rae can feel a headache coming on from all this thinking. Why does this shit have to be put in her lap? Why couldn't she be one of the normal people who got a mate and then rode into the sunset with them? She knows the answer before she even finishes the question because she's able to handle it.

The notion of a moon goddess seems archaic, but Rae has to admit that she's often wondered if the legends were true. Did a wolf once fall in love with the moon upon seeing her beauty? Did she grant him a second form as a reward for his undying love hence making their species? That was the bedtime story Rae had been told and in turn had told the girls on many occasions, but could it be true?

Maybe.

But if it was true, then maybe that was the reason Rae was given this life. Maybe the moon goddess only gave you what you could handle. Maybe, Rae was just built to handle this better than most. Or maybe, Rae is just looking for some kind of justification for this whole messed up situation. Rae drops the whole subject as her headache only intensifies.

She needs a drink.

"Is that . . ."

Rae looks up at the sound of Colton's voice, but he doesn't look back at her. His eyes are focused in surprise at something across the yard. Rae tries to see what he's seeing but when she does, her own jaw drops. It's Cleo and a guy holding hands and laughing while Cassidy is propped up on the guy's hip. Rae rolls her eyes when she sees Cassidy running her hands over the guy's shaved head. She'd love to say that surprises her, but she doesn't.

"It appears Cleo has a new boyfriend." Rae sighs.

"Not quite," Colton says tightly. "That's Andy."

"Andy?" Rae repeats in confusion before it dawns on her. "Wait, your friend? The one with the flower scent? What is he doing with my sister?"

"From the healing bite mark on her shoulder, I'm going to guess that he couldn't really help himself with this one."

Rae snaps her head back in the couple's direction. Her jaw drops as her eyes take in the scabbed over crescent shaped mark on her sister's bare shoulder. No way! Rae practically drags Colton towards the couple, not even listening to his attempts at soothing her. There's nothing to be soothed right now because Rae isn't upset, she just wants to know when the hell this happened!

Cleo is laughing as she turns her head in Rae's direction, but her smile slips off her face as her eyes land on Rae's face. Cleo's blue eyes look anywhere but at Rae, but that's fine because Rae has other means of getting information. Moving her attention to Andy, her sister's supposed mate, she smiles widely at him.

Andy lets Cassidy down, and she comes running towards Rae. Rae scoops Cassidy into her arms and balances her on her own hip. Cassidy looks much happier, not mentally scarred or anything, so that's good. Rae puts her lips to her sister's ear and decides to do a little digging before she confronts.

"Who is the boy with Cleo?" she whispers.

Cassidy cups Rae's ear as she answers, "His name is Andy. He's really nice. He's her boyfriend. I told her I'd give her a cootie shot later."

"Good call," Rae whispers back before coming to a stop before them and smiles widely. "Hello."

"Uh, h-hey, Rae," Cleo says with a shaky smile.

"Hello," she says cheerfully before turning to Andy. "I'm Rae, Cleo's sister, I don't think we've met."

"No, we haven't," Andy says, a wide smile coming across his face as he sticks his free hand out towards Rae. "I'm Andy. I'm actually Colton's best friend."

"I wouldn't say best," Colton mumbles only to receive Rae's elbow in his gut.

"It's lovely to meet you," Rae says as she shakes his hand. "So, Andy, tell me, do you often go around marking girls without their families' knowledge, or is my sister special?"

"R-Rae!" Cleo stutters out with wide eyes before glancing over at Andy. "I'm sorry. She's just trying to embarrass me."

"*Me?* Embarrass *you?*" Rae asks innocently. "You must have me confused with someone else."

"Rae, believe me. I would have loved to have spoken to you first, but you know how it can be," Andy says with a goofy smile in Cleo's direction.

Rae narrows her eyes at him. "I do. Andy, are you aware that Cleo is seventeen?"

"Yes," Andy says sheepishly. "We talked about that."

"And?"

"Not that it's any of your business, Rae, but we've decided to wait," Cleo tells her with an eye roll.

Rae feels herself warm up a bit to Andy. "Well then, I really can't complain about much, can I?"

"Oh, I'm sure you can find something," Cleo grumbles.

"Andy, can you do me a favor?"

Andy gives Rae a cautious look. "Uh, sure?"

265

"Keep her in line for me, will you? She never listens to me, but maybe she'll listen to you."

"I'll try my best," he says with a respectful dip of his head.

"Then you have my blessing." Rae smiles before walking over to pinch Andy's cheek. "You are just too cute, I can barely stand it!"

Colton clears his throat from behind her. "I'm standing right here."

"I'm aware, but I'm cooing at a grown man right now."

Cleo facepalms herself. "Oh my god, could you get any more embarrassing?"

Rae just gives her a creepy grin. "You have no idea."

"There you two are!"

Rae turns around to see Jessica speed walking towards them looking flustered. "I've been waiting for you two to come back since we got the news of Hudson's shift. How is he?"

"Fine." Rae shrugs before looking around. "Don't know where he's run off to, though."

Colton smirks down at her. "I'm sure he's in good hands."

"What's that supposed to mean?"

Colton's response is cut off by Jessica. "We can discuss 'Where's Hudson' riddle later. We've bigger fish to fry right now."

"Being?" Colton asks.

"The acceptance ceremony!" Jessica bursts. "I've been keeping your father on hold longer than he can sit still waiting for you. The people are getting antsy. They want to eat, but I want to do the ceremony first. I have Sawyer fighting them off with a pretty impressive fireplace poker."

Colton runs a hand down his face and sighs. "Please tell me you're kidding."

Jessica blinks her blue eyes at him once. "Does it look like I'm kidding?"

266

"Well, we should probably get to it then, huh?" Rae asks, cutting in as she notices how frustrated Colton's getting. "The sooner we begin, the fewer people Sawyer has to maim."

"Now we're getting somewhere!" Jessica cries in relief before grabbing Rae's hand and tugging Rae behind her. "Come along."

Rae glances behind her, asking Colton for help but he just shrugs in an "I know but there's little you can do" way. Turning back around, she nearly trips over her own feet as she spots Hudson hand in hand with another young man. He's extremely handsome, and obviously very smitten with her brother.

"No way," Rae breathes, and Hudson's head snaps up to meet her wide eyes.

Hudson's face turns bright red as he shrugs at her. Rae narrows her eyes at him and points at him while mouthing that he has some serious explaining to do. He really does have some serious explaining to do, because what the hell? Does no one tell her anything anymore?

"I told you he was in good hands," Colton whispers in her ear.

Rae glares at him. "You knew?"

"I had an inkling." He shrugs.

"I feel so left out," she grumbles.

"Not for long, sweetheart," Jessica says with a smile over her shoulder, not even disguising the fact she was eavesdropping.

Apparently, that's a family trait.

As Rae stumbles her way up the stairs to the platform, she spots Dalton already standing there. His brown eyes are filled with humor as he sees his wife dragging Rae up on stage. He's also dressed up in a white button up shirt, but he's kept it comfortable with jeans though she's sure he's never worn them before. They look straight off the hanger they're so clean.

"Glad you could join us," He murmurs as Jessica pulls her to a stop beside him.

"I wish I could say the same," Rae says with a shaky smile, making the alpha chuckle lowly.

"It'll be quick," Dalton assures her. "I'll just ask you for some things, and all you have to say is accept that you'll do them."

"You're not going to ask me to do anything weird, are you?"

Dalton frowns at her questionably. "Like what?"

"I have no idea," She rushes out with an exhale of air. "I'm just asking."

Dalton pats her back a few times. "I won't ask you for anything you can't handle."

"Right." She nods before taking a few more calming breaths. "Thank you, by the way, Sir."

"For what?"

"Being so kind to my family and me. You can't imagine how much that means to us."

"Not as much as you being paired with my son means to me," Dalton says with a sincere smile.

Rae's overwhelmed babble is cut off by Jessica's loud and commanding voice. Everyone goes quiet as Jessica stands in the form of Dalton, Colton, and herself, while facing the gathered members of the pack. There's a lot, Rae thinks in a panic, there is a lot more than she thought there would be.

"Welcome all to the acceptance ceremony!" Jessica calls into the mass of people.

Rae forces a shaky smile to her face and prepares to face her new pack.

She just hopes she doesn't screw it up.

CHAPTER TWENTY-NINE

"Can you come forward please, sweetheart?" Jessica asks with a bright smile over her shoulder in Rae's direction.

Rae just stares blankly at her for a few seconds before Jessica gives her a wide-eyed look and waves for her to join her. Realizing that she's not only talking to her but wants her to step onto the front of the stage, Rae feels her panic heighten. Forcing a no-doubt creepy smile, Rae stumbles forward before slipping her hand in Jessica's who squeezes it reassuringly as she pulls Rae to stand beside her.

"This beautiful woman has been chosen by fate to be the mate of my son and the alpha heir, Colton," Jessica announces with pride, but Rae just feels her face go burning hot as the crowd begins to hoot and holler. Jessica sticks a hand up and they all quite down. Turning to Rae, Jessica gives her a soft smile. "I have often prayed that someone worthy would be paired with my baby boy, and I haven't been disappointed. Rae Applebee, you have answered my prayers, and I can't be more thrilled to see my son's mark on your shoulder."

At the mention of the mark, Rae chuckles nervously and looks over at the crowd who are now focusing their attention fully on her. Realizing she should say something back, she clears her voice and tries to think of something to say. Preferably something that doesn't make her look like a half-crazed idiot.

"W-Well." She squeaks before clearing her throat. "Jessica, uh, I mean Alpha, I'm incredibly h-honored that you would say that. I can say that I'm thrilled that you didn't hate me at first glance."

Rae winces at her words, but the crowd begins laughing, making her want to hide in a hole somewhere. Glancing over at Jessica, she sees her grinning at her before pinching her cheek. "How can anyone hate anyone this adorable?"

More laughs come from the crowd, but when she glances at the crowd, Rae's embarrassment drops as she lays on a situation. Jace is standing in front of Cleo and Andy, looking pissed as hell. Rae can't make out what he's saying with all the other noises and people around. Her senses are too overwhelmed to pick out anything that secular, but she can see it all in his body language. He's pissed that Andy didn't talk to them first and despite how much Jace may pretend he dislikes Cleo, that's still his sister.

"Rae?"

Rae tears her eyes away from the scene and looks over at Jessica. "Uh, yeah?"

"Are you ready to be initiated into the pack?"

"Y-Yeah," Rae says before speaking a little louder. "Yes."

"Great!" Jessica chirps before turning to Dalton and Colton behind them. "You're up honey."

Dalton smiles and quirks an eyebrow at his wife. "You sure? I'd hate to ruin your moment in the sun, dear."

"Don't start," she warns him before turning to Rae to whisper. "You'll do great. Just follow his lead, and it'll be cake."

Rae just nods before glancing over at Colton. Colton gives her a sympathetic smile before wording "you're doing great" and winking at her. Rae gives him a shaky smile in return before she spots Dalton's figure approaching out of the corner of her eye. He gives her a reassuring smile as well, and Rae starts to feel a little bad. Here they are accepting her into their pack and all she's acting like they're about to execute her.

Straightening her back, Rae tries her best to push away the feeling of a hundred or more eyes on her and focus on the alpha in front of her. Taking a deep breath, she meets Dalton's gaze and finds him already smiling down at her, amusement and a little pride in his own dark brown eyes.

"Rae Applebee, do you accept this pack as your own? Do you swear to keep these lands protected as though you were born of them? Do you swear to protect your fellow pack members as you would any other member of your family? Do you swear loyalty to your alphas above all others?"

Rae swallows thickly as she wonders if her father said "yes" to these same things. Is that why he agreed to give her away? Is that why he put the pack and his alpha's wants above what was right for his family? Could Rae do the same if it came down to it? She exhales unsteadily as she meets Dalton's encouraging gaze. No, she couldn't do that to her children, but in this pack, she's sure she'll never have to make that choice.

"I swear."

Dalton smiles briefly before putting on a more stern expression. Reaching on his side, Rae's eyes widen at the view of a large wooden-handled knife in a sheath clipped to his belt. Taking the knife out, Dalton gives her a reassuring look while slowly unsheathing the frankly huge knife.

"It should only hurt for a minute," he murmurs before speaking louder. "And do you, Rae Applebee, accept this pack as your family, to be of our blood as we are of yours."

"I d-do," she stutters as the knife comes closer but is shocked when he drags the metal blade across his own palm. A line of blood springs up, and Rae feels a little queasy looking at it but tries to keep taking deep breaths.

"Your hand, please."

Rae gives him her shaky hand, and he grabs it with his much larger one before placing the cold metal onto her palm. Rae squeezes her eyes shut and turns away but faintly hears Colton's low growl. She would roll her eyes at that, but she's too busy trying not to bite through her lower lip as Dalton drags the blade across her palm.

It doesn't really hurt, she supposes, but it's more the idea of someone cutting her that she doesn't like. Besides with a knife that big, how can she not be at least a little freaked out? When Dalton removes the blade, he takes her hand in his and presses their cuts together before they can heal. Rae gasps and clutches her head as she feels the pack's mind link attach itself to that of her wolf. It feels like a short but super intense headache, but once it clears, she can feel her wolf's contentment.

Her wolf's always felt more comfortable as part of a pack, anyway.

"You did good, kid," Dalton tells her lowly before turning towards the crowd and holding up their still joined hands. "I present, Rae Applebee, a new member of our pack!"

Cheers explode out of the crowd, making Rae flinch back a little. She looks through the groups of people and tries to spot her siblings. She first spots Hudson and who she's assuming his mate clapping with smiles on their faces. When Hudson sees her looking at him, he gives her a dorky wave before blushing when his mate kisses his cheek. Apparently, she's going to have to set some ground rules with those two because mates or not, Hudson is too young for anything . . . intimate.

Moving her gaze over to where she last saw Cleo and Andy, she sees them gone and Jace as well. Rae frowns as she thinks about where they could have gone and what exactly is happening. The possibilities become nearly overwhelming, and she's half tempted to just jump off the stage and go looking for them when she realizes she has the pack link now. Focusing on Andy's image in her mind, she sends her thoughts straight to him.

Where is my sister?

It takes him a minute to answer back but when he does, it's clear he's a little busy. *With me but we have a bit of a situation.*

Situation?

Jace is trying to fight me.

Rae would facepalm herself if she wasn't on stage right now. *Okay, give me five minutes, and I'll be there. You're not hitting him back, are you?*

Are you kidding? I could lay this kid's ass out in seconds.

Yeah, okay, Floyd Mayweather, calm it. I'll be there in a few.

Yes, Beta.

Rae stills at the title before coming back into the moment. Dalton releases her hand, and Rae forces her most serene looking, but still most likely crazy looking smile before bowing her head in his direction. Dalton inclines his head a little towards her as well before gesturing for her to head back to Colton. With her head still inclined forward, Rae walks backward until Colton grabs her cut hand by the wrist.

"Does it hurt?" he asks while inspecting the already closing wound.

"No, but we have to go."

"Go? Where?"

Grabbing his hand with her non-healing one, she starts leading him off the stage. Jessica frowns at them, but Rae sends her a reassuring grin as she continues to drag him down the few till steps they hit the ground. Continuing to pull him, Rae tries to latch onto their scent and catches a trail heading into a nearby area of woods. She's only slightly relieved to know that they thought ahead enough to go somewhere else for their pissing contest.

"Rae, what's going on?"

"Jace is trying to fight Andy."

Colton laughs before seeing her glare. Cutting his laughter off, he puts on a more serious expression. "Why would he do that?"

"Jace is very protective of us. When our dad ran off, he got it in his head that he was supposed to become our protector. So

273

now, if anyone even looks at us weird, he throws up fists faster than he thinks."

"Are you sure he's not a shifter?" he asks with a frown.

Rae shakes her head. "I don't think he is. He didn't have any of the classic signs like Hudson did. Not that I would have noticed anyway, apparently. God, I really should pay more attention to these kids."

"You're doing great," Colton soothes. "They're just a lot to handle."

"Isn't everyone these days?" she grumbles before spotting Jace and Andy circling each other with Cleo crying on the sidelines. If she had a nickel for every time she came upon this scene, she'd be a millionaire, Rae thinks with a tired sigh. "Alright, everyone, break it up!"

"Oh thank god!" Cleo cries as she comes running towards Rae. "These idiots won't listen to me."

"Hey!" Andy and Jace yell in unison before glaring at each other.

Rae rolls her eyes and takes her hand from Colton so she can put both of them on her hips. "What are you, seven? No fighting!"

"Rae, he marked her! The son of a bitch didn't even ask or talk to us!"

"I'm aware, and we've already had a chat about that," she tells Jace with a stern look. "I already gave my blessing, Jace. Leave it alone."

"Are you fucking kidding me right now?" He explodes at her. "He's just going to use her and dump her like trash just like all of those other pieces of shit. Can't you see that?"

"Watch your mouth," Andy snaps lowly.

"Make me, you—"

"Enough!" Rae yells, getting both of their attention. "Jace, Andy is Cleo's mate. You're going to have to accept that. Hudson, for your information, has also found his mate, so try to get over and accept that while you're at it too."

"Really?" Jace asks with a smirk. "Is she hot?"

"*He*," she corrects. "Is very handsome."

Jace's auburn colored eyebrows both arch in surprise before speaking, "He? As in a guy? As in two guys together?"

"Yes, that's the very wordy explanation of your brother being gay, but yes." Rae sighs with a dry look in his direction.

Cleo lets a giggle, making Rae slide her eyes in her direction. "Really?"

"Yes, really," Rae tells her sharply.

"Would it be rude to say I totally called it?" Cleo asks with a smirk.

"You knew?" Jace demands.

Cleo shrugs. "I had an idea. I mean, he's always disappearing, and I saw him hanging around this really cute boy in town one day, and the guy's arm was around him. I figured he might be bi-sexual maybe, but gay . . . that's so awesome."

"Awesome? How is this awesome?"

Rae narrows her eyes at her brother. "Jace, don't be a dick about this, he's still your brother, who you love."

"I know that!" Jace snaps. "I don't love him any less, but I can't really welcome this with open arms, Rae. Do you realize what high school is like? People aren't as understanding as we want them to be. I don't want him going through that."

Rae's initial anger melts away as she steps towards Jace with a slight smile. "I know you want to protect him, all of us, but you have to let things happen as they happen. He's still our brother, and he's happy. I know it's a lot to process, but we can't make him hide who he is just because of other people. We stand by his side and help him through it just like he would do for any of us."

Jace runs his hands through his hair before running them down his face. Playing with his lip ring, Jace glances over at Andy. "I'm still not okay with you just marking her like that."

275

Rae rolls her eyes. "I'm sure he's learned his lesson and will never do it again."

Colton and Andy start laughing, and Cleo rolls her own baby blues with a smile. Jace, on the other hand, narrows his eyes at Rae. "You think you're being funny, but I'm serious."

"Okay, Mr. Serious, now that this is all settled, are we allowed to go back and enjoy the party or are there other issues you want to bring to the table?" Rae drawls, while crossing her arms over her chest.

"Not right now, but I'll let you know."

"Fantastic," Rae says sarcastically before turning to Colton. "Shall we?"

Colton smirks at her and takes her hand in his. "Of course."

* * *

Colton can't hide his pride as he watches Rae mingle among the pack. Cassidy is balanced on her hip, twirling a strand of Rae's hair with her finger while laying her head on Rae's shoulder. Colton can't stop the image of Rae one day having their kid on her hip as he looks at them. He tries to convince himself that those thoughts are years away, but he still has them.

Who wouldn't, though, if Rae was their mate?

"Stop looking so love struck, loser. You're going to make her think she's got you wrapped around her little finger."

Colton turns to his brother Sawyer and glares at him. "Like you're any better with Vivienne."

"Yeah, but I'm married." Sawyer grins, his mouth full of food.

Colton grimaces and turns back to look at Rae. "She'll be a good alpha female, won't she?"

Sawyer sucks some ketchup off his thumb before shrugging. "Well, she won't suck at it."

276

"Can you be serious for once?"

"Nope," Sawyer answers immediately. "So what's crawled up your ass?"

"Besides you?"

"Of course."

Colton sighs heavily before motioning for Sawyer to follow him. Once they're on the outskirts of the party, Colton spills everything in a low voice, "Rae wasn't supposed to find me the night of the run."

Sawyer's dark brows pull into a frown. "What are you talking about?"

"Well, I told you about how I smelled another wolf nearby when I found her."

"You were in a forest filled with other wolves, that doesn't shock me."

"Yeah, but this one didn't smell like a normal wolf, it smelled like a rogue."

"And you didn't tell me this before?"

Colton shrugs looking a little sheepish. "I was a little distracted."

"Mates do that." Sawyer smirks before sighing heavily. "So you smelled a rogue, what does that have anything to do with Rae?"

"She told me some things. Things her dad told her about her mate. He told her that she was going to have to fight to survive, and that her mate would be cruel. He said that she would have to leave him soon."

"Sounds like a whacko protective daddy to me." Sawyer shrugs.

"Yeah, but that's not all. I told you about White Stone's issues, right? The territorial attacks and Kendrick's constant reassurance it would be taken care of? Also, he was pretty adamant about Rae not accepting my mark or leaving with me. Something didn't seem right but with everything else . . ."

"So, what are you saying?"

"I think that Rae was supposed to be a bargaining chip. Like they used to do in the old days to ward off other packs or rogues. Give them a girl to use for their . . . amusements and keep them busy."

"Colton, that was outlawed centuries ago. You could face some serious consequences for that. You think that self-righteous prick Kendrick would risk his head on a pike for that?"

"I think a desperate tyrant will do anything to keep his kingdom intact."

Sawyer frowns as he thinks it over and Colton does the same. The thought of Rae being put up as a sacrificial lamb like that makes his blood run cold, and his wolf wants to rip everything apart. He'll never allow that to happen, and knowing Rae, neither will she. She's strong, and she's capable. Colton has no doubt that if anything did happen, she'd fight tooth and nail every step of the way like an alpha female should.

"Colton." Sawyer finally sighs. "I think you need to tell mom and dad."

Colton doesn't like it, although he has to agree.

But he has something to do first.

* * *

Rae goes on her toes and tries to spot Colton, but she can't see him anywhere. Going flat on her feet again, she glances over and notices that Cassidy is asleep on her shoulder. With a small smile, she decides to go lay her down and excuses herself from the conversation she's having with an older pack member.

While walking toward the pack house, Rae spots Poppy running around with some of the other kids with a huge grin on her face. Rae smiles at the image of her sister being so happy and hopes that the rest of her siblings feel that way. Still, she worries about Jace. Hudson and Cleo have mates to make the transition easier but Jace is alone, and that isn't a settling thought.

Maybe some people have roads they have to navigate alone, she thinks.

Humming softly, Rae carries Cassidy up the stairs and rubs her back, so she stays asleep. Their mom used to do this too, same song and everything. No matter how old the kids got, if they were sick, they got their back rubbed, and this little made up song hummed to them. It used to drive Jace nuts, and he always says he was too old for being sang to. That didn't stop him from sleeping like a baby every time, though.

Rae uses her foot to push open the girls' room and looks around it for the first time. She'll have to give Jessica a big hug and a thank you because it's perfect. The walls are white but with painted scenes of *Alice in Wonderland* all around the room. The scene of Alice talking to the white rabbit is right above the bed that carries Cassidy's smell, and Rae begins putting her down there.

Rae gently removes Cassidy's white sandals and places them on the fluffy white rug by the bed before grabbing the light blue comforter to pull over her. Cassidy stirs a bit in her sleep and opens her eyes a little to look at Rae. Rae smiles down at her baby sister and brushes her fingers over Cassidy's now messy braids.

"It's okay, baby, go back to sleep."

"Rae, can we stay here forever?"

Rae smiles a little. "Of course we can, sweet pea."

"Will Colton stay with us?"

"Of course he will. He's not going anywhere."

"Will you stay?"

Rae frowns at the question. "Of course I will."

"You won't leave like mama?"

"No," Rae whispers, tears coming to her eyes. "No, baby, I would never leave you."

"Promise?"

"With all my heart."

Cassidy nods and closes her eyes again. Rae hears her breathing even out, and Rae lets out a shaky sigh while wiping away a few rebellious tears that have fallen against her will. Getting to her feet, she leans over and kisses Cassidy's temple before heading for the door. Glancing back at her sister, she feels an ache in her chest, knowing how much Cassidy must miss their mom.

They all miss her.

Closing the door as quietly as she can, she slides down against the door and sits on the floor. She wishes she could tell Cassidy about their mom without feeling like she's ripping her own heart out. Maybe she'll continue the tradition their mom started, she thinks, as she realizes Cassidy's birthday is coming up. Rae's eyes widen as she realizes that 'coming up' means it's actually five days away. Shit, she's going to have to talk to Jessica about planning something.

"Rae?"

She lifts her head to see Colton coming up the stairs with a concerned look on his face. She rolls her eyes and lays her head back on the door. "Can't escape anyone here."

"Nope." Colton smiles as he comes to crouch in front of her. Lifting his gaze to the door he nods towards it. "She fall asleep?"

"Out like a light."

Rae squeals as Colton reaches out to wrap his arm around her waist so he can pull her to him. Before she can say anything, his lips are on hers, and it doesn't take her long to kiss him back. Wrapping her arms around his neck, she moans lightly against his mouth when he deepens the kiss. Colton lifts her off the ground, and Rae automatically wraps her legs around his waist.

He carries her to their room and lets her slide down to her feet. Rae shivers at the loss of warmth as he moves away from her to shut the door. With his hands on the back of the door and his back to her, her confusion only grows. What's going on with him? Walking over to him, she lays her hand on his back, making him tense and decides to just ask him.

"Colton, what's going on? Rae," he says hoarsely before turning to face her. "I need you to do something for me."

She waits for him to elaborate but when he doesn't, she asks, "What?"

"I need you to mark me. Right here, right now."

Rae just blinks at him.

She thinks she's in too much shock to do much else.

CHAPTER THIRTY

Colton watches her face carefully as she takes in his demand. As he takes in her shocked expression, he realizes he probably should have prettied up a bit. He should have, but his wolf has other ideas. The idea of Rae marking them as well as the threat of danger has made his wolf downright troublesome. His wolf is done waiting, and for Colton, that makes this whole situation much more difficult.

"What?"

Colton lets out a frustrated sigh and runs his hand through his hair. "I want you to mark me."

"Yeah, that part I got."

He narrows his eyes at the teasing smirk on her lips. It's cute, he likes when she smirks, but right now it just makes him agitated. "Rae, with everything going on I want to be sure that if something did happen, you could reach me. and I could reach you. This is completely practical."

Rae arches one dark blonde eyebrow at him. "Well, when you put it like that . . ."

"Rae, this is serious."

"I know it is, but you can't just throw me in our room and demand that I mark you. When I mark you, it will be out of my affection for you, not practicality. I like you, Colton, a lot, but that doesn't mean you can forgo romance just because you already have me in your grasp."

"I'm doing this to protect you."

"From what? Kendrick and his rogue lap puppy? Did you not get the memo about us moving away from them? My family and I are here now with your pack, and maybe I'm being overconfident, but I'm quite sure your pack can fight off a few rogues."

"That doesn't mean anything, Rae." He grits out, his jaw clenched tightly. "Do you really think Kendrick isn't crafty enough to send someone to get you? Maybe even someone from my pack? He's desperate, Rae! Desperate enough to give you to rogues as a chew toy, and you want to just ignore it?"

This time, his words seem to get through to her. Rae moves towards the bed and turns her back to him as she thinks. Colton doesn't say a word; he wants her to understand why they have to do this now. It's not like he didn't want to give her some kind of romantic setting for his marking, he did, but situations change. He can't risk not being able to contact her, especially since he's gotten new information.

After talking to his brother, Colton decided to go collect some more information. He's been gone for almost a week from his pack, and now that he is back, he's been understandably distracted with Rae. No one can blame him for that, and no one does, but he's behind on his workload. As beta, Colton has responsibilities, this that his father doesn't want to handle or has no time to handle fall on his shoulders. Apparently, the rising number of rogues surrounding the pack territory since Rae's arrival falls into one of those categories.

"There's something you're not telling me," Rae says quietly, but getting Colton's attention. He lifts his gaze to see her trying to read his expression, but he keeps his face as placid as he can. He needs her to stay calm. "Colton? Is there?"

"Yes," he eventually admits.

He can't help himself. She just has to look at him with those large brown eyes of hers, and he'd spill his literal guts on the floor for her if she asked it. He can't look her in the eye though when he says it, but he can't keep it from her. She needs to know the situation so she can be ready if anything does happen. He doesn't want her getting caught unaware at any point.

"What is it?" She prods when he doesn't immediately elaborate.

"Since your arrival, there has been reports of higher counts of the rogues on our boundaries. There used to be a handful, maybe twenty circling around if we were lucky, but it's been growing overnight. Now it's closer to fifty, and it's continuing to grow. I believe that they're either here for a distraction or to build muscle for a siege."

"But . . . that's insane."

Colton walks towards her and cups her face in his hands. He looks deeply into her eyes, so she understands and believes what he's about to say as much as he does. He needs her to know his intentions because again, he doesn't want her to be caught unaware.

"I will protect you, Rae. I will protect your family, and I will protect this pack with everything I have. Nothing will take you away from me, I won't allow it, but we need to take precautions."

"And if I mark you, I can contact you if I'm taken."

"Yes." He sighs, relieved that she finally understands his position. Laying his forehead against hers, he brushes her hair out of her face. "I wanted it to be special for you like it was when I marked you. I really did."

Putting her hand on top of the one cupping her cheek, she presses her face into his palm. "I know."

"I'll make it up to you, I swear it."

"How?" she asks, her eyes brimming with tears.

He gives her a slight smile. "I don't know yet, but I will."

With a little laugh, she sniffles before a huge grin comes across her face. "I can be patient then."

Leaning down, Colton presses his lips to Rae's. She moans lightly against his mouth, and Colton's wolf growls lowly at the

284

sound. When he had marked Rae, Colton had a hard enough time not taking it further, but he kept his resolve. Technically, Colton is a virgin. He's never had sex with anyone, but he has done other stuff with girls. He needed release, he won't deny that, but sex? That was something he wanted to give to his mate and only her.

Doesn't mean he didn't want it, all the damn time.

Breaking their kiss, Rae's voice is breathy. "But the party."

"Screw the party," he growls against her lips before crouching a little to grab the back of her thighs. With a little squeal, she automatically wraps her legs around his waist. Holding her in the middle of the room, Colton groans at the contact. The fact she's only in a dress and a pair of underwear isn't exactly helping his focus either. All he'd have to do is move it up a few inches . . .

"What about your mom? Won't she come in here?" she asks as Colton moves to laying kisses on her neck.

He doesn't answer her with anything more than a grunt before getting back to the task at hand. Rae's hands move into his hair, and her legs tighten around him when his lips hit her mark. He smirks against the now completely healed bite mark before baring his teeth to lightly bite the sensitive skin.

Rae arches her back as she lets out a breathy moan, and Colton figures this is the time to just go for it. Walking over towards the bed, he lays her down on her back before crawling on top of her. Her chest is heaving with labored breaths as she stares up at him with lightening brown eyes. Her wolf is on edge, it's right there in the now more caramel color of her eyes. All she needs is that extra push to come all the way to the surface and do what has to be done.

"Colton." Rae groans as his hands move under her skirt to knead the flesh of her thigh. Seeing this as an encouragement, he moves his hand higher up and can't stop his lustful growl as he's met with a thin lace. So easy to tear away, the only barrier to doing what he's been dying to do. "C-Colton, please."

Colton's now yellow eyes move up to meet the eyes of her wolf staring right back at him. He knows what she wants, and he's tempted to do that but he can't. Not now; not with a whole damn party of people downstairs just dying to irrupt. No, if he can't make his marking special, then at least he can give her that to look back on fondly. Still, it's clear that she's getting uncomfortable, so he decides to compromise.

Spreading her legs a little with his fingers, he reaches between her legs to rub over the fabric of her underwear. Colton watches Rae throw her head back as her hands claw at anything in reach. He gazes on her as she gets closer to coming apart at the seams with determination to push her over the edge. Besides, he can't think of anything better than knowing that he can bring her that much pleasure.

"Colton!" she cries and squeezes her legs around his arm.

She's close, very close.

Colton isn't really surprised when she suddenly pushes him onto his back and straddles his lap. Her dress has ridden up to pool at her waist, and he runs his hands up her sides as she looks down at him. Yellow eyes, that of her wolf, shine brightly back at him before she reaches down and grips his shirt. With one quick pull, his shirt is torn in half, and he smiles up at her, feeling a bit smug.

"I'm not stupid enough not to know what you're doing, mate."

Her voice is rougher than it is normally, and he knows that's because her wolf is now in control. His own wolf growls at him in his head demanding to be let out too, but Colton won't allow it. If he lets his wolf take over then, he'll fully mate them without a second hesitation. If Colton is a little weaker in resolve, maybe he'll allow him, but he promised he'd make it up to her somehow.

Waiting is the only thing he can really think of at the moment, so that's what he's going with.

Rae runs her nose up his chest and inhales his scent deeply, making him clench his hands into fists at his side. He can't even touch her anymore. He's that close to the edge of just saying "fuck it" and taking this the rest of the way. When she licks his shoulder, he shivers at the sensation while his wolf whines in impatience. Colton glares at the ceiling, knowing exactly what she's doing. It appears that Rae isn't the only tease he'll be acquainted with for the rest of his life.

"Rae," he growls as he grips the back of her head to press her against his neck. "Now."

"Are you sure?" She sings softly before dragging her teeth against his skin.

Colton practically convulses at the feel of the shocks that sends off but manages to whine his response, "For fuck's sake, yes."

He doesn't hear any response for a few seconds before her teeth abruptly slice into the skin of his shoulder. Fisting her hair in his hand, he keeps her against his neck while his other hand tightens around her waist. He's sure he's leaving bruises and grabbing her so hard, but at the moment, he doesn't care.

Colton can feel the other half of the bond connecting her to him, and with it, her thoughts come flooding into his mind. Before it was partial mental pictures, some vague emotions, and maybe some general attitudes, but that was it. Now it's like he can see everything she's feeling as though those feelings were his own. It's overwhelming, but he tries his best to keep his head on straight.

Let go, she tells him through their link while her teeth stay embedded in his shoulder.

With more effort than it should be, slowly, he allows his body to relax. The pleasurable shocks of her touch, and the euphoria of the bite make him feel on the verge of losing his mind. No one told him it would feel like this. No one said it would be this strong, this consuming, and this fantastic.

287

Rae slowly pulls away from his shoulder and Colton lets out a grunt as she does. The area on his shoulder is tingling warm, and he feels a warm feeling flow through his veins. As she licks his shoulder clean of his own blood, he stares at the ceiling in bliss. Total relaxation, that's what this is, and he can't say he's not enjoying it right now.

Opening his suddenly heavy eyelids, he sees Rae sitting up on his lap with a smile playing on her blood stained lips. He reaches a weighted down arm up and tries to beckon her down to him. She gets the hint and laughs a little as she leans down to give him a quick kiss. He whines a little when she pulls back, but she only laughs at him again instead of returning to him like he wants.

"Told you it was exhausting." She smirks at him.

"I believe you," he mumbles, his mouth feeling slack.

She laughs a little and rolls her eyes. "Do you want to sleep?"

He shakes his head, but his eyelids are already drooping close. "No. I'm okay. I just need a minute."

He can't see her face, but he hears her sigh as she shifts herself off his lap to lay beside him. Moving his arm out of the way, she tucks herself into his side and lays her head over his head. Her hand lays on the bare skin of his stomach, making his skin come alive under the contact of it.

Silence comes over them, and he tries to keep himself conscious. If he's honest with himself, he's a little embarrassed that he's this drained by a marking. He figures it's from not sleeping much the night before. Colton was too busy the other night watching her sleep and staring at his mark on her shoulder. Now he's paying for it by pretty much falling asleep like an exhausted toddler.

"Do you want me to stay with you?" Rae asks quietly, making him step back from jumping off the steep cliff.

He wraps his arms around her and nods. "Please."

"Colton?"

"Hmm?"

"I'm glad it was you," she whispers in his ear. "I'm glad it was you who found me in the woods."

The edge of his lips twitches up as he pulls her tighter against him. "Me too."

"I owe you so much," she tells him as he begins losing the battle with consciousness. "And I'll pay you back for all of it somehow."

Colton falls asleep before he can respond, but if he could talk, he'd tell her that she doesn't owe him anything.

She's already given him everything.

* * *

Rae knows exactly when Colton has fallen asleep. His thoughts aren't of her or her words anymore. He's in la-la land now, and as tempting as it is to peek into his dreams, she holds back. Instead, she reaches up and traces the lines of his features and memorizes his face. She wants to remember this for the future. When she's old and gray with only her memories to keep her company, she wants to have every detail saved up.

A light knocking on the door has Rae's head snapping in its source's direction. Colton twitches but doesn't wake up, so Rae decides to answer it before does. Marking is surprisingly exhausting, and he'll need his sleep. Gently removing herself from Colton's grip, she tip-toes over to the door and pries it open.

"Oh, there you are!" Jessica grins.

Rae puts a finger to her mouth and whispers back, "Colton's sleeping."

The alpha female's bright brown eyes take in Rae's state, and a smirk comes over her face. "You marked him, didn't you?"

Rae's cheeks go red, but she nods. "Yes, ma'am."

289

"Well, good for you," Jessica says with a pat on Rae's shoulder. "He's lucky to have you, dear. Though as the hostess of a party, I do have to scold you for doing now of all times."

"He insisted." Rae shrugs as she tries to straighten out her mess of a hairdo.

Jessica frowns a little. "Insisted?"

Looking over her shoulder, Rae peeks back into the room and sees Colton still asleep. Rae steps into the hallway and closes the door behind her as gently as she can before turning her attention back to Jessica. She flinches back when she comes face-to-face with a wet wipe.

"You have a little blood on your face, honey," the older woman tells her with a sheepish smile.

"Oh, uh, right. Thanks."

"No problem, dear. So why did he insist?"

Rae bites her lip and stares at the wet wipe as she debates on telling her. Jessica is alpha female, and as such, she should be told when her pack is in danger. Rae's pretty sure Colton hasn't told anyone of his theories about Kendrick yet, but this is becoming more serious. Fifty rogues and more coming? That's not just a small matter, and this is becoming a serious issue.

"You can tell me anything, honey," Jessica soothes, apparently seeing her apprehension. "Including telling me when to bud out."

Rae shakes her head and speaks quietly, "No, you have a right to know."

"To know what? Rae, you're worrying me."

"How much do you know about Alpha Kendrick of White Stone?"

CHAPTER THIRTY-ONE

Rae watches Jessica blink slowly at her before wrapping her arm through Rae's. Leading Rae back down towards the stairs, Jessica answers, "Well, I haven't had much to do with Kendrick, but I did do a lot of dealing with his father."

Rae grimaces at the mention of the previous alpha. "Then I feel sorry for you."

"Dalton simply couldn't be in the room with the man for longer than half an hour before he'd be ready to rip out his throat. Nasty piece of work that man was," Jessica says with a little shutter. "So for the good of peace between the two packs, I took over those little visits. I have to admit that he almost met the business end of my fists a few times."

Rae smiles a little at that last bit before focusing again. "Do you think he would succumb to rogue demands?"

"What do you mean?"

"I mean, do you think Kendrick's father would have made a deal with the rogues just to keep his pack lands safe?"

Jessica gives her an odd look. "Well, I can't really speak of the actions of others, but I wouldn't put it past him to consider it. Why do you ask?"

"Something's come to my attention recently that I hadn't even considered," Rae tells her as she comes to a stop on a stair and faces the older woman. "Something having to do with me, the rogues, and my old pack."

"What is it?"

Rae lets out an uneven breath and instead asks, "Did Colton tell you about our meeting with Kendrick?"

Jessica's face transforms into a picture of mama bear rage. "You mean suggesting a rejection? Yes, Colton told me and let me just say if Colton weren't so persuasive, I would have called the council of alphas on his ass. Of all the nerve . . . I would have beaten him right then and there if I had been in either one of your shoes."

"What do you mean by 'persuasive'?"

"He told me he was going to try to get you out of there," Jessica says with pride. "He didn't like how that alpha was treating you, and of course with your siblings more vulnerable than you, he didn't want to take chances. He was very concerned with all of your safety, so I told him to bring you here as soon as possible."

Rae nods as she feels warmth spread through her chest at how much Colton cares not only for her but her siblings. It would be one thing for him to just take them on just to get on her good side. It was a feeling she had and still had, up until she saw how Colton acted with Cassidy and Poppy. There was nothing other than affection on that man's face when he was with them, and it eased her worries to see that.

And if Rae has anything, it's worries.

"Jessica, I don't think I was meant to find Colton that night of the run."

The alpha frowns at her. "Of course you were, Rae. Mates always find their way to each other right when they're meant to."

"Colton and I think that maybe it was all a ploy. Alpha Kendrick has been having issues with the rogues for years, problems that go back to his father's rule. My dad had been training me, preparing me for something that I didn't get until now. Colton thinks that maybe I was meant to be kidnapped that night by rogues."

"'The Gift' ritual was outlawed long ago!" Jessica gasps. "Are you sure that's what he had planned?"

"I had doubts, but I'm putting so many things together that seems irrational to just disregard it."

Jessica shakes her head, tears rim her eyes as a distant look fills them. "If it's true, I can't even imagine what you'd be going through right now. What kind of alpha does that to one of his own?"

"Colton just thinks he was desperate."

"No, you don't understand, Rae. Rogues aren't right in the mind. They're usually kicked out of packs for unsavory behavior. Rape, murder, and unfair challenges. They aren't the kind of people you would want to be around, and now some of them have started raising families outside of the packs. Indoctrinating them into some sick way of life."

Rae's never seen Jessica disgusted or angry before, and it is a sight. She's pretty sure she would never want to be on this woman's bad side. That's how most alpha females are, though. Once a woman has been full mated to an alpha, she must begin to train like any other alpha. She has to know how to defend, govern, and be a diplomat. She's as well trained, if not better trained, than the alpha male himself. These days though some are just interested in the glamor of the position.

Like a certain alpha female Rae doesn't care to think about at the moment.

"That's the reason why they outlawed 'The Gift' ritual. They would give a young woman of strong family breeding to rogues who threatened the territory. It kept wars and deaths to a minimum, but the women wouldn't survive, and if they did, they were never the same. Rogues aren't gentle with their war prizes, Rae."

"I would have found a way out," Rae whispers more to herself. "I wouldn't have given up until I had escaped. I wouldn't have left my family like my dad left us. I would have found a way to come back."

"Of course you would have," Jessica says with a sniffle. "I have no doubt you would have."

Rae takes a deep breath, runs a hand through her hair, and gets her fingers caught in a knot. "I want to bring the rest of my family here. I know it's a burden, I know that, but I can't think of anything else to do. My aunt, my uncle, and my cousin are all there still. My dad is ill. I haven't heard anything from my aunt, but I'm sure he doesn't have long left. If I could just bring them all here, I could keep them safe and out of reach of Kendrick."

"Of course you can, dear. More pack members is never a burden to us, but what do you mean about bringing your father here?"

Rae sighs. "After my mom had died, he slipped into deep grief. His wolf took over, and he went feral. He's sick and half mad, but he's still my dad. I can't just leave him there."

Jessica shakes her head, her cheeks still glistening with spent tears. "Didn't Colton tell you? Didn't anyone tell you?"

"Tell me what?"

"Rae, your father died shortly after his attack on you."

"What?"

"In the cells. Kendrick said he died in the middle of the night."

Rae steps back from Jessica in shock and her heart shatters in her chest, but she refuses to believe it.

"No," Rae says with a vigorous shake of her head. "No. He's lying. He's lied before, and he'd lie again. My dad isn't dead."

Jessica reaches out and tries to comfort her, but Rae pushes her hand away. "I'm so sorry, honey."

"No, he's not dead!" she yells, making Jessica jump.

"Please calm down," Jessica pleads, but it falls on deaf ears.

Rae is already running down the stairs with tears trailing down her face. No, she refuses to believe it. If it were true, why

294

wouldn't Cleo or Jace or even Hudson tell her? Why would they lie to her and say Jolene would watch after him? Why would they let her linger in this guilt about leaving him behind for this long?

"Whoa, slow down there, *Speed Racer*, you almost knocked me down."

Rae pushes her way past Sawyer and stalks into the party looking for her siblings. She wants to hear it from them, from their mouths, that their dad is really dead. She wants to hear their explanations for not telling her. She wants a fucking reason why she was left in the dark about this when it should have been told to her as soon as it happened.

The rational part of her calls her a hypocrite from being upset about not being told. She didn't tell them he was alive, and they didn't tell her that he supposedly died. It's two sides of the same coin, but why does this betrayal feel so much deeper then?

Looking around, Rae spots Jace with Hudson and his mate on the edges of the gathering. She can feel eyes on her flushed and tear-streaked face, but she doesn't care. She doesn't care if she looks weak or crazy for crying. She just wants to know the truth.

Jace's blue eyes widen as they land on her and he comes jogging towards her to cup her face. "What happened? Did that son of a bitch hurt you?"

Rae pushes his hands away and glares at him. "Is it true?"

"Is what true?"

"About Dad," she spits at him. "Is it true?"

Jace immediately seems to realize what she means and hangs his head. Rae scoffs as new tears spill free from her eyes. Glancing over at Hudson, she sees the same contrite look on his face as silence falls over the party around them. Rae shakes her head as a sob escapes her mouth.

"Why wouldn't you tell me?"

"We thought it was best," Jace says quietly. "You were healing, and then you were so happy, Rae. You deserved to be happy at least one time without it being tainted with dad's shit."

295

"I deserve to know the truth!" Jace looks away from her, and she turns her eyes back to Hudson. "You knew too. Did Cleo know?"

"Yes," Cleo says from behind her, with Andy at her side. "Yes, I knew."

Rae lets out a bitter laugh. "You were so fucking cruel about me not telling you he was still alive and now, you're the one who was holding back information. How does it feel to be the hypocritical bitch now, Cleo? How does being knocked off your high horse feel? Did it fucking hurt like it should have?"

Andy's about to speak up in defense of Cleo, but she holds him back and speaks for herself, "Yes, I didn't tell you. Yes, I felt like shit for not telling you, but now I understand why you didn't want to tell us. I understand why you did everything you did for us now."

"Yeah?" Rae asks before sneering at her. "Well, it's too fucking late for that."

"Rae—"

Rae puts a hand up to stop Hudson's approach. "Don't touch me. None of you even come near me. I've sacrificed my life for you. I have given everything I had to give, and when that wasn't enough, I gave you more. Your gratitude and understanding aren't needed. I don't need it. I don't need any of you."

Rae starts walking away, but Cleo grabs her arm to stop her. "Rae, please—"

"No!" she yells in her face as she pushes her hand away easily. "I don't want to listen to you anymore. I'm done!"

Rae runs towards the surrounding woods. Her clothes rip to pieces as she shifts into her gray furred second form. Her wolf lets out a pained whine at the loss of the man she had also grown attached to, but it's nothing compared to Rae's grief. He was a son of a bitch, sure, but he was still her dad. He taught her how to swim, taught her how to ride a bike, and even though he hated it, he would read her stories. That was the dad she clung to, the one she's grieving.

And now he's gone.

* * *

Colton wakes up alone in his bed. Reaching over to the empty side beside him, he finds it cold and long without use. His first instinct is to panic, and that's exactly what he does. Jumping off the bed, he runs for the bathroom first, hoping she's in there, but she isn't. Of course, looking around the room, he realizes that it's much darker in here than it was before. How long was he asleep for? Shaking the question out of his head, he decides it doesn't matter.

Where is she? Opening up the mind link, he sees that she's closed it off, but he can still sense her emotions. Grief, anger, pain, and sadness are easily distinguishable through the link.

The immediate fear is that she's been taken, right from under his nose. Swinging open the bedroom door, he comes upon an odd scene. The whole Applebee family, Andy, Joseph, and even Colton's family are outside a guest room door. Colton takes in the scene quickly before finally speaking up and getting all their attentions.

Colton's sister-in-law, Vivienne, is in deep discussion with his mother. His father has a drowsy looking Cassidy in his lap and an upset looking Poppy at his side. Sawyer is sitting beside Jace against the stairwell banister. Hudson and Joseph sit on the other side of Jace, and Joseph has his head on Hudson's shoulder. Cleo is quietly crying in Andy's lap as he rubs her back and looks like she's ready for another breakdown.

"What the hell is going on?" Colton asks getting all eyes on him. "Where's Rae?"

"Some fucking mate you are." Jace hisses and starts to get up but Hudson grabs his shoulder.

297

"Jace." Cleo hiccups in warning before looking up at Colton. "She found out."

"Found out what?"

"About dad. She found out he's dead."

"I'm so sorry," Colton's mom says solemnly. "I thought she knew."

Colton's hands curl into fists at his side. "And no one thought to come and get me?"

"We tried," Sawyer grumbles from his position. "You were out, man."

"For shit's sake," he mutters to himself as he runs a hand through his hair. "She's in the room?"

"Yeah, we found her in the woods about two hours ago," Hudson says quietly, his brown eyes rimmed red. "She wouldn't let any of us near her other than Poppy or Cassidy. We got her dressed, but she didn't want to go to your room. She said she wanted to be alone."

Shaking his head, Colton steps over all the stretched out limbs in the way and heads for the door. Pounding on it with the side of his fist, he hears nothing from the other side of the door. Not even a floorboard creak or sigh.

"Rae?" he calls. "Come on baby, open up the door."

That gets a reaction. Stomping footsteps come towards the door before it swings open. Colton's heart sinks to his gut at the sight of his mate looking so upset. Her nose, eyes, and lips are swollen red from her tears. She's only dressed in an oversized neon yellow t-shirt that lands just above her knees and is covered in dirt. Her hair is dirty and sticking up in every direction as she glares at him.

"Get away from me." She hisses at him.

"Rae, please just—"

"You knew," she snaps at him, a tear falling from her eye as she does. "You knew, and you didn't tell me."

"I just wanted to protect you."

298

"From what?" she asks. "Because all you ended up doing was breaking my trust in you."

"I'm sorry," he whispers, reaching out to her.

Rae steps out of his reach and glares at him again. "I don't want your apologies, Colton. I just want you to leave me alone."

Slamming the door in his face, she disappears from sight, and he hears her broken sobs muffled behind the door. His heart breaks at the sound, but he can't reach out to her. She's shut him out mentally and now physically. His wolf whines loudly in his mind, but he pushes the beast away in favor of focusing on his own guilt. Turning around, he slides down the wood of the door and drops his head into his hands.

His father reaches over and puts a hand on his shoulder. "She'll come around, son."

"No, dad, I don't think she will."

And that very thought has him fighting back his own tears.

CHAPTER THIRTY-TWO

Two days.

Two fucking days.

That's how long his sister has been in there. Jace growls at the door as he continues to pace up and down the hallway trying to think of some way to get her out. Up to this point, he's pretty sure he's tried everything he can think of. He's pounded on the door, pleaded, threatened, and said he'd wait for her until he rotted out here, but nothing has worked.

He wants to blame someone, or anyone really, for this, but he can't. It's on him, Cleo, and Hudson. No matter how much he wants to, he can't even blame Colton for this. The poor guy just had to go with it. Colton had wanted to tell her the minute she was up and healthy again, but he was quickly shut down. Jace and his siblings decided to wait until she was accepted into the pack first. He wasn't lying before. He really did just want his sister to have her moment in the sun without all this mess on her shoulders.

Was that really so much to ask for?

With a heavy sigh, he puts his back against the wall and slides down it until he's seated on the floor again. Colton is there with him, on the other side of the closed door, looking like shit. Jace has watched the guy go from distraught to the brink of a mental breakdown. The guy hasn't slept or eaten, other than use the bathroom and hasn't moved from his place by the door.

As the days have passed, it's accurate to say Jace has grown to respect Colton more and more. At first, he can admit he wasn't a fan. How could he be? This cocky alpha shit head was going to come and take his sister from them? Who did this prick think he was? Then he saw them together when they didn't think he was watching. He saw how Colton looked at his sister, and he softened towards the guy.

Not too much, though.

Just a little.

Footsteps up the stairs has Jace looking for the source while Colton sits in his own pity party. To say Jace is unhappy to see Jessica's face would be an understatement. She's the reason behind this whole mess. If Jessica had waited just one more day, then they could have broken it to her gently. They would have hopefully avoided this whole fiasco, because if there is anything Rae hates more, it's people outside the family discussing family business. Kind of ruined that with that whole scene yesterday, though, did she?

Jessica sighs heavily as she takes in the both of them before coming to crouch in front of her son. Jace feels bitterness enter his heart at the sight of the two of them. He wishes his mom was here to come help him with this situation, but she isn't here. It's a fact Jace had to come to terms with quickly.

While Cleo was ruining her life and Hudson pulled deeper into himself, Jace had to step up to the plate as the man of the family. Rae was great with the girls and providing for them, but Jace simply doesn't take handouts. He got a job as soon as he could and though Rae fought him on it, he tried to help as much as he could. Little things like Hudson's sports equipment or the new freaky *Barbie* Poppy wanted. It wasn't much, but it was something he could do to ease her burden.

"Colton, you can't keep doing this," Jessica says softly, breaking Jace out of his thoughts. "Rae wouldn't want this."

Colton's head snaps up, and he glares at his mother. "Rae didn't want to be told her father was killed either but you did that, didn't you?"

"Colton, I said I was sorry. I—"

"What? You didn't think?" Colton nearly yells before looking away from her with a clenched jaw. "Mom, you know I love you, but I need you to get away from me right now."

"Colton—"

"Mom, please."

Jessica closes her eyes, and Jace sees a tear roll down her cheek before she nods. "Okay, if that's what you want."

Jessica gives Jace a fleeting glance as she walks past him and begins heading back down the stairs. It's better that she doesn't speak to him, really. Jace isn't too sure he can refrain from laying into her about keeping her nose out of their business.

On a surface level, Jace has a soft spot for Jessica. She's been good to his family, great with his little sisters, and accepting of Rae. It's all he could ask for from an alpha female, but the nosey mother-in- law routine has run its course from him. Jessica may be alpha female of this pack, but she's not part of their family. She needs to know her place with them if they're going to continue to stay here.

Looking over at Colton, Jace sees a tear fall from his eye and internally groans. Fuck, he's going to start crying again. Jace can hardly stand it anymore. Something needs to happen, or he's going to lose his mind. Deciding he's had enough of this shit, he gets up off the floor and stalks off to his room.

The place is still a mess. He's never had a room this big before. He feels weird putting his shitty hand-me-down stuff in a room this nice, so he's kept most of it in the boxes still. Ripping open one of the boxes, he finds exactly what he's looking for and gives it a relieved grin. This will definitely get shit moving. He's surprised he didn't think of it before. Maybe he wasn't desperate enough yet.

Jogging out of his room, Jace holds up his lock picking set to Colton who looks confused. Jace doesn't take the time to explain before kneeling in front of the door and digging in the little pouch for the right tools. When he finds them, he starts getting to work.

"What are you doing?" Colton croaks with wide eyes.

"I'm getting her the hell out of there. You may be okay with waiting until she starves herself to death, but I'm not. It's been three days, Colton. We can't just sit here anymore."

"She doesn't want to come out, Jace. I've already fucked up so much. I can't risk her hating me anymore for this."

Jace sighs heavily and turns to the wreck of a man beside him. "Listen, man. I like you, I do, so I'm going to give you a bit of advice. There are times when Rae takes things too far. She pushes herself until she literally can't go any farther just for a stupid point. She's stubborn as shit, just like our dad was. I'm all for giving a woman what she wants and everything, but there's also a time to step up and take control."

As Colton seems to be considering his words, Jace goes back to screwing around with the lock. He's had to do this so many times back at the old house it's almost like second nature. But what do you expect when you have a six-year-old sister who demands hours of bathroom privacy? She's not the only one who has to take a piss in the morning, and Jace has limits to his patience.

When the lock clicks, Jace smirks at the door before getting to his feet. He's about to take hold of the doorknob when he has a moment of hesitation. Shit, what if Colton's right? She obviously wasn't ready for this. What if she just pushes him farther away? Jace knows she doesn't mean the shit she said at the party, but that doesn't mean he wants to hear more of it.

"Screw it," he mutters before grabbing the doorknob and pushing open the door. The room smells kind of stale, and it's dark as he steps into it. He can't see her anywhere in the room, and that has him panicking. Shit, what if something happened? Would she have made a run for it?

303

"Go away." He hears a weak voice demand. "Leave me alone, Jace."

He rolls his eyes at his sister's ability to always know it's him. It's his scent, he knows that. Apparently, he smells like a mixture of bad body odor and maple. He's heard enough shit over the years to know what his own scent trail smells like. In fact, it's become one of his least favorite things about living with werewolves as a result.

"No," he tells her casually. "We're done with the game now, Rae. You need to get up and get over it."

She sits up and glares at him. His eyes are slowly adjusting to the darkness, and he can just make out her pissed off expression. Well, too bad for her. If tough love is what she needs, then tough love is what she'll get. Stepping closer to the bed, he stops when he sees her eyes flash a glowing yellow and knows to keep his distance. He's already got a healing wound on his chest from his last tangle with a wolf. He's not in the mood to add another one to the list.

"Get over it?" she echoes through clenched teeth. "Who the fuck do you think you are?"

"Your brother, Rae. I'm your brother, and I'm telling you to get over it. Dad was going to die. He was half dead already and in a day or two, he would have been dead with or without the fight with you. Did we lie? Yes, okay? We lied, but we did it for you. The same thing you would and have done for us."

Jace stops and waits for a response but gets nothing, so he continues.

"I get it. Fuck, Rae, I get it, but you can't just sit in here and wallow in self-pity. Colton is a fucking mess. I'm a fucking mess. And Cleo? Man, if you thought she was a mess before, you should see her now. She refuses to shower and her body odor is making everyone, but Andy, avoid her like the plague."

He stops again, hoping for a laugh, but all he gets is a tired sigh. Deciding to take his chances, he steps closer to the bed and sits on the edge. His nose wrinkles a bit when he realizes that Rae

304

hasn't bathed either and in this heat, she's starting to stink too. Coughing a little, he turns his head and looks at her, knowing that she can see him perfectly fine.

"We love you, okay? You said you did everything for us out of love, and I'm telling you now, we did this for the same reason. We just wanted you to be happy, and for two glorious days, you were. You weren't the overstressed mess you normally are. You were like the old you. The version of you that you were before you got your wolf, before mom's death, and before all this mating bullshit. We missed that. We missed you, Rae."

When he doesn't get a response, Jace runs a hand through his greasy, dark red hair and sighs heavily. "Shit, Rae, I don't know what to do anymore. I'm out of ideas here. If you want to stay in the room, then that's your deal, but please think about us before you do. Poppy thinks you hate her and Cassidy doesn't understand anything about what's going on. Hudson isn't talking to anyone again. I can't force you to come out of here, I know that. I just thought . . . it was worth a try, I guess."

Realizing this didn't do either one of them any good, Jace gets up to leave, but Rae grabs his arm, stopping him. Looking down at her, he sees that the light from the cracked open door is highlighting her face. His first observation is that she looks like hell. His second observation is that she's crying again. Without hesitation, he hugs her as she immediately breaks down into sobs on his shoulder.

"I-I'm s-sorry," she cries brokenly as she clutches the back of his shirt.

Jace shushes her and rubs her back. "It's okay. I'm the one who should be sorry here, okay? We should have told you as soon as we knew."

"I've been so selfish."

Jace can't help his snort. "You are anything but selfish, Rae. In fact, I'm insisting that as long it's not holding yourself in rooms for days, you should be more selfish."

305

Rae laughs a little and Jace leans back to smile down at her. Wiping some of her tears off of her cheeks, he kisses her forehead. God, she really does smell awful. Shaking his head, he leans back and looks her straight in the eyes.

"And for the love of god, take a damn shower."

She snorts out another laugh, making him laugh for the first time in days himself. Both hear the door creak open a little further and turn to see Colton standing apprehensively in the doorway. Jace feels Rae tense in his arms, and he immediately moves to soothe her.

"He's been a wreck, Rae. He's not mad, just worried. Give him a chance to explain himself, huh? Besides, it wasn't his idea."

Rae just nods a little, but her eyes don't move away from Colton. Seeing this turning into some dramatic, romantic reunion, Jace looks for the next available exit. As Colton steps closer to them, Jace pries Rae's hands off him and inches towards the door. Yeah, this is about to become some sappy shit he wouldn't even illegally download to see.

Once the love sick creatures are all caught up in each other, Jace escapes the room and takes a deep breath of air. He really hopes she takes his advice about that shower. Deciding to get some real fresh air, Jace heads down the nearly endless stairs towards the front door with a little bounce in his step. He feels much more relaxed knowing his big sis is up and actually out of the room. Maybe Colton can actually get her to eat something while he's at it.

"Jace?" Hudson calls quietly as Jace hits the last stair. "Is she—"

"She's fine," Jace tells him quickly.

Hudson's shoulders immediately slouch. "Oh, thank god."

"No need. Just thank Jace and his trusty set of burglar tools."

Hudson huffs a laugh. "I'd say I was surprised, but I'd be lying."

"And we're in enough trouble for that," Jace says with a wink.

"Jace do you think . . . Will she still be mad? She said—"

Jace cuts him off again, knowing exactly where he's going with that. "She said a lot of shit she didn't mean, kid. Just forget she even said it, because believe me when I say she feels shitty enough as it is."

Hudson nods and Jace takes that as confirmation enough. Jumping off the last step, he starts heading for the front door but stops when a thought hits him. Looking around, he realizes that everyone is out of the room, so he takes it as his chance to bring up the subject.

"By the way, Rae told me, about your . . . boyfriend," Jace says awkwardly.

"Oh, uh, yeah," Hudson mumbles nervously, rubbing the back of his neck. "His name's Joseph. He's my mate, actually."

"Mate," Jace says to himself before shoving his hands into the front pockets of his jeans. "He a good guy? Treat you well so far?"

"Yeah," Hudson says with a small goofy smile. "Yeah, he's a really good guy."

"Older than you?"

"Just a few years."

Jace narrows his eyes. "How much older?"

"Two years," Hudson answers reluctantly.

Jace blows out a breath before laughing a little. "Well, at least it means I can beat the shit out of him if he steps out of line, huh?"

Hudson smiles a little. "Yeah, I guess."

"Well . . . good talk."

"Yeah," Hudson agrees with that smile still on his face. "You going out?"

"Just for a quick walk."

"Okay, well, be safe."

Jace waves over his head as he heads out the front door. Taking a deep breath of fresh air, he decides to go left and wander around a little bit. About a half hour in, he's circled the large cleared out front yard about six times, and he's about ready to head in. He's had some time to think and get all the kinks out of his limbs over this time. Now all he needs is about eighteen hours of sleep, and he'll be good to go.

The cracking of a twig catches his attention, though. Turning towards the surrounding woods, he frowns when he can't see anything. Still, he feels the urge to check it out. If this were a horror movie he was watching, he'd be calling himself a dumbass for checking out the "suspicious noise in the distance," but here he is doing it anyway. He just hopes some big ass Sasquatch doesn't eat him.

"Hello? Anyone there?"

Yeah . . . He is so going to be gutted.

Suddenly, he's pinned face first against a nearby tree with his arm bent behind his back painfully. Okay, what the actual fuck is happening right now? Struggling to get out of the hold, the person presses his face harder into the sharp bark, and he decides to call a truce.

"Okay, okay, fuck. I'll be good."

Jace stumbles a little when he's suddenly let go, and he turns around to see a small figure nearby. They're half covered in darkness, but he can tell that they smell fucking rancid. Actually, he's pretty sure a giant mutant raccoon covered in its own piss just tackled him. Fighting the urge to take a chemical bath, he tries instead to take in his attacker.

"Who the hell are you?"

At his question, the person steps into the moonlight, and Jace feels like he just got smacked in the face with a brick. All rational thought goes out of his head as a tiny girl comes into view. The first thing that gets his attention is a pair of bright yellow eyes that slowly fade into a lighter color he can't distinguish in this lighting. Her dark hair is cropped short with random pieces sticking out here and there messily.

That's when he realizes how dirty she is. She's pale, he can tell that, but that's under all the dirt she's got rubbed all over her skin and clothes. She's dressed in a pair of baggy ill-fitting jeans held on with an oversized belt and a soiled white lace trimmed tank top. Oh, and she's barefoot.

"Where the hell did you come from?" Jace asks quietly, completely forgetting his ability to use an inner monologue.

She tilts her head to the side and frowns. "Who are you?"

Her small voice pulls at something in his chest, and in effect, his voice comes out hoarsely. "Uh, Jace. Who are you?"

"Mackenzie."

"Mackenzie, huh?" he murmurs and watches in fascination as she shivers. "Are you cold?"

She only shakes her head.

"Uh . . . Did you want to come inside?" he asks, and after looking at how skinny she is, he adds, "We have food."

He watches her eye widen at the idea of food, but she collects herself and shakes her head. "I'm not allowed."

"What? Why?"

She steps back, looking uneasy. "I have to go."

Jace is gripped with panic he can't describe. Something about this girl makes him want to take care of her. He wants to feed her, bathe her, and keep her close to him. It's a bizarre feeling. He's never felt this . . . protective about a girl outside of his family, especially one he doesn't even know. His next words spill out of his mouth before he can stop them as the panic only grows.

"No! Look, I'm sorry. I just . . . you look hungry. Everyone's asleep, it wouldn't be a bother. I'm a really good cook," he says with his most charming smile.

Her full lips pull up into a small smile, but she shakes her head. "I can't. I have to go."

309

"Will you be back?" he asks hopefully before wincing at how stupid he sounds.

She bites her lower lip in consideration before looking him in the eyes. "Yes, I'll be back, and when you see me, you better run."

"Run?" he repeats with a frown. "Why would I run?"

"Because I won't be coming alone."

Jace doesn't get to say anything else because before he can even let her words sink in, she's already gone. Jace runs a hand through his hair and runs it down his face with a sigh. Well, he thinks with a rueful laugh, that has to be one of the weirdest encounters of his life. But that doesn't stop him from having dreams about her that night, and until he sees her again, he's sure that won't be changing anytime soon.

CHAPTER THIRTY-THREE

Rae watches her brother disappear from sight and turns her full attention on Colton. She can see him barely through her blurry sore eyes, but his body language tells her all she needs to know. She's put him through a lot. As soon as that realization hits her, Rae drops her head into her hands and starts to cry again. She honestly doesn't know where she keeps getting the tears when this is all she's been doing since she's been in here. Yet here she is, crying again.

"I'm so s-sorry."

"Shh," Colton soothes as he rushes over and kneels on the floor in front of her. "Hey, it's okay."

"No, it's not," she says, curling her legs up against her chest. "I said horrible things to them and to you. They won't forgive me. I said I didn't need them. I pushed you away. I . . . I was so horrible to everyone."

Colton hesitantly reaches out to her before dropping his hand. "They'll forgive you, Rae. You've forgiven them for the times they've yelled at you or said horrible things. They'll do the same for you."

Rae notices that Colton is keeping his distance and frowns. He didn't mention himself forgiving her. Maybe he hasn't. She was so cruel to him, pushing him away like that. For the past two days, she's felt his misery, his guilt, and his shame, but didn't do anything about it.

At first, she locked herself away to grieve in private. First, she did it in her wolf form and then later in an actual room. Then she felt Hudson's emotions through the familial link and Colton's through their mate bond. After that, she was just ashamed. She had acted out of character and out of spite, not her usual way, but one she couldn't stop.

She knows it's wrong, what she said to her family and to Colton. The way she spoke to Jessica, her alpha female, was most likely a punishable offense. She didn't want to face the consequences of what she did, and that's what's kept her locked in this room until this moment. It's been her own self-disgust. How can she face the people she's hurt the most?

"This was different," she insists quietly at Colton's statement. "I snapped at them for the same thing they damned me for. I didn't tell them he was alive, and they didn't tell me he was . . . dead. How is it fair that I can act like that? I'm supposed to be the rational one. I'm supposed to be the strong one. How am I supposed to be strong when they've seen me be so weak?"

"You weren't weak."

"I let the situation get to me, Colton," she says, almost more to herself. "Rogues are coming for me, you said so yourself. My dad practically sold me to them because of his alpha's orders, and now he's dead. He taught me everything I know. Before mom died, we were so close, even after I first shifted. He treated me like I was strong, and it was his belief in me that made me think I really was. Now . . . I don't know what I am anymore."

"You're my mate, Rae."

Rae sighs. "Colton—"

"No, listen to me," Colton demands, surprising her a little. "You are my mate, but you're also more than that. You have raised those kids on your own since you were sixteen. You have kept their bellies full and their feet planted on the ground. You have done things and experienced things I can't even imagine, but you've survived it all. Do you understand me? You don't need your dad to know you're strong."

"Then what do I need?" she asks, looking him right in the eyes.

"You don't need anyone but yourself, Rae."

Rae drops her forehead to her knees and feels more tears fall down from her eyes. How many times had she wished someone had told her that before? How many times did she want someone to approve of her? How many times did she wish she didn't need that approval? She can feel his hand hovering over her, but he drops it again.

Lifting her head, she really looks at Colton for the first time since he's come in here. It's dark in the room, but the light from the open doorway has illuminated half of his face. Dark circles and bags sit under his dark blue, almost gray eyes from his lack of sleep. He looks pale, much too pale to be healthy and a little gaunt. How long has it been since he's eaten? Most likely as long as it's been for her, she thinks with guilt. She should have known better than to put him through this. He must hate her for torturing him like this.

"Colton, you haven't said anything about you yet," she says with a sniffle.

His light brown eyebrows pull together. "What about me?"

"Do you forgive me?"

Colton drops his head and lets out a frustrated sigh. "You have nothing to be sorry for, Rae. Especially concerning me. We kept the truth from you because we didn't want to face what it would do to you. You spent years taking care of him. You did everything you could to keep him alive. No one would blame you for grieving for him."

"I knew he was going to die," she whispers. "I knew he was going to die. I'd prepared myself for it so many times to go out there and find him dead. I was so sure it would happen right before my eyes but when Jessica told me . . . it felt like nothing like I thought I was prepared for. God, and the things I said to them, Colton. How are they going to forget what I said to them?"

"As far as I know, they already have," he tells her. "They're just worried about you, Rae."

"They shouldn't be."

Colton rams his fists into the bed on either side of her, making Rae's eyes widen double their size. Lifting his head, Colton glares at her. "Stop fucking talking like that. Of course, we care about you. Of course, we worry. We love you, Rae! All of us, even the pack has been worried sick about you! Don't you understand what you mean to this pack, to your family, and even me? Don't you get it?"

"I-I just . . ."

"Jace said you were stubborn, and I knew that already but god, this is getting ridiculous."

"I'm sorry."

"And stop apologizing," he grumbles, already more calmed down. "I told you that I don't need an apology."

Rae watches him for a few minutes, waiting for him to completely calm down. She's never seen him that riled up, other than back at Kendrick's office. He's always seemed so level-headed that it's borderline frightening to see him like this. Once she's sure that he's okay, she lowers her head, hoping to catch his eye. When she does, she drops her legs in front of her and moves closer to the edge of the bed.

"Do you really forgive me?"

"Rae—"

"Please, just humor me on this," she says quickly, cutting him off. "Do you?"

"Of course, I do."

Taking a deep breath, she leans forward and gives him a light but solid kiss on the lips. Colton reacts immediately. His arms wrap around her waist before pulling her off the bed, so she's seated in his lap as he sits back. With her legs wrapped around his waist, he adjusts her so they're chest to chest. He doesn't deepen the kiss, and she's not complaining. She's sure both of them have neglected to brush their teeth for a few days so a make-out session wouldn't be a good idea. Rae doesn't need more than this, though.

She just wants to be held.

"I'm sorry," Colton whispers as he lays his forehead against hers.

Rae frowns at him. "For what?"

"Not telling you."

"It's okay, I—"

"No, it's not okay," he says fiercely, cutting her off. "I made a promise to myself when you accepted me that I would never lie to you. I broke my own promise, but I'm going to win your trust back, Rae. I swear I will. No matter what it takes, I'll do whatever you need."

"You don't have to do this."

"Yes, I do."

Tilting her head Rae asks, "Why?"

"Because I don't want there to be anything between us. You're going to be by my side the rest of my life, Rae. Not behind me, but beside me as my equal, and you deserve to know everything I know. We can't function as alphas of this pack or as a couple if we don't have trust in each other."

Rae gives him another short but satisfying kiss before pulling back. "Thank you."

"Nothing to thank," he says, rubbing the tip of his nose against her. "But I do have a favor to ask."

"What?"

"Can we get some food? I'm starving."

Rae laughs for the second time in two days. "Yes. Yes, we can."

* * *

The next morning, Rae wakes up to the sunshine and chirping birds outside her window. Colton is beside her in their bed with his arm draped over her middle, and his face buried in her neck. She smiles a little at the feel of having him so near when for days she's been depriving not only herself, but him as well. Her wolf growls at the reminder in Rae's head, but she simply rolls her eyes at it.

She's had to listen to her bitching enough as it is.

Pushing her upper body upright, she feels Colton's arm tighten around her and smiles down at him widely. She figured this wouldn't be an easy escape, but one she needs to attempt anyway. Trying to be as gentle as she can manage, she pries Colton's arm off of her and places it over her pillow. It carries her scent enough that it would keep his wolf off her trail for a little while.

Getting out of the bed slowly, Colton's phone on the side table catches her attention. She wonders what time it is and gasps when she realizes that they've been asleep for a whole day. It's not the next morning anymore, it's the morning after that morning. Rae frowns at the string of thought, does that even make sense? Shaking her head, she puts down his charging phone and heads quietly towards the bedroom door.

Slowly shutting it behind her, she sighs with relief when she doesn't hear him stir. Looking both ways down the hallway, Rae runs a hand through her hair and gets it caught in one monster of a knot. She grunts a little as she tries to free her fingers but instead pulls a few strands from her scalp. Shaking the loose hair free from her hands, she heads for the door at the end of the hallway.

Slowly cracking open the door, she sees Poppy and Cassidy asleep in their twin beds and feels her stomach twist with remorse. She should have come out sooner for their sake, at the very least. Moving over to Cassidy's bed, Rae sits on the edge and lightly pets her sister's messy dark blonde hair. This has been a ritual in the Applebee home since Rae was little.

316

Every birthday, her mom would come into her room early in the morning, wake her up, and tell her the story of how she was born. As more siblings came, the ritual became more like a mini-party with the older siblings adding in their recollections as well. It's something Rae has kept alive, especially with the younger girls, too little to remember what it was like when their mom would do it.

Cassidy's dark brown eyes suddenly start to blink open and widen when they land on Rae. Without a word, the now seven-year-old tackles Rae into a hug. Hanging on to her like a spider monkey, Cassidy lays kisses all over Rae's face, making Rae laugh quietly. Pulling back a little, Rae grins at her baby sister and brushes back some unruly curls from her face.

"Hey, baby girl," Rae whispers.

"Poppy said you were sick," Cassidy whispers back with a pout.

"I was," Rae says with a sad smile as she locks her hands behind Cassidy's back. "But I'm feeling better now."

Cassidy runs her tiny fingers under Rae's eyes. "You look sleepy."

"Do I? Well, you look like a beautiful princess on your special day."

Cassidy grins widely. "I do?"

"Yup. A beautiful, smart, wise ruler of a castle that has more sparkly vampire suitors then you can handle."

"I don't want a suit, Rae, I want a pony."

Rae smiles at her sister's misunderstanding before asking, "A pony? No more boys?"

Cassidy shakes her head and makes a face. "Boys are gross."

"Since when?"

"Since Connor threw mud at her," Poppy's very awake voice says smartly.

Rae looks over at Poppy and lifts a brow. "Who's Connor?"

317

"One of the boys here. He's eight."

"And he threw mud at you?" Rae asks Cassidy who nods. "What did you do?"

"She kicked him in the knee," Poppy says with a laugh.

Rae laughs too and smiles at Cassidy. "You did?"

Cassidy crosses her arms over her chest and nods once. "He was mean."

"Well, I should be telling you not to hit other people, but since he started it . . ." Rae trails before raising a hand up. "High-five."

Cassidy slaps Rae's hand and grins proudly.

"Now," Rae says as she shifts them to sit at the top of the bed. "Shall we get to the story?"

"Yes!" Cassidy cheers. "I love the story!"

"Of course you do," Poppy says with an eye roll as she puts on her glasses. "It has you in it."

"You have to be nice to me, Poppy. It's my birthday! Right, Rae?"

Rae nods seriously. "Right. Now come over here and listen to the story, Poppy."

Poppy comes over to sit on the edge of the bed with an over dramatic huff, but Rae can see the anticipation in her eyes. She likes this just as much as Cassidy does. Even the ever-macho Jace likes the morning story no matter how much he pretends to hate it. Sitting back against the headboard, Rae cuddles Cassidy against her side and closes her eyes.

"It was a Wednesday," she begins. "The day was rainy and gray, but mom didn't let it stop her from having all the windows open in the house. She liked to listen to the rain. That was when—"

The door opening has Rae stopping mid-sentence and opening her eyes to see Hudson coming into the room. His brown eyes widen at the sight of Rae out of her room, but he quickly collects himself. Stuffing his hands in the pockets of his unzipped hoodie, he looks down at his feet.

318

"Um, can I join?"

Rae gives him a small smile. "Of course, you can. Hop on in."

He looks surprised again, but comes to sit next to Poppy at the end of the bed.

Closing her eyes, Rae continues with the story, "That was when you gave a huge kick right under her left rib. Mom was so surprised by it, her water broke right then and there all over Grandma Applebee's prized antique rug. Mom knew she had some time before you'd really start to come into the world, so she tried to clean the rug. She knew Grandma Applebee gave the rug to mom and dad as a wedding gift, and she couldn't stand the idea of it being ruined. So she—"

"Oh!"

Rae looks up to see Cleo and Jace standing in the doorway with matching wide blue eyes. Cleo's start to brim with tears the longer she looks at Rae, but Jace just smirks at her. Rae returns his smile with one of her own before waving for them both to join them. Of course, the room on Cassidy's bed is getting slim, so they both move to sit on Poppy's bed instead.

"Where was I?" Rae asks Cassidy as they both settle into their spots.

"The rug," Poppy replies when Cassidy shrugs while playing with a piece of Rae's hair. "Mom was sad about the rug."

"Ah yes, the rug. Well, mom was almost in tears over the rug, so she tried to clean it. Dad came home for lunch, and that's how he found mom who was standing ankle deep in soapy water, crying, and trying to wash out the rug. When he asked her what happened, she told him her water broke. He picked her up right there and carried her straight to the car in the rain."

"Aunt Jojo had to pick us up from school," Jace adds in with a smile. "She was half out of her mind."

"Why?" Cassidy asks with a scrunched up nose.

Jace shrugs. "Because Jojo is always half out of her mind."

319

"Oh," Cassidy says with a nod. "Then what happened?"

"Well, you were so excited to meet us you came out in two hours flat," Rae says with an exaggeratedly excited expression. "You wouldn't cry either. The doctor had to smack your butt, and when he did, you peed on him."

"Ew!" Poppy and Cassidy exclaim in synch.

"Dad didn't think so," Hudson says with a grin. "He cracked up every time he told the story."

All of her three older younger siblings' eyes fall to Rae as soon as their dad is mentioned but she just nods. "He did, and for the first year of your life, dad called you his 'little sprinkler'."

Jace, Cleo, and Hudson all visibly relax into laughter, and Rae feels bad for making them that uncomfortable. Pushing past the feeling, she continues with the story, "When we got to the hospital, mom was holding you and dad looked so proud. I got to hold you first, though, and you opened up your big brown eyes to stare at me. I knew you were my favorite sibling ever since then."

"Hey!" All four of her other siblings yell at the same time.

Rae just shrugs with a smile. "What? You know you all come in at a strong second in my sibling affections."

The rest of the morning is full of laughter and funny stories. It's a bittersweet feeling for Rae as it is every year when one of her siblings has a birthday. Their mother is gone, and now their father as well. All they have now is each other and Rae swears to herself that she'll keep them safe. Come rogue, crazy alpha, or even a damn war. Rae will keep them safe no matter what it may cost her.

CHAPTER THIRTY-FOUR

"Again!"

Rae looks over at her baby sister and can't stop the laugh that bubbles out of her mouth. She can't help it. Cassidy just looks so cute! All the girls got her ready this morning for her big day with Cassidy picking out everything, and Rae is unsurprised with her choices; blue fairy wings on her back, a bright pink dress with four tulle skirts underneath to make it really poor, and mismatched striped knee-high toes socks. This ensemble, of course, is topped with a little plastic crown pushed into the root of the messy blonde bun on the top of her head.

She looks adorable and utterly Cassidy.

"I can only flip the pancake so many times, kiddo," Jace tells her with an eye roll.

"Just one more time?" Cassidy begs, adding in an extra flutter of her eyelashes.

Jace purses his lips before sighing heavily. "Fine."

Cassidy grins and claps her hands excitedly before turning to Rae. "Am I going to have a party?"

Rae stops short and glances up at Jace who gives her a subtle nod. Turning her attention back to Cassidy, she puts on a huge smile. "Of course you do, princess."

"Really? Will there be cake? What about a pony? I told you how much I like ponies right? I rode one of Jessica's ponies, and it was so pretty and big! Jessica even let me feed it. You have to keep your palm like this. Rae? Do you see? This is how you feed a pony, or it'll bite you! Poppy was scared, but I wasn't scared. Rae! Look!"

"I see," Rae assures her, just trying to get the poor girl to take a breath. "You were very brave, and I'm sure if the ponies aren't at the party, we can go see them later."

Cassidy blinks innocently at her from her spot on the breakfast bar. "But you can't come, Rae. You'll scare them."

Rae arches a brow. "I'm sure someone who won't scare the ponies will be able to take you. You're the birthday girl, I'm sure no one can say no to the birthday girl."

"Really?"

"Really, really."

"Yay!"

Rae flinches back at Cassidy's sheer volume before she feels Colton and his wolf stirring down their mate bond. Sitting up a bit straighter in her seat, she smiles a little as she stares blankly at a cabinet across the way. This is only her second time using the bond, but she already feels so connected to him that it feels like she's done it a million times. As his panic begins to build, though, she realizes how worried he really is about the approaching threat the rogues present.

Mentally, she adds that to her checklist of things to talk to him about.

Calm down. I'm fine.

Where are you? he demands, making her roll her eyes.

"If you're so concerned, then come and find me. Here's a hint, I'm in the house."

He doesn't say anything for a second, but when he does, he sounds relieved, *Downstairs, huh?*

She scowls at the cabinet. *"Don't dig in my head for answers! That's cheating!"*

It wasn't stipulated in the rules that I couldn't, he says with a smile in his voice.

Rae huffs a laugh. *Just get your nice-looking ass down here. It's my sister's birthday.*

I know.

How did you know?

I'm Beta, I know everything.

And with that, he shuts off the mind-link.

Butthead.

Tuning back into her surroundings, Rae realizes all of her siblings are staring at her weirdly. Her face immediately begins to heat up, and she realizes how much like a crazy person she must seem. Just sitting here scoffing and scowling without a reason apparent to anyone else in the room.

"What?" she snaps with a frown.

Poppy responds first with a question of her own, "What were you doing?"

"Talking to Colton."

Cassidy leans forward and gets mere centimeters from Rae's face. "Do you have a saddle light in your head?"

"A what?"

"You mean *satellite*," Poppy corrects her with an eye roll before looking right at Rae again. "Is it that mind link thing?"

Rae lifts a brow. "Who told you about that?"

Cleo raises a hand. "Guilty as charged on that one."

"And that subject came up how?" Rae asks while crossing her arms over her chest.

Cleo shrugs. "I was asking Andy why I could hear his voice in my head. Mom and dad never talked about it, you know, and he said it was the mate bond. He can hear my thoughts as clear as a bell since he marked me, but I can only see impressions or hear passing thoughts. It's weird."

"Let me guess," Rae says as she turns back to Poppy. "You were eavesdropping?"

Poppy just gives her a wicked grin. "Guilty."

"I was going to ask you about that," Hudson says as he comes around to stand on the other side of Rae. "Will it get clearer or will it always be such a mess? I can hear everything Joseph is thinking even if I don't want to."

"Wait a second here," Rae says throwing her hands up before staring at Hudson wide-eyed. "You marked him?"

Hudson's smile is sheepish. "Guilty."

"I haven't even met him yet!"

"You will!" Hudson assures her quickly. "You'll like him. I know you will."

"Whatever happened to waiting anymore?" Rae grumbles as she drops her head into her hands.

"Well, we can't all be prudes like you," Cleo sings as she looks at her nails. "How long did it take you to let him mark you? Like a month?"

"A week, maybe a week and a half," Rae admits with a mumble. "But that's not the point. The point is at least I let him meet you first!"

"You were just delaying the inevitable, and we all know it," Cleo says smartly. "And we *all* know it."

"I was not."

"You were," Cleo responds simply.

"I was not!"

"You were," Jace and Hudson agree in unison.

"I hate all of you, and I denounce you as my siblings. Poppy and Cassidy, you are now my only sisters, and you shall be taught loyalty."

"Can we at least keep Jace?" Poppy asks before smiling widely. "He cooks."

"I can cook," Rae responds stubbornly.

"No, sis, you burn," Jace says before slipping another perfect pancake with his spatula. "There's a difference."

"Says you."

Jace snorts a laugh. "Says anyone who's had your cooking."

324

"Oh shut up, maple syrup, we all know what an ace you are in the kitchen. No need to rub it in our faces."

Jace's face goes red from the old nickname and Cassidy scrunches up her nose as she leans towards Jace to sniff him. "He doesn't smell like maple syrup. He smells like that good smelly spray."

"Damn right I do," Jace says with a nod as he places the newest pancake on top of the already huge pile.

"Anyway," Rae says with some stress in her tone before turning to Hudson. "When did this whole marking thing go down?"

"When you were . . . uh, sick."

Rae's expression falls. "Oh."

"Rae, we just wanted to say that we are so—"

Rae shakes her head and smiles at Cleo, cutting her off. "You don't have to be sorry. I said some awful things."

"Yeah, but we were straight up . . ." Cleo trails off and glances at Cassidy's expectant face before continuing, ". . . butt faces, and we know we should have told you as soon as it happened. It was a big . . . mess up on our part not to. We feel awful. Right, guys?"

"Right." Hudson nods while Jace doesn't say anything.

He doesn't have to, as far as Rae is concerned. They already mended their fence.

"We wouldn't even fault you if you wanted to call us every bad name in the book," Cleo continues despite a short glare in Jace's direction. "I mean, I've said so many awful things to you that it'd be only fair that you say something like that to me."

"I'm not going to call you names, Cleo," Rae says flatly. "We're not in elementary school."

"I am!" Cassidy says loudly.

"We know," Poppy drawls with an eye roll.

"The point is," Rae says with a little laugh. "It would be kind of hypocritical of me to be mad when I kind of did the same things to you, wouldn't it?"

"Not really," Cleo says with a shrug. "I mean you did it to protect us. He was straight up feral, and as you can see, we are idiots." Cleo accentuates the point by holding up her still healing arm and pointing to Jace's chest. "So it was for our best. We didn't tell you because we're selfish. Totally different situation."

"Cleo . . ."

"Just say you forgive us and we'll drop it," Hudson pleads. "We've felt awful the past few days."

"Yeah, forgive us," Cassidy says with a pout.

Rae frowns at the birthday girl deeply. "What am I forgiving you for?"

"Um . . . for taking so long in the bathroom?" Cassidy answers innocently.

Rae palms her face with a short laugh before lifting her head to smile widely at her sister. "Okay, you are forgiven. Everyone is forgiven, and now we shall never talk about it again as long as we all shall live."

"But that's a long time." Cassidy whines as she drops her head onto Rae's shoulder. "I can't wait that long."

"You'll live," Rae says flatly before pushing Cassidy lightly off her and towards the plate of pancakes Jace just placed beside her. "Now look what Jace made you."

"They're so pretty!" Cassidy yells as she takes in the four syrup dosed pancakes with sprinkles on the tip and a square of butter. "Can I eat them?"

"Well, that or give them to me because I'm terribly hungry," Cleo says, rubbing her stomach for extra effect.

Cassidy stares at her blankly until Cleo tries to reach for her. With a scream, Cassidy takes the plate and starts stuffing her face. She grins at Rae, mouth full and a few teeth missing, making Rae want to laugh. Secretly, Rae hopes Cassidy never loses her bizarre personality. It's good to have an eccentric in the family.

"What smells so good?"

All six siblings turn to see a shirtless Colton come strutting into the kitchen with a lazy smile on his face. Rae's eyes look over every visible bit of skin hungrily before meeting his eyes. The dark blue flashes yellow for a second, telling her that he knows exactly where her thoughts are. Rae's wolf growls lustfully in her head, and she bites her lower lip to stop it from escaping her own mouth.

Now is so not the time.

"Colton!" Cassidy cheers, mouth still full when she sees him. "It's my birthday!"

"I heard." He grins before coming over to ruffle her hair. "Happy birthday, munchkin."

"You messed up my crown!"

"Still look beautiful, though," Colton tells her before his eyes move over to Rae and winks at her.

Cassidy isn't buying it though and crosses her arms over her tiny chest. "Did you get me a gift?"

"You bet."

"Is it pretty?"

"Very pretty."

"Does it sparkle?"

"Maybe."

"Can I have it now?" Cassidy asks hopefully, fluttering her eyelashes.

Colton smirks a little but shakes his head. "Nope."

"Rae!" She gasps before pointing to Colton. "He's mean!"

Rae rolls her eyes. "No, he's not. Not everyone who doesn't give you what you want is mean."

Cassidy blinks her large brown eyes. "Yes, they are."

"Oh my god," Rae mutters before laughing lowly. Lifting her head, she sees Colton watching her closely and doesn't need to read his mind to know why. "Stop looking at me like that. I'm fine."

"Are you sure?"

327

"Positive," Rae says simply before looking over at Cleo. "What is the theme for the party?"

"What do you think? Princesses, of course!"

"Does that mean we have to dress up?" Rae asks dismally.

"Since I found a box outside my door this morning with a surprisingly not hideous dress in it, I'm assuming so."

Rae frowns. "I didn't get a dress this morning."

Colton clears his throat. "That's because I've had it hanging in the closet since the night before. Mom dropped it off just in case you were... feeling better."

"Oh," Rae says in surprise. "Well, that's good . . . I guess."

A silence settles in the atmosphere of the kitchen before Jace suddenly cuts in with the most vital question ever uttered.

"Pancakes?"

* * *

Rae studies herself in the bathroom mirror and pulls at the shoulders of her dress again, trying to get used to them. The dress itself is actually really pretty, but that doesn't help the fact that it is indeed a dress. She dealt with wearing a dress to the acceptance ceremony thinking she would have a bit of a reprieve before having to do it again. She was wrong.

It's a sapphire blue satin dress with black roses and birds patterned on the fabric and off the shoulder sleeves. It fits her perfectly with the hem ending just below her knee with some black lace trim. It looks nice on her, she can admit that, but she looks at the occupying shoes with distrust; Black stiletto heels sitting on the toilet bowl mocking her.

Three knocks on the door have her looking away from the shoes and opening the door to see Colton on the other side. She gasps lightly at how good he looks. Dark washed jeans and a black button-up shirt that only seems to make his eyes look even darker than normal. Or maybe that's just his pupils dilating as he takes his sweet time taking in her attire.

"Does it look stupid?" she asks with a wince.

He shakes his head and silently walks towards her. She barely has time to ask what he's doing before he pushes her up against the nearest wall, and his lips press against hers. Rae is more than a little surprised by how hurried and insistent his kisses are. When he suddenly dips down to lift her, she even lets out a squeal against his mouth as he grips her ass under her dress.

"C-Colton, what—"

"You look so beautiful," he growls before kissing her again.

Rae melts a little into this kiss as he deepens it and wraps her arms around his neck. Then the sound of her sisters' laughter as they run down the hall get her back some of her senses. Pulling back from him, Rae tries to catch her breath while also trying to reclaim the ability to form words. Colton busies himself with running his nose up and down the side of her neck, which is distracting on a level all its own.

"We need to head down," Rae says unsteadily when he begins laying light kisses on her mark.

"We could," He says lowly. "Or we could do this. Three guesses on which one I would prefer."

"I don't have to guess." She laughs breathlessly before pulling back as far as she can to look down at him. "But as much as I'd like to, we can't. We have to head down."

Colton drops his head on her chest with a groan. "Do we have to?"

"It's my sister's party, so yes."

"She won't mind if we're late."

"She will, and you know she will."

He just groans again, making her laugh.

"Poor baby," she coos and pets his still damp hair.

"Will you make it up to me?" he asks, lifting his head to look her right in the eye.

329

"What are you suggesting?"

His cheeks go a little pink, and he shrugs. "Just . . . an idea."

Rae bites her lower lip before kissing him quickly on the mouth. "We'll see."

Sliding back down to her bare feet, Rae pulls away from him. She laughs a little at the stunned look on his face before beginning to walk away. She makes it out of the bathroom completely before he comes running after her and grabs her by the waist to stop her from leaving.

"So that's not a 'no,' right?"

"Not a 'no'." she confirms.

He frowns a little. "But not a 'yes'?"

"Not a 'yes'," she repeats with a small smile before adding. "More like a maybe with high probability."

His smile goes goofy, and Rae uses the opportunity to pull away from him. She opens the door and is about to step out when Colton speaks up again.

"Aren't you forgetting your shoes?" he asks, pointing to the bathroom where the devil shoes are sitting.

"Are you kidding?" she asks with a smirk. "This is a Cassidy party."

CHAPTER THIRTY-FIVE

As Colton makes his way towards the activity center where Cassidy's party is being held, he feels Rae nibble on his ear lobe. His footsteps slow down considerably, and he finds his breathing become more and more labored. She stops biting him only to giggle in his ear, and he realizes her asking for him to carry her on his back was most likely a ploy to drive him insane.

"You're pushing your luck," he warns her a little breathlessly.

She balances her chin on his shoulder and lets out another impish laugh. "Am I?"

"Yes, and if you keep doing that, we'll never get there."

Rae lets out a heavy sigh, but he can sense her smile. "Well then I better behave myself, shouldn't I?"

"Well, I didn't say that."

Rae laughs again but doesn't respond. A smile spreads across his face at the sound of her laughter. It's a relief if he's honest. He has thought she'd be miserable even after they got her out of that room, but she's only made his pride in her grow at how quickly she's bounced back. She'll be an amazing alpha female, and he can't wait to see her in action when she takes over the role.

She's already an alpha female as far as he's concerned anyway.

The activity center holds tons of the pack's events. Pack meetings, training, school activities, and even extracurricular stuff like dancing. Colton clenches his hands into fists at the idea of dancing. He's a horrible dancer, despite Vivienne on many occasions attempting to teach him. He has no rhythm and more often than not makes a fool of himself.

Glancing over at Rae's face on his shoulder, he silently prays she doesn't ask him to dance with her. He doesn't know if Sawyer will survive if his older brother tries to get him shit about it again. Sawyer got away with only a broken bone last time, and that was because Vivienne stepped in. Colton knows better than to mess with her. She doesn't play fair, and in her wolf form, Vivienne is way faster than Colton despite any brawn he may have over her.

Colton carries Rae the rest of the way into the building and hears her surprised gasp in his ear. All twenty of the kids of the pack are running around in the center of the room while the rest of the pack, meaning the teenagers and adults stand around the perimeter of the room. A large disco ball is hanging over the dance floor, and that's where Colton spots Cassidy, spinning in a circle while staring up at it.

Rae slides off his back and runs up to Cassidy to grab her up in her arms. Colton watches the two of them with a smile on his face. Rae starts to spin Cassidy in her arms and the birthday girl lets out a happy laugh as she puts her arms out. The image of Rae doing that with their own child comes to mind, and the thought steals his breath away.

He wants that. He wants that with Rae much more than he thought he would. Up to this point, in fact, he has never thought he'd want kids. He couldn't relate to them on any level. Then he met Rae's sisters. Cassidy only had to ask one adorable question to have him wrapped around her finger. Poppy, on the other hand, he feels like he understands. She's serious and sarcastic with a fierce loyalty that he was initially surprised to see in one so young. If any of their kids are like those two, he thinks he'd be a lucky man.

"She seems better."

Colton turns to see Jace standing beside him and watching his sisters with a slight smile. Colton turns his attention back to the scene and nods. "She is. All she needed was a shower, some food, and whatever happened this morning before I came down."

"She still thinks we hate her?"

"No," Colton says with a sigh. "But she thinks you should."

Jace scoffs and shakes his head. "She's too altruistic for her own good sometimes."

Colton lifts an eyebrow, making Jace scowl at him. "What? I know words."

"Never said you didn't," Colton says innocently before looking at Rae again. A song comes on over the loudspeakers. It's incredibly catchy and highly annoying, making both men grimace.

"Who the hell is the DJ at this thing?" Jace complains.

Colton nods towards one of the preteen girls messing with the stereo system. "Looks like it's party goers' choice."

"Ugh."

"Are you two actually going to just stand here all day and complain the whole time?" Cleo says as she walks towards the two in a green lace party dress. "I mean, come on, how stereotypical of you."

"Cleo," Colton greets stiffly, still not her biggest fan.

Cleo rolls her eyes and crosses her arms over her chest. "Listen, Colton, I'm with Andy, your best friend, and you're screwing my sister. Let's at least pretend that we like each other for their sake."

"I'm not *screwing* your sister," Colton growls. He does not like her wording at all.

"We're all adults here, Colton. I'm just calling a spade a spade."

"Cleo." Jace sighs, kneading his forehead. "Go be annoying somewhere else."

Cleo grins and comes over to ruffle Jace's hair. "I could, but then you'd be missing out on all the fun, little brother."

Jace swats her hands away. "Touch me again and lose the hands."

"Oh," she says with mock fright. "I'm *so* scared."

"Baby?" Andy calls as he comes to join the group. "Your sister wants you."

"Which one?"

"Uh . . . Poppy, I think?" Andy says with an apologetic shrug.

Rolling her perfectly lined eyes, Cleo goes up on her toes and kisses Andy's cheek before walking away. Colton notices that she's not wearing shoes either and frowns. What is it with them not wearing shoes?

"It's a Cassidy law," Jace enlightens him as he follows Colton's gaze. "She doesn't like shoes and since it's her birthday . . ."

"But you're wearing shoes," Colton comments before gesturing to the black converse on Jace's feet.

"Yeah, well, I was her pony today, so I got a pass."

Colton shakes his head with a grin before turning to Andy. "Hey, man."

"Hey man yourself," Andy greets with a grin.

Colton pats his friend's shoulder. "I gotta be honest with you, man. I'm not sure whether to give you condolences or congratulate you on your mate pairing."

Andy shrugs and takes a sip of beer from a pink solo cup. "I'm happy and definitely not complaining, so I guess I don't need either."

"She doesn't drive you insane?" Jace asks flatly.

Andy chuckles while shaking his head. "Not at all. She's smart and calls me out on my shit. I like that."

Colton eyes the wide grin on Andy's face speculatively. "You said you were waiting, right?"

"Yeah. Joint decision. I don't want her to feel like I want her only for sex, and she wants to get to know me first. She isn't just some one-night screw, so I don't intend on treating her like one."

"Dude!" Jace snaps, covering his ears. "That's my sister!"

"Oh, grow up."

Colton pats Andy's shoulder again, feeling more pleased with the situation. "Well, again, good luck."

Andy watches Cleo across the room talking to Poppy with a small smile on his face. "Thanks, but I don't think I'll need it."

Out of the corner of his eye, Colton sees Hudson and Joseph pass the group. Colton likes Joseph as it happens. He's younger than Colton but Joseph's mom and Colton's mom are friends, so they know each other on a friendly basis. He's just glad Hudson was paired with someone closer to his age. Sometimes, the age gaps can cause disciplinary issues for older mates who don't think they should have to wait. It may be a private matter, but when rights aren't respected, Colton has no problem stepping in to handle it.

"Whoa, there," Jace says as he grabs Hudson by the collar to stop him from walking away any farther. "Where do you think you're going?"

Hudson frowns as he takes in the line of men in. "To say happy birthday to my sister?"

"Don't you want to introduce us to your boyfriend?" Jace asks with a glare at the boyfriend in question. "I don't think I've been formally introduced."

"Uh, right. Joseph, this is my brother, Jace. Jace, this is my boyfriend and mate, Joseph."

Joseph waves at him with a slight smile. "Hi."

"Okay, this has been fun," Hudson says with red cheeks. "See you!"

Jace tightens his hold on his brother's collar, keeping Hudson still as Jace gives a threatening smile to Joseph. "I assume

335

he told you who I am and what I'm about from the way he's trying to scurry off."

"He may have mentioned it," Joseph says with humor in his hazel eyes.

"Then you know that if you mess with him in any way I don't like, I'll break your nose and both your legs without breaking a sweat, right?"

Colton notices Joseph trying really hard not smile. "I'm aware."

"Good," Jace says lowly before letting go of Hudson's collar. "I suggest you keep that in mind."

"Will do." Joseph nods before grabbing Hudson's hand. "Come on, I want to meet this adorable little sister of yours."

Both boys walk away, and Colton smirks at Jace. "Real smooth."

The younger man shrugs. "What? It's only fair they know where they stand with me."

"Right."

"Colton!"

Colton turns back just in time for a tiny body to jump into his arms. He holds Cassidy up, and she wraps her legs around him and kisses him all over the face, surprising him. She leans back and gives him a huge grin, missing baby teeth and all.

"This is the best party ever!"

"I'm glad you're enjoying it." He smiles.

Rae comes to stand beside them. "Your mom said this was all your idea."

"Wait, you talked to my mom. Are you—?"

"I'm fine," she assures him with a patient smile and an eye roll. "We worked everything out. I don't blame her for anything no matter how much she apologizes. It's you who needs to make it up to her."

He frowns. "What do you mean?"

"You know what I mean," she says with a little glare before changing the subject. "You've done a wonderful job with everything. Maybe you should be planning all the parties around here."

Colton shrugs, but his neck gets warm with a blush. "I just told my mom what Cassidy liked. I didn't actually do anything."

Rae leans up and kisses his cheek. "Well, thank you all the same."

"Colton, what's the difference between a raven and a writing desk?"

Colton frowns at the tiny person in his arms. "Uh . . . I don't know. What's the difference?"

Cassidy smiles widely at him. "I don't have the slightest idea."

Rae reaches up and brushes a few tendrils of loose hair from Cassidy's face. "She's been stumping everyone with that one. It's driving Sawyer crazy."

"It's okay to be mad," Cassidy says smartly. "All the best people are."

"Is she quoting something?"

Rae rolls her brown eyes. "*Alice in Wonderland.*"

"I want to be the Mad Hatter when I grow up."

Colton tilts his head. "Wouldn't you rather be Alice?"

"No."

Okay then.

Colton's attention is taken off of Cassidy when an alert comes down the pack mind-link. All the shifter adults and even some of the teens go stiff as does Rae and Andy beside him. A rogue has been spotted by the west border trying to break into the territory by one of the sentries. Colton lets out a growl and feels Cassidy jump in his arms at the sound. Giving her to Jace, Colton grabs Rae's hand and starts dragging her towards the exit.

"Do you think—?"

"Yes," he snaps, cutting her off and tightening his hold on her hand. Stopping mid-step, he turns around and faces her. "Do you want to come or stay here?"

"I want to come," she says, immediately making him smile.

She really will make an amazing alpha female.

Turning to Andy who's following behind Rae, he gives him his orders. "Stay here with five shifters of your choice watching the perimeter. I don't want this to be some kind of distraction so there can be a more direct attack."

"Yes, Beta."

"And make sure everyone stays in the building. Wandering guests make the best targets."

Andy bows his head at him, no longer his friend, but his subordinate. "Beta."

Colton grasps Rae's hand tighter and leads her out of the building with five more people following them out. The rest stay behind inside the building and keep an eye on things there while Andy starts to follow through with his orders. Colton isn't himself anymore; he's in leadership mode. In his head, he's barking orders to anyone who's dealing with the captured Rogue.

They got close, too close for comfort.

"How many is it?" Rae asks after a while.

Colton sighs. "Just one, but they got much closer than we thought they could."

"How close?"

"Too close."

Rae doesn't respond, but he can feel her anxiety. Opening up the mind link, he sees Rae's thoughts are on her siblings' safety, particularly Poppy and Cassidy. Their father trained the older siblings on how to defend themselves well enough that she doesn't worry as much. Colton feels himself relax marginally at that realization. He may have been a shit father, but he can say one thing for the man, he was smart enough to actually take the time to train his kids.

When Colton spots a group only two miles from the activity center, he feels his anger begin to grow. It's unacceptable that a rogue was able to get that close, let alone that close to the children. Rae's hand tightens around his, and he manages to reel in his anger a bit. He needs to keep an even head if he's going to get to the bottom of this. Narrowing his eyes on the thin stringy wolf pinned by one of his shifted sentries, Colton feels his anger begin to boil over.

Glancing at his dad, Colton silently asks for permission to take control of the situation. Dalton nods his head and takes a few steps back, so everyone else is aware of Colton's control. It's his right as Rae's mate to take control since it is her that these pieces of shit are trying to get at. He's just relieved his dad didn't take it as a sign of Colton's challenge.

Colton isn't ready to be alpha just yet.

Coming back to the situation at hand, Colton curls his lip up in a snarl. "Shift."

When the rogue doesn't immediately do as commanded, Colton nods at the one pinning him, Paul. Paul tightens his bite on the rogue's neck, and the rogue lets out a high-pitched whine. Colton lets go of Rae's hand and steps forward so he's able to stare the rogue in the eye.

"Shift!"

The rogue closes their eyes, and Colton sees their body begin to shake. Paul lets the shifting body fall limply from his jaws and steps back as Colton keeps his body coiled to strike if needed. The skinny wolf turns into a skinny, dirty man. Colton curls his lip up in disgust at the foul scent of him.

"Get him some clothes," Colton orders no one in particular.

It's Vivienne who comes back to the group a minute later with some clothes in her hands and tosses them at the rogue. No one says anything as the rogue pulls on the loose basketball shorts to cover himself from the chill of the autumn air. Once he's dressed, Colton takes a step closer and crosses his arms over his chest.

"Name?"

"Steven."

Colton takes in the man's long messy blonde hair and runs his tongue over his teeth. "How did you get so far into my land, Steven?"

"I don't answer to Beta scum," Steven spits.

Colton chuckles darkly before ramming his fist into the side of the rogue's face. Steven falls to the side and hits the ground with a thump. Colton straightens himself up as Steven does the same with a chuckle.

"Still not feeling talkative," Steven sings before his eyes land on Rae. "Well, aren't you a pretty one. Much better looking than in your picture."

Colton punches him again and stands over him shaking with rage. "You don't look or speak to her again, or I'll rip your throat out myself!"

"Why?" Steven asks as he straightens himself up again into a kneeling position. "She's not yours. Not really."

Colton's about to rip his head clean off his shoulders when Dalton steps in. Rae grabs Colton's arm and pulls him back as Dalton begins the questioning. "Why are you here?"

"My alpha wanted to be sure she was worth all the trouble," Steven says simply before looking at Rae again. "He'll be pleased to know she is."

Colton tries to go for him again, but Rae keeps him where he is. Gritting his teeth, he points a finger at the smirking little shit. "He won't get near her."

"Alpha?" Dalton asks with a scowl. "Rogues have no alphas."

Steven's bloody face splits in a grin. "We do now."

Dalton grabs the rogue by the neck and lifts him, so his feet are above the ground. "Name your alpha."

"His name is alpha." Steven chokes out before Dalton releases him. Steven rubs his neck and laughs. "But my alpha is a fair sportsman, so I'm here to send a message. We're coming for what we were promised, and we don't care which of those little bitches we get."

"You were lucky this time, but next time we'll be ready for you," Dalton warns him coldly.

"I got this far into your territory, and I'm not even the best fighter we have. Who says that another one of my kind won't come close enough to steal one of those pretty little sisters of hers as a replacement?" he asks before glancing over at Rae. "The alpha loves his gifts with golden hair."

Now it's Rae who steps forward, but no one stops her. Grabbing his hair in her hand, she pulls his head back so she can look him straight in the eyes. "You come near them, and I will rip you to pieces with my bare hands."

Dalton glances in Colton's direction with raised eyebrows. Colton feels his pride grow until he literally can't have any more respect for his mate. He knows she'll do it too. When it comes to her family, Colton has no doubt that Rae will decimate anything that comes between her and their safety.

"I'd like to see what you do when you're face to face with the realities we have planned for you," Steven says with a chuckle. "You'll be the one ripped to pieces, that I can promise you."

Rae lets out a growl before suddenly grabbing his head and snapping his neck. She lets him fall to the ground with a limp thump, her body shaking with barely contained rage. When she turns to face in Colton's direction, he's not surprised to see her eyes are the bright yellow of her wolf.

"Dump him on the other side of the boundary line," she orders before walking away from the rogue's dead body. "That way, his alpha knows how we treat rogues on our side of the line."

Rae walks past Colton and back towards the party without another word. Giving the dead rogue on the ground one last glance,

Colton starts following after her. They don't say anything on the way back but both know that this isn't the last rogue they'll have to deal with.

The war has only just begun.

CHAPTER THIRTY-SIX

Jace isn't stupid. He's not a genius, but he's not stupid. He knows something is going on. Half of the damn party don't just leave, including Rae and Colton, for nothing. Jace keeps eyes on the pack members stationed at the main entrance and knows there is no way in hell he'll be able to get past Andy. He's too wise to Jace being full of shit to let him out.

It seems fate is on his side, though, because Andy suddenly leaves his station and goes outside the building. Okay, Jace thinks, maybe this lineup he can deal with. Some kid, maybe a few years older than Jace blocks the door. Now this, he can definitely deal with. He's about to approach him when a hand grabs his arm, stopping him.

"Where do you think you're going?"

Jace turns to face Cleo, looking far from impressed. "What's it to you?"

"I don't want you getting into something you can't handle."

"Like what?" he asks flatly. "Please, suddenly mighty and wise Cleo, enlighten me with your unending guidance."

Cleo narrows her eyes and purses her lips. "What is your deal? I'm just trying to protect you."

"I'm not interested in your protection, and just so we're clear, I also don't trust your sudden attitude change. I think it's fair for me to be asking what it is you think you're doing instead of the other way around, don't you?"

Cleo lets go of his arm and crosses her own in front of her chest. "Jace, you're my baby brother, and I love you, but you are frankly a huge dick."

He rolls his eyes and starts to turn away from her. "Glad we got that covered."

She grabs his arm again, stopping him, and he grits his teeth while she speaks, "You can't just go out there. I don't know if you remembered this or not, but you and I don't have wolves. If shit is out of our depth, then we could be ripped to pieces. Do you remember what dad did to us? He nearly ripped your heart out of your chest."

Jace's chest aches with the reminder of their father's attack, and he instinctually rubs over the still healing wound. When his dad attacked a large part of him, he couldn't believe it. Was this the guy who gave him his first beer? Was this the same guy that taught him how to throw a proper punch? No, it wasn't. He knew it as soon as he looked into his dad's feral wolf eyes. It's one of the reasons Jace hasn't mourned like most people would think he should. His dad was long gone, and as far as he is concerned, he lost his father three years ago.

So what's the point of mourning?

Taking his arm back from Cleo, Jace glares at her. "I'll be fine."

Walking away from her, he's stopped again but this time, feels less annoyed about it. Poppy grabs his hand and pulls him away from his front door destination only to drag him by the drink station. Pulling him down till he's crouching in front of her, Jace is alarmed by the look on his little sister's face. Why does she look so scared?

"What's wrong?"

"I think rogues are here."

"Rogues?" Jace repeats slowly. "Poppy, where the hell did you come up with that idea?"

"I heard Andy talking about it. He said the alpha needed his assistance with a rogue situation just before he left. Dad used to talk about them all the time. That's why he was always so mad when Rae stayed out when it got dark out."

"Wait, how did you overhear Andy without him noticing you?"

Poppy shrugs. "I don't know, but none of them ever notice me."

"Okay . . . Well, what else did they say?"

"One of the other ones said that the 'beta's family' had to be secured. What does that mean, Jace?"

Jace repeats the words in his head. They have to mean him and his siblings, but why? Jace goes through everything he knows about rogues and doesn't like them being mentioned with his family. From what their dad had told them about rogues, Jace knows they're the scum of the werewolf world. He's never seen one from before, but he's sure he doesn't want to meet one either.

The real question is, why would they be a threat specifically to them? Besides the fact that Rae is the soon to be alpha female to this pack, they aren't that special. Their mom was a human and their dad was an enforcer for a different pack. There's not real concrete reason as to why rogues would want to use them for anything. Well, other than to drive Rae insane.

Shaking that thought out of his head, he looks Poppy right in the eyes as he reassures her, "You have nothing to worry about."

"But—"

"Poppy, you have nothing to worry about. You know Rae and Colton would hurt anyone who came near us."

"But what if they did?" she asks, tears brimming her eyes. "I don't want anyone to die."

Jace frowns and lays his hands on both of her tiny shoulders. "No one is going to die, and no one is going to hurt any of you. If, by some miracle, those rogues did get past Rae or Colton, they'd still have to get past me, and no one beats me."

345

Poppy wipes away a tear from under her glasses. "Colton did."

"Yeah, well, I let him win."

"Jace?" she asks with a little sniffle.

"Yeah, kiddo?"

"I left Cassidy's present back at the house, can you go get it?"

Jace frowns. "What? I saw you—"

He cuts himself off as it dawns on him what his sister is doing. Poppy smiles at him a little before she closes her eyes and hugs him as she dramatically starts to cry. Jace tries to stop the proud grin that comes across his face as he hugs her to his chest and gets to his feet. He always knew Poppy was going to be a smart one, he knew it from the day she decided her first word would be his name.

Heading for the front door with Poppy in his arms, Jace gives the guy stationed in his way a helpless look. "Hey, do you think you could let us head back to the pack house? My sister forgot her birthday present for the birthday girl. She's really upset about it."

"She'll be so mad!" Poppy wails from his shoulder.

Jace has to fight the urge to roll his eyes. Okay kid, tone it down a bit, would you? Looking the guy in the eye he puts on a pleading expression. "Come on man, I don't want her upset. Give me a break here."

The guy eyes both of them before giving a reluctant nod. "Fine, but go straight there. You have fifteen minutes before I send someone after you."

"Thanks, man, you're a lifesaver."

Putting Poppy down, Jace kneels in front of her. "I'm going to go get your gift now, okay?"

Poppy sniffles. "You will?"

"Yup. Only take a minute."

"Really?"

Jace narrows his eyes a little when he sees her little smirk. "Yes."

"Okay," she agrees with a shrug. "Be back soon, or you'll miss the cake!"

And with that, she's off, running to go play with Cassidy. Jace gets up with a sigh and sees the guy's speculative eyes watch a now perfectly happy Poppy running around. He has got to teach the kid to keep character longer, he thinks with a mental groan.

Turning to the guy he shrugs. "Kids, right?"

The guy just gives him an impassive look. "Fifteen minutes."

Jace has a lot of things he wants to tell this guy but bites his tongue. He has other shit to deal with. Pushing past the doors, he gets out of the building and has no intention of heading for the pack house. That being said, though, there are a considerable amount of pack members outside of the building obviously on watch. He really can't run off with them ready to jump on the first escapee. So he keeps on his way towards the pack house.

Once he's reached the pack house, he walks in. The house is empty, which is a relief because he won't be staying in it long. He starts jogging through the house towards the kitchen when he hears a door suddenly slam open, or maybe shut. Dipping behind the kitchen counter, he tries to stay hidden while he listens.

"Rae, it's going to be okay," Colton's voice says from somewhere in the house.

"No, it is not going to be okay!" Rae yells back. "He threatened my sisters, Colton. It was one thing when they were coming after me, but my sisters? That's a step too far. If he or any of his followers step one toe over the line, I'll rip their throats out with my bare hands!"

"I would never let that happen."

"Really?" she snaps. "Because I'm pretty sure what that piece of shit did! He got within two miles of the building where my sisters are. Two miles! I thought you said this place was secure."

347

"It is secure, but we can't account for everything Rae," Colton says calmly.

Jace scowls as he processes this new information. These rogues want Rae? Why? Why hasn't she mentioned this before? Jace scoffs at the last question. Of course, he knows why she hasn't told them. She's trying to protect them like she always is by putting all the weight on her own shoulders. It's as worrying as it is unsurprising that she would be hiding something this big from them. Still, he can't find it in him to be mad at her. Wouldn't he do the same thing in her shoes?

"I can't risk something happening to them, Colton," Rae says, her voice bordering on a sob. "I can't lose anyone else in my family. I can't do it. I'm not strong enough to survive this time especially when I could do something to stop it."

"We'll figure something out. We'll meet with my father and make a plan. No one is going to hurt your family, Rae. No one."

Jace doesn't hear any more talking, and he takes it as his cue. Getting off the floor, he keeps low to the ground while making his way to the back exit door coming off the kitchen. He had a feeling he'd use this door as soon as he laid eyes on it. He just didn't think it'd be for something like this.

When he's out of the house again, he lets out a sigh as he runs a hand through his dark red hair. He'll need to talk to Rae about the situation once she's calmed down. If there's anything he knows about Rae at this point in his life, it's that talking to her when she's upset is like talking to a brick wall. You just have to let her get all that shit out of her system and then calmly discuss. Otherwise, she'll use her stubbornness to railroad you into a corner.

Jace scoffs, just like their dad.

Pacing in a small patch of woods near the pack house, Jace tries to think of a way to approach his sister with this when he hears a branch snap. Looking around, he doesn't see anyone, but his stomach does a churning motion under his dark blue button up shirt. He scans the area for any sign of anyone else but can't see them at all. It's turning into mid-day now, and the light should be good enough to spot anyone, but he can't see anything. Still, he can feel that someone is here.

"I know you're here. Show yourself," he demands into the air.

He hears a few rustling tree branches from behind him. Turning around, he feels his heart squeeze in his chest as he sees someone fall out of a tree. The tiny being lands on her bare soiled feet with a thump before straightening herself out. He can see her clearly now, and from the messy black hair on the top of her head, he has no doubt it was Mackenzie.

She's dressed in a dirty yellow t-shirt and cut off shorts that are way too big for her skinny frame. The t-shirt hangs off, exposing her slender, pale shoulder. Her short hair is sticking out in every way, and she looks even more severely underweight in the sunlight. After she straightens down her t-shirt, she looks him straight in the eye, and Jace feels like he just got slapped with a raw fish. Bright green eyes meet his before briefly flashing yellow.

She's a wolf, he realizes, though he's pretty sure he knew that before. He just wasn't sure if what he saw was a trick of the limited light or just him being sleep deprived. Now looking at her though in broad daylight, he knows that she is indeed a shifter.

"What? Wolf got your tongue?" she asks with a slight smirk on her thin face.

"Where are your friends?" he spits at her.

Smirking, Mackenzie shrugs. "I must have lost them on the way here. I'm pretty fast, you know. Maybe they couldn't keep up."

"Why are you here?" he demands, narrowing his eyes at her. "And how did you get past the sentries?"

"What? You mean you're too dumb to find their own tail guard dogs?" she asks with a little laugh. "Honey, I've been doing this for as long as I can remember. There isn't anywhere I can't get into. Getting past your security was as easy as pie."

"That doesn't answer my first question."

"No, it doesn't," she admits before shifting on her feet a little. "Listen, I'm not here to do any harm. I'm just here to talk."

"Talk?" he echoes with disbelief. "You broke into pack territory at the risk of your life just to talk? I don't believe that for a second."

She smirks a little. "I'd be disappointed if you did."

He ignores the butterflies in his stomach when he sees her smile and narrows his eyes at her. "So, what are you? A rogue?"

"Does it matter?" she asks quietly, looking down at the ground.

He can't control his answering sneer, "Yes, it fucking matters. I need to know what I'm dealing with so I can figure whether to kill you now or call someone else who can do a better job of it."

"And why would you do something like that?" she asks, tilting her head to the side as she watches him warily. "I haven't done anything to you."

"I know that you pieces of shit want my sister. What I want to know is why? She isn't mated to any of your men."

"Well . . ." Mackenzie says with a click of her tongue as she sits on a nearby boulder. "She's not mated to anyone, but she sure was promised."

"Promised?"

"Yup. Turns out your barbie doll of a sister was promised to the up and coming head of the rogues as insurance. We don't attack some pathetic pack's land if alpha gets her on his arm. Her being mated to a legitimate alpha heir isn't exactly what he was expecting, but that's the hand we've been dealt. Now we have to go to war."

"War?" Jace echoes. "What's so important about Rae that he can't just pick some other woman or even better, wait for his mate?"

"Alpha's mate died young many years ago, and it just happens your Rae looks just like her. He's not going to stop until

350

she comes to heel or he'll kill her trying. I think it's an 'if he can't have her, no one can' sort of thing."

Jace narrows her eyes at her. "Why are you telling me all this? Aren't you on their side?"

Mackenzie shrugs a bony shoulder. "I like you, Jace, and despite what you may think you know about rogues, we're not all bad."

"Says the girl who said she would be bringing an army next time I saw her," he mutters.

"Yeah, well, I wasn't expecting to come back here."

"So why are you?"

Mackenzie runs a thin small hand through her hair with a sigh. "I just . . . I needed to see you."

He narrows his eyes at her. "Is this some kind of Jedi mind fuck or something?"

She laughs a little and shakes her head. "No. I wish it were, but I'm all out of mind tricks today. You've caught me on a bit of an off day."

A silence settles in, and he blurts the first thing he can think of.

"How old are you?" he asks suddenly. The tips of his ears heat a little as he realizes what he just blurted. Why should it matter how old she is? She's the enemy.

Mackenzie's heart shaped face lifts up in a wide smile. "Seventeen."

"Oh."

"Why? How old are you?"

"Uh . . . not seventeen."

She tilts her head in that unnerving way again. "Younger?"

"I'm sixteen."

She smiles a little. "Well, that's not so bad."

"Listen, Mackenzie." He sighs, shoving his hands in his jean pockets. "You seem like you don't want to be mixed up in this, so I have to ask you not to come here again. Security is going to be tripled, and if they catch you, they won't be as restrained as I've been. They will kill you."

"Why do you care?"

He frowns at her question, though it's the same one he's been asking himself this whole time. Why should he care? He doesn't know why, but he does. Something about this tiny and obviously ill-treated girl makes him want to take care of her. He wants to protect her and take her from wherever the hell she comes from. He also wants to kiss those full pink lips of hers, but that's an urge he's trying to bury deep down in himself. He can't be thinking about that when she's this close, or he might lose control of himself and do it.

"I don't care," he lies. "I just don't want your blood on my hands."

She frowns a little, looking almost hurt before getting up off the rock. "Two days, Jace. You'll see me in two days, and when you do, you need to take your sisters to hide. I don't care where you hide or how much it hurts your pride, but you have to keep them safe. Alpha wants a girl with golden hair, and if he needs to get to one of the little ones to get it, he'll do it."

"What about you?" he asks. "When it comes down to it, and your alpha asks you to come after me, will you?"

"I don't know," she says quietly. "But I hope I won't have to make that decision."

He watches her run deeper into woods and hopes the same thing. He really doesn't want to have to kill her, and he really doesn't want to be killed by her. Either way, he thinks with a sigh, at least she's given him something to help his sister keep them safe. Two days, his mind repeats, two days until the shit hits the fan.

CHAPTER THIRTY-SEVEN

Alpha listens to the muffled screams from nearby, but it's a sound he's often heard over the years. He's had to fight his way to the top and to earn his place as a leader among barbarians. He has given up everything for his position, even his name. Everything and yet, he's distracted.

Glancing down at the faded photograph in his hand, he runs the pad of his thumb over her face softly. He took this picture when they were young, both eighteen years old, and he's kept it on his person ever since. Her soft smile, wild blonde hair blowing in the wind, and happy blue eyes look back at him. What he wouldn't give to have that moment back, to enjoy it more fully.

What he wouldn't give to have *her* back.

Annie was his mate. His one and only goddess-given mate. He found her at the run that year, dressed in white with a pink masquerade mask on her face. She wasn't a shifter like him, but she was strong. He could tell that about her right away; the way her blue eyes lit up with fire when she was angry or softened into sapphire when she was happy. Alpha clutches the picture tighter at the memory as emotion sticks in his throat.

Annie is dead now, but Alpha refuses to be without a mate. He's created a pack for himself, one that he has built from the ground up. He's proud of what he's built, proud of what he's accomplished and now he needs someone to share it with him. Rae

Applebee is exactly what he needs. She looks so much like his Annie. He thought she was a dream when he first saw her.

He's convinced that she is his second chance, a gift from the moon goddess, sent to make things right for him. Why else would things have fallen into place so perfectly? Convincing Kendrick was easy. His father had originally agreed to the pairing and was going to allow Alpha to take her when she was sixteen, but then she shifted. Alpha couldn't believe his luck. This time, she would be strong enough to survive childbirth, not like his Annie.

Alpha decided to wait and give her time to grow a bit before she would be ready for him. He decided to wait for the run. It would be just as it was when he met Annie. *She* would be just like Annie; and if Rae weren't, she would learn to be. Alpha has waited too long for his second chance to have a bad attitude ruining this pairing. Kendrick had warned him about Rae's attitude, but Alpha is sure that once she got to know him, she would bend to his will. He doesn't want to hurt her, but he's not above it.

"Alpha, Kenzie is back."

"Mackenzie?" Alpha asks, perking up a bit. "Send her in."

The flap of the tent opens to show Mackenzie, Alpha's favorite soldier. She's quiet, stealthy, and observant. It's exactly what one would want in a spy, and after years of training, Mackenzie has risen above the rest of her class. Mackenzie comes deeper into the large tent and stands up straight with her hands clasped behind her. Bowing her head, she keeps her eyes on the ground.

"Alpha."

"Report."

"The scent cover was a success. I was able to make it within mere feet of the pack house."

Alpha sits back in his chair with a smirk. The scent covering came to him years before when he was just a lone rogue. He had been hunting wildlife in a dense forest area when a bullet grazed his shoulder. He had never even caught the scent of the

354

hunters in the area, but they were up there in their stands pointing guns in his direction. It was a common practice for hunters, he later found out. Hiding their scents from their prey so they would be unprepared. Alpha had Mackenzie and his other soldiers try as many methods as he could find, but this one seemed to be the best and least detected.

"Good." He sighs before lowering his voice. "Did you see her?"

"No, Alpha."

"Where is Steven? Perhaps he saw her."

Mackenzie shifts on her feet. "Steven was caught by the sentries."

"And?"

"His body was found just outside the boundary lines. We believe it to be a warning."

Alpha snorts. "A warning? They should be the one receiving warnings from us if they do not give us my mate."

"She's already mated to the beta, Alpha. Perhaps you should find another who can satisfy you," Mackenzie says quietly but he hears it, and his reaction is swift.

Rising to his feet, he slaps her hard across the face, making her fall to her knees before him. Her nose is bleeding, and her lip is split, but she doesn't cry out. She's been trained not to feel pain, and as his best student, she does not disappoint. Still, she has yet to learn her place when it comes to Alpha's affairs.

"She is mine!" he snarls down at her. "She was made for me, and she will belong to me!"

"She isn't Annie," Mackenzie whispers.

Alpha growls and grabs her by the neck, making her feet dangle above the ground. "She is close enough."

"Steven warned them." She gasps out. "He warned them that you wanted someone with golden hair. What if they dye their hair? What if they cover their scents like we have learned to do? We can't lose more men!"

355

Alpha's grip tightens on her throat making her wheeze as he continues to snarl at her. "We will do everything that is necessary to reclaim what I was promised. I know her scent, and it is her that I want. If I have to threaten her with the taking of her sisters to ensure her obedience, then I will do it."

Alpha throws Mackenzie away from him. She lands with a grunt on the hard floor below and coughs as she tries to catch her breath. Alpha calmly goes back to his chair and sits as he watches her collect herself. She's young and has no idea what loss is. It took a great amount of strength on his part not to lose himself to his wolf, promising the beast that he would bring them happiness again. He's built his wolf a pack, given his leadership, and now he must give his wolf a mate.

He cannot fail, or he will be lost forever.

"Can you get in again?" he asks once she's collected herself.

Rubbing her throat, Mackenzie reluctantly nods.

"Good." He nods. "Then do it, and this time, make my intentions clear. Either Rae comes to me, or I will be forced to take extreme measures to make sure she does."

More muffled screams meet his ears, and he smiles. Kendrick was very accommodating when it came to his request, but Rae was a fool to leave family behind. The woman was the hardest to subdue, but once she was, the men fell in line quickly. Now all they have to do is convince them to act as Alpha needs them to, and he believes everything will fall into place and Rae into his arms.

Wiping the blood from her nose and lip, Mackenzie gets to her feet and waits for command. "What do you want me to do, Alpha?"

Grabbing the picture again, Alpha stares at it as he answers, "Go back and tell them we have some people they'll be very interested in having back."

"You mean, be captured."

"Yes."

"What if they kill me?"

Alpha's eyes snap up to meet hers and narrow. "Then you would have died for your pack. An honorable death."

Mackenzie visibly wilts under his glare. "Yes, Alpha."

Turning his gaze back to the image of Annie, he speaks, "I suggest you head out now. Darkness will be coming soon and with it, the closer you'll be able to get to their center. Unnerve them, make them fear and do me proud."

"Y-Yes, Alpha."

He glances up at her one more time. "Go."

Mackenzie turns on a heel and walks out of sight. Alpha balls the picture in his hand and closes his eyes as his wolf growls and fights for control in his mind. He needs to hurry and have Rae by his side before he can't hold him back anymore. His wolf is getting too close to escaping his tight mental cage and Alpha fears what may happen when he does.

CHAPTER THIRTY-EIGHT

Rae kneads her forehead as she listens to Aunt and Uncle's answering machine again. Why aren't they answering? Jolene never lets the phone go past a third ring, especially since it's the fourth time Rae has called over the space of an hour. They would have answered normally. It is Cassidy's birthday after all.

Hanging up the phone, Rae decides to go an alternate route and heads for her and Colton's room for her address book. Her cheap phones have broken way too many times over the years to not keep a second record of everything. Besides, Rae likes to try to be prepared for everything, though most of the time she fails. Grabbing the book, she heads back to the office Colton deposited her in the first place.

Colton is somewhere in the house, maybe already heading back to the party to collect her older siblings. She doesn't want to ruin Cassidy's party or worry her, but they all need to know what's going on. She can't risk them wandering around at the wrong time and getting snatched. The thought has her hand tightening around the phone in her hand as the rogue's "warning" replays in her mind.

No one is touching her sisters, she'll kill them before they even get the chance.

Finding the number, she starts dialing it and listens to the ringing as it echoes down the receiver. Looking around the room, she has to admit that the office itself is nice. It's plain, clean, organized, and obviously Colton's. She sits on the edge of the wide desk and puts her feet on the office chair while waiting. When the line picks up, she smiles. Despite her best attempts, she has to admit, she missed him.

"Hello, you've reached Graham Jones's house of pleasures. How may I help you?"

"You, my friend, are a loser."

"Baby cakes!"

Rae smiles goofily into the phone. "Hey, Graham."

"Well, what do I owe the honor? Did that mate of yours already screw up? I could be there in a few hours ready to rescue you from your tower."

"That won't be necessary," she assures him. "I was actually wondering if you'd seen Garrett, Jolene, or Everett. I've been calling them for a while now, and I'm not getting through."

"Did something happen?" he asks, suddenly serious.

"No," she lies as she bites her lower lip. "It's Cassidy's birthday. I just thought they'd want to talk to her."

"Oh," he breathes, apparently relieved. "Well, that's good to hear."

"Why would you think anything was wrong, Graham?"

She hears a moment of hesitation before he says, "Give me a minute."

Rae frowns and listens to some shuffling on the other end of the phone before there's the tell-tale click of a door. Why would he have to hide himself just to talk to her? The awful feeling that maybe Graham knows about what's happening comes into her thoughts. It's possible, though. He's related to Kendrick's beta, and Graham is of higher privilege for that reason. He could know things that Rae, as the daughter of a mere enforcer, would never know.

"Okay, it's safe now," he says in a hushed voice.

"Graham, what's going on?"

"To be honest, I'm not sure, but something is happening over here. Kendrick is training us all like crazy, and though he says it's just to bulk up defenses, it feels sketchy as shit."

"What about my family, Graham?" Rae asks sharply, her anxiety building with every word he speaks. When he doesn't answer right away, Rae feels tears prick her eyes. "Graham, where's my family?"

"I don't know," he whispers into the phone. "Last I saw them they were summoned to the alpha house. No one's seen them since, and I've been asking around."

"Did you check the house?"

"Yeah, had to break a window to get in, but I did. Nothing's been touched."

Rae dashes away a fallen tear with her hand and asks, "Why didn't you call me earlier, Graham? I gave you the number here before we left. You should have called as soon as you knew something was up."

"That's the thing, Rae. I asked Kendrick about them in my own way, you know, and he said they were gone visiting you. That's why I checked the house. Nothing was gone. Even the damn suitcases were in their place. Rae, is something happening over there? Something you're not telling me?"

Rae runs a hand through her hair and stares up at the ceiling, trying to stop the tears from spilling. "Yeah, shit's hitting the fan here too, and my guess is Kendrick's the pushing force behind it all."

After a quick explanation of the whole situation and some choice words from Graham, Rae finally stops pacing the perimeter of the room. She stares out of the windows and tries to think of a way to find Jolene, Everett, and Garrett before something serious happens to them. She just can't believe Kendrick would stoop that low just for pack security. It's one thing to protect a pack. It's another thing to betray those same people for that protection.

"Shit," Graham says for the fifth time.

"Yeah."

"So what do we do?"

Rae bites her lip, weighing her next words. "That depends."

"On?"

"If you can leave that pack or not."

Graham's silent on the other end of the line for a few seconds before speaking, "Rae, my family is here. My sister and my parents are here. I can't just leave them here, especially if what you're saying about Kendrick is right."

"You doubt it?" she asks sharper than she intended.

He sighs. "No, I don't. That's the scary thing."

The door opens, and Rae glances up to see Colton entering the room. He notices her being on the phone and frowns. She feels like she's been caught red-handed doing something even though she knows she's not doing anything wrong. Of course, that doesn't stop her face from heating up.

"Rae? Hello?"

"Uh, yeah," Rae says before clearing her throat. "I'm here."

"So what do we do?"

"Who is it?" Colton mouths to her, making her squirm.

She scowls at him and turns her head away from him before speaking into the phone again, "I think for now it's best to stay there. Pretend nothing's wrong and you suspect nothing. That's all you can do right now. We don't want Kendrick to think you're being disloyal and take it out on anyone else."

"Fucker would try it too," Graham mutters irritably before sighing. "What about you? Will you be okay?"

Rae tries to sneak a peek over her shoulder only to find Colton standing right in front of her. His blue eyes are intense as the gaze into hers. He crosses his arms over his chest as he stares her down, but Rae doesn't bat an eyelash. She's actually intimidated a little by the look on his face, but she's not going to show it. Why would she when that's most likely exactly what he wants her to feel? Get her to spill her guts.

361

Too bad she's just too smart for him.

"I'll be fine," she answers Graham, not breaking her eye contact with Colton. "Just worry about yourself and stay out of trouble, okay?"

Graham lets out a light chuckle. "Well, that's impossible."

"Humor me and try."

"Yeah, I'll try. Talk to you later, Muffin."

Rae rolls her eyes and smiles. "Yeah, talk to you later, Graham."

When she says his name, Colton raises an eyebrow at her. Pressing the end button on the phone, Rae places it beside her on the desk and leans back on her hands. She meets her mate's gaze squarely and is rewarded with an amused tilt to his lips. It becomes a full-blown smirk when he comes to stand between her legs. He places his hand on either side of her on the desk and leans in so they're nose to nose before he actually says a word.

"Graham?"

Rae's lips twitch up into a small smile. She surprises him though by laying her head on his shoulder. Colton's arms automatically wrap around her, and Rae inhales his scent. The indescribable but calming scent he carries that makes her body feel like the weight of the world has been lifted off.

"Hey, what's wrong?"

Rae slowly sits up again and meet his eyes. "I called Graham. I was trying to get to Jojo or Everett or even Garrett, but no one is answering at the house. Graham and Garrett are close, so I thought he would have at least seen them."

When Rae suddenly stops, Colton grabs her chin and makes her look him in the eyes again. "And?"

"He said they were summoned to the alpha house. No one's seen them since. Kendrick's telling people they're here to visit me but obviously, that's a lie. I have a bad feeling about it, Colton. I mean, what if Kendrick—"

"Stop," Colton orders. "Don't think like that."

"You think he's below it?"

"No." He sighs. "No, I don't, but I also don't want you torturing yourself with thoughts like that. I'll have some of my best and most discrete trackers try to find them. If they don't, then freak out as much as you want, but until we have exhausted all other options, try to be positive."

Rae gives him a weak smile before pressing their foreheads together. "You're too good for me, you know that."

"I don't know about that."

"And I'm definitely too good for you."

He leans back and smiles. "Oh, really?"

"Definitely."

He licks his lower lip and narrows his eyes at her. "Earlier, when I came in here, were you challenging me?"

Rae frowns at the question. "No. Why would you say that?"

"I clearly wanted to know who was on the phone with my mate, but instead of telling me, you turned away from me. Don't you know that turning your back on not only your mate but also your beta is very bad manners?"

"Meaning?"

He shrugs. "Just an observation."

"Well, you don't seem that upset about it," she says as she crosses her arms over her chest.

"Do I?" he asks, his amusement now painfully clear. "You seem to like challenging me."

"Challenging you or being challenging?" Rae asks with a tilt of her head.

He grins. "Both."

She lets out a pitying sigh. "How horrible it must be for you."

"It has its advantages," he murmurs as his lips come closer to hers.

"Does it?" she breathes, very caught up in the moment.

"Yup."

"Ew! They're going to kiss!"

Rae closes her eyes and growls under her breath. Still, she turns her head towards the office entrance to see four of her five siblings pile into the room. Wait, four? Sure enough, Poppy comes walking in with her arms crossed in behind Hudson. Rae's eyes narrow on Hudson for a second. Is that a hickey on his neck?

"You told me to go get them," Colton mutters, not sounding too pleased with his own mission being accomplished.

"Yes, I did." She sighs before sliding off the desk to stand on her own two feet. Facing her family, Rae runs a hand through her hair and just decides to come out with it. "Alright, how much do you already know?"

"Rogues are here," Poppy says bluntly, shocking Rae a little.

"How did you find out?"

"I heard some people talking about it." The nine-year-old shrugs.

"Oh, o-okay," Rae stutters out before turning to Cleo.

Cleo's shrug echoes Poppy's. "Only what Andy told me. He said you and Colton were dealing with a rogue on the perimeter. He also said I wasn't supposed to be walking around alone. What's all that about?"

"That's one of the reasons I wanted to talk to you guys," Rae says hesitantly. She can feel her palms begin to sweat a little. She's not looking forward to their reactions.

"They're here for Rae," Jace says stiffly from his position in the back of the room, getting all of their attention. "And if they can't get Rae, they'll take one of you. They want a blonde for their alpha and apparently, have their eyes set on someone from our family."

"Jace how—"

"And we have two days before they strike."

364

Rae feels like the air has been knocked out of her lungs. She stumbles back a little and sits down in the large desk chair behind the chair. Two days? Only two days? She glances up at Colton. Two days isn't long enough. She needs more time. She needs more time to be with the people she loves because what if they lose?

"How do you know all this?" Colton demands.

"I know because someone told me."

"Who?" Rae asks him thickly. "Who told you?"

"Mackenzie," Jace mumbles. "She's a rogue."

"What?" Rae, Hudson, and Colton all yell.

Cleo comes up with her own spin, though. "What the actual fuck, Jace?"

"Are you crazy?" Rae yells at him, getting to her feet again. "You could have been killed or taken!"

"But I wasn't."

Cleo scoffs and crosses her arms over her chest. "Screw the rogues, I'll kill him myself."

"Cleo, enough," Rae snaps before trying to catch Jace's gaze in her own. "What else did she say?"

Jace plays with his lip ring before sighing heavily. "She said that the alpha picked you because you look like his . . . dead mate. That's why he's so obsessed with you. He wants you for himself, and he'll do anything to have that."

"Shit," Hudson mutters and Cleo echoes the sentiment.

"Anything else?" Rae asks, trying to keep her panic to herself.

Jace glances up at her and reluctantly adds, "She said that if her alpha doesn't get you, he'll kill you and anyone who stands in his way."

Silence. That's what fills the room.

Rae sits back down in the office chair and stares at her hands gripping the edge of the desk. Her knuckles are white, and she can feel her whole body beginning to shake. She's never felt like this before; not when her mom died. Not when she learned her dad was dead. Never in her life has she felt this scared and angry in her life.

"Rae—"

"I'm fine," Rae croaks. "I'm fine. I just need a minute."

"No one is going to lay a hand on any of you," Colton growls, his own stress clear in his voice. "Jace, I want to know everything that happened between you and the rogue. Hudson, you're going to need to join the pack."

Rae's head snaps up, and she glares at Colton. "No. He's too young."

"Rae . . ."

She looks at her baby brother and shakes her head. "I said no. You can't join a pack under these circumstances, and you're only fourteen. I don't want you buried under all that responsibility."

"I can handle it," he insists. "Rae, my mate is here, my family is here. Why wouldn't I want to join this pack?"

"Because if you join this pack, you'll have to fight."

"And I'm willing to do that."

"Yeah, well, I'm not," Rae snaps.

At the mention of Hudson fighting, an array of bloody images flashes through her mind. She pushes them away. That won't happen, she tells herself. She won't let him become some casualty on the battlefield. Especially when it's for this stupid of a reason. It should have never even come to this, she thinks. She should have just given herself up as soon as she found out.

"Knock it off. I'm not allowing it, and you shouldn't even be considering it," Colton growls, obviously hearing her thoughts. "And if you think I'm even letting you out my sight now, you're poorly mistaken."

"It was just a thought," she grumbles defensively.

"Well, stop thinking it."

He turns to face her siblings again, and she pulls a face behind his back. Ass.

"So what do we do next?" Cleo asks.

"Honestly, the best thing we can do is train you guys up," Colton says while running a hand through his hair. "Get you ready to defend yourselves if the time comes."

Jace grins and cracks his knuckles. "Now we're talking."

"Will I have to train too?" Poppy asks softly.

"It's probably a good idea," Colton answers with a twinge of sadness in his tone and expression.

He doesn't want to have to train her. That much is clear. Rae feels the guilt well up in her. It seems ridiculous to think it all comes down to her looking like some crazy guy's dead mate to put everyone she loves in so much danger. Maybe she should just scar herself or dye her hair. He probably knows her scent though or at least has henchmen who know it. With obsession usually comes preparation and with how everything's gone so far, for a crazy guy, he's pretty smart.

"I'll do it." Rae sighs.

"What? You'll take the ring to Mordor?" Hudson asks. All eyes turn to him, and he blushes bright red. "I . . . we . . . Joseph likes *Lord of the Rings*."

"Okay then," Rae says, barely able to stop the urge to laugh and claps her hands together before rubbing them together. "This is going to be fun."

"Shit." Cleo groans.

"What?" Hudson asks, still a novice in anything other than the basics.

"This is going to be brutal," Cleo whines.

Jace grimaces, apparently remembering how training used to go. "She's going to kill us."

"Better me than some rogues." Rae points out.

"I'd almost prefer it," Jace grumbles.

"It can't be that bad . . ." Colton trails before glancing at Rae. "Is it?"

She sits back in the desk chair and puts her most evil smile. "You have no idea."

CHAPTER THIRTY-NINE

Rae eyes the glinting metal in Cleo's hand as she shifts her weight from foot to foot. Both of them are sweating and panting, but Cleo looks like she's exhausted. Rae has never stopped training. She also joined in sparring with other pack members at White Stone when she could. Mostly though, she either sparred with Graham or stuck to more solitary skills. She never wanted to be caught off guard just in case, and now, all the effort is paying off.

"We need a break, Rae," Jace pants from the sidelines with Hudson and Poppy.

Rae shakes her head. "No."

"Come on," Cleo whines. "We've been at this for three hours!"

"And we'll go for longer unless you can prove you can pin me."

"With a knife?" Cleo asks dryly as she waves the switchblade in front of herself.

"Yes, with a knife. Now, are you going to attack anytime soon or not?"

Cleo loses her stance and crosses her arms. "But why a knife?"

Rae sighs and straightens up from her crouched position. "Because you're not a wolf, and you never will be, Cleo. It may seem harsh, but these are the facts. You don't have a wolf form to rely on, and if the rogues break the perimeter, you need to know how to defend yourself."

"But why a knife?"

"Wolves have strength, you know that. In hand-to-hand combat, you would be overtaken easily. A knife or any weapon will even the odds a bit."

"Oh," Cleo breathes before getting back into position. "Well, that's all I needed to hear."

Rae rolls her eyes and also gets back into her crouched position. Without warning, Cleo charges and Rae steps out of the way quickly before grabbing the back of Cleo's shirt to throw her to the ground. Cleo rolls and is swiftly back on her feet, ready to go again. Cleo starts swiping the knife cross ways at Rae, causing Rae to dodge the blade a few times before the sharp edge sweeps across her upper arm.

Rae hisses and looks down, but it's already healing. She doesn't stop it from burning like a bitch, though. Apparently seeing Rae's distraction, Cleo strikes again and lands a kick to Rae's lower back, making her stumble forward.

Rae smirks at this and straightens up to face Cleo, whose smug look quickly falls off. Rae tilts her head to the side and beckons her sister forward. It's a dare; they both know it. Cleo narrows her eyes before starting her attack again, but Rae is ready for her. Crouching low, Rae grabs Cleo's leg and pulls it behind her, making Cleo fall on her face with a grunt.

Cleo mutters some few choice words under her breath before she's on her feet again. Switching hands, Cleo grips the knife tighter in her more dominant hand and attacks. Rae catches her arm and flips her on her back before getting on top of her. Rae uses control of Cleo's arm to bend the direction of the knife's tip until it's against Cleo's throat. Cleo goes rigid and stares up at Rae wide-eyed.

"Don't look so scared." Rae smirks. "You landed a blow, good job."

370

"That's what she said!" Jace yells, making both of them laugh.

Poppy frowns as she looks between her siblings. "I don't get it."

Rae waves her hand, panting. "Don't worry about it. Cleo, you're done for today."

"Really?" Cleo asks. At Rae's nod, she jumps up in the air. "About freakin' time!"

"I want you out here at 5AM tomorrow, though."

Cleo stops celebrating to scowl at her. "You're evil."

Rae just grins. "Welcome to training."

"Fuck, who's next?" Jace groans.

"Hudson," Rae says before reaching up to wipe the sweat from her forehead. "Wolf forms."

"But I already shifted with you," Hudson protests weakly, looking just as exhausted as the others.

"Yeah, and you're going to do it again. You didn't land a blow. When you can pin me, you can go. Those are the rules."

"Shit . . ." Hudson says lowly before reaching up to remove his shirt as he heads behind a nearby tree.

Rae follows suit and soon, both wolves emerge. Hudson's multicolored second form and Rae's dark gray wolf step back into the makeshift sparring circle. His wolf seems to instinctively know of her position as a dominant wolf. Hudson's ears lay flat back, his tail goes between his legs, and his body posture is slumped. He's being submissive to her, to show respect, and Rae's wolf takes his attitude with great pride. She likes being in control and in power.

You ready? Rae calls down the familial link, trying to focus both herself and her wolf.

Hudson nods his head twice before jumping into attack position. His upper body is lower to the ground, and his ears stick up straight as he bares his teeth at her. His snout is wrinkled, and his tail is straight out behind him. Rae internally smirks at his posture. Talk about a one-eighty personality flip.

Rae starts circling him, something he doesn't seem to like since he snarls at her. She waits until she's behind him before striking. It's a cheap move, but one that he needs to be ready for. Grabbing his hind leg, she makes his body slam into the ground with a yelp. She backs off and waits for his response. As expected, it's angry and not very well thought through.

He jumps at her, but Rae already is on her hind legs pushing back. She uses all her force, and within seconds, he's on his back. She presses her paws into his shoulders, pinning him, and snarls down into his face. Hudson's brown eyes are wide as they look up at her. He didn't expect her to be this hard on him, but this is how it's done. How it's always been done.

No more, Rae, come on, he begs.

No, you need to pin me down.

I can't do it! We've tried for hours and I just can't do it!

Rae growls at him and gets off him. *Then you can't fight.*

Hudson rolls back onto his feet and runs back behind the tree. He emerges dressed in his basketball shorts and nothing else. He's dirty, sweaty, and obviously pissed off. Rae does the same and goes behind the tree to shift back and get redressed in her yoga shorts and sports bra.

Stepping back into view, she's practically boiling with anger as she addresses her family. "Do you think a rogue will stop if you're tired? Do you think he or she will wait for you to catch your breath? They're waiting for you to get tired, for you to let your guard down, and as soon as you do, they'll go for your throat. If you can't take that, then you're more of a hindrance in this battle than a help."

"You're being a bit harsh, Rae," Cleo says flatly.

"No, I'm not!" Rae yells. "I'm trying to get you ready! I refuse to lose another one of you! I'll give myself up before I even think of the idea of losing you! You are my family, and I will bleed every drop of my blood to keep you safe!"

"And you think we wouldn't?" Jace snaps. "You think all of us wouldn't do the same for you? Why else do you think we're out here killing ourselves for you? We care just as much, Rae!"

"I'm not saying that!" Rae yells, frustrated and stressed. "I . . . I . . . I just can't do it again. I can't do the funerals, the loss, and the grief. We've done too much of it. We've sacrificed enough, and I refuse to have any of you sacrifice anything else."

They all go quiet, and Rae feels tears prick her eyes. She doesn't know how much more of this she can handle. Brat teenagers, pushy alphas, and potential asshole mates, she can handle. This, though? A war? Over her? It's too much.

"We're trying," Hudson says quietly, breaking the silence. "We're trying, but we don't have enough time."

Rae dashes away a few escaped tears from her cheek. "I know. I'm sorry. I know I'm pushing you all too hard, but I can't allow you to be defenseless when faced with danger. This pack and myself? We come second to your safety. I will do whatever I have to do to keep you safe. No matter how much it makes you hate me."

Cleo rolls her eyes. "We don't hate you."

"Really? Because I'm pretty sure you told me you hated me earlier," Rae tells her dryly.

"Well, yeah, you were making us run laps. Do I look like I run?"

Rae lets out a reluctant chuckle before putting her hands on her hips as she regards her siblings. "I'm sorry. I'm sorry for pushing you, but when the shit hits the fan, I need you to be ready. That being said, you won't be on the front lines with the rest of the pack. Cassidy and Poppy will be inside with the other kids, and Poppy, I need you to protect Cassidy the best you can."

Poppy nods, looking much too serious for her age. "I can do that."

373

"Cleo and Jace, your job will be protecting the kids and the untrained humans. They'll be in the alpha's rooms, and if you see anyone approach, you attack, got it?"

"Yup," Jace and Cleo chorus.

Rae turns to her littlest brother. "Hudson? I can't have you on the front lines."

Hudson sighs, but nods. "I get it."

"So you'll be outside with the other younger shifters protecting the pack house. You have brute strength, and your reflexes are good. I don't think you'll have any problems, but we need the best at the front, holding the line."

Hudson nods solemnly. "Okay."

"What about you and Colton?" Poppy asks softly. "Will you be okay?"

"Yeah," Rae lies with a smile. "We'll be fine."

None of the older siblings call her on her bluff. It's a blessing.

Rae is brought out of her thoughts when she catches a whiff of something. It's strong and nasty smelling. She can't trace it, though. It seems to disappear in and out of range. It may be a dead animal, or maybe just an odd scent on the breeze. That happens on occasion. That conclusion is tossed aside though when Rae sees a flash of black out of the corner of her eye.

She doesn't hesitate. Changing form quickly, she takes off after the wolf, who is surprisingly fast. Rae is even more shocked when the petite wolf starts using trees to propel itself forward. Now that she's never seen before. Picking up her speed though, she manages to get the wolf's tail in her jaws and pulls. The wolf yelps, and Rae tosses the wolf straight into a tree. The wolf is quickly back on its feet, but Rae has it pinned within minutes, snarling down at the wiry animal.

Sending an alert down the pack line, Rae keeps the wolf pinned as she waits for Colton to arrive. It's only a matter of time, of course. He's fanatical about her protection lately. Rae takes in the wolf below her and notices that not only is this creature underfed, but it's also extremely laid back for a rogue that's just been captured. What's even odder is that it's not giving off any distinguishable scent. That's . . . impossible.

"Rae!"

Rae doesn't look up at Colton's call but answers him through their link, *I'm fine.*

Colton's mind is clouded with anger, concern, and relief. Rae can sense it all as she does a quick scan of his mind. It's as much to assure herself as it is to him. Rae's wolf reaches out down the link as well to sooth Colton's wolf, who is equally on edge. She doesn't blame him; she'd be just as worried if the roles were reversed.

"Shift," Colton snarls at the rogue as more pack members come to create a hopefully inescapable perimeter.

The rogue gives Rae a pointed look she doesn't like. Rae lowers her head snarling, so she's snout to snout with the rogue. Colton pushes his own attempt at soothing down the mate bond, and Rae reluctantly backs off. She still doesn't like this situation at all. Something about it doesn't seem right.

The rogue starts to shiver and shake before her bones start to pop back into human form. Rae can't help the whine she lets out. The young woman is just so unhealthy looking. She's skinny, true, but also horribly scarred, particularly on her torso with so many scars. Looking at what looks to be whip marks on the girl's back, Rae can feel her own back tingle in empathy. She must have been in so much pain.

Colton doesn't seem to feel the same though as he tosses the naked girl an oversized t-shirt to cover herself. Winter is near, and with how unhealthy she is, the girl is shivering from it. Colton steps in front of Rae and glares at the young woman as Andy comes around to hover behind the rogue.

Colton nods towards a tree and Rae heads off back there to get dressed. She finds a pair of Colton's boxers and an oversized

375

Rage Against The Machine t-shirt waiting for her. His scent is on both of them, and as she tugs them on, she inhales it deeply. Colton's already speaking to the rogue as Rae comes out to join them again.

"Name," Colton demands.

"Mackenzie."

"Why are you here?"

Mackenzie shrugs her bony shoulder. "Just passing through."

Colton snarls, "Put her in the cells, I'll talk to her later."

Andy grabs both of Mackenzie's arms and starts pushing her towards the holding cells, hidden under the garden shed. It's allegedly empty from what Rae's been told, but she'll find out soon enough herself. There's no way she's not going to be there for this girl's interrogation.

"Hey, be gentle, guy," Mackenzie purrs before winking at Rae. "It's my first time."

Colton pulls Rae into a hug, but she doesn't look away from Mackenzie as she's being lead away.

"Are you okay?" Colton asks, searching her face for any injury or negative emotion.

Rae nods her head and lays her head against his chest. Closing her eyes, she makes a plan in her head about how she's going to get away from him tonight. She has questions, ones that Colton can't be there to hear when she asks them. Ones that will upset him, but ones she needs to know and Mackenzie has the answers.

CHAPTER FORTY

Rae sits back in her chair and stares at Mackenzie down, trying to figure her out. The girl can't be older than her brother Hudson. She's tiny in not only built, but also in height barely reaching; if Rae had to guess, five feet. Her black hair is cut short and messily as it sticks all over the place in a way that makes Rae think it was cut with a knife instead of scissors. The really remarkable thing about her though are her eyes. Bright green eyes that seem to stand out even more against the filth smeared all around the girl's face.

"I thought you had questions," the girl prompts after a few minutes of silence. Rae narrows her eyes. She doesn't like the girl's tone.

"How old are you?"

Mackenzie scoffs and rolls her eyes. "Not much of a question."

"But one I suggest you answer anyway," Rae tells her coldly.

Sighing, Mackenzie turns around and sits on the bench in the farthest part of the cell. "Seventeen years, five months, and twenty-three days old. Want me to break down in minutes and hours for you too?"

Rae ignores her irritation and asks, "Have a last name?"

Mackenzie shrugs. "Don't need one. It's not like I'm ever going to get a job or anything. I don't have a birth certificate."

"None at all?" Rae asks slowly.

"Nope," Mackenzie chirps. "I was born in the woods, and I'll die in the woods. That's how we nasty rogues live, you know. Like animals."

"What about your parents?"

Rae watches the girl stiffen. "What about them?"

"Where are they?"

"Mom died in childbirth and my dad . . . Well, who knows where he is."

"Was he a shifter?"

"They both were. I have an older sister, though, and she isn't. She was put up for adoption, so who the hell knows where she is."

Rae frowns. "Why would they put her up for adoption?"

Mackenzie shrugs again. "Alpha's orders. No weak links in the pack. Humans are easy marks and casualties in our pack. They often don't survive, so it's for the greater good for everybody if you think about it."

"Speaking of your alpha . . ."

"Oh, now we're getting to the good stuff." Mackenzie grins.

Rae arches a brow. "You seem very excited to share your alpha's secrets."

"Secrets?" She snorts. "Why do you think I'm here, Rae? Do you honestly think if I didn't want to be caught, I would have been? I've been infiltrating your pack lands for weeks now, and you've only just caught me. What does that tell you about me? No, what does that tell you about your security? And here I thought you guys were some hot shot pack. I have to say . . . I'm not impressed."

"And still, you felt the need to have conversations with my brother," Rae tells her tightly.

Rae watches Mackenzie squirm in her seat a little and is immediately suspicious. She watches the younger girl look anywhere but her at the mention of Jace, but why? It doesn't make sense until suddenly, like a revelation, it does. Rae lets out a humorless laugh and sits back in her chair as she lets that fact sink in. It would be Jace to end up with a rogue.

"What?" Mackenzie snaps, clearly uncomfortable with the direction of the conversation.

"That's why you've been coming here more frequently isn't it?" Rae asks while smirking at her, "For him. To see him."

"I don't know what you're talking about."

"Does he know?"

"Shut up."

"Come on," Rae sings with a grin. "It's just us girls. You can tell me."

"Shut up!"

"He's got to have an idea. I mean, he only told me about you when it was absolutely necessary. How many times have you talked to him? Once? Twice? Maybe a handful of times? He's pretty charming."

"You don't know anything," Mackenzie spits at her, her eyes going the color of the wolf inside.

Rae just keeps on smiling. "I think I know way more than you think I do, Mackenzie. I think you're scared, and I also think that since Jace is human, your alpha wouldn't approve of this little pairing. So, how often have you talked to him? Better question, how many times have you betrayed your alpha and not told him?"

Mackenzie grabs the cell's bars, and Rae hears the sizzling of her flesh against the silver. Mackenzie stares Rae down, completely ignoring the burning of her hands to snarl at her. "I am loyal to my alpha, and only my alpha!"

Mackenzie lets go of the bars and with jerky movements, walks back towards the bench. Sitting down on it, Mackenzie looks at her already blistering hands, emotionless, and Rae sits in her chair in shock. The smell of burning flesh hangs in the air and it's nearly overwhelming enough to make Rae dry heave but doesn't. She has more questions, but she also doesn't want Mackenzie hurting herself anymore.

Like it or not, this is her brother's soul mate and what hurts him, hurts Rae herself.

"Will you reject him?" Rae asks quietly.

"Do you want me to?"

"No," Rae admits with a sigh. "But I have a feeling that doesn't really matter, does it?"

Mackenzie shakes her head. "No, it doesn't."

"So, will you?"

Mackenzie's voice is barely above a whisper. "I don't know."

"When the day comes that your alpha strikes, you know Jace will be in danger, don't you?"

The younger girl glares at Rae, her eyes going yellow again. "Of course, I know. Why do you think I warned him in the first place about when we'd strike? Despite what you may think of me, I'm not completely heartless."

"Then why are you doing this at all?" Rae asks pleadingly. "I love Colton, he's my mate, and my second chance. Why can't you just let it and me, be?"

"Because you are Alpha's second chance," Mackenzie mutters. "His last chance, really. Without you, his wolf will finally succumb to madness, and everything will be lost. We will become hunted and killed without discrimination, just like it used to be. Just like it always was before Alpha took control and saved us. To you, he's a monster, but to us? Those in his pack? He's our savior, our one chance at living."

Rae gives her a dry look. "You want me to believe that you were all banished from your original packs for no good reason?"

"Of course not," Mackenzie says with a snort. "I know some of our pack members are pieces of shit. I also know that our life outside the packs isn't easy, especially for those who are from the outside coming in. Women have died living with us because of

380

the people in our pack, but what I'm talking about is the second generation. The ones like me who did nothing wrong other than be born. Why must we be punished?"

"Because you don't keep innocent!" Rae yells and stands up from the chair. "You become nothing more than lackeys for some deranged alpha. Little soldiers who put up fronts of righteousness when we both know that your alpha is breaking up a fated pairing!"

"Sacrifices have to be made for the greater good," Mackenzie whispers.

"Bullshit!"

Mackenzie lifts her mostly healed hand and nervously tugs on some strands of her hair. "I don't want to talk anymore."

"Well, tough shit, because I'm not done."

Rae sits back down in the chair and tucks her hair behind her ears before sighing heavily. It's clear that whatever this alpha is doing isn't right. He's taking young shifters and turning them into a calculated army. He's given them an idol in himself and a message to live by. Rae snorts as she realizes what this really is. This "alpha" isn't running a pack; he's running a cult.

"One day, huh? That's how long we have?" Rae asks.

Mackenzie nods, looking at her hands in her lap.

"And I assume you were meant to be captured for a reason," Rae deduces, only to get another nod. "So, why would that be?"

"Alpha wanted you to know that the offer to surrender is still open."

Rae snorts. "Surrender."

Mackenzie swallows thickly and nods. "Yes, and he feels very confident about the fact that you will, in fact, surrender."

"Because?" Rae prompts when she doesn't automatically elaborate.

"Because he has your aunt, uncle, and cousin in the camp," Mackenzie tells her in a small voice. "And if you don't surrender, he'll kill them."

Rae doesn't know what to feel first. Rage? Sadness? Grief? She can't decide on one, so she goes with them all, all at once. Standing up from the chair, she throws it across the room, making Mackenzie jump in her seat. Rae is about to rip off the damn cell door to wring this girl's neck until she tells her everything, but suddenly she's grabbed around the waist.

"Let me go!" Rae yells.

"No," Colton's voice tells her resolutely. "The cells are lined with silver."

"I know that! Now let me go!"

"No."

"Let her go, Beta," Mackenzie says sadly. "She deserves some kind of justice."

"Tell me where they are!" Rae screams at her.

Mackenzie shakes her head. "I can't."

"You can and you will, or I will rip you limb by limb!"

Another pair of hands grabs Rae as she almost fights her way free from Colton. These aren't as strong, but ones she won't fight as much. Jace waits until she's done fighting and turns around before pulling her into his chest. Holding Rae close to him, Rae starts to cry and cling to him. Jolene, Everett, and Garrett could all be dead by now. And for what? For her? She's not worth all this.

"Colton, take her inside," Jace says quietly as he pulls back to look Rae in the eyes. His light blue eyes are blurry with his own emotion, but he doesn't let it spill out. He's always been so much better at that than Rae.

Colton surprisingly does as Jace says and grabs Rae up in his arms. She wraps her arms around his neck as he picks her up in a princess carry. Rae buries her face in the crook of his neck and inhales his scent. She needs to calm down and think of a plan. Think of some way to save everyone, even if that means sacrificing herself.

* * *

Mackenzie watches the beta male and female leave the cell with guilt sitting heavily on her chest. She didn't want to be the one to tell her, but that's what she was here to do. Mackenzie thought she'd be dead the minute the words passed her lips, but she isn't. This is almost worse.

"Is it true or just another trick?"

Mackenzie lifts her gaze to look up at Jace, her mate, and feels her shame only triple. These are his relatives too, not just Rae's. She had a hand in torturing her own mate's family. The thought is so overwhelming she hangs her head and feels her stomach churn with disgust at her own actions.

"It's true."

"And what about the other stuff?"

Mackenzie scoffs lightly. "You know, you have a very distinctive scent. It's like maple with a mix of something all your own. It's easy to track, and even easier to catch when someone is eavesdropping on a private conversation."

"Was it true?" he demands.

"What? That you're my mate?" she asks sharply, glaring at him. "Does it matter if it's true or not?"

He doesn't answer and just stares at her with open hostility. It's obvious to her that, no, it shouldn't matter to him if she is. It shouldn't matter to her, but it does. It matters to both of them that they are mates because they feel the pull. Her wolf calling to his soul and his everything drawing her to him. That's how it's supposed to be with mates, and it's just unfair.

"Yes," she says quietly. "Yes, it's true."

"Then why are you doing this?" he demands, his voice going thick with emotion. "Mates are supposed to care about each other, take care of each other, but yet, you're trying to tear my family apart and kill them. Why the fuck would you do that?"

"You don't understand."

"Then make me understand!"

Mackenzie pulls at her hair nervously again. "You had a dad, right? A man who you cared about, would do anything for because you loved him? No matter what he did to you, you convinced yourself he did it out of love. You convinced yourself that he would sacrifice himself right back for you even if, deep down, you knew it wasn't true."

"That's what Alpha is for me, Jace," she tells him truthfully. "My father wasn't there, and Alpha chose me out of everyone else. He made me strong, independent, and able to defend myself. The world I live in, it's not like your world. While you had forehead kisses and warm meals, I had punishments and scraps. You can never understand my reasons because you can't imagine the life I live."

"Then why continue to live it?" he asks faintly.

"Because it's the only life I know."

Mackenzie wraps her arms around herself and touches the area on her hip where one of her deeper scars are. She can feel the horrific bumpiness of the skin, even through the oversized t-shirt she has on and tries not to think about the pain it caused. She deserved these lashes for disobedience. She learned her lesson then, and despite any misgivings she may have, she won't face the whip again.

"So you won't help us?"

Mackenzie shakes her head.

"Then I don't want you."

Mackenzie lifts her tear filled eyes and gives him a weak smile. "I'd be disappointed if you did."

Jace turns away from her to leave the same way as his sister and her mate. He hesitates for a second and Mackenzie thinks he's going to say something, but he doesn't. Instead, he shakes his head and refuses to look at her one last time before leaving. As the heavy metal door blockading her in slams shut behind him, she can hear her wolf howling in grief in her head.

384

Pulling her legs up against her chest, Mackenzie does something she hasn't done in many years. The grief is too much for her to bear, but she knows she deserves to bear it anyway. So she lets her tears fall down her face, feeling more alone than ever.

CHAPTER FORTY-ONE

Colton carries Rae all the way up to their room in silence. He has so much he wants to say to her, but he's afraid it won't come out right. He wants to tell her that they'll get her family back. He wants to tell her that he'll protect her no matter what. He wants to tell her that her sisters and brothers will be safe, and all of this will end with a victory. He wants to tell her all these things, but what if he can't do all those things? What if they'll just be empty promises? He can't do that to her.

He uses his elbow to push open the bedroom door, and by now, Rae's not crying anymore. She's still shaking a little, but he thinks that's just residual energy from her anger. Walking deeper into the room, Colton carries her over the bed, but when he tries to put her down, she holds him tighter. So, Colton just keeps standing and holds her until she's ready to let him go. It's the least he can do.

He heard it all, of course, the whole conversation. As soon as she left their bed after she thought he was asleep, he knew where she was going. He kept his distance, careful not to let her catch his scent and kept their link sealed shut. Jace caught him following and tagged along when he mentioned Mackenzie, something that didn't sit well with Colton.

If she wasn't a rogue, Colton would have almost feared for the kid's safety. Rae is a beast when it comes to her family and Colton knows that. Mentioning anything happening to Jolene, Garrett, or Everett would obviously send her over the edge. It didn't surprise him when it did just that, but he didn't want Rae hurting herself. Not even if it was to justly rip that girl's throat out.

With a sniffle, Rae leans back, and Colton's heart clenches at the sight of her. Her cheeks are red, her eyes sore, and her lips swollen from her crying. Laying his forehead against hers, he lets his wolf push forward enough to soothe her equally distraught wolf. As their wolves seek to each other's needs, Rae starts to relax in his arms even more.

Colton doesn't let her down as he sits on the edge of the bed and settles her in his lap. She continues to just stare at him with bloodshot brown eyes. He decides to soothe her as best as he can and kisses her forehead. She just blinks at him, and he kisses the apples of each cheek as well. He kisses each of her temples and then finally her chin, before pulling back to look at her. Her eyes were closed, but as he pulls back, they open slowly to lock onto his.

He gives her a weak smile, and she exhales, a bit unsteady before making a move. She places a hand against the side of his face and leans forward a bit to kiss him on the lips. It's light at first, barely there, before it swiftly hardens into a more demanding kiss. Colton grunts in surprise against her mouth but quickly closes his eyes when she bites his lower lip. Rae deepens the kiss, and Colton groans at the taste of her.

Rae pushes him down on the bed and straddles his lap before sitting up to look down at him. She's just dressed in a pair of ripped jeans, a white tank top, and one of his oversized hoodies. He grabs the top of her jean clad thighs and looks up at her with confusion. What is she doing?

She bites her lip, and Colton's eyes move to the area with renewed interest. Unzipping the hoodie, she strips it away and throws it behind her before turning to face him again. She tilts her head a little and licks her lower lip again, soothing her previous bite. Colton's wolf growls in his head at the sight. He wants to bite her lip. Actually, he wants to bite everything she'll let him bite. He just wants to taste her.

Rae seems to be thinking the same thing because she leans down and starts kissing him again. The kiss quickly deepens again, and Colton's hands act of their own accord. Grabbing her upper arms, he feels her smooth skin against his palm before flipping her onto her back on the bed. She lets him do this and even lets out a little mewl at the action. Colton's eyes light up at the sound, and his wolf growls lustfully in his head.

"I just want to forget about everything outside of this room," she tells him, a bit breathlessly. "Just for a little while."

Colton brushes her hair out of her face and nods before kissing her again. Half laying on top of her, Colton deepens the kiss. She opens her mouth willingly when he asks for entrance with his tongue. She buries one of her hands into his hair while the other one scratches his back through his t-shirt. The t-shirt is now an issue. So, pulling back, he reaches behind his head and pulls the shirt off and tosses it to the other end of the bed.

Rae takes in the newly exposed area hungrily, and her eyes flash gold as they meet his again. Now, *that* is sexy. She reaches one hand up and starts at the edge of his jaw and slowly caresses down his entire torso. Every bit of muscle or contour is treated to the feel of her fingers against them. Colton closes his eyes, and his arms begin to shake with the effort it's taking not to move a muscle as she explores.

"Colton," she whispers, making him open his eyes again. "You know where I want this to go, right?"

He swallows thickly and nods.

"And you know that I've done this before, right?"

Colton's whole body stills, and he looks at her blankly. Had he suspected? Yes, he had. Was he sure? No. Now, to have those thoughts confirmed though is a bitter pill to swallow. It's true that waiting for your mate is a bit of an old custom but one he took seriously. He never thought about what he would do if his mate was a virgin.

"I didn't know I was a wolf then," she says quietly.

He doesn't say anything.

"I can't change it, though, no matter how much I want to now."

Still nothing.

"What am I doing?" She sighs. "I shouldn't have to apologize for it. I didn't know you existed, and you didn't know I existed."

Colton just watches her face as she starts to get embarrassed and also a little angry. Her face flushes, and her dark blonde eyebrows furrow as she looks up at him. She starts to wiggle out from under him when he presses his body weight down on her, keeping her where she is. She scowls up at him, but he swiftly gives her a kiss before speaking before she can.

"You're right," he tells her quickly as she opens her mouth. "You shouldn't have to apologize for it. It was your decision before you even knew you were a wolf. There was no way you would know you'd be mated to me and I don't hold it against you."

"But—"

He puts his hand over her mouth, stopping her from talking. He's honestly not mad, just a little disappointed. Would it have been nice to have mutually had their first time together? Yes. Is his wolf pissed that someone was there before him? Possessively speaking, yes.

That being said, Colton is just a wolf who is occasionally a man. He's a man who becomes a wolf, and that's what he has to often remind himself. He has to see this from a human point of view, which Rae was when she made that decision. Can he be mad at her for her past? No, because that's what it was, in the past. Rae shifts under him, and he realizes he needs to get out of his head and explain himself.

"I'm not talking yet," he enlightens her with a grin. "As I was saying, I'm not upset about me not being your first. I don't think of you as some prize that has to be in perfect condition. It was the past. Over and done. So let's just move on."

389

She stares at him in what he thinks may be shock. She collects herself though and mumbles something against this hand, looking miffed. Deciding to lighten the mood a little, he leans down and angles his ear towards her covered mouth.

"What was that, baby? I couldn't hear you," he teases, only to receive a bite on his hand. He pulls it back and pouts. "That wasn't ever nice."

Rolling her eyes, Rae sighs. "Yeah, well, your hand was all sweaty."

"I'd apologize, but we both know you love it."

She smacks his arm, and he laughs. When Colton stops laughing, he just smiles down softly at her. Some people would probably think his Rae is plain, but to him, she's perfect. Large brown eyes, messy blonde hair, all the pink now completely gone from the sunny strands, and a pouty mouth. She doesn't have the dark circles under her eyes anymore, and she's not as pale. She looks beautiful, but then again, he thought she did before. He has a feeling he'll always think she is.

"Do you really mean that?" she asks quietly, regaining his attention.

Colton frowns. "Did I mean what?"

"That you didn't care?"

He doesn't like the wording. Of course, he cares, but if that makes it easier to move on, he'll go with that. He simply shrugs and concentrates on rhythmically moving his thumbs against her cheekbones. The rest of his fingers are buried in her hair. The sweet strawberry scent of her shampoo mixed with her naturally crisp apple scent is making his mouth water. He really just wants to get back to the making out and whatever else she was willing to do.

He really wants to get back to that. A lot.

"Why not?" she asks, still confused. "I mean a lot of guys, especially alphas, would have rejected me for that or even banished me."

"Because it doesn't matter, Rae. It was the past."

"But—"

"Do I have to cover your mouth again?" he asks with an arched brow.

She pouts. "No."

Before she can even think about speaking again, Colton starts kissing her. She's tense at first, but when he moves to her mark, she melts into him. He nips, licks, and kisses the mark of his wolf on their mate. This is all that matters, he tells himself. All that matters to him is that she belongs to him now and for the rest of their lives. She doesn't belong to that idiot she was with all those years ago. She belongs to him, and that itself is a powerful aphrodisiac.

Rae's nails scratch down his back, and Colton growls against her mark, making her shiver as it reverberates through her body. His fingers remove themselves from her hair to the tops of her jeans before brushing against the skin under her tank top. He can hear her heart speed up when he experimentally skims the skin just under her breasts. Rae gasps sharply when he decides to make a bolder move and grab one of the pale globes in his hand.

Colton's thumb brushes over her nipple, and she arches her back even more. He bites her earlobe quickly, making her jolt before claiming her mouth with his. He swallows her moans as he continues to play with her breast, and he can feel her practically shaking under him the longer he goes on.

He would be grinning ear to ear if his mouth wasn't busy at the moment. Foreplay he can do; he's well versed in that. It's the actual sex he's nervous about. He doesn't want to be shit on their first time, so he's made a plan, just in case. Get her off first.

Rae grabs Colton's hand off her breast, and he unlatches his mouth from hers to look down at her in question. Her brown eyes are bright gold as they stare back at him, and he groans out loud how sexy she looks like that. She continues to look him in the eye as she guides his hand down her stomach until slowly leading

391

his fingers under the waistband of her jeans. He gets the idea quickly and is eager to please.

Undoing the button of her jeans, he dives his fingers under her pale pink underwear before finding where he needs to be. Rae groans loudly and throws her head back as he starts to move his fingers against her. He works at her mark with his mouth at the rhythm of his fingers, and when he finally slips one finger into her, he bites down on the sensitive mark. She moans loudly, and her thighs press together as he feels how wet she really is, just for him.

Suddenly his hand is gone, and Rae is pushing him on his back. Her tank top is pooled around her hips, exposing her full breasts, and the top of her jeans are undone as she looks down at him. When she starts to slide off his lap, he lets out a noise between a whine and a whimper. Where is she going? Come back here!

That thought stops short when she starts pulling her jeans off her long legs. Colton's eyes watch the light blue material with anticipation as it reveals another bit of skin for him to explore. She leaves her underwear on, but does pull the tank top off so those baby pink underwear is all she has on. Her hair is a mess on the top of her head, and her lips are swollen from their kissing. Colton groans out loud again as he looks at her. She's perfect.

"Come here," he orders hoarsely and holds a hand out towards her.

Biting her lower lip, she shakes her head.

Colton immediately scowls. "Why not?"

"Because I don't want to."

His scowl gets deeper as he repeats himself, "Why not?"

"Because I want you to come and get me."

Gone is the scowl and replaced with a surprised look. "You want me to chase you?"

"I want you to catch me," she corrects.

His eyes flash gold, and she sees him smirk as his wolf pushes forward at the challenge. Slowly rising from the bed, Colton rises to his full height with excitement coursing through him. She takes a step back, but his face holds so much mischief that he knows she's not really scared. When he fakes a start, she squeals and jumps, making him laugh. She laughs too before crossing her arms across her breasts, and he pouts. He doesn't like when she hides herself from him, especially parts with darkening hickeys on them.

"Are you going to be a good boy and give the lady a head start?" She asks primly.

"No."

She gives him a scolding look. "And why is that?"

"Because no matter where you go, I'm going to find you."

Her dark eyes turn a little sad. "Do you promise?"

"Yes," he says without a moment of hesitation and walks over to her to cup her face in his hands. "No matter where you go, Rae, I will find you, and I will protect you."

Rae turns her head and kisses his palm, making electric shocks shoot up his arm. Colton leans down and gently kisses her lips before exhaling shakily. It's amazing to him that even though she's half naked in front of him, a simple kiss can still take his breath away.

Tilting his head a little, Colton places his lips against the shell of her ear and whispers, "Now run."

She bites her lip and shakes her head. "No. I have a better idea."

Wrapping her arms around his neck, she jumps up. Colton catches her and cups her behind in his hands as she wraps her legs around his waist. She starts kissing him, and he's taken back by the amount of force she's using. It's almost desperate, the way she's kissing him. He gets with her tempo quickly though, and soon, he's walking towards the next available surface. This one just so happens to be his desk.

Placing her on the edge of it, he puts his hand between them and starts rubbing her through her underwear. She gasps out loudly and starts rocking her hips against his fingers while her own hand starts rubbing over the front of his sweatpants. Colton moans loudly and starts pressing himself harder against her hand. She surprises him though when she suddenly dips her hands into his sweatpants and boxers to grip him. When she starts moving her hand, he throws his head back and groans.

Fuck, he thinks distantly, if she keeps doing that he won't last long at all.

"Stop," he begs hoarsely.

She stills her hand but doesn't let go of him. Dropping his head, he presses their foreheads together and tries to catch his breath. He was close, too close. He can't lose control like that again. He needs her to come first, but she's being stubborn. Not a big surprise, but no less aggravating. He had a plan!

"Did I do something wrong or . . ."

"No, baby," he says breathlessly as he shakes his head. "No. I just . . . this is my first time and I . . . I just want to make it last with you."

"Oh."

"Yeah."

He expects some kind of assurance, but instead, he gets her lips on his again. He groans and welcomes her tongue in his mouth before she pulls back to meet his eyes. "Take me to the bed then."

"What?"

"Unless you want to lose it on your desk," she suggests innocently before looking at the desk in question. "It does have possibilities."

"Fuck." He groans.

"Maybe later then?" she asks with a tilt of her head.

Colton growls and lifts her off the desk before practically throwing her on the bed. He lies on top of her and starts kissing her again as he starts to strip off her underwear. Throwing it to the ground with the rest of the discarded clothing, he also tries removing his sweatpants and boxers.

"Shit," he says, pausing.

"What?"

"I don't have any condoms."

"We do, but you don't need them."

"We don't?"

Rae shakes her head and looks a little annoyed. "No. I'm on birth control. We're good to go. Now go."

"Oh," he breathes before shrugging. "Good enough for me."

He resumes trying to get his pants and boxers off. He's a bit clumsy, and it takes a few tries to kick them off but once they are, he kisses her with a newfound determination. He really does want this to be great for her. When he presses himself against her though, he can feel his patience start to run a bit thin. He wants to mate with her . . . now.

"Rae."

Her name is all the question he needs to say. Rae nods to him and with one swift move, he pushes himself inside her. Fuck, he thinks, she's tight. At least he thinks she is. He has no one to compare it to, but he's having a hard time pushing himself in. So much so that he's worried he's hurting her.

"I'm fine," she assures him breathlessly. "Shit."

"Are you sure?"

She moans and arches her back, making him go in deeper. She feels amazing wrapped around him like this. Much better than he ever thought it would feel. He knew it would be amazing with Rae, she's his mate after all, but this is insane. When he pushes all the way in, they both groan.

"Okay," Rae says hoarsely. "Now, pull out slowly and then back in."

Colton is panting at this point but follows directions. When he pushes back in, she moans loudly, and he savors the sound. He looks at her for direction but she just nods, and he takes that as a sign to do it again. They continue this for a few minutes but soon, she's begging him to go faster. He watches her face as he starts to really pound into her. Her face is flushed, her mouth is open, and her eyes are squeezed shut. A few strands of her hair are damp with sweat and stick to her face, and he finds the image is just turning him on all the more.

God, he loves her.

Rae's nails scratch his back hard enough that he thinks she may have broken skin before she tightens around him. She lets out a few short moans before stilling underneath him, and Colton fights back a sigh of relief. He wasn't too sure he could have hung on much longer. Speeding up his entry, he closes his eyes and seeks his own release.

After a handful of seconds, he groans loudly and stills on top of her. Burying his head in her neck, he tries to catch his breath while listening to her try to do the same. She smells fantastic all sweaty like this. He inhales her scent deeply and groans again in satisfaction that she's completely and utterly his now.

She belongs to him, and he belongs to her. It's really that simple, and he'll be damned if some dickless rogue alpha is going to take that away from them. Colton pulls out of his mate and lies beside her before turning to pull her into his side. Rae snuggles into his side, and Colton wraps the comforter around them.

As Rae falls asleep next to him, Colton swears to the powers that brought them together, that he'll do anything to not lose this because he doesn't make promises he can't keep, and Rae needs a champion.

CHAPTER FORTY-TWO

Rae wakes up feeling the best she's felt in years. Warm, loved, and comfortable, are the words that come to her mind. Opening her eyes slowly, she comes face to face with the image of a sleeping Colton. A small smile touches her lips as she looks at his sleeping face. His brows are furrowed a little, and his lips are pouted, making her bite her lower lip, so she doesn't laugh. He just looks so adorably ridiculous.

Reaching out towards him, Rae traces the shape of his light brown eyebrows and smiles when they unfurrow. Her fingers run down the length of his nose before caressing his lips, and she feels them part. His warm breath heats her fingertips, and she feels her wolf stir in her mind. Rae's wolf pushes her to memorize his face, and Rae does as she's told. She doesn't want to forget anything. Not even a freckle.

She used to do this because she wanted to remember it for when she was old. Now she's doing it because she knows that, despite any plans they may have for defense, their chances of winning aren't great. Melancholy starts to come over Rae, and she drops her hand from Colton's lips as she fights the urge to cry.

Today is the last day they have together before everything topples on top of them. Mackenzie said they had two days, and the sand has officially run out in the hourglass. A tear slips down Rae's face, and she quickly wipes it away with a quite sniffle. She inhales shakily and tries to push away all those feelings, knowing they won't do her any good.

When Colton starts stirring beside her, Rae rubs her eyes and sighs heavily. Turning her head, she meets Colton's concerned dark blue eyes and forces a smile. She doesn't even know why she bothers to do it. Colton sees right through it, and she knew he would.

Cupping her cheek in his hand, he frowns. "What's wrong?"

Rae puts her hand on top of his. "Nothing."

"You're lying."

"I'm aware."

"Rae . . ."

"Colton," she counters thickly before asking, "Sundown?"

"That's what Andy said. The rogue was very forthcoming with information."

Rae closes her eyes painfully at the thought of Mackenzie. With a clearer head, Rae realizes that Mackenzie isn't the reason why her family is in danger. She's just a symptom of a sickness that's gripped a heartbroken man. Rae's mind wanders towards how Jace is handling all this. That girl, one of their enemies, is his mate. His other half.

"We're going to get through this," Colton assures her, bringing her out of her thoughts.

"Colton, promise me something."

His expression immediately turns wary. "What?"

"Promise me that if anything happens to me, if they end up taking me, that you'll look after my family. I need to know they'll be in good hands if I don't make it out of this in one piece. I need to know that you'll protect them."

"Why are you talking like this?"

"Colton, please, just promise me that you'll do that for me."

"No," he snaps as he sits up. "No, I won't promise it because you won't need me to take care of them. You'll be here."

"The outcome isn't going to be that assured, Colton. We need to think about what could happen if they win."

"No."

"Colton—"

"I said no!" he snarls, getting out of the bed.

Rae watches his every move as he quickly dresses himself. Pulling on a pair of boxers, he turns back to her, scowling. Rae sits up in bed and has no doubt she looks a mess. She can feel her hair sticking up in every direction, and her body feels a little sore from last night. Also, she's naked underneath the blanket, and she pulls it up to her collarbones, blushing. Probably not the time to get shy, but oh well.

Leaning down on the edge of the bed, Colton glares at Rae, and she averts her gaze to her lap. She should have known he'd react this way, but she needs the reassurance that he'll take care of her family. She won't let anything to happen to them, no matter what that may cost her.

"I don't want to talk about it, Rae. I don't want to even think about this going the wrong way. You, screaming my name as you're ripped from me... it haunts my dreams. I won't lose you because I can't go on without you by my side."

"Why?" Rae whispers, not even sure why she says it.

"Why?" he repeats with a frown, apparently as confused as she is. "Because I love you, Rae. Isn't it obvious?"

Rae's heart stops in her chest. He'd implied it. Showed her with his actions, but he'd never said it. He never said that he loved her, explicitly. A part of her is observing, rather dryly, that he waited until the eleventh hour to say it, but it's a very small part of her. The rest is blown away that he would really love her and openly admit it.

Suddenly, he comes crawling onto the bed and cups her face in his hands. His thumbs wipe away the unexpected falling tears from her cheeks. Rae closes her eyes and tries to get her head together enough to respond, but all that keeps coming out are little sobs.

"You really didn't know?" Colton asks sadly.

"I . . ." she trails off before letting out a sob. Taking a deep breath, she opens her eyes and gives him a small smile. "You have the worst timing in the world."

"That's all I get?" he asks with a pout.

Rolling her eyes, Rae pulls his head down and kisses him soundly on the lips. Of course, she loves him. She's been in love with him since the morning she saw him in her kitchen with her little sisters. It was a small love at first, but it's grown steadily over their time together to the point that she couldn't be without him.

The kiss deepens, and Colton pushes Rae back down on the bed. There isn't any more discussion about promises, the ensuing battle, or the possible outcomes if they lose. All there is, is Rae and Colton, just for a little while longer. Just until they're ready to face the fact that that this may be all they have left.

* * *

The rest of the day goes by in a blur for Rae. She puts her siblings through their paces again, this time including a very put out Cassidy. Rae's youngest sibling was not happy about the disruption in her birthday party, or being left out of "the fun" as she calls it.

Apparently, watching her older siblings be tossed around by Rae is hilarious to Cassidy, and maybe if Rae wasn't as stressed as she is, she'd agree. They all seem to be able to feel it, the impending danger. Cleo has even been buckling down and taking the lessons seriously.

After Jessica comes to collect Cassidy for a nap, something Rae still thinks the overactive kid needs, Rae stops taking it easy on her other siblings. Over the course of the day, Rae has felt her pride grow for her siblings. They've all improved.

Cleo has been sparring with Hudson half of the day and half with her. Hudson and her have been switching between both Jace and Cleo. Since both are shifters, they can heal, and Rae doesn't want them taking it easy on each other in fear of injury.

Poppy has been the one to surprise Rae the most. After lunch, they start doing senses training. It's something their father used to do with them when they were kids and Poppy excels at it. Senses training is when one person stands in the woods, blindfolded, while the others try to take them by surprise. Only relying on senses, the person must block hits and land at least one hit. Poppy, up to date, has been kicking ass. She even knocked Jace on his ass a few times, and Rae has never been more proud.

"What are you, a freaking ninja?" Jace grumbles as he gets up from yet another Poppy tackle.

"She wouldn't be getting you if you were paying better attention."

He ignores Rae and turns back to Poppy to demand, "How do you do it?"

"It's just . . . easy," Poppy pants at him with a shrug.

Rae winces at that. It is easy for Poppy. Rae has an inkling that she knows why as well. The signs, though more subtle with Hudson, are there for Poppy. Rae's suspicions about Poppy having the gene just gets more justification as the afternoon has worn on. Rae just hopes she'll be here to guide Poppy through her first shift like she did for Hudson. Shaking the thought from her mind, Rae adjusts her headband in her hair and puts her hands on her hips.

"Let's call it a day."

All five of her siblings look at her with matching frowns. It's moments like this that Rae realizes how much they all look alike. It's hard to see it when they're individual, but as a group like this, you can tell an Applebee on sight. They all have the same frown, one that they inherited from their father. His scowl was legendary.

"But we aren't ready yet," Cleo says as she pushes a stray bit of hair behind her ear.

"We'll be as ready as we'll ever be," Rae tells her. "They're coming at sundown."

"How do you know?" Jace asks, stepping forward.

Rae hesitates but eventually tells him, "Mackenzie."

Jace's whole face shuts down, and he looks away. Rae can see his pain, she can almost feel it inside herself, it's so strong. She's pretty sure he didn't reject Mackenzie, he was raised better than that, but she's positive he said some things he regrets to her. Either way, she decides to ask.

"Did you . . ."

"No."

Rae sighs heavily. "Well, that's good."

Jace glares at her. "Is it?"

"What am I missing here?" Cleo asks, looking between the two of them.

"Jace—"

"Shut up, Rae!" Jace snaps, running his hand roughly through his hair.

"Seriously, what's going on?" Cleo asks again.

"He found his mate," Rae tells her quietly.

"You did?" Hudson asks, trying to catch Jace's tortured gaze. "Who is it?"

"A rogue," Jace spits.

Cleo's expression twists into horror. "The one they caught yesterday?"

Jace grits his teeth. "Yes."

"Holy shit."

Rae winces, but has to agree with Cleo's word choice. It's not a good situation to be in, especially with the incoming battle only a few hours away. Looking up at the sky, she knows that she only has a few hours, maybe three, before the siege. She needs to say her goodbyes now. Dalton will want to go over strategy soon, and they need to lock down the pack house. There won't be any other time, and Rae wants to do it right.

Taking a deep breath, Rae suddenly walks towards Jace. Wrapping her arms around his neck, she hugs him tightly. It's something she hasn't done since their mom's funeral. Jace has always been physically distant. He's never been a fan of physical affection, but if this is their last night as a family, Rae wants him to know she loves him. His returned hug is slow, but once she feels arms wrap back around her, she closes her eyes.

"Rae . . ."

"I love you, baby brother."

"I . . . love you, too."

"She loves you too," she tells him. Jace tenses but Rae keeps going. "If she didn't, she wouldn't have warned you. If she didn't care, she wouldn't have risked everything by crossing into our borders just to get to you. You don't have to accept her right away, Jace. Just let her try."

Jace tightens his arms around her, and Rae inhales his maple scent before pulling back and putting her hands on his shoulder. Looking him in his bright blue eyes, Rae tries to tell him how much she trusts him to do the right thing. It's his decision, she knows that, but she hopes her words have helped a little.

Stepping back from Jace, she looks over at Poppy. Rae gets down on her knees in front of her sister while she gives her a little smile of assurance, but Poppy's blue eyes are already tearing up. Poppy wipes her cheeks with her small hands before pushing up her large brown glasses. Rae sighs and brushes back a strand of her sister's dirty blonde hair from her face.

"You're such a big girl, you know that?"

Poppy nods, her chin wobbling as more tears escape.

"You're going to be such a strong woman," Rae says, her own tears running over.

"Please, don't leave me, Rae," Poppy begs.

"I'm sorry, baby, but I have to go."

"I'm not like you, Rae. I'm not strong. I'm scared."

Rae grabs Poppy by the shoulders and kisses her forehead. "I'm scared too, but that doesn't mean I'm not going to be brave."

Poppy wraps her arms around Rae's neck, and Rae hugs her little sister tightly. She inhales Poppy's scent but frowns when she notices how faint it is. It's been getting fainter over the past few months but not noticeably. It's only now that Rae has her nose buried in her sister's neck does she even notice the subtle change. Deciding not to dwell on it, Rae pulls back from the hug and kisses her sister's forehead again.

"You take care of Cassidy for me."

Poppy nods and wipes away more tears.

Rae nods too before getting to her feet again. She gives a teary-eyed smile to Hudson who's already on the verge of crying. He shakily reaches out and grabs Rae's wrist before pulling her into his body for a hug. Rae hugs him back and brushes his hair with her hand. Kissing his cheek, Rae pulls back and gives him another smile, this one more genuine.

"Joseph is one lucky man."

Hudson chuckles before wiping away a stray tear from under one brown eye. "Not as lucky as Colton."

Rae laughs too before ruffling his hair. "Keep your flanks protected, okay? That's your weak point."

"I will."

Rae wipes her face with her clammy hands and turns to Cleo who is trying so hard not to cry. As the resident cry baby in the family, Rae is surprised Cleo has been able to keep it together as long as she has. Cleo's arms are wrapped around her middle, and her eyes are on her shoes as she chews on her bottom lip.

"Cleo . . ."

"I'm not going to say goodbye," Cleo says quietly. "Don't ask me to do it."

"Why? You never do what I say anyway," Rae says with a huff of a laugh.

Cleo glares at her. "It won't matter if I say it because nothing is going to happen to you."

"Please, for once in your life, be reasonable."

"No," Cleo denies, shaking her head. "I don't have to be anything."

Rae can't help her eye roll. "Now, you're just being ridiculous."

"I don't care."

"Cleo." Rae sighs. "Would it kill you to just say goodbye like a normal person and not start a fight?"

"I . . ." Cleo trails off before looking up at Rae. Her eyes are filled with tears, and her mascara is already starting to run. "I'm sorry."

"For what?" Rae asks with a frown.

"For being such a bitch to you."

Rae laughs a little. "It's fine."

"No, it isn't. I was awful to you. I was awful to everyone, and I feel like shit knowing that I can't help you with this. You're sacrificing everything for us, again. I don't just want to sit here and watch it happen, Rae. Not anymore."

Rae walks closer to Cleo and cups her face in her hands. Cleo's lower lip trembles, and Rae pulls her into a hug. It's been even longer for Cleo and Rae when it comes to physical affection. I think the last time they hugged like this, Rae was thirteen and Cleo was eleven. Cleo grabs onto the back of Rae's shirt and sobs into her shoulder, making Rae fight her own tears. God, how much more of this does she have to take? It's the reason she's not saying goodbye to Cassidy. She couldn't handle it. Rae knows she couldn't handle that. This is almost proving to be too much.

"You are the best sister I could ask for," Rae tells her, tears audible in her voice. "You pushed me and drove me insane, but I wouldn't trade you. Not for anything or anyone else in the world."

"Don't leave me alone," Cleo begs. "Please don't make me do this on my own."

405

Rae pulls back and takes her sister's face in her hands again. "You're not alone. Not anymore. You have Andy, and you have the rest of the family. You don't need me to be strong, Cleo. You've been strong all on your own."

Cleo shakes her head. "I'm not. I won't be."

"You will."

"Promise me you'll try your best to come back, okay? Even if it's a lie, just promise me that you'll come back."

Rae lets out her own sob before smiling at her sister. "Have I ever let you down?"

Cleo hugs her again, and Rae tries to commit the embrace to memory. Even if she does make it out of this, she's not sure when this will even happen again. Eventually, Rae hears Dalton call for her down the pack line and forcibly removes herself from Cleo's hold. Stepping back, she looks at all of her siblings one last time before turning on a heel and walking away from them.

Rae closes her eyes when she hears Cleo and Poppy's crying and tries to block it out. Standing up a bit straighter, Rae stops her crying and pushes away her pain to summon her strength. She doesn't know when she'll see her brothers and sisters again. She doesn't know if she ever will, but she'll do her best to make sure that no one will ever threaten them again.

Over her dead body.

CHAPTER FORTY-THREE

Cleo closes her eyes and tries to stop the tears that continue to fall. She hasn't been able to stop them since Rae left Cleo and her siblings back in the woods. Cleo walked away soon after Rae disappeared from sight. She's been sitting under this large redwood tree ever since, just thinking about the situation.

She wishes there was something she could do to help her sister, but she can't. Cleo knows she doesn't have the guts to sacrifice herself in place of Rae. She's not even sure this crazy alpha would even take her. Most likely he'd just kill her or use her as bait to get Rae to go to him. Cleo won't risk any chance of Rae giving in without a fight.

It's getting later in the day, but the sun is still high in the sky. When it falls to the tree lines, Cleo knows that she won't be allowed to be here by herself anymore. Wiping away a stray tear, she folds her legs underneath her before reaching up to tighten her ponytail. She just needs some time to herself, to breathe in the air, and try to gather her strength.

She did this a lot after her mom died and her dad disappeared. She would often be by herself, in her room, just thinking. Trying to understand why her dad could just leave them like that without even a second thought. An image of him when he heard that their mom had died is something, even three years later, Cleo can't erase from her mind.

Is that what Colton will look like if they lose? Will he lose his mind too and leave them all? The thought is a chilling one for Cleo. Despite appearances, she really likes Colton for Rae. They suit each other so perfectly and give each other exactly what the other needs. It's all Cleo could have hoped for her sister, all she would have wished for her if she'd been in her right mind these past few years.

It's something that's been dawning on her since Rae was gravely injured by their dad's wolf. It wasn't instantaneous, though. Just little things that Cleo has been noticing after that initial wake-up call. Watching Rae with Cassidy and Poppy. How she handled Hudson's shift. And how she's been dealing with both Hudson and Cleo herself, finding their mates. All of it just reminded Cleo how much she needs Rae. She could never have done any of that if Rae wasn't there.

The idea of losing her now is an overwhelming feeling to contend with. Cleo fights back another sob building in her throat as the idea seems to anchor itself in her mind. She can't do this again. She can't lose another person in her family. She lost her best mom to random chance and her dad to madness. She can't lose her big sister to yet another thing out of her control. She's not sure she'll survive it this time.

"Cleo!"

Cleo's head lifts up at the sound of Andy's frantic voice. She doesn't respond to him; she knows that he'll find her. He can always find her, no matter where she tries to hide. It's one of the things, among many, she's grown to love about him.

When she hears his footfalls growing closer, she quickly attempts to wipe all traces of her recent crying from her face. It's no use, though. Like Rae, she's a horrible crier, and it takes a while for the swelling to go down. Still, she tries to hide her emotions from Andy, no matter how useless it is. He always sees through it anyway.

When he comes into view, Cleo can feel her heart pick up in speed in her chest. It does that every time she sees him now. Even since they started sharing a room, she still gets butterflies just seeing his face beside her. It's something she never thought she could have, but now it's here, right in front of her.

"Hey, hey, what's wrong?" Andy asks as he comes to kneel before her and takes her face in his hands.

She gives him a shaky smile. "I'm fine."

"Bullshit."

Cleo rolls her light blue eyes at him. "You always think I'm lying."

"Not always," he corrects. "Just when you are."

She laughs a little. "Good point."

He swipes his thumb against her damp cheeks and frowns. "What's wrong?"

"I . . . Rae said her goodbyes."

"Goodbyes?"

She nods. "She said she wouldn't be able to do it later."

"She'll be expected on the front line as soon as dusk falls. She needs to prepare."

"I know," Cleo mumbles, her eyes getting blurry again with tears. "It just felt so final, you know?"

"She's going to be okay, baby, you'll see."

"And if she isn't?"

Andy tightens his hands on her face and forces her to look up at him. "Don't say that. You're just only going to upset yourself."

"But what if you lose? What if we all lose? I can't lose her. I can't lose you."

"You won't lose me, and you won't lose Rae," he insists.

"You can't promise me that."

Andy narrows his dark eyes at her in consideration before suddenly moving forward. Cleo closes her eyes as soon as his lips connect with hers and her toes curl in her sneakers. She'll never get

409

used to this, she thinks. How many times has she kissed someone and begged that she could feel something, anything that could take away her pain? She didn't know at the time, but what she was wishing for was Andy, because with just a simple kiss, he can take it all away.

Cleo wraps her arms around his neck, and he wraps his arms around her waist. Pulling her into his lap, Andy makes sure there's barely an inch between them. Cleo straddles his lap, but it isn't sexual or demanding. Even the kiss is soft and sweet, reassuring almost. He just wants her to know that he's there. He's done this a lot the past few weeks, Cleo notes. Just holds her and never demanding more.

It's nice sometimes, she realizes, just to be held.

Laying her forehead against his, Cleo keeps her eyes closed. "Thank you."

She can feel his eyes on her. "For what?"

"Being here, I guess."

"I'm not going anywhere, Cleo. I've told you that."

"I know." She sighs. "It's still hard to believe, though."

Andy grabs her chin and angles her head back. Cleo opens her eyes and sees Andy's perfect face go serious. "I'm not going anywhere, Cleo. I want you and only you. You belong to me, and I belong to you. I can't say it any other way. I don't know how to make you believe me."

Cleo bites the inside of her cheek as she reaches up to touch his smooth dark skin. She traces the shape of his high cheekbones, the length of his nose, the shape of his eyes, and finally the fullness of his lips. Leaning forward, she gives him a brief but meaningful kiss on the lips. He whines a little when she pulls back, and Cleo smiles at the sound of it.

"What was that for?" he asks, his voice rougher.

She shrugs. "Just another thank you."

"Well, feel free to thank me like that anytime."

Cleo laughs. "I'll remember that."

"I love you, you know that, right?"

Cleo stops laughing and feels her cheeks heat up as she shrugs. "Yeah, I guess."

"You guess?" he asks flatly.

She shrugs again.

Suddenly, Andy flips them over and presses her against the ground as he hovers over her. Running his hands through her long blonde hair, he looks down at her adoringly. The look affects Cleo more than it probably should have; she can't help that. She likes that look on his face. It's one she hasn't seen a lot, one that she hasn't earned in a long time, but one she treasures all the same.

"You guess," he repeats sullenly.

Cleo smiles up at him and shrugs again. "Yup."

"Are you trying to drive me crazy?"

"Is it working?"

"Maybe."

"Then maybe." She grins.

Grabbing her face again, he looks her in the eyes as he repeats, "I love you, baby. No one else but you."

She sighs heavily. "I suppose you're going to promise me that it's the truth, aren't you?"

His lips twitch up a little at the ends. "Yes."

"How predictable."

He nuzzles her neck and laughs. "Can't please you, can I?"

"It appears not."

"There's nothing I can do?" he asks as he kisses along her jaw line.

Cleo's breathing starts to become a bit labored as she shuts her eyes. Little shocks move across her skin with each kiss, and she can feel herself getting more turned on with each precise peck. It's driving her insane, especially because they haven't done anything beyond this.

Despite any appearances or assumptions her family has made about her, Cleo has only had sex with three people. All three

411

were boyfriends that she was with for longer than a month. She's done other things with other boys, but not sex. That she saved for people she thought she really liked. Kip, the guy she was seeing before meeting Andy, being an exception.

Cleo didn't really like Kip, but after Rae had embarrassed her at school, she wanted to get back at her. Petty and really shitty of her, Cleo can admit that now, but at that time it seemed like a good idea. Problem was that as soon as they started getting there, Cleo freaked out. She didn't really want to do this, did she? She tried to get Kip off of her and that she didn't want to do it anymore, and that was when Jace came in. He'd heard her saying no and thought that she was being hurt.

Cleo cringes even thinking about the whole episode, it was so embarrassing. She learned her lesson, though. She needs to be ready to take that step, and though she knows she loves Andy, she wants it to be perfect when they finally make that choice. She wants to make it special, just for him.

"You're trying to distract me," Cleo says breathlessly when he nips at the mark on her shoulder.

"Am I? I thought I was just showing you that I can please you."

Cleo weakly smacks his shoulder. "Pervert."

"Sexually frustrated is the term I'd use."

She rolls her eyes at his mumbled words. "Yeah, well, get over it."

Lifting his head, he looks down at her reassuringly. "I'm not complaining, baby. I know how much it means to you to wait."

"I just want to be sure that this is real."

He leans forward to nip her earlobe before pulling back to smirk at her. "Did that feel real?"

She glares at him with a pout. "Not fair."

"I never said I played fair."

Biting her lip, Cleo sighs. "I suppose . . . that I love you too."

He looks surprised at first before a brilliant smile comes across his face. "You suppose?"

"Take it or leave it."

"You're killing my ego here, you know that, don't you?"

"Knowing you, a little ego check wouldn't do any harm," she drawls.

Andy laughs, making his body shake above hers before grinning down at her. "Are you trying to take me down a peg?"

Cleo eyes him warily. "Depends if you need to be."

"Not today," he says quietly, rubbing his nose against hers. "Today, I just need you to stay safe. Can you do that for me?"

"Can you promise me the same?" she asks, feeling fear grip her heart.

"I can promise that I'll be doing everything I can to come back to you in one piece."

"I don't need you in one piece, Andrew. I need you alive," she snaps, feeling edgy even talking about it.

"Shit. You full named me," he notes in mock fear. "You must mean business."

She slaps his arm. "Don't be cute. I'm being serious."

Andy sighs heavily and starts running his fingers through her ponytail again. "I know, baby. I know."

"So? Can you promise me you'll come back alive?"

"Only if you can promise me that you'll stay safe."

Cleo bites on the inside of her cheek again and nods. "Fine. I promise to stay safe."

"Then I promise to come back alive," he agrees with a smile. "Seal it with a kiss?"

She pretends to think about it before grabbing the back of his head and meeting him half way. The kiss deepens and Cleo feels tears start to well in her eyes again. She can't lose him. She can't lose anyone. She doesn't have any grief left to give, and she's too selfish to give anyone up.

As the day starts to fade into dusk, the two stay wrapped up in each other, pretending just for a little while, that everything isn't about to change. And as the sun hits the tree line, howls start to be heard. Howls of an incoming army.

CHAPTER FORTY-FOUR

Rae tightens her grip on the edge of the couch and mumbles to herself. She's alone in the living room at the moment. Everyone else is either getting their orders from Dalton or saying goodbye to their loved ones. Rae, meanwhile, is just trying to get mentally prepared for the horrors of what's about to happen.

Rae isn't a fool. She knows that with war comes casualties, and that means from her pack as well. This, of course, weighs heavily on her mind. She doesn't want to be the one responsible for the deaths of loved ones. She doesn't want to be the one who is haunted by the screams of the injured and dying. She never wanted that, but that's what she knows is sure to come. That's what war is after all, death, destruction, and loss. She just never thought she'd be the cause of it.

Squeezing her eyes shut, Rae can feel a tear escape from under her eyelid, and she quickly bats it away. Now isn't the time for crying. She's the beta female, and soon, she'll be alpha female. She needs to be strong. Crying or being weak is something her pack doesn't need to see. Taking a few shaky intakes of breath, Rae manages to calm down a bit and runs through the plan Dalton laid out earlier.

Mackenzie told them they would be coming from the north end of the territory. Rae knows she could be lying of course, but it doesn't seem like it. A few sentries have been noticing a lot of activity on that side of the boundary. That's why Rae, Colton, and

Dalton will be stationed there, facing the threat head on. Dalton's delta, or third in command, Lana, along with Andy, will be in charge with keeping the remaining boundary lines secured.

Hudson, along with the younger shifting wolves, are in charge of protecting the pack house. The younger wolves will be managed and under the command of Vivienne. Inside the pack house, Jessica, Cleo, Jace, Sawyer, and Joseph, along with all other able-bodied non-shifting pack members will be ready in case the line is broken. All the kids, Poppy and Cassidy included, are to be locked away in the basement with two more able-bodied non-shifters guarding there. The kids are the most important to the pack and as such, are the best protected.

As Rae repeats this over and over in her head, she tries to let that calm her down. All of her family members will be fine if the front line isn't broken, and that's what her goal is. She doesn't want that alpha getting anywhere close to the pack house, even if she has to take him down herself. Of course, this is where her frustration comes in.

Dalton, as well as Colton, have ordered her to stay as far away from the alpha as possible. They don't want the risk of him just grabbing her and running. Rae doesn't want that to happen either, but she's also not going to sit there and rely on someone else if he comes straight for her. She's going to fight him until she can't fight anymore. If she's going down, she's taking him with her.

Tingling trails move down her cheek, and she opens her eyes to see the concerned blue eyes, belonging to Colton, staring at her. His fingers grasp her chin and angle her head up, so she's looking him in the eyes. She tries not to show how afraid she is of what's coming, but when her lower lip starts to tremble, she knows she's failed. With a pained expression, Colton pulls Rae into a hug, and she buries her head in the curve of his neck.

Inhaling his indescribable scent, Rae tries to stop her tears before they fall. She lies to herself and says everything will be okay. Her family will be fine, she tells herself. She'll get Jolene, Garrett, and Everett back in one piece and no one will lose their mates. At this moment, she doesn't care if all of those things are impossible. She just needs them to get out of this room and face the incoming threat.

"I'm not going to let anything happen to you," Colton swears lowly in her ear.

"What about you?" Rae whispers back. "I can't go on without you."

"You can if you have to, Rae. I don't want you getting lost in the grief."

Rae pulls back and gapes at him. "What?"

"You heard me," he says roughly, almost unwillingly. "If something happens to me, I don't want you sulking for the rest of your life. You're going to have to move on."

"What the hell are you talking about, Colton?"

"Just promise me that you'll try," he pleads, grabbing her face in his hands. "Just promise me that if I die today, I can pass on knowing that you won't give up. Your family needs you."

"But I need you," she insists, her vision getting blurry again.

Colton sighs and lays his forehead against hers. "Please, Rae, just promise me."

Placing her hands over his, Rae closes her eyes in agony. She feels a tear roll down her cheek as she nods, agreeing to the impossible yet again. Can she move on when her other half is dead? Her father wasn't strong enough to do it, and he was the strongest person she knew. Rae's not too sure she can or would even want to try but she made a promise, and if it happens, she'll have to do her best.

Colton connects their lips, and Rae is sure he can taste her tears. She wraps her arms around his neck and buries her hands in his hair. She tries to memorize his taste, his smell, and even the feel of him. Just in case, she tells herself, it's all just in case. When he pulls back, Rae opens her eyes and looks him in the eye squarely.

417

She watches his eyes shine gold for a second before going back to their cool blue. It's his wolf reassuring her, she realizes.

"I love you," she whispers lowly. "I love you so much."

Colton gives her a sad smile. "I love you more than you can comprehend."

Despite herself and the situation, Rae laughs a little. "I don't know about that."

"I do," he insists before grabbing one of her hands in his. "We have to go."

Rae takes in a deep breath and collects any and all fortitude she can. Wiping her cheeks with the edge of her t-shirt, she straightens her back and gives Colton a nod. She's ready for this. Colton kisses her temple swiftly before starting to lead her out of the pack house and into the expansive front yard. Rae's feet stumble a bit when she sees the whole pack assembled before her as the sun starts to set in the sky with only an hour or so left.

An older woman, maybe in her fifties, bows her head towards Rae as she comes to a stop beside her. "Beta."

Rae clumsily bows her head back, but she doesn't know the woman's name, so she leaves it at that. Colton starts pulling her through the crowd, and as they move past each person, they call out to her and bow. Rae's overwhelmed by the respect and reverence she sees on their faces as they greet her. It almost brings her to tears all over again.

When she spots Hudson in the crowd, he gives her a small smile and bows his head. "Beta."

That's the tipping point. Her tears spill over, and she gives him a small pitiful smile before nodding at a forlorn looking Joseph beside her brother. He returns the gesture and also gives her a small smile. Jace is holding Poppy and Cassidy's hands as Rae passes by them.

Jace surprises Rae by bowing to her, and it takes Rae a minute to return it. Poppy's crying again and is too busy wiping her eyes to do anything. Cassidy, on the other hand, starts to squirm as soon as she sees Rae. Rae frowns a little and wonders where Cleo is.

Eventually, Cassidy gets her hand free before running to Rae. Rae crouches down and catches Cassidy as the little girl jumps up on her. Cassidy lays her head on Rae's shoulder, and Rae looks skyward in an attempt to stop these damn tears once and for all.

"Don't go," Cassidy whines quietly. "I don't want you to go."

Rae reaches up and dashes away a fallen tear. "I'll come back."

"You promised you wouldn't leave, Rae. You promised you wouldn't leave like mama."

"I'm not going to leave," Rae says roughly, trying not to break down. "Jace, come take her."

"No!" Cassidy yells and starts fighting.

"Jace!" Rae calls, her voice almost a sob, as she starts prying Cassidy off her.

Jace comes over and grabs Cassidy, but she's fighting him as hard as she can. Cassidy slaps and kicks as hard as she can, trying to get back to Rae. Rae turns away from Cassidy and tries to head forward, but she can still hear Cassidy wailing from behind her.

"Let me go! Rae! I'll be good! I promise I'll be better! Please come back! Rae! Please!"

Rae covers her mouth to stop an escaping sob and Colton pulls her closer to him. When they come to a stop before the alpha and alpha female, Rae is a mess. Jessica is also crying and reaches out to cup Rae's face before kissing her forehead. In the back of her mind, Rae wonders how many times Jessica has had to say goodbye to her sons in the past.

"I'll take care of her, Rae," Jessica promises.

Rae just nods. She's too upset to do much else.

Howls sound in the distance, and all the shifters in the area turn in the direction of their source: the north. Mackenzie, it turns out, wasn't lying. Rae isn't comforted much by the idea, but it's

419

good to know that Jace isn't mated to a liar. Alpha Dalton squares his shoulders and gives Rae a nod. She returns it just before Colton starts to pull her off the side of his parents. It appears the alpha has something to say.

"Tonight, the rogues have stepped over a line. They crossed our boundaries and have sought to take what does not belong to them. They have come for our beta female. They have come to destroy what fate has designed, and they have come seeking war. We are not weak; we never have been. And tonight, we show them how strong we really are. We show them what happens to those who step over the line. We show them that death is the penalty, and we will show them without mercy."

Howls, cheers, and yells fill the air, and Rae closes her eyes as she soaks it in. She can feel their loyalty and their conviction through the pack link. It strengthens her and gives her a sense of conviction of her own. She'll do anything to protect this pack, and she'll do it all without question.

Dalton turns to both Rae, and Colton with grave eyes and gives them another nod. Both of them know what to do and give each other one last longing look before facing forward. Rae closes her eyes and starts running towards the north. Her body shakes and contours as she runs and soon, she's on all fours as her clothes start to rip from her body.

When she opens her eyes, she's at a lower level, and she can feel the freedom of her second skin take over. Turning her head, she sees Colton's large brown wolf running beside her. To the left, she sees the massive figure of her alpha's wolf. He's a black wolf with powerful gait and a fierce look on his face. Not someone Rae would want to mess with, that's for sure.

The howling of the rogues doesn't only start to intensify, but it also seems to be coming from every direction. Rae slows down her speed and looks along the tree line quickly. It's still too close to dawn. At night, wolves have great vision. During the day, even better sight, but at dusk or dawn, they have a hard time. Rae can't make out anything.

It's starting . . . Rae's whispering down the pack line as realization dawns. *They aren't going to wait for night. They're going to attack now!*

No one can respond to her before a wolf comes out of the bush and barrels into Rae. She lands on the forest floor with a yelp and hears Colton snarl, but he too is quickly attacked. The scrawny wolf on top of her snaps its jaws at her, and Rae snarls back at it as it pins her down by her shoulders. Moving her head as far as she can, Rae grabs its front leg in her mouth and bites down.

The wolf yelps loudly and jumps off her, blood running down its front leg. Rae can taste its blood in her mouth, but it only excites her wolf more. Before the rogue can collect itself, Rae charges and attempts to wrap her jaws around its neck. It moves at the last second but gives her its side. Using her claws, she drags the sharp ends down the side of its ruddy fur and feels more blood coat her.

When it does finally manage to gain some space, she quickly wraps her teeth around its muzzle and drags it down to the ground. Once she has it pinned, she buries her teeth into its neck and doesn't hesitate to rip its throat out. It lets out one last whine before it stops moving. Rae can hear its heart slow down until finally, as it bleeds out, it goes silent.

Backing away from the dead rogue, Rae turns around to spot Dalton dispatching of three rogues at the same time. She looks around to see the other five shifters of her group also battling rogues. Rae spots one of their pack members on the ground already dead. Looking away from the sight, Rae looks for Colton. She runs through the mayhem and spots his wolf battling another large gray and white one.

Rae lets out a snarl and runs towards them but is stopped when a rogue bites her ankle. It drags her away from Colton just as a rogue drags its claws down Colton's side. Rae flips around the best she can and tries to swipe at the rogue, but her body doesn't allow that kind of contorting. It's moments like this the human form is almost preferable to the wolf one. More flexibility, definitely.

Suddenly, her body is dropped to the forest floor, and the pain in her ankle is gone. She twists around in time to see Dalton with the rogue in his jaws. He's shaking the beast's body all over. When he rams its body into a large tree, Rae hears its neck snap and sees its body go limp. Dalton drops the body and looks Rae in the eye quickly before turning away as another rogue comes up behind him.

Rae gets to her feet and ignores the pain in her back leg as she tries to run for Colton again. He's battling two rogues now, and Rae uses her body weight to push the one anchored to Colton's back off him. She's able to quickly bury her claws into the wolf's belly—a weak spot, and is about to retract her paw from it when something comes down the pack line.

They've broken the line! East side.

Rae snarls and removes her claws from the now dead rogue. *How deep in are they?*

Sentries at the pack house have spotted them, Andy tells her bluntly before his attention is taken off of the conversation.

Shit! She starts running for the pack house when she hears Colton's wolf yelp. She stops and turns back to see a rogue biting his ear and dragging him to the ground. Rae can't leave him on his own. At this rate, he'll never make it. Growling lowly, Rae starts running back for Colton as she starts to reach out for Hudson down the familial line.

Hudson, you hear me?

Yeah, I hear you.

They're coming. Rogues are approaching. From the east.

Shit!

Protect your flanks!

Hudson hesitates to answer, but when he does, his voice is full of fear. *I will. Stay safe, Rae.*

You just stay alive.

Rae shuts down the link just in time to slam her body into the wolf on Colton. She manages to push it down a slope on the other side of where Colton is. When she knows it's out of the way, she looks over at Colton and sees him panting and bloody. Her wolf whines out loud before she can stop it as Colton's head snaps up, looking a little ashamed. Looking around, Rae notices that all the rogues in this area are either dead or have run off.

Are you okay? she asks as she turns back to Colton. Walking closer to him, she starts licking the wounds on his muzzle, hoping to speed up his healing.

Yes.

Good, now protect your fucking flanks, Rae snarls at him as she steps back. *You and Hudson will be the death of me, I swear.*

Are you okay? he asks after a minute.

They broke the line.

Colton lets out a huff out of his muzzle. *I know, I heard.*

Move out! Dalton's voice orders as his wolf form moves past them.

Rae looks over Colton one last time before following after the alpha. They still have a few more miles before they reach the northern boundary line. There will be more attacks and more chances for them to take out more of the alpha's entourage. They've already lost one. How many more will they lose?

423

CHAPTER FORTY-FIVE

Hudson can hear the pack's sentries speaking down the pack line and feels his wolf become edgy. The rogues have broken through the front line, and that means that pretty soon they'll be at their doorstep. He turns his attention to Vivienne, who is standing in front of him and the group of younger shifts. Her wolf is red in color with gray around her eyes, making the agitation there seem even more noticeable.

Surround the perimeter of the house, she growls down the line. When they hesitate, she turns to face them and lets out a snarl before her voice comes down the mind link again. *Now!*

The younger wolves jump into action and begin to follow her command. Hudson decides to stay closer to the entrance of the pack house. The fact that the rest of his siblings, as well as his mate, are in there comes to the forefront of his mind. He doesn't want anyone getting past this door, and the only way he can make sure that doesn't happen is if he does that himself.

Hudson widens his stance and keeps his eyes on the tree line when he hears a faint voice in his head. It's not as strong as the pack line, but he's pretty sure that if he concentrates on it enough, he can make it out. It only takes a few seconds to figure out that the voice is familiar to him. It's Rae!

Hudson, you hear me?

Hudson's body relaxes when he hears her voice. *Yeah, I'm here.*

They're coming. Rogues are approaching. From the east."
Shit!

He says it before he can even think about it. From the east, he repeats to himself. That means they'll be coming straight in his direction, and he's pretty sure they're going for a direct offensive. That means that most of the issues will be mean guarding the front entrance. Unless that's what they want, a distraction. Hudson can feel his fear rise, but he attempts to push it down. She doesn't need to know he's scared shitless right now.

Protect your flanks! Rae barks at him, concern and agitation clear in her voice.

I will, he tells her before wincing at how terrified he sounds. *Stay safe, Rae.*

You just stay alive.

She cuts off the familial link quickly after that, and Hudson feels his panic triple. Shit, shit, shit. What is he going to do? Rae was right, he thinks. He's not well equipped enough for this. Like most things in his life, Hudson wants it to be perfect before he puts something into practice, especially if it's life or death.

Swallowing thickly, he closes his eyes and tries to calm himself down. He thinks about Joseph, his mate. If he were in his human form right now, he'd be smiling at the very thought of his name. They haven't been together long, but the time they've spent together have been perfect. Joseph even let him mark him. Now, Hudson's glad he's not in human form. If he were, he'd be blushing.

They haven't completed the mating yet. It'll probably be a few more years before they do, but they make out a lot. Hudson can feel his wolf getting distracted by the memory before growling at him to focus. He tries to oblige, but it's difficult to do. Joseph has been such a pillar of strength for him since he's been with him, that it seems like second nature for his mind to turn to him at this moment. Hudson can't imagine what he'd do if he lost Joseph. The very idea has his wolf snarling.

425

Opening his eyes, Hudson focuses on the task at hand. If he can't stand up to these rogues for himself, he can do it for Joseph and his family. He won't let them get hurt because he was weak. Rae, over the years, has been the protector and the one to shield them from pain, but this time, it's his turn to stand on his own two feet and protect. It's his turn to be strong.

The sound of the pack link coming alive again grabs his attention, and Hudson looks around for Vivienne to see her pacing in front of him. He can see her worry for those inside and her annoyance with anyone letting the rogues get this far. They were never supposed to get this far. Suddenly, Vivienne stops and dips her head lowly as a snarl passes her lips.

They're here.

Hudson's ichor colored eyes look around, trying to spot them, but it's still a dimming dusk. It's hard to make out much in this lighting, but he tries anyway. When he does spot one, it's too late because they're already heading straight for the pack house. What shocks him though is that it's not changes shifts but also shifters in human form. He can tell they're shifters from their yellow eyes and speed, but he doesn't understand why they aren't shifted. What are they planning?

Vivienne's wolf takes off with another snarl and goes for an incoming rogue. That seems to be the cue for the rest of the group to start fighting as well. Every other shifter around the pack house runs out into the front yard while the rest cover the perimeter. Hudson is among the ones who have to hang back. He prefers this, since in sparring he's much better at defense than offense. He just needs to remember to protect his flanks.

He's keeping an eye on most of the action, but he's surprised when he sees a dirty middle-aged, blonde woman approach him. Her eyes are bright gold, and she bares her teeth at him in warning. That's not what's getting his attention, though. What catches his eyes is the silver blade in her wrapped up hand. His wolf snarls at the very sight of the silver and Hudson lets that sound escape past his mouth. The sound is loud and nasty enough that it almost scares himself.

"Come here, little puppy," the woman goads, licking her lips, as she looks him the eye.

Hudson takes the bait and snaps his jaws at her, missing her by a hair as she steps back from him. She attempts to swipe him with the blade, but he manages to move out of the way just in time as well. Hudson lifts his paw and manages to rake his claw down the side of her arm, making her shriek before falling to the ground. Hudson approaches her hesitantly, and she grabs her arm as it leaks impossible amounts of blood. He thinks he may have hit an artery or something.

The sight of her blood makes him sick. He doesn't know if he can do this. Can he do this? Looking down at her again, he sees her struggling to get to her feet and knows he has to do something. This woman is trying to hurt his family and trying to kidnap his sister. He can't just let her go just because he doesn't have the stomach for all this violence.

"Weak," she spits at him as she gets to her feet. "I hope your sister will be as easy to take down as you, mutt."

Hudson's wolf reacts to her words before Hudson himself does. Letting his wolf take over, Hudson takes a step back and lets him handle the situation. His wolf lowers his head and positions himself as though ready to pounce. The woman grips her dagger tighter and blows a frizzy strand of blonde hair from her face, ready for his attack.

Hudson's wolf snarls before lunging at her, and he manages to knock her down. Of course, that's before she shoves the blade of her knife into his shoulder. Hudson's wolf howls and Hudson screams in his head at the pain. Silver is not something you want even touching your skin, let alone under the surface of it. It burns, and with too much exposure can give a prolonged painful death to those who have been tainted with it.

"Long live Alpha!" she screams from underneath him.

427

Hudson bares his fangs, and without even a second thought, he wraps his jaws around her throat. She screams again, this time in pain, but Hudson pays it little mind. Instead, he just tightens his bite on her neck until he hears a snap and then she lets out a breathless gasp.

She's still twitching underneath him as he backs up, but he doesn't make it far. With the silver embedded in his shoulder, he can't use his left front leg. He only makes it two steps back until, without warning, he collapses.

* * *

Joseph feels pain radiating his shoulder and doesn't have a doubt that it's Hudson. Mates sharing pain isn't uncommon. He's seen it happen all the time, and since his mom is the pack doctor, he knows how debilitating it can be. Grabbing his shoulder, Joseph grits his teeth as a sweat breaks over his forehead. It fucking burns!

"Joseph?" Hudson's brother Jace calls while rushing over to keep him upright. "What's wrong?"

"Hudson," Joseph gasps out. "Something's wrong. He's in pain."

Joseph wishes his mother was here; but as a full-grown shifter, she's tending to the wounded on the battlefield. Joseph's dad, Ray, is here though, but he's guarding the kids in the basement. The other human pack members are just hanging around; none of which he's particularly close to. His few friends are outside with the other young shifters. Joseph closes his eyes at the thought. He hopes all of them make it. Even Melanie, and he hates that bitch.

"Fuck!" Jace yells, clearly distressed.

"What?" Joseph hears Cleo ask as she comes over to stand near him.

"Hudson's hurt," Jace snaps as Joseph hears him stalk out from the room. Where the hell does he think he's going, Joseph thinks.

Cleo grabs Joseph's hand and tries to help him get upright, but her hands are shaking. "Is he . . ."

"No," Joseph says roughly. "He's not, but I don't know what's wrong. Something burns."

"Silver. It has to be," Alpha Jessica says hoarsely. "How could they use silver against their own kind?"

"They're no good pieces of shit, that's how!" Jace snarls as he comes back into the room.

"What the hell do you think you're doing?" Cleo demands, leaving Joseph's side.

"I'm getting him the hell out of there! Now let go!"

Joseph hears some struggling but ignores it. The pain is still there, but through their mate bond, he knows Hudson is alive, just not well. The idea has Joseph's whole body shaking with rage. No one hurts his boyfriend and gets away with that shit.

Gathering all the strength he can, he straightens himself upright and runs a hand through his dark, sweaty hair. He's well trained in hand to hand; all none-shifting members of the pack are, but Joseph also has other skills. Ones that he has no problem using, especially now that Hudson's in danger. If it had been up to him, he would have been using it from the start, but as usual, the alpha likes to underestimate the humans in this pack.

Pushing past Jace, Joseph moves out of the living room and heads to an adjoining room. The safe in the wall is passcode entry, and since it's also where his mom keeps the harder medicinal drugs, he knows the code. Pressing the code in, he hears the latch unlock and pulls open the door before spotting his weapon of choice.

Joseph curls his hands around the bow itself. Testing the tightness of the bowstring, he puts it over his shoulder and grabs his arrows. Of course, they're not just any arrows. These ones are special.

Grabbing all his gear, he walks back into the living room and hears the conversation suddenly stop. He ignores it though and finishes putting on his arm guard before meeting Jace's wide blue eyes. Cleo looks shocked as well, but Jessica just looks annoyed. Sawyer, on the other hand, just looks like he knows exactly what Joseph is about to suggest and loves it.

"You want to help him?" Joseph asks, rolling his shoulder. He can still feel the residual sting. "Do you want my help to get him out of there?"

Jace eyes him a little before nodding. "Yeah."

"Then you're going to have to listen to me. I have wolfsbane-laced arrows, and I'm a perfect shot. I'll follow out behind you."

"Can I trust you to cover me?" Jace asks doubtfully. "With a bow and arrow?"

"Hudson is my mate, Jace. I would never do anything that would harm him. Letting you die would be one of those things. Now get over your overprotective bullshit, and help me save your brother before I lose him forever!"

Jace lifts both his eyebrows in surprise before nodding. "Fine, but if you get me killed, I'll come back to haunt your ass."

"Noted," he says with a roll of his hazel eyes. Lifting up his arrows he nods at Jace. "You ready?"

"Oh yeah," Jace says with a huge grin before cracking his knuckles. "By the way, Joey, I think I'm coming to like you more and more, kid."

Joseph grimaces at the nickname but doesn't call him on it. Instead, he straightens up and tries to regulate his breathing. Closing his eyes, he pictures Hudson's smiling face. His happy brown eyes and messy brown hair. Joseph exhales and knows there isn't any more time to spare.

"Cleo and Sawyer, guard the door. When we're clear, close it and lock it," Jace throws over his shoulder.

"You're not my alpha," Sawyer grumbles but does go towards the door with Cleo tagging along behind him.

"No, but I am." Alpha Jessica sighs before looking Joseph in the eyes. "Be careful. We can't lose any more pack members today."

Joseph bows his head at his alpha female. "Yes, ma'am."

Pulling the first arrow from his bag, he gets it ready in his bow and gets ready for what he's sure is a massacre outside. Who is massacring what though is the real question. Jace counts lowly to himself but Joseph can hear it, and it's helping him focus.

"One . . . two . . . three."

* * *

Hudson's body is wracked with pain. His wolf is trying to shift him back into human form, but with the silver stuck in a muscle, it's stopping him from fully shifting back. His wolf wants him to pull out the knife so they can try to heal, but it's not working. He can't get his hand to shift back long enough for him to get a grip on it. He actually pushed it deeper in the one time he did almost have it. It's causing more pain at this point, and Hudson is almost done even trying.

He's so wrapped up in his own pain that he doesn't even notice the incoming rogue wolf until it wraps his jaws around his hind leg. The rogue starts pulling at his back leg and Hudson lets out a sharp whine when he hears the bone snap. What follows is an odd noise. One he can't pick out specifically but one that definitely tells him something is coming.

Suddenly, the jaws loosen up though, and Hudson angles his head to see the wolf has an arrow in its eye. Hudson lets out a yelp in shock at the sight. Where did the arrow come from?

Looking around, he sees a set of human feet coming towards him. A pair of black converse, if he's not mistaken.

Hudson lets out a growl when someone touches the silver knife in his hand and with one hard yank, pulls it out of his shoulder. Hudson quickly shifts back into human form, and his wolf starts to take over the healing process. The healing isn't much better in the pain department, but at least it's not killing him. Arms slide under Hudson's naked body, and he's pulled off the cold grass of the front lawn.

"You know, I never thought I'd ever have to see you naked again after we stopped bathing together."

Hudson lets out a tired laugh at the sound of Jace's voice. "Asshole."

"That may be, but this asshole is saving yours."

Hudson grimaces but doesn't say anything. A huge part of him is just happy his big brother is coming to save him while the smaller part of him is wondering why Joseph isn't doing it. Hudson hears the incoming footfalls before Jace does, and he's about to open his mouth to tell him so when a rogue barrels into them. Jace and Hudson are both knocked over, but just before the rogue descends on them, an arrow cuts through the air. It spears right through the rogue's temple.

"What the . . ."

"Your boyfriend is one ace shot with that bow, I'll give him that."

Joseph? Hudson turns his head and sees Joseph with concentration on his face as he pulls another arrow out of his bag. Hudson only has a second to take in how hot he looks like that before the reality of the situation sets back in.

"Get up!" Jace orders, grabbing Hudson's hand and accidentally pulling the still healing shoulder wound hard enough for it to start bleeding again. "Oh, for fuck's sake!"

"I-It takes longer to heal with s-silver," Hudson says, feeling lightheaded.

432

With an aggravated growl, Jace crouches down and hauls Hudson over his shoulder, even though Hudson is still very much naked. "If you fucking fart on me right now, I swear to god I'll kill you!"

Hudson would laugh, but he's too busy trying not to pass out right now. He's about to lose consciousness when he's suddenly set down on something hard and cold. Is it leather? He can't tell, and at this point, he really doesn't care. He feels a blanket wrap around his lower half, and the doors being slammed shut from somewhere in the room.

"Did you lock it?" a woman's voice asks.

"Yeah," a voice he recognizes as belonging to Cleo answers. "Is he okay?"

"Bleeding like a pig, but he's fine," Jace tells her distractedly as Hudson hears fabric being torn. "Nice shooting out there, Katniss. Almost gotten eaten a few times by the rabies brigade."

"Shut it and be happy I didn't let them take a chunk from you."

Hudson smiles a little at the second male voice. Joseph, he knows it's him. Reaching out towards the source of the sound, he tries to touch his mate. His wounded wolf and Hudson's battered body need the closeness of their mate. Hudson can feel the shocks move up his arm as Joseph grabs his hand and holds it tightly in his own.

"You've lost a lot of blood," Joseph says faintly.

Hudson takes in the concern on his mate's handsome face and smiles a little. "I'll be fine. Just need time to heal."

"Either way, I wish my mom was here. I'd feel better knowing she could help."

"She has others to worry about. I'll be fine," Hudson assures him, "It's just a little stab wound."

Joseph brushes his free hand through Hudson's dark oak colored hair. "You know, Rae is going to have your ass for not watching your flank."

Hudson rolls his eyes. "Yeah, well, as long as she's here to say it to me in person, I'll be fine."

"You're an idiot, you know that?" Jace snaps. "You could have died!"

"I know," Hudson says with a sharp gasp as Jace tightens the tourniquet around his shoulder. "But I'm not."

"Do you realize what would have happened if we lost you?" Jace demands.

Hudson searches his brother's ashen face. "I know. I'm sorry."

"You have to learn to take care of yourself out there. I won't always be here to get you out of shit like this."

"Jace—"

"I mean, how stupid could you be?"

"Jace!" Hudson yells, getting his attention finally.

Jace eyes him. "What?"

"Thank you."

Reluctantly, Jace smiles a little. "Yeah, well, you owe me one."

Hudson is about to answer when the sound of breaking glass and a few surprise screams grab everyone's attention. Hudson tries to get up, but Joseph pushes him back down. Cleo and Jace share a quick look before they run for the kitchen where the noise is coming from. When both are out of sight, Hudson tries to get off the couch again, but just before he's on his feet, Joseph grabs his non-injured arm.

"You're still healing," Joseph tells him tightly as he wraps Hudson's arm around his shoulder. He starts leading him away from the living room, and it takes Hudson a minute to realize that Joseph's taking him towards the basement.

"They're in the house, Joseph. I need to help my brother and sister!"

"They have this covered," Joseph assures as he continues to pull him towards the basement.

"Please, let me help," he pleads.

Joseph's face contorts into pain. "I'm sorry, baby, but I . . . I can't."

Just before the basement's secure metal door slides behind them, Hudson hears the sounds of struggle and fear grip him. Joseph is right, he can't do anything useful in this condition, but it's better than doing nothing. Still, he knows he won't be able to change his mate's mind. So, as he's lead down the basement stairs towards the safe room with the kids, elderly, and pregnant women, Hudson can do nothing but send a prayer.

CHAPTER FORTY-SIX

Colton is panting and struggling to keep up as the group continues to move towards the north. The bite on his left ear from the rogue is causing issues with his hearing. He's pretty sure that its teeth may have gotten into the ear and damaged something. He's not sure, but it's throwing him off balance, and it's distracting enough to have him off his game. He's becoming concerned the longer that the wound continues not to heal like his other wounds have.

Colton!

Colton is taken off guard, not only by Rae's voice in his head, but also by a rogue that tackles him to the ground. Colton lets out a yelp as he lands on his freshly healed ribs, making his body spasm with the sudden pain. Razor sharp teeth wrap around his neck and claws start dragging down his chest. With the skin being thinner there, he knows he has to stop the rogue's claws before they cause real damage.

The rogue growls suddenly and leaps off him in the direction of Rae's wolf. Colton quickly rolls onto his feet, and just as the rogue is about to attack his mate, he springs forward. Colton pushes on the rogue's back to get attention off of Rae and back on him. Rae is busy with her own rogue now, and Colton needs to keep all the others from taking advantage of her distraction. He lunges at the rogue and wraps his jaws around the rogue's neck, drawing blood.

Using all the strength he can, Colton targets an artery in the neck and feels blood fill his mouth when he punctures it. He can sort of hear the heart of the rogue, but the sound is fading in and out. It's disorienting for Colton and it has his wolf on edge. Neither of them likes the idea of being impaired in some way.

When he's sure the rogue is dead, Colton unlatches his jaw from around his neck and lets the rogue's body fall to the ground with a thump. He steps back from the body but stays poised, just in case another one of this one's group decides to jump out. He doesn't want to be taken by surprise like that again. He put Rae in danger just then, and that's something he doesn't want to repeat.

He doesn't want that rogue, or any rogue going near Rae, but it seems inevitable given the situation. He knows she can take care of herself. He's seen her take out at least ten rogues with his own eyes today, but the urge to protect is a hard one to shake.

Colton wishes he'd been better about training. As an alpha's son, he was trained to defend himself and he can, but it's nothing compared to Rae's training. He's seen how she and her siblings were trained and Colton isn't too sure he would have survived it.

Are you okay? Rae asks through their link, voice breathless.

Looking around, Colton spots his dad and Jonah, his father's favorite enforcer, dispatching of the last two rogues. Colton's tongue juts out, and he licks the blood from his muzzle, not really concerned about if it's his blood or not. Finally, he turns to her and answers her with a breathless voice of his own.

Yes, but I think that I have damage to my ear. It's throwing me off.

Rae's dark brown eyes shift up before lifting her muzzle so she can lick the wound. Pulling back, she looks at him with a little frown. *You're not healing.*

I know.

Why?

I don't know, but now isn't the time to deal with it.

Rae hesitates for a second before asking, *Can you keep going?*

437

Yes.

Colton, if this is about pride—

I can do it, he snaps, growling a little at her. *Besides, I think this is what he wants.*

Who? Alpha?

Yes. I think he wants to wear us down so when we reach him, we'll be too exhausted to put up much of a fight.

Rae lets out a huff through her muzzle. *He's not only insane but intelligent. Just what we need.*

What's going on? Dalton asks, cutting through their private conversation and using the pack link. *We need to keep moving.*

Colton thinks that Alpha wants us tired when we face him, Rae tells him quickly.

I thought the same, his dad agrees thoughtfully. *It's a good strategy, I'll give the son of a bitch that.*

How many miles until the meeting point? Colton asks directly.

Another four and a half miles. We can make it there in a half hour on foot, but if the attacks keep coming, maybe it'll be an hour.

Shit. Rae groans and Colton presses his side against hers as a way of comfort.

Dalton's eyes look over both Rae and Colton and turn assessing before asking, *How are you two holding up?*

Fine, Colton answers shortly.

Nothing I can't handle, Rae adds.

Colton looks her over and winces at the sight of her. She's covered in her own blood and the rogues'. Her fur is matted and stained with mud and dirt along with some dead leaves. She's breathing really hard, and her tongue is hanging out of her mouth. He also spots a pretty nasty bite mark on her back leg. His wolf snarls in his head at the sight.

Rae, is your leg okay? he asks through their private link.

I'm fine.

Rae—"

438

Rae ignores him and speaks directly to Dalton, *We need to keep moving if we're going to end this tonight. With them already surrounding the pack house, we need to get to this lead rogue before day break. Don't you agree, Alpha?*

Dalton looks slightly bemused by her tone but nods once. *Yes. Let's get moving.*

Dalton and Jonah start to walk ahead, and Rae moves to follow them, but Colton stops her. Walking in front of her, he blocks her path and instantly annoys her. He doesn't care if she's annoyed. He wants to know why she's putting herself at this kind of risk when she could seriously damage her body.

We're wasting time sitting here talking when we could be getting this shit over with! she snarls at him down the link as she moves to walk around him. *He has my aunt, cousin, and uncle in his hands, and my siblings are fighting for their lives! I want this finished, and worrying about my fucking leg isn't going to get us anywhere!*

You could lose your leg, Rae. I've seen it happen.

Then I lose it defending my family, she growls.

Colton watches her run up behind his dad and Jonah with a visible limp in her gait. She's too stubborn to let anything get in the way of her doing her duty, even if it's one she doesn't need to be doing. She could have stayed at the pack house and kept safe while they took care of the problem, but it would have never worked. Rae would have found a way to get to the front line and get involved. It's one of the many things he admires about her.

Shaking his head and trying to get the sound of ringing out of his ear, he quickly follows after them. He has a feeling following Rae will be something he'll need to be well practiced in for the future. A future he still has all the hope in the world will be one they can share together.

* * *

439

Mackenzie can hear nothing in the underground cells, but she knows that all kinds of chaos are breaking out overhead. She can feel the nearness of her pack above her and hear their communication through the pack link. She knows they've broken through the line and made it past the untrained pups around the pack house. What she doesn't know is where Jace is and if he's okay.

The idea that he may not be has been torturing her since he walked out of the cells and told her he didn't want her. The memory causes a physical pain as well as an emotional one. She doesn't blame him for not wanting her, and in fact, has only amplified her self-loathing and confusion.

Her wolf is equally confused. Having been cared for and looked after by Alpha, Mackenzie has never thought of anything beyond her loyalty to him. She never even thought about having a mate or what that might mean. She only ever thought about how she would survive and advance.

Now, things have changed. Jace is muddying the water, and Mackenzie is finding her loyalty tested by her human mate. Was this what Alpha meant by loyalty above all? If so, Mackenzie may fail this test. In fact, as time passes and the separation between her mate and her stretches on, she's not sure she can hold out much longer.

The sound of the upstairs door opening meets her heightened hearing, and Mackenzie gets off the bench to get to her feet. Maybe this pack will use her as a bargaining chip. If they do, then they're stupider than she thought they were. Mackenzie, more than anyone else, knows that Alpha doesn't negotiate. He simply takes.

The intensifying buzzing in her mind tells her that it isn't someone of this pack, though. Whoever is coming down the stone steps into the cells, is someone from her own pack. When Mackenzie spots a buzzed blond head and a scar on the left cheek, she knows it's Wade. She's rather indifferent to Wade, but isn't surprised he's come down here. He's often ordered to do the shit errands in the pack.

"Glad to see you're still alive," Wade drawls as he looks her over. "They've been feeding you too, I see."

"Fuck off and let me out."

"So much for being thankful," he mutters as he goes to grab the keys from their place on the wall.

"What's going on up there?" she demands as she gets closer to the silver tinted bars of her cell. "How far have we gotten?"

"Last report was that they'd made it into the house."

"The house?"

"The pack house," Wade tells her with a shrug as he tries the first key. "Nothing but non-shifters and kids in there. Should be easy."

Mackenzie sees Wade move to the next key and swallows the growl of frustration growing in her throat. This is why Wade is never tasked with big things. He takes forever to get anything done.

"Ah, here we are. This one should be it. Oh no, that's not it."

"I'm surprised Alpha told you to come down here," Mackenzie says as she tries to keep a grip on her anger.

"He didn't."

"What?"

"Your mother asked me for a favor. She knew you were alive, and this was the best place to start to look for you. I owed her one."

"Where is my mom?"

Wade shrugs. "Don't know. Don't care."

Mackenzie narrows her green eyes at him. "So Alpha doesn't know you've come down here for me?"

"Nope. He'd probably let you rot down here if it were up to him," Wade says before giving her a little smirk. "So I guess it's you who's going to be owing me one this time, huh?"

441

When Mackenzie hears the click of the lock and the cry of the metal hinges, she pushes her way out of the cell. She feels immediately relieved not to be closed in anymore, and the urge to change forms and run freely comes to mind. Instead, she looks over at the very expectant looking Wade with disgust.

"What?"

"I said you owed me, didn't I? You know how these things go."

Her disgust only grows knowing what he's implying. Since women are seen as disposable breeders once they reach eighteen, sexual favors as payment have become commonplace in the pack. Mackenzie has never done it and has no wish to, but Wade doesn't look like he'll be taking a rain check.

"We're in the middle of a war right now," she tells him flatly.

"Not my problem." He sighs, reaching down to undo his pants.

Rolling her eyes, Mackenzie grabs Wade's face in her hands and with one swift move, snaps his neck. He falls to the ground with a thump, and she sees his legs start to twitch from the suddenness of it all. Stepping over him, Mackenzie goes up the stairs and when she finally reaches the top, pushes her way out into the open.

Now she needs to find the pack house.

* * *

Rae throws another rogue off her with a snarl and staggers on her feet. She's getting tired, and she knows that the only thing helping her push on is her adrenaline. Just two more miles, she tells herself, just two more miles. That's all she has to make before she faces whom she has to face. Her wolf becomes giddy at the idea of being able to kill this alpha herself, and Rae isn't arguing. She wants to destroy this deranged king where he stands just as much.

Move out! Dalton orders down the line, and Rae forces her legs to keep moving her forward.

She's exhausted, but she has to keep going. She has to, because this is her demon to face. She's protected her family for the past three years from every threat that's come their way, and she'll protect them from this too. It's her duty as the head of the family and as the reason of this war.

She's so wrapped up in keeping herself upright and moving that she doesn't even realize everyone has stopped running until she runs into Dalton's enforcer. Colton comes and presses his body against her smaller one, helping her keep herself upright. She absorbs his comfort willingly and tries to bring her labored breathing under control the best she can.

A slow clapping comes from somewhere in the distance, and Rae lifts her heavy head to see a large group of both wolves and people standing before her group of five. The one whose clapping though is an older man who is pushing through the crowd. He's dressed in just a pair of ripped up baggy jeans, leaving his abdomen and feet bare to the elements. His hair is buzzed close to his head but obviously a lighter color and gives Rae the opportunity to clearly see the horrific scar cutting across his face.

"Glad to see you could join us, Alpha Woodward," the man says with a wide grin. "I had a bet going."

Dalton just snarls in response.

"Kendrick, it seems you owe me a few dollars," the man calls out behind him. "Care to settle our debt now or later?"

Rae growls lowly as she sees a familiar face push forward through the crowd to stand by the man. Alpha Kendrick's eyes immediately land on Rae, and he keeps his face carefully blank. "What's a debt between brothers?"

Brothers? Rae's mind halts at the word and her eyes dart between the two men wildly. She doesn't really see any resemblance, but that doesn't mean much. The fact that the other man is older raises the question as to how Kendrick is alpha if this man is Kendrick's older brother. Not that the answer matters much to her at the moment. All of this, no matter how well explained, will probably never make sense to her.

"Well, brother-in-law, but all the same. It's me who owes you for getting Julie off my hands," the man says with a laugh before his light blue eyes land on Rae, and she hears his breath catch in his throat. "Even her wolf looks the same."

Rae growls loudly at him, letting him know what she thinks of his comment. The man grins at the sound and looks more pleased than Rae is comfortable with. It's obvious to her that this is the alpha, brainwasher of the rogues and the one who claims her as his own. The idea of which makes her shiver in disgust.

"Rae," Alpha breathes, his eyes softening as he continues to look at her. "I've waited a long time to see you in person. To speak with you."

Rae just stares at him.

"I'm a fair man. Fairer than most, and I'm willing to make peace and leave this land without harming another person in this pack if you want that." As he speaks, Rae eyes him doubtfully, and when he sees it, he grins. "You don't look convinced."

Deciding to say her piece, Rae closes her eyes and starts to shift back into her human form. Since she's so exhausted, the process takes longer, but once it's done, she feels as though she can breathe deeply for the first time in hours. She doesn't think much about the fact that she's naked as she stands before the group, covered in blood and grime. Instead, she stares the so-called alpha in the eye and waits for him to speak again.

"You're injured." He nearly growls as he sees the state of her leg.

"I've had worse," she snaps at him, making him bring his eyes back up to meet hers.

He tilts his head in an unnerving way. "You seem upset. I gave plenty of warning, Rae. This could have been stopped ages ago."

"By what? Giving myself to you willingly? Tearing myself away from my mate and my family because of a promise I had no consent in?" she growls. "I would rather fight every one of your rogues on my own than willingly come to your side."

"You're brave. I can respect that."

"I don't need your respect. I need you to leave!"

He rolls his eyes and crosses his arms over his chest, looking exasperated. "That's not going to happen. A deal is a deal, and I've been waiting long enough for you as it is. So, here's what I'm going to do. I'm going to give you one more opportunity to do what is meant to happen, or I rip everything and everyone you love to pieces before your eyes and take you anyway."

"Fuck you."

Alpha hangs his head and sighs heavily before looking up at her again. "Final answer?"

She clenches her hands into fists and glares at him in answer.

"Fine," he mutters. "Have it your way."

With one gesture of his hand, twenty wolves cross the northern barrier and head straight for Rae's small group. Rae closes her eyes and forces her body to slip back into her second form. It's painful and takes a lot out of her, but it's needed. Especially when a rogue-allied wolf slams right into her.

CHAPTER FORTY-SEVEN

The sound of broken glass gets Jace's attention off his injured brother and has his head snapping towards the kitchen. Glancing towards Cleo, he already sees the determination come over her face, telling him that she's not going to wuss out on him this time. It's a relief, really, because at this point, he's not in the mood to deal with her bullshit. They have a lot of people to protect.

Glancing over his shoulder, Jace is relieved to see Joseph taking Hudson towards the basement. His body relaxes momentarily knowing that at least three out of his six siblings are going to be well protected during this shit show. Grabbing the baseball bat he'd intended to use to get Hudson in the first place, he doesn't hesitate to jog towards the kitchen while Cleo trails after him.

"You ready?" he calls over his shoulder at her.

"To kick ass?" she asks, cracking her knuckles. "Always."

Smirking, he pushes open the kitchen door. It hits the back word with a slam, and Jace looks over the scene before him. At least seven shifters in human form have broken through the kitchens boarded up windows. He knows they're shifters from the yellow of their eyes, elongated fangs, and claw bearing hands. One of them has a young woman in their grasp when Jace and Cleo come in. That's the one whose eyes seem to spark with recognition.

"Applebee," the rogue snarls at him.

Jace's eyes widen at the fact that the rogue knows who he is. Depending on how long this crazed alpha has been stalking Rae, he supposes it shouldn't be too surprising. Still, it's unnerving knowing that this piece of shit knows anything about him.

Jace eyes the rogue speculatively as he speaks before tightening his grip on the wooden bat in his hand. "Seems like you know who I am but I don't know who you are."

"I am one of Alpha's army."

"How exciting that must be for you," Jace comments dryly.

The rogue snarls at him again, spit flying out of his mouth, "You will show my alpha respect!"

Jace narrows his eyes at him. "Your alpha is the last person I'd show respect to."

Jace sees Cleo inching towards the knife drawer and purses his lips. She's not being very subtle about it, but then again, that's not really her style. Cleo is an attack and grab kind of fighter. She's more concerned with getting the job done than living through the whole experience. He'll have to watch her back more than he anticipated, he thinks with a curse.

"I know all about your family," the male rogue spits at him, as his yellow eyes move towards Cleo. "I know that you have been trained."

"Good," Jace says, focusing a cold glare at the rogue. "Then you know that if you don't let that girl go in five seconds, I'll beat your skull in. Or did they not tell you about that part of my training?"

The rogue bares his teeth at him and throws the girl away from him. Her head cracks against the wall before she falls to the floor in a heap. Jace feels Jessica step towards the girl, but puts the bat up to stop her. If anyone out of this group needs to be protected, Jessica is that one. If she goes down, the alpha goes down and then this whole pack is up shit's creek without a paddle.

"Good doggy." Jace smirks.

447

Luckily, the rogue falls for his goading and with a growl escaping his lips, goes for Jace. The other six rogues turn their attention towards the small group of four and Jace almost grins. Could they be any more idiotic? As soon as the rogues come for them, Cleo runs for the knife drawer and pulls out a peeler knife to throw. Jace flinches back in time for the knife to barely miss his face and hit the male rogue right between the eyes.

Jace gives her a dry look. "Really?"

"What?" she says with a shrug and grabs a fillet knife. "You moved out of the way."

"What if I didn't?" he snaps as he swings the bat across a female rogue's left cheek. She does a dramatic spin and Jace winces when her head cracks against the kitchen counter. Yikes.

After grabbing a few more knives in her hands, Cleo slides and crawls up on the kitchen counter. She focuses her knives on the rogues coming in through the broken window. Blocking a few swipes of a burly rogue's claws, she manages to slide the fillet knife across the man's belly. He growls at her before dragging his claws across the arm she lifts to block her face.

Cleo screams, getting Jace's attention off the rogue he's got on his knees with one well-placed blow to the knee. The rogue in front of Jace takes the opportunity to slide his own claws across Jace's thigh. Jace yells loudly in pain before turning the bat around and slamming the end cap of it repeatedly into the rogue's face. The rogue's face is covered in blood, but he's still not going down. Jace grabs the bat by the grip and swings it across the side of his skull. The loud crack tells him all he needs to know before the rogue falls to the already bloody kitchen floor.

"Well?" Jace pants out, as he looks over at Cleo.

Cleo slides the blade of her knife across the burly rogue's throat, throws his body to the ground, and looks over at Jace. "Well, what?"

"What if it had hit me?"

She sighs heavily. "Is this really the time for being a fucktard, Jace?"

Jace just blinks at her. "Yes."

With a growl of frustration, she steps over the burly rogue's body and throws the bloodied fillet knife at a rogue trying to get in through the window. It hits the female blonde in the neck, making blood spurt everywhere. Finally, Cleo turns to Jace and gives him an annoyed look.

"I guess it would just add to another hole in your face for you to use to annoy us even more," she snaps at him.

Jace's split lip rises in a smirk. "Awe, I love you too, sis."

She rolls her bright blue eyes before they widen. "Duck!"

Jace goes down in a crouch just in time to miss an attacking rogue coming in from behind him. The rogue slides across the kitchen counter and crashes to the floor. Cleo takes out a carving knife from her little pile and sticks it in the back of the rogue's neck. His feet twitch a little, but it's clear that he's dead or paralyzed from the neck down.

"What the fuck?" Cleo pants as she rises up again, wiping the blade on her jean shorts. "Are they getting in somewhere else too?"

"I don't know, but if they are, we need to get up there," Jace answers.

"Guys!" Sawyer yells, running into the room, blood sliding down his face from a head wound. "Upstairs!"

"Upstairs?" They both ask before Cleo adds, "What about down here? We can't keep this place unprotected!"

"Good point," Sawyer allows before sighing. "Fuck it. I'll stay down here with you, Lo. Jace, you go up ahead."

"Where's Jessica?" Jace asks.

"I put mom downstairs with the kids and Hudson."

Jace nods before asking, "Joseph?"

"Upstairs," Sawyer says quickly as he spots a rogue trying to sneak in. Without hesitation, Sawyer pulls out a 25-caliber gun with a silencer and shoots the rogue between the eyes. "Now stop wasting time and get your ass up there!"

Jace hesitates and looks over at Cleo. No words are said, but he can see the assurance in her eyes. It's a false assurance, of course. She's scared too of what could happen if they're not together and watching each other's backs. Still, both of them know that they have to make sure the rogues don't get past them. If they do, Poppy, Cassidy, and Hudson will be next on their hit list, and neither of them wants that.

"Jace!" Sawyer snaps, getting Jace out of his thoughts.

"Yeah, I'm going," he responds quietly, reluctantly backing out of the kitchen. "You take care of her."

Sawyer's brown eyes soften slightly. "I will. Now focus on watching your own back."

"I will."

And with that, Jace turns and jogs out of the kitchen. He immediately runs into two rogues, both female. One is a brunette while the other has short buzzed blonde hair. The blonde one looks like she's been pretty badly injured already, if the blood staining her loose-fitting muscle tee is any kind of indication. He really doesn't want to hit women, even if they are attacking him. He already knocked one out in the kitchen, and he feels like shit about it.

Fuck, he thinks. He'd always wanted two girls at once, but this is not the way he'd pictured it.

His hesitation is their entry point though, and they both attack him at the same time. One pins him down while the other tries to get the bat out of his hand. He holds on to it with all his strength, but when the blonde bites his wrist hard enough for him to hear a crunch, his hand gives in. The blonde throws the bat across the room before clawing over and taking his arms into her hands, pinning them above his head. The brunette sits back on his chest with glowing yellow eyes. Jace's eyes widen when he sees her claws come out from her nail beds, jagged, and already covered in blood.

450

Shit, he thinks, *this is the end.* This is how he's going to go. Again, not how he thought this would go. Closing his eyes tightly, he prays that his mom's spirit or ghost or whatever you pray to, watches out for his siblings. That's all he can think about now that he may die, his family. Who will protect them now?

Then someone screams. Jace's eyes open, and he sees bloody claws inches away from his face with another smaller hand gripping it tight. Jace blinks at the sight before he hears a sickening crunching echo through the room followed by another scream. That's when he realizes that someone is stopping his death. What crazy kind of bullshit is this?

"Hey Wendy, do me a favor and get the fuck off my mate." He hears a familiar voice snarl lowly.

Before he can even blink, the hand is tossed away from his face and the brunette's neck has been snapped. The weight is suddenly off him, but his hands are still being pinned. He can feel blood pouring from his arms from the blonde's claws digging into his forearms.

"Mate?" the blonde asks with a laugh. "A human as the great Mackenzie's mate? How thrilled you must be."

Mackenzie? What the fuck is she doing here? How did she get here? That's the better question, he thinks.

"If you've heard of me, then you know I don't share. Now, let him go, or I rip your throat out. If I were you, I know which one to choose."

"Me too."

The buzzed blonde sneers, suddenly grabbing Jace's hair and so his head is snapped backward. He grunts loudly at the pain it causes, but when she digs her claws into his neck, he's a bit more concerned with that. "Death or nothing, right, Mackenzie? Alpha and pack above all."

"Not this." He hears Mackenzie snap. "Not above this."

"Easy to say when it's your mate, isn't it?"

"Belinda . . . Please, let him go."

451

"No," Belinda says in Jace's ear. "Long live Alpha."

Jace closes his eyes again, preparing himself. But again, Mackenzie is faster than he expected her to be. When he feels Belinda's hands loosen on his hair and hears her body slam onto the floor behind him, he relaxes. Shit, that was close. Opening his eyes, he comes face to face with Mackenzie whose bright green eyes are looking over him for injury. When she reaches out for him though, he moves just out of reach.

"Jace . . ."

"What are you doing here?" he snaps, cutting her off.

She scowls at him. "Saving your ass. You're welcome by the way."

Getting to his feet, he moves away from her, looking for his bat as he responds, "I didn't thank you, and I don't intend to."

"That's really charming of you," she tells him dryly.

When he spots his bat, he grabs it and grips it tightly in his left hand. Turning to face her, he looks at her with cold eyes. Her hair is a mess on the top of her head, and her clothes are splattered with blood along with her petite face. Jace won't admit, but he's looking for injuries on her too.

Despite what he tells himself and what he wants to feel, he still cares to know she's okay. After all, she is one of the reasons all this shit is happening in the first place. She's the one who put his family in danger.

Narrowing his eyes, he moves towards her. "I don't thank rogues."

"And I don't save weak human men," she responds softly, her eyes falling to his lips for a split second. "So I guess we're even."

Jace's lips thin out, and he moves past her towards the staircase. With one foot on the bottom step, he pauses and speaks, "Are you here to help or not?"

"Help," she answers automatically.

Jace sighs heavily and closes his eyes for a split second. "Fine, but don't expect anything from me."

"I don't."

With a quick nod, he jogs up the stairs with her following him. He can feel the tie between them strengthen and overwhelm him with her closeness. Part of him is pissed she's here, muddying up his feelings, while the other half of him feels more invincible knowing she's here. He ignores the latter part as he pushes forward up the stairs towards the sounds of the growls and war.

CHAPTER FORTY-EIGHT

There are times when stubbornness has to be set aside. There are times when someone's pride has to become secondary to their loved one's needs. And there are times when, despite what you want for yourself, you have to do what's the best for the group, for your loved ones. As the rogue slams into her, Rae realizes that fact. She can't go on like this and neither can her alpha, her pack members, her family, or her mate.

Pushing back the rogue with her body weight, she shifts back into her human form and screams in pain as she does so. Naked, covered in blood, and in great amounts of pain, she falls to the ground below heavily. Her body is twitching from all the shifting in such a small amount of time, but she has no choice. If she wants to speak, she has to be in human form and in this moment, she has a lot to say.

"Halt!" she hears Alpha yell, and all movement stops around her. "Get my mate some clothes."

Rae ignores his title for her and focuses on righting herself. Her nails dig into the damp dirt below her while her arms shake with the effort of pushing herself upright. All is dead silent as she attempts to right herself, but it's not until she feels the cold feel of a wet muzzle against her stomach does she get the help she needs. Looking over, she sees Colton's large brown wolf looking at her with distressed dark blue eyes. Knowing her as well as he does, he can probably imagine what she's about to do.

Rae can only hope he doesn't screw it up somehow.

"Have you given up?" Alpha calls as Rae manages to get to her knees. "Will you come to me willingly?"

An un-shifted rogue man comes towards her and throws her a pair of sweat pants and a dirty white shirt. Pulling them on, Rae can feel no cleaner and tries to gag at the smell clinging to the clothes. They're obviously not from one of the stashes her pack hides around the woods. These are rogue clothes, and the fact that she has to wear them disgusts her.

Rae shakes her head after she's completely dressed. "No. I'm not coming to you willingly or giving up."

He frowns. "Then I don't understand."

"I won't come to you willingly, but I will make you a deal."

He lifts a brow at that. "Go on."

Taking a deep breath, she tests putting all her weight on her legs. When she doesn't fall over or sway, she straightens her back and faces him without hesitation. Alpha seems even more confused by this but says nothing as Rae draws on any reserve strength.

It was an old law, one that Rae would never have known about if her dad wasn't so obsessed with pack laws. Still, it's one she kept in her back pocket in case her mate wasn't what she wanted. She wasn't going to be taken by force, and with this law on the books, she was sure she never would be. She just never thought she'd have to use it like this.

"You want to take me, but I refuse to go," she begins. "That means that as a sought after party, I can call a challenge to your claim. If you want to take me against my will, I have the right to fight back through direct challenge. You and me sparring until one of us gives in or one of us dies."

No!

Rae closes her eyes and tries to ignore the sound of Colton's voice in her head. She knew he would react this way, and that was why she didn't want to tell him about it ahead of time. She thought about giving in, but she couldn't have lived with herself if she had done that. She thought about challenging him directly without Dalton or Colton present, but the reality that the alpha may cheat was very possible. So instead, she waited until the moment that she's already exhausted, weary, and barely conscious to pull out her ace. It isn't ideal, of course, but what else can she do? What else are her options when everything and everyone she loves is on the line?

"And why would you think I would agree to that?" Alpha asks carefully.

"Because it's a fifty-fifty shot, isn't it?" Rae counters. "I could give in. You've worn me down with your attacks just like you wanted. I guess you'll have to bank on how much self-preservation I have."

"If I win, I get you without complaint, is that correct?"

Rae grits her teeth but answers, "Yes."

"And if I lose, what do you get besides your freedom?"

"I want my aunt, my uncle, and my cousin."

Alpha smirks a bit. "What makes you think I have them?"

"I know you have them and I want them back now. Alive."

"Not unharmed."

Rae narrows her eyes at the humor on his face. "Considering your reputation, I think it would be foolish of me to ask for the impossible, wouldn't it?"

The humor disappears from his face before he whistles and makes a signal with his hand. Rae looks around and is relieved when she hears her aunt Jolene's voice cursing up a storm. The relief is quickly clouded with anger when Rae sees the state of Jolene. She's bloody and only dressed in a tank top and some soiled ripped jeans. Her dark brown hair is a mess on the top of her head, and Rae can see that she's been beaten.

Garrett and Everett are equally beaten to hell, and it appears that Everett is half unconscious as he's dragged in front of her. Garrett is only dressed in a pair of boxers and is covered in dried blood. His black curls are matted to his head, and he too seems to have trouble keeping his eyes open. The guilt Rae feels at the sight of them is almost overwhelming. She should have protected them before any of this happened. She should have done more.

Jolene suddenly stops struggling with the rogue holding her when she sees Rae and gapes at her. "R-Rae?"

The tears in Rae's eyes threaten to pour over as she nods. "Yeah, Jojo, it's me."

"Get out of here!" Jolene yells. "Don't you have any idea what they want to do with you?"

"Of course, I know," Rae tells her softly before roughly wiping away a runaway tear. "Why do you think you're coming home with me?"

Garrett's hoarse voice cuts in then. "What have you done?"

Rae softens her eyes as she looks at her cousin. "Nothing that didn't need to be done." Rae turns her attention to Alpha and hardens her features. "Let them go."

Surprisingly, Alpha doesn't seem offended by her commanding tone but instead seems pleased. "Already a fine leader. You heard your alpha female. Release the prisoners."

Garrett and Everett fall to the ground in heaps and Jolene hobbles over to go over to them. Rae wants to help, but she has to stand her ground. She's toeing the boundary line enough as it is. If she crosses it, she has no doubt that Alpha won't hesitate to simply take her, and it'll all be over. Garrett manages to help his mom help drag his father towards Rae's side, and once they're over the line, Rae rushes over to help.

"Give him to me," Rae demands quietly as she tries to move Garrett out of the way.

Garrett glares at her. "You've done enough."

"I didn't—"

"Giving in to him like that like an idiot is a step too far, Rae. What good will it do any of us if you sacrifice yourself like that?"

"I'm not. I'm challenging him."

"It's the same damn thing," he snaps. "And I'll never forgive you for it if you lose."

Rae smiles a little. "If you think I'll give in, then you're the real idiot."

Garrett sighs and nods once towards her before leading his father past her. Jolene doesn't say anything either. Instead, she just cups Rae's cheek in her hand with tears in her hazel eyes. Rae presses her cheek against her aunt's palm, absorbing the warmth before it's removed and Rae is left cold.

Colton, take them back to the pack house, she says through the mate bond's link.

I'm not leaving you alone."

Colton, please—

No! I'm staying with you until you kill this son of a bitch. Standing by the sidelines and proud. You remember?

Rae smiles a little. *Yeah, I remember.*

I love you.

I know you do, Colton. I just wish I was worthy of that.

Rae—

Colton's words are cut off when Alpha yells at her, "You do belong to me!"

Irritated and beyond angry, Rae screams back at him, "I belong to no one!"

Silence meets her proclamation before she sees the alpha smile widely. "Then you denounce the man you claim to be your mate?"

"No."

"You just did by saying that, you stubborn imbecile!" Kendrick snarls from beside Alpha, glaring at her in disgust. "All of this could have been avoided if you had just done what I ordered."

458

"You are nothing but a rogue lap dog," Rae tells him with a cold smirk. "Why would I do anything you tell me?"

Kendrick's face goes red, and he's about to step towards her, but Alpha puts his hand out, stopping him. Rae wishes he hadn't stopped him. Maybe then she'd get her chance to rip that piece of shit a new asshole. She'd enjoy it too. Her wolf gives a gleeful growl in her head in agreement. The growl is weak though, and Rae knows that her wolf is just as tired, if not more so than Rae.

"Enough," Alpha orders, his light blue eyes never leaving her. "You've said your piece, now fall back in line."

The look Kendrick gives the rogue Alpha is so venomous it almost makes Rae laugh. The spoiled brat in Kendrick is all represented in that look. The pampered alpha's heir who got everything without question is now being ordered around. The sight is something Rae wishes she could have seen before all this happened. In fact, at this moment, she wishes she could just go back to the day of the run and do it all over again. Maybe then, things would be different.

"You have something to say, Rae?" Alpha asks, bringing her out of her thoughts and back to the reality of her situation.

"Yes."

"Then say it."

Rae doesn't like the order in his voice but pushes it aside to meet his eyes directly. "I belong to no one, that's true, but I chose to be with my mate. The one my wolf, my heart, and my soul, have chosen to spend my remaining days with. We have completed the mating and—"

"Enough!" Alpha snarls, clearly unhappy with this proclamation.

"No!" Rae yells back, managing to get to her feet. "I am beta female of this pack, and with time, I will be alpha here as well. This is my fated life. This is my fated pack. This is my fate, Alpha. You have to let me and this insane mission of yours go!"

459

He shakes his head while his eyes flicker between gold and blue. She can see the struggle clearly on his face, and when he drags his dirty fingernails across his scalp, she feels tears come to her eyes. Her dad did the same thing before he ran off.

He used to pull at his ear and twitch uncontrollably just like this alpha before her. It's then that Rae realizes what this really is. This isn't even about her. This is about a desperate man trying to hang on to his last string of sanity. Sympathy for this pained man before her rises up in her, but it's not something Rae wants to claim. She doesn't want sympathy for a man who she has no doubt she'll have to kill.

The alpha eventually lifts his head, and Rae sees tears building in his eyes as he looks at her. His face looks to have aged years right in front of her. The once sure and capable alpha is now nothing more than a lost man looking for his lost love. There's a saying that comes to Rae's mind at this moment. A saying her dad used to throw around without thinking, but one that fits this moment perfectly.

Without a moon for a wolf to howl to, what does the wolf have left to love?

This man has no moon, and so he's trying to take someone else's.

"I can't do that," Alpha says quietly, making Rae's heart drop and her last shred of hope shrivel up. "I love you too much to give you up. I'm sorry."

A tear falls down Rae's face as she closes her eyes. Wiping it away with one dirt-covered hand, she opens her eyes again and meets his gaze. "If you loved me at all, you would have let me be happy."

"I can't do that."

Looking up to the darkened sky above her, Rae responds quietly, "I know you can't."

"Just take her and get it over with, Alpha," Kendrick spits while looking at Rae. "Kill the boy, kill the alpha, and give me what was promised."

"I told you to be quiet," Alpha says lowly.

"All this talking is a waste of time when you could be doing so much more!"

"I won't warn you again to learn your place, Kenny."

"I am Alpha!" Kendrick yells, his hands curling into fists at his side. "I won't be spoken down by you of all people anymore!"

Rae watches in mute horror as the rogue alpha grabs his brother-in-law by the throat and lifts him easily in the air. Kendrick's feet dangle below him as he stays suspended off the ground, fighting for release and air. Rae stumbles back a few steps and feels fur on her lower back. Turning around, she sees Colton keeping her upright as she sways on her feet. She's exhausted. Her body has been through so much healing and injury in such a small amount of time. She's not sure how she's been able to stay upright as long as she has but she can't give in now.

She has to settle this in the only way she can at this point.

The gasps of people and growls of wolves get Rae's attention, and she looks up to see the rogue alpha's claws buried deep in Kendrick's belly. Blood is running down the front of the man's shirt and trickling to the ground below. Alpha blood has been spilled before her eyes and left to color the same land bathed by the moon above. The tragedy and irony of which are not long on Rae in the least bit.

If the moon goddess does exist, she thinks, she must be so disappointed in her sons and daughters.

"I am Alpha," Rogue Alpha tells the paling face of Kendrick before dropping him to the ground.

Something inside Rae is not only horrified by this but also offended. Kendrick may have been a shitty leader and an even worse person, but he was still her alpha back at White Stone. As much as she wanted not to have that lingering loyalty in the back of

461

her mind, it's still there. Besides, this seems like such an undignified way to be killed for an alpha. It actually disturbs way to her core to witness it. And apparently, Dalton feels the same way.

Her alpha's snarl echoes through the woods, making Rae jump and be steadied again by Colton. Dalton breaks the surreal silence by attacking the rogue nearest to him and wrapping his jaws around its throat. Everything is thrown into chaos immediately. Rae falls backward to the ground when Colton moves away from her to stop an incoming rogue. Her legs feel completely limp and though she knows it's only temporary, it's scary for her to be this helpless.

Gripping the grass, Rae tries to drag her body towards a nearby tree. She hopes that at least then, she'll be able to get at least upright again. She only pulls herself a few feet before tears start streaming down her face and sobs leave her lips. She can hear the whimpers, snarls, and yelps of wolves surrounding her and knows of the devastation happening around her. Yet, she can do nothing about it.

Suddenly, teeth wrap around her ankle before Rae screams in pain. Without warning, she's being dragged towards the boundary line and tries to grab anything she can nearby to stop that from happening. When her hand runs over a hard object, she hisses when it cuts her. Acting quickly, she grabs it and realizes it's a broken knife blade. It's covered in someone else's blood, but it's still sharp enough to be used.

Gripping it tightly, Rae is dragged across the field. She hears people screaming her name, but she can't find the courage to answer them. Instead, she allows herself to be taken across the boundary line with every intention of not coming back. Now she has a different plan, and she's even more positive she won't survive it.

"Mine!" Alpha growls as he throws the rogue off of her to take her in his arms. Rae kicks at him. She's trying to make him stay away from her, but he grabs her by the legs and stills her kicks.

Growling again, he pins her down with his weight before coming nearly nose to nose with her. "Mine!"

"Let me go!" she demands, clawing at his face with her free hand, she tries to keep him from trying to mark her.

"No!" he snarls in her face, his eyes going gold. "Mine! My Annie!"

"I'm not Annie!" Rae screams in his face, tears falling down the sides of her face. "I'm not Annie!"

Alpha's face goes pale, and his eyes gloss over. "Annie?"

"I'm not her," Rae tells him softly. "I'm not yours."

She sees a hint of sanity, just a glimpse, before his eyes go yellow again. Rae feels all hope disintegrate from her body. He's too far-gone. It's over, and now she'll have no choice but to end this her way.

"Mine!"

"No," Rae says quietly with a shake of her head. "I'm not yours."

Revealing the tip of the broken knife blade in her hand, she lifts her hand and while looking him in the eyes, drives it into his neck. Alpha's eyes widen, and a light gasp comes out of his mouth, but no other sound escapes him. Rae lets out a sob as blood trickles down from Alpha's neck and mouth onto her.

Pushing him off of her, Rae scrambles away from him and tries to catch her breath. There is an unnatural silence that comes over the clearing, and Rae knows that all eyes are on them. Still, she can't be sure he won't try to attack her to the end. That is until he hears his voice calling out to her.

"Annie . . ." he whispers while reaching for her.

Rae, in his last moments, decides to play the part. Moving towards him slowly, she comes to sit beside him and can't stop the tears falling down her face. She doesn't touch him. She still doesn't trust him enough to do that, but he's bleeding out so fast she can't imagine he'll be alive much longer. She hit an artery. She knows his death will be one more added to her conscience.

463

"Annie . . ." He gasps and she sees a tear far from the corner of his eyes. "I'm . . . so . . . sorry."

Rae says nothing, but she does let out a sob.

And with one last breath, an alpha dies.

CHAPTER FORTY-NINE

"Andy!"

Andy turns his head and feels a smile come to his face when he sees his girl come running towards him. He's bandaged all to hell, and since his eye was almost taken out by a rogue's claw, that's bandaged too. Though his sight of her isn't completely clear, he's still no less relieved to see her. His wolf relaxes in his mind as Andy's eyes inspect her. She's spattered with blood and has a few bandages, but she looks to be fine. He didn't doubt she wouldn't be fine either.

His mate isn't one to be taken down easily by anyone.

"Jesus H. Christ, Andy!" She sobs as she comes to a stop by his cot. "What the hell did you do? Crawl in a meat grinder?"

Rolling his dark brown eyes, Andy smiles widely at her. "I'm fine."

"The hell you are!" she yells, tears coming into her clear blue eyes. "Why didn't anyone get me sooner?"

Andy notices people looking at them with strange looks, but Andy couldn't give one hint of a fuck about them. He's actually happy to see her look as concerned and frightened as she is. Not because he likes to see her upset. It's just that over the short time of their relationship, she's been characteristically distant. He knows it's just her protecting herself and her heart from hurt, but it doesn't make him feel any less excited about this development.

"Well?" she asks, trying to hide her crying from him.

"I told them to wait until you were all bandaged up first. I didn't want you coming to check on me with you injured, Cleo."

"That's just bullshit." She hisses, running her hand through her long blonde hair. "I nearly lost my mind when they told me you were injured."

Andy's grin only widens. "I know, babe."

"You know? You knew, but you still didn't think to have anyone tell me sooner?" she snaps, giving him a weak glare. "I would kill you if you weren't already injured."

"Well, now's your chance," he tells her, spreading his arms as wide as he can. "You have me at a disadvantage."

Cleo's eyes assess him coldly for a minute before she sighs. Her shoulders relax, and her hands fall off her hips to go limp at her sides. With another sigh, Cleo gestures for him to move over a bit before coming to sit on the side of his cot. Andy can't wipe the grin off his face even if he tried. She cares about him, she loves him, and this is her way of showing it beyond telling him as much.

As if he didn't love her enough already . . .

Putting a hand over the large bandage on his right pectoral muscle, Cleo lets out a stuttering breath. "You scared the shit out of me."

"I know baby, and I'm sorry about that," he tells her, his gaze softening.

"I thought that maybe you . . ." she trails off, her eyes watering again. Suddenly, she smacks him on his uninjured shoulder. "Would it kill you to at least keep the mate bond open? You could have at least sent me a mind text to tell me you were okay!"

Andy chuckles before holding a hand to his broken ribs. Cleo's eyes widen, and her hands start to flutter over his body looking for injury, and it only makes him laugh more. God, could she just stop being so adorable? She'll kill him at this rate.

"Oh my god Andy, stop laughing!"

Andy shakes his head and tries his hardest, but it takes a while to calm his laughter down. Who the hell calls a mind link a "mind text?" God, he's marrying her tomorrow if she'd have him. She's still young, and he knows that won't happen without Rae's consent, but a man can still hope. Eventually, he promises himself. It's just not soon enough.

"I'm sorry, baby."

"Are you okay?" she asks, looking him over wildly.

Reaching up, he takes her hand off his chest and entwines it with his. "I'm good."

Cleo's eyes soften, and she gives him an incredibly rare shy smile. "I love you, you know that, don't you?"

"Yeah, I know."

Cleo leans down and kisses him, her lips lingering there a bit longer than he thinks she intended. Lifting a hand up, he buries his large hand into her thick golden hair and keeps her where she is. He loves kissing her. He loves holding her. He loves knowing she loves it too. It's not exactly the manliest thing to admit maybe, but he's not going to be ashamed to say he loves his mate. Never have, never will.

"You know," Cleo says after pulling back to cradle the uninjured side of his face in her hand. "I almost feel sorry for you."

Andy frowns up at her. "Why?"

Cleo smirks at him. "Because now you're stuck with me forever."

Andy laughs before grinning at her. "Doesn't seem like that crap of a deal to me."

"It's still early," she tells him with a slightly sad smile.

"Well, you have the rest of our lives for you to prove me wrong."

* * *

Once the battle is settled with Mackenzie on the losing side, she doesn't know what to do with herself. She has no alpha, no pack, and everyone who's been left alive has either fled or has been captured. Despite the claim she feels she has on Jace, she knows that he most likely still doesn't want her. Why would he? She's a rogue. She's a rogue who is also without family, resources, and can claim little to zero education. She can barely even read.

What good is she without any of that?

Running a hand through her dirty hair, Mackenzie figures it's best for her to leave now. She has no place among this pack, and she doesn't deserve to be by anyone's side. Once she knows the attention is off of her and can slink away into the dawn, Mackenzie makes her escape.

She's too exhausted to switch forms, and she still has injuries that need to heal, so she stays in her human body as she walks. She can hear the birds singing and the cold forest air in her lungs. It's going to snow soon, she realizes. A small smile comes to her face as she imagines how beautiful it must be here when it snows.

She wishes she would be able to see it, but she knows how impossible that is. In fact, she's not even sure she'll survive the winter. She's not sure many of the others from her disbanded pack will either. They've outlived their usefulness, and now they're meant to be wandering souls in a world that has no room for outcasts like them.

Her wolf feels him before Mackenzie herself does. Mackenzie's shoulders tense, and she stops hobbling through the woods long enough to give the chance to say his piece. They may have a lot to learn about each other, but it doesn't take a genius to realize that Jace isn't about to let her leave with the last word.

"You're leaving?"

Mackenzie closes her eyes at the sound of his voice and nods once. "Yes."

She doesn't turn to face him and keeps still as the silence grows between them. She can feel his feelings faintly through their fairly strong bond, but she knows she has to be wrong. Why would he be nervous or scared? There's nothing out here but her and him. Is this the same guy who beat the shit out of adult shifters with a baseball bat just a few hours ago?

"Why?" he eventually asks.

"Because there's no place for me here," she tells him with a bitter smile on her face. "I have nothing to offer here and no one to take me in. I think it's best I leave and try to make my own way in the world."

"Alone?"

"It wouldn't be the first time."

"You don't . . ." he cuts himself off, and Mackenzie waits patiently for him to continue. "You don't have to be alone."

"Why?" she asks, looking at him over her shoulder. "You want to come with me?"

His answer is quick and hits her right in the heart. "No."

"Then why offer?"

"I wasn't."

"Then say what you need to say, Jace!" she snaps, turning around fully to face him. "What is it you want from me? What more can I give you? I have to warn you now that I don't have much more to give. I'm tapped out. So, leave me alone and go back home where you belong."

Mackenzie turns back around and starts hobbling deeper into the forest. Her leg was injured shortly after entering the upstairs with Jace, but she didn't draw attention to it. She just kept watching Jace's back and her own the best she could. There was nothing else she could do, but now, she can feel the burning of the healing process, and the pain can no longer be ignored.

She's made it a few feet before she suddenly feels a hand on her shoulder, pulling her to a stop. She growls lowly at him in warning and tries her best to keep her calm, but it's hard. If he doesn't want her, fine, but does he really have to torture her like this? Can't she be allowed to at least have a sliver of dignity?

"What do you want?" she snaps.

He hesitates before asking, "Where will you go?"

She shrugs, not looking at him. "I don't know yet. I hear the coast is nice."

"I don't want you to go to the coast."

Mackenzie closes her eyes, begging the goddess for patience. "It's not really up to you, Jace."

"Why not," he demands, turning her to face him, though she manages to avoid eye contact. "Aren't I your mate?"

She snorts. "Not really. You've made your intentions clear, Jace. Now, just let me go and stop being so damn dramatic. It's over and done."

"It's not over and done."

"You don't want me!" she yells at him, finally looking into his light blue eyes and repeats herself quietly. "You don't want me."

He searches her face for something before speaking again, "I didn't reject you. Not formally."

"I don't need a formal rejection to get the hint," she tells him, pushing him away from her. "I'm a rogue, and you're a human related to an alpha. People like us aren't meant to mix."

"Who are you to decide that?" he snaps, glaring at her. "You're not the only one in this mess, you know."

"Oh, shut the fuck up and go back home to big sister, you brat!" She snaps back at him, her own anger and patience coming to a head. "I don't owe you anything anymore! I paid my debt to your pack. It's over!"

"No . . . It's not."

Before Mackenzie can say another word, Jace grabs her hand and pulls her against him. She looks up at him wide-eyed while he seems to be debating something. Finally, with a lowly muttered swear word, Jace leans down and kisses her. Mackenzie keeps her eyes open, her shock overriding any happiness she may feel about it. What does this mean? Pulling back, Jace looks down at her with a wrinkled nose.

"You smell."

Mackenzie just blinks at him. "What?"

"You reek."

She arches a brow. "Thanks?"

"You don't brush your teeth often, do you?"

"Uh . . ."

"We'll work on it."

She just stares at him. "What?"

Rolling his eyes, a barely there smile comes onto his face. "I'm willing to try. You came back here and saved my life even though you didn't have to. You gave information that helped us win. You helped save this pack, Mackenzie. Why wouldn't I want to at least try to be with you?"

"I . . ." she trails, off her mouth going dry. "Really?"

"Yeah," he says with a shrug, entwining their fingers together. "Why not, right?"

"Yeah," she agrees, staring at their hands with a growing smile. "Why not?"

* * *

"Damn donkey artichoke testicles!" Hudson yells as Joseph tries his best to help clean his mate's wounds.

Joseph glances over at Poppy and Cassidy nearby and tries to suppress a smile at the looks on their faces. The girls haven't left Hudson's side since they both came down here, and Joseph has proven just as susceptible to their charms as everyone else. Poppy has even volunteered to be his nurse for the day to help take care of her big brother.

"What's a test-a-bill?" Cassidy asks, her face adorably scrunched in confusion.

"Testicle," Poppy says matter-of-factly. "It's a boy part."

471

"Like his face hair?" Cassidy asks.

"No, girls can have face hair too."

"Under the arm hair?" she asks before adding to Joseph. "Boys can only have that."

"Girls have it too," Poppy says with a heavy sigh. "Don't they teach you anything at school?"

"I know how to spell elephant!" Cassidy says before sticking her tongue out at Poppy.

Poppy rolls her eyes under her large brown glasses. "Then spell it if you're so smart."

"I could, but I don't want to," Cassidy tells her, crossing her arms over her chest.

"Do it."

"You're not the boss of me!"

"Girls!" Hudson yells, gripping his head, making both the girls go quiet to stare at him. "Girls, I love you, but can you just stop . . . talking? Please?"

Tears start to form in Cassidy's dark brown eyes, making Joseph's heart clench. "Am I making you sick?"

Hudson's face softens. "No, I just . . . I really want to hear you spell elephant."

"Really." Cassidy sniffles. "Like really, really?"

"Yeah." He sighs, sitting back on the cot they have him sprawled on. "Spell away."

"Girls," a voice Joseph recognizes as belonging to Alpha Jessica calls from the top of the stairs. "Can you come up here? I need your help."

Poppy pushes back a few strands of dark blonde hair from her face and gets to her feet. Looking down at Joseph, she twists her mouth doubtfully. "Are you going to be okay without my help?"

Joseph is momentarily surprised by her maturity but eventually nods. "Yeah, I'll be fine."

"Okay." Poppy nods before putting her hand out for Cassidy. "Come on, let's go."

"Will you be okay, Hudson?" Cassidy asks as she too gets to her feet.

"Yeah," he assures his little sister. "I'll be fine."

Both boys watch Cassidy and Poppy walk up the stairs before leaving their sight. Joseph shakes his head and chuckles before putting more cleaning alcohol on one of the cotton balls. He's about to get back to work when Hudson grabs his wrist, and he looks up into Hudson's dark brown eyes. He can see where Poppy gets that maturity from. Joseph feels like it'd take him a lifetime just to uncover everything Hudson's thinking, maybe longer.

"Thank you," Hudson says, rubbing his thumb rhythmically on Joseph's wrist. "I owe you my life."

"You don't owe me anything."

"No, Joseph, I do," Hudson insists. "I owe you so much."

Joseph licks his lower lip and breathes, "Do you want to pay me back?"

Hudson's eyes flicker to Joseph's mouth for a second. "Yes."

"Then stop squirming," Joseph whispers before putting the cotton ball to the wound.

Hudson inhales sharply and grips the sides of the cots before glaring at him. "I hate you!"

Joseph just grins. "Yeah, but I love you."

* * *

Rae isn't awoken by a specific smell or sound. Instead, she wakes up from her deep sleep due to the silence. It's the peaceful silence that invades her senses and the warmth surrounding her body. Her first thought is that maybe she's dead. It feels like an

473

eternity since she last felt this comfortable and safe, so it's the only explanation her still groggy mind can come up with.

Opening her eyes, Rae blinks away the blurriness there and looks around. She's in the room she shares with Colton. With a deep inhale, she lets Colton's scent settle in her lungs. He's been here, she realizes. It's been a few hours, but he's been here, checking on her. His scent has even seeped into her hair from him brushing his hand over the greasy strands.

Sitting up a little, she looks over the edge of the plush comforter and notices how tranquil the room is and also how dark. Has she been asleep long? It's hard to say since there are no hints as to what day it is. The incidents come back to her then, the memories of her tangle with the alpha, the blood on her hands, and the death of Kendrick. Mostly it's the fear she remembers and tears start to fill her eyes. She's not sure if the tears are from relief or just a leftover of the spent adrenaline, but either way, they're welcomed. The wetness on her cheeks telling her that she did survive.

Opening her mental tether to Colton, Rae reaches out to him to tell him she's awake, but not before making her way to the bathroom. She needs a shower and some time to process this whole thing. She knows her siblings are okay, she's already noticed their fairly new scent trails in her room as well. She's counted all five many times, just to be sure and takes even more solace in the fact. Having something happen to her would have been bad. Having something happen to her siblings because of her, that would rip her apart.

Stripping off Colton's oversized t-shirt from her body, Rae looks at herself in the mirror while the shower runs behind her. She doesn't know how to feel about what's in front of her. She's not at her best. That much is clear from her waxy looking skin and the deep circles under her eyes.

She still has some dried blood along her hairline and in the crevices of her neck. Looking down at her hands gripping the sides of the sink, she's not surprised to still find dark dried blood under her nails either. It's clear to her that someone tried to clean her up but couldn't get it all. Rae smiles a little at the idea that it was most likely Colton. Knowing him the way she does, she doesn't doubt he would have fought tooth and nail for the right to wash her down. In fact, she's surprised he's left her side, but knows that he wouldn't have done so without a good reason.

Once the steam of the shower fills the room, Rae comes out of her thoughts and steps into the spray of the water. She nearly groans at the feeling of it on her weary body and leans on one hand as it runs over her head and down her back. It doesn't take long before she hears the bathroom door slam open. It's followed by the faint smell of Colton's scent and the nearly overwhelming excitement of her wolf practically running circles in her mind.

The glass shower door flies open, and Rae blinks wide eyes at Colton as he stands behind her. His chest is rising rapidly, and his eyes have gone yellow as he stares at her frozen form. Rae is trying to think of something to say, but her mouth just moves without any sound coming out. She wants to apologize for scaring him like she did. She wants to explain why she put herself in danger. She has so much to say, but she can't seem to get it out.

"Rae . . ." Colton says with his voice low and hoarse.

"I—"

Rae is cut off by Colton coming into the shower, fully clothed, and pulling her into his arms. The water wets his hair and makes his shirt stick to his chest, but he doesn't seem to care. His hold on her is a bit harsh, and maybe even desperate, but Rae doesn't mind. She feels the same. Laying her head against his soaked chest, she wraps her arms around his waist and hugs him back. There was a part of her going into this battle that thought she wouldn't be able to do this again. Closing her eyes, Rae relaxes into him, knowing that it really is over, and nothing can come between them again.

"Colton, what happened?" Rae asks quietly though she knows Colton can still hear her.

475

"What's the last thing you remember?"

Rae swallows past the lump in her throat. "Alpha . . . he was apologizing to me. He didn't know it was me, though. He kept calling me Annie. He still thought I was Annie."

"He was a sick man."

"He had a very sick and lonely wolf," Rae corrects in a whisper. "He was just trying to stay sane. My dad would have done the same if he's been his right mind enough."

"Rae—"

"My dad, Kendrick, Alpha, and the losses of this war; they're all dead because of me. They're dead because I wasn't strong enough to end it when I should have. I should have disobeyed Kendrick. I should have taken my siblings and ran as soon as dad left and mom died. All of this would have been avoided."

"Rae, none of this could have been avoided."

"How many did we lose?" she demands, challenging.

"Thirty-three have been counted dead or missing."

Rae's heart drops to her gut, and she closes her eyes. "Injured?"

"Fifty-nine injured, fifteen of which are critical."

A tear rolls down Rae's cheek and blends into the showerhead's spray. "This is my fault."

"Rae—"

"I should have left before the run. I should have just left. All those families . . . Colton, how am I supposed to live with that? What am I supposed to say when they ask me what they died for?"

Colton leans back and cups Rae's face in his hands. His eyes are soft as he looks down at her and she sees tears pricking his own sea colored orbs. How much has he suffered about this? How much pain has he been in while she slept? How much has he had to deal with alone? The idea that she may have abandoned him in his hour of need is too much for her to stomach. Some alpha female she is; she thinks in disgust.

"You tell them that they fought for their pack, Rae," Colton says, his voice thick with his own grief. "You tell them that they fought for their freedom. The pack was meant to be dismantled, Rae. Kendrick was going to absorb our pack into White Stone, growing his territory three-fold. On the surface and in Alpha's mind this was about you, but in the bigger picture, it all boiled down to greed. We fought for our land and our pack, Rae. There is nothing to be ashamed about."

Rae's chin is wobbling as she looks up at her mate, the one chosen for her by fate. Her heart swells and as if it was even possible, her respect for him grows. Her wolf has known from the beginning that Colton was their other half from the beginning. As Rae looks up at him herself with fresh eyes, she knows that her wolf was right. No one else would be here for her now like he is. No one else outside her family would give a damn enough to even try.

Laying her head back down against his chest, she kisses the spot over his beating heart. She loves him. She loved him before when she first told him, but now she's deeply and unconditionally in love with him. There is no going back for her now and the illusion that she could have before this point seems even more ridiculous. Colton belongs to Rae and Rae belongs to Colton from this moment and until there are no more moments left.

"What about me?" Colton asks from above her, his arms still holding her close. "If you had left before the run, I wouldn't have found you."

Rae lifts her head and gives him a small smile. "You would have found me. You promised."

Colton's mouth tilts up into an answering smile. "You're right."

Biting her lower lip a little, Rae coyly looks up at him. "Won't be the first or last time you'll be saying that."

Colton chuckles before lowering his head to capture her lips with his. Rae moans lowly against his mouth as her hands reach up to bury themselves in his hair. The kiss is ended too soon for Rae, but it's served its purpose. She feels dazed and flushed from the embrace. She has no doubt she's blushing right now, but she's not embarrassed by it.

"What was that for?" she asks.

Colton shrugs and gives her a crooked smile. "For being mine."

EPILOGUE

The next night, everyone is gathered in a clearing on pack land. A large funeral pyre has been erected in the middle and seems to be reaching almost six feet in the air. It's a beautiful and macabre sight, but all who are there know what it stands for. This is how the shifters of the world say goodbye to their dead. Each religion and culture have their own way of sending their loved ones back home, and this is the way of the wolf.

Rae stands next to Colton and behind the alpha male and female. Dalton's delta, Lana, stands with her young son beside her. All are dressed in black, and all eyes are on the pyre as Sawyer lights the torch. He brings it to his father Dalton, and it's clear that this is a solemn occasion to all as the clearing remains in revered silence.

Fire is a cleanser, a way to release the wolf soul trapped within the body back into the arms of the Moon Goddess. It's a very sacred ceremony that Rae has never been given the privilege to see in person. Her mother had been given a human burial, and most of these were done in privacy. The rest of the pack is only allowed to pay their respects once sunrise has come, and the pyre is nothing but embers. This is now how Dalton is doing it, and Rae respects his reason why.

They died for the pack, and they will be released with the honor of that pack surrounding them.

Rae looks up at the stars shining up in the sky and wishes they had been able to do something like this for her dad. He would have been owed such a respectful passing. Before the illness and despite whatever he may have gotten her into, Rae knows that his life surrounded the pack. She likes to think that maybe Kendrick would have acknowledged that and done right by her dad, but she doubts it. Kendrick didn't acknowledge the worth of others very much. Not even when his own life was at its end.

Dalton's hands wrap around the torch tightly as he looks into the flames with the stoic dark eyes of a leader. As he begins to speak, even the wildlife around them falls silent and in respect of this great alpha. Rae watches her alpha and father-in-law with pride as he speaks and buries her own thoughts for those for the ones on the pyre.

"Tonight we honor our fallen," Dalton begins. "They offered their blood, their pride, and finally, their lives for this pack. I have no words that can articulate what their sacrifice means not only to me, but to this pack. United we stand and united we should fall, but this isn't the way life works. We stood united, and only the bravest and best of us fell. So, with nothing less than pride, I light this pyre and release the wolf spirit from its cage and back to the arms of our loving goddess."

With Dalton throwing the torch onto the pyre, everyone watches as the hay, wood, and the shrouded bodies begin to burn. None of the rogues, Kendrick, or Alpha are among them. Their bodies were burned the night before, and their ashes left for Mother Nature to sort through. Maybe a bit callous, but it's the way it's always been with the dead of the enemy. It's a way of respecting their sacrifice but denouncing their action, nothing less and nothing more.

Dalton throws his head back and howls up at the bright shining moon in the sky. It's an old custom, and depending on the howl, a way of telling the goddess to take care of our pack members in the hereafter. The rest of the pack follows suit, and Rae grips Colton's hand tighter as she too throws her head back to howl into the sky. May you find peace, she thinks as she watches the dancing embers disappear into the night.

Gone are the sins of yesterday in hopes of seeing the virtues of tomorrow.

* * *

Later that night, Poppy and Cassidy are in bed, but neither is asleep. Poppy has her back to Cassidy, but she knows she's awake from all the moving around. Now she's just waiting for her to say something. Poppy knows it's only a matter of time before Cassidy says something annoying.

"Poppy?" Cassidy asks, breaking the silence.

Poppy rolls her eyes, figures.

"What?"

"Will be safe now?"

Poppy turns around and notices the worry on her sister's face. With a light sigh, she throws off her blankets and gets out of bed. Waving her sister over, Poppy gets into the bed with Cassidy, who snuggles right up to her. With one small hand, Poppy runs her fingers through her sister's unruly curls and tries to calm her down.

"Of course we'll be safe."

"Are you sure?" Cassidy asks.

Poppy looks out the window and knows that that's probably not true. If people can come for them like this once, there's a chance it could happen again. For some reason, the idea really makes Poppy mad. Pushing that thought away, though, she instead focuses on her little sister and hugs her a bit closer.

"Don't worry, Cass. I'll protect you," she promises in a whisper. "No matter what happens, I'll protect you."

THE END

Do you like werewolf stories?
Here are samples of other stories
you might enjoy!

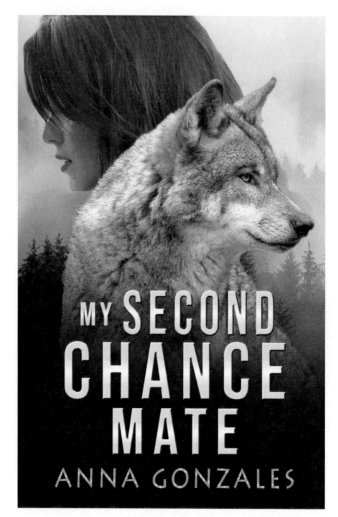

MY SECOND CHANCE MATE

ANNA GONZALES

CHAPTER ONE
Rejected but Moving On

HARMONY

Waking up in the morning has never been easy for me and now it feels as if there's no point in doing it at all. I didn't always feel this way. I used to love life. I enjoyed hanging out with friends and even going to school. That changed the day I met my mate. What is a mate? It's supposed to be the best part of being a werewolf, which is what I am. We are born in human form and can transform into a wolf at the age of twelve. From that point on, it's a waiting game until we find our mate. A mate is a special someone who completes you; the one you was made for and vice versa. I should be happy to have found mine. Unfortunately, my story is unique and I don't mean that in a good way.

*   *   *

One Year Ago . . .

I met him at the age of sixteen. He was everything I could've hoped for. Seventeen years old, 6'1', gorgeous gray eyes, dark black hair, nicely tanned skin, washboard abs, and strong long legs. Perfect, right? I thought so too. We found each other outside the airport baggage claim area. Our eyes met and it was electrifying. We moved towards one another as if pulled by some force until we were only a foot away.

"Mate," we both whispered. He reached out to touch my cheek and I leant into his palm. It felt right; like home. I was so happy that I closed my eyes to savor the moment when he suddenly tensed and dropped his hand. I opened my eyes to ask what was wrong just as he took a big step back. I stared at him in confusion and was about to ask what made him move away when the sound of a familiar voice made the words freeze on my lips.

"Babe, I see you've met my sister. Isn't she adorable?" My older sister, Megan, gushed as she gave me her usual too-tight, can't breathe type of hug.

"Did you say babe?" I asked.

"Yes, silly! Aiden, you didn't introduce yourself?" She laughed while playfully swatting his chest. "Harmony, meet the best thing to come out of this whole mandatory wolf camp that mom and dad sent me to. My boyfriend, Aiden James," she announced happily while grabbing his arm.

My wolf growled at the sight of her touching my mate, but I couldn't say anything right now. I love my sister. She's my best friend and she looked so happy. I couldn't do anything to ruin that. Don't get me wrong; I had some serious questions to ask but I would get my answers when the time was right. Even if I had to tie Aiden to a chair to do it. There was a satisfactory rumble from my wolf just by picturing it. I couldn't believe that, out of all people my sister could have met at this camp, she had to meet and fall in love with the one wolf meant for me.

The camp they attended was a first of it's kind. It was created for two types of wolves. The first was for someone like Aiden, a future alpha. These types of wolves would one day be the leaders of their pack and had to be taught to control their added power and authority so that it wouldn't be misused. The second was for wolves born from two werewolf parents who both carry the recessive gene. It causes their child to be born completely human, and my sister was one of those children. The whole thing was complicated enough as it is, and finding out I was the mate of a future alpha my sister was currently dating only added to the complication.

Aiden and I quickly exchanged hellos as if the spine tingling encounter between us never happened. We grabbed their bags and headed to the car. The ride was uncomfortable mainly because the love birds decided to share the back seat and cuddle. I exchanged looks with Aiden a couple times in the mirror, and though he would smile at my sister, the looks he gave me seemed sad and resigned. His mood confused me but I expected to get an explanation soon.

We made it to our pack house where they were having a big barbeque to welcome my sister and Aiden back. Aiden is the only nephew of our alpha, and because our alpha's mate is human, she could not conceive a child. Our law states that the next male in line would be the alpha's younger brother, Aiden's dad. However, he was killed by rogues when Aiden was thirteen so by law, Aiden is the next heir. It is strange that we never had the opportunity to meet before but that's due to the fact that Aiden's mother took him back to her pack shortly after his father's death. She was unable to deal with the memories of her lost mate that surrounded her wherever she went. Her story was sad and was still used today to teach young pups the ups and downs of mating.

After about an hour into the barbeque, my sister made a run to the store with our mom, and it finally gave me a chance to get Aiden alone. I dragged him to a clearing, a little far down from our pack house, and laid above him.

"So, what are we going to do? I love my sister to death but we're mates. We can't deny that. I don't want to hurt her but the pull I feel for you is so strong I can't ignore it," I started rambling.

"I can," he said.

I continued, not quite hearing him. "I mean, I know this is going to be difficult and create a lot of drama but I'm so happy I've found you a—"

He cut me off and repeated those two words, loud enough so I could hear them. "I can."

"You can? Can what?" I asked, confused.

"I can ignore it. This pull between us," he stated. He proceeded to rip my heart out of my chest with the rest of his words. "I never had a choice in many things in my life. I didn't choose to lose my dad, or have to leave my pack, or be put into the role of alpha but I chose your sister. I fell in love with her all on my own with no influence from anyone. I refuse to change how I feel just because my wolf wants me to. I want to be with the one I love because I say so and not because a bond is forcing me to."

I stared at him. I was shocked and hurt. "Are you saying what I'm thinking? Are you rejecting our bond?"

He sighed. "Look, I don't want to hurt you, Harmony. I spent time with your sister, and I got to know her and fell in love all on my own. If I'm with you, it's not by choice anymore but by fate. I refuse to let fate control anything else in my life. I'm sorry but that's just how it has to be."

To say I was hurt was an understatement. What came next was just anger. "You refuse? What about me? Do you know how long I've dreamed of meeting my mate and finally feeling the love only he can give me? Only you can give me? And now you tell me I can never feel that because fate has dealt you a cruel hand and you're rebelling? And so I'm the one who has to pay for your misfortune? I have never done anything in my sixteen years of life to deserve that, but does it matter to you? Obviously not!" I cried out.

"Look, Harmony. I—"

"No, you look. I'm sorry you had to go through all that but that's what I can be here for. I can help heal the pain you've been through and support you through the role that was forced onto you. No one will be able to understand you like I, your mate, can. Let me do this for you. For us," I pleaded.

"I just can't, Harmony. I've already chosen the future I want, and that future is with your sister," he replied firmly.

"What about our bond? It's going to be hard to fight it. My wolf is trying to get through, and I'm sure so is yours. How are you going to deny him?" I questioned.

Nothing. And I meant nothing could have saved me from the pain his answer caused. "Well, I'll fight him off until I completely mate with Megan. Once I mark her, he will be easier to control, and as more time passes, our bond will eventually weaken."

"True, but you forgot one important detail. Or maybe it's not so important to you since you won't be affected but what happens to the rejected mate, Aiden? What will happen to me? Let me remind you, being that I don't have a choice in the rejection," I lashed out in anger, "my wolf will weaken. When you mark Megan, I will feel as if my chest has been ripped open. You will have your love for Megan to help get you through the weakened bond, but I won't be able to find another wolf mate since we are only given one in our *lifetime. Even though the bond will deteriorate, I will still hurt every day. I will have to see you together and be reminded of my rejection time and time again. Is that really what you want for me? I know you feel something for me. I saw it at the airport. Are you absolutely sure this is what you want to do?"*

"It's what I want," he whispered. "I've thought about this my whole life."

I tried one last plea."What about kids, Aiden? Megan is human. You won't be able to have a pup with her. How will you carry on your alpha line?"

"I'll deal with that when the problem arises."

"So you'll give up your mate and any future blood children just to spite fate?" I asked, hurt and shocked.

He nodded. "Yes. I'm really sorry. I just can't be with you." There was a hint of sadness in his voice.

"It's not that you can't. You just chose not to," I whispered in defeat. "So you're finally getting to choose for yourself, and that choice forces me into a life of pain and misery," I said as I looked him in the eyes. I thought I saw some indecision and pain, but it was quickly replaced by resignation and determination. I looked away as the tears started to fall. "Fine." I turned back to face him. "I will accept your rejection of the bond but only because like a mate should; I only want your happiness. You see, that's what mates are supposed to do: Protect each other, care for one another, and put each other first. I will endure the pain of the future for you, and I hope that it haunts you every night while you live your happily ever after with my sister." And with that said, I shifted into my light brown wolf and ran further into the darkness of the woods.

*   *   *

Shaking my head of the unwanted memories, I think about my life since then. I haven't done anything drastic to my appearance. I still wear my brown hair long and straight, no contacts cover my light green eyes, my full lips are still only covered in clear lip gloss, and I haven't changed from skinnys and tanks to ripped jeans and grungy t-shirts. No, the only change is my attitude.

The sweet carefree nature is gone. I now know how real life can be and it isn't a fairytale. My enthusiasm for life is gone. When you look into my eyes, you'll see emptiness that hides the constant pain.

I no longer live with my pack. Six months after my rejection, Aiden marked my sister and the pain was unbearable. I couldn't be around him and see him happy anymore. Yes, there were times when I was near him and could feel his wolf fighting for control but Aiden always pushed him back. I begged my parents to let me leave the pack and join my maternal aunt's pack— Her mate's pack in Hawaii, to be specific. My parents didn't understand why at first because I never told anyone about my rejection. I made up the excuse of it being hard to be around Aiden and Megan knowing I haven't found my mate yet. At least it was half true.

That's where I am now. A new pack, a new school, and hopefully, a new life. I should have an optimistic attitude, but I no longer have the illusion of happily ever after. Hope is something I seriously lack in the present. There is one good thing to come from all this.

"Harmony, get your lazy ass up so we can get to school. I don't want to miss all the fresh meat awaiting me. My game is on fire today. Just don't stare too hard at me 'cause you might be blinded by all this hotness."

There it is. My cousin Jared. He's the only one who knows about my rejection because, unlike my aunt and uncle, I can't hide the pain from him. He knows me too well, and it took all of my wolf strength to stop him from jumping on a plane to beat the crap out of Aiden. It's good though because he constantly takes my mind off of things with his crazy man whorish ways and wise remarks. His friends are awesome too. And are total eye candies. A few tried hitting on me when I was first introduced to the pack, but Jared gave all them death glares. He warned his player friends that I was completely hands off unless any of them were planning on putting a ring on my finger. I laughed at all the deathly ill expressions in the room after that announcement. Commitment is equal to a bad case of crabs in their minds. I can't wait 'til they meet their mates. It'll be fun watching them get tamed.

I get dressed in some black skinnys and an off-shoulder white top with a black tank underneath. I put my hair in a loose bun, gloss my lips, and slip into a pair of black gladiator sandals. As I'm tucking a fly away hair behind my ear, the opening of the front door announces Jace, Nate, and Brad's arrival. I make my way to their voices and find them in the kitchen as usual.

"Bro, I'm telling you. This year we're gonna score so much pu—"

"Lady in the room!" I shout, interrupting what I'm sure was gonna be one of Nate's more colorful terms for *vajayjay*.

"Right. Sorry, Harm. As I was saying, we're gonna score so much chicks because we're now seniors," Nate corrects himself excitedly.

"Well, I know I will, but I'm not too sure about you ugly mutts. Just don't stand too close to me and you'll have a chance since my sex appeal is just too massive," Jared boasts, a l in his usual arrogant self.

"Really, Jared? I know what's massive about you, and it's not your sex appeal or your weiner. Don't try to deny it. Our moms showered us together when we were little, and if I remember correctly, which I do, it was very, very, very tiny," I say, making sure I emphasized the size with my thumb and pointer fingers.

"Hey, that's because I haven't changed yet. Trust me. Massive isn't even a big enough word to describe it now," he argues, a tiny bit offended.

I cringe. "First of all, gross. And second, your ego is the only thing that's massive. I'm worried if you don't bring it down you might not be able to fit your fat head out the door."

"She's right. Besides, we all know my sexiness outshines all of you," Brad informs them.

"No way. I score the most ass . . . I mean chicks every year," Jace argues.

"That's only cause you don't have standards and will screw anything with two sets of lips," says Nate with a raised brow.

This sets off a whole new conversation about what's doable and what's not, followed by pushing and headlocks. These boys are too much and, even though I'm not excited about the day ahead, it promises to be entertaining.

If you enjoyed this sample, look for
My Second Chance Mate
on Amazon.

ASHLEY MICHELLE

His
to Claim

CHAPTER 1

"—Shift."

I was jolted out of my daydreaming by the sound of a loud voice ringing in my ear. I turned around with raised brows to find Darlene, the shift manager of the small family-owned diner, staring at me expectantly with a tray of dirty dishes in one hand. I had clearly missed the important parts of whatever she had been saying to me.

A sheepish grin worked its way up my face. "What was that?"

She rolled her eyes and blew a stray hair out of her face. "I *said*, do you mind covering the end of my shift for me? My babysitter called. Apparently, Graham is running a pretty high fever."

I nodded my head. "Sure, no problem." It wasn't like I had any plans for the evening anyway, other than obsessively checking the mail. There were only two weeks left before graduation, and I was yet to hear from any of the colleges I had applied to.

Darlene let out a small sigh. "Thanks, Scarlett. I owe you."

I waved my hand. "Don't worry about it. I know how hard it is on you being left to take care of Graham while Troy is away. I'm happy to help lighten the load." Her husband had to travel a lot for his job, and that left Darlene with extra parenting duties.

She gave me a grateful smile as she turned away with the tray of dishes. "You're truly an angel, Scarlett."

I snorted at her comment. "I already agreed to cover you. You don't need to kiss my butt anymore, Darlene."

She gave me a playful wink before turning away, disappearing through the kitchen door. I slowly turned back around with a sigh. This was going to be a long night of nothing but the virtual emptiness of the diner.

I was happy when a familiar face shuffled through the front door of the diner, setting off the little bell that hung above the door. He lifted his hand to his head, ruffling his dark hair which was starting to look shaggy around the edges. This boy would look like a mountain man if it weren't for my constant influence in his life. He met my gaze briefly as he reached out and grabbed one of the cheaply made menus from an empty table. He flipped through the pages quickly before setting it back down.

I pulled the pen and pad from the front pocket of my stained apron. "What can I get you, Wyatt?"

He shrugged as he moved closer toward me. "I think a cup of coffee will be fine. It's been a long day."

"It's going to be a bit longer. Darlene asked me to cover the end of her shift," I commented with an apologetic smile. Wyatt had promised to pick me up after my shift ended while I was running out the door this morning.

He let out a sigh, running his hand through his hair. "Of course, she did. Well, there *is* a meeting tonight. Guess it's going to be extra long for both of us, sweetheart," he replied with a sarcastic grin as I poured him a cup of coffee and placed it on the counter in front of me.

Darlene approached us carrying her purse, her jacket slung over her arm. "You know the coffee here is shit, Wyatt. I don't know why you keep ordering it when you only ever have a sip and leave the rest."

Wyatt ignored her comment. The two of them were always at each other's throats for reasons unknown to me. He pressed his hands to the counter, breathing in deeply. His nose scrunched up a bit, and he looked over at me. "You smell." I frowned at my cousins greeting as he sat himself down on a stool at the breakfast counter, grabbing the coffee.

"Gee, you really know how to compliment a girl," I grumbled, my voice dripping with sarcasm. My cousin and I had a very close relationship, considering that my parents had taken him in after his father ran off and his mother got sick. He returned the favor when my parents died, taking me into his home and raising me like I was his kid sister.

"God, Wyatt…" Darlene remarked as she threw her arms into the sleeves of her jacket, pulling up the collar. "Even if a woman does stink, you shouldn't comment on it. And you wonder why you're still single."

Her words brought a smile to my face, and I gave him a sharp look. I snickered as I turned away from my cousin who was pouting at the blunt reprimand he had received. I could see Winston, our cook, slaving away over the grill through the small hole, singing along to some garbage being gurgled out of the old boom box he kept in the kitchen. The diner was my home away from home, and its motley crew was my self-created wolf pack even if they were only humans.

"Wyatt," she said his name in a flat tone. Darlene had never cared much for my cousin. Maybe it's because he had a knack for putting his foot in his mouth… or maybe because they had gone "grown-up" together and he'd been quite the fool back in his younger years.

"See you tomorrow, Scarlett. Thanks again," she called.

I turned around to give her a quick wave. "See ya, Darlene. Tell Graham I said hello and hope he feels better," I called back as she exited the front door, the bell ringing again.

Wyatt lifted his gaze to mine, staring at me expectantly with wide eyes as if he was waiting for something. I stared back at him, shifting my hands to my hips. "Why are you looking at me like that? Do I have something on my face?" I reached up with a hand and wiped it across my cheek, checking to see if there was any food splatter. It was a hazard of the job.

"Can't you feel it, Scarlett?" he asked me in a soft voice so that no one else could hear. Hell, if it weren't for my extra-sensitive senses I probably wouldn't have heard him either.

I narrowed my eyes in confusion at his question. "What are talking about? Are you feeling okay, Wyatt?" I reached out and placed my hand on his forehead. He pulled back with a furrowed brow and looked at me as if I had two heads.

"After all the complaining and whining I had to listen to from you... are you seriously telling me that you don't feel even the slightest bit different?" he asked a little louder in an exasperated tone, waving his hand in the air dramatically. I had no idea what he was going on about or why he seemed so upset.

I looked around the small room at the other patrons who seemed content to ignore his outburst. I leaned forward, stuffing my notepad back into the pocket of my apron. "I don't know why you think I should feel different, but I feel the same as I always do. Unless you want to count the fact that my feet feel like I've been walking barefoot on hot coals. These ten-hour shifts have been killing me," I whined at him.

He gave me a slow blink, shaking his head. "Seriously, Scarlett?"

"What?" I questioned with a tired tone.

"Your scent—"

I held up a hand, cutting off his thought mid-sentence.

"I know. I know. I smell, but in my defense, you would smell too if you worked with greasy food all day," I snapped at him, growing tired of the conversation he was having with me. If I wanted to be insulted, I'm sure I could easily find one of my peers to satisfy that need without a problem. Human or shifter, they were all eager to tear someone else down to elevate themselves.

He shook his head at me. "No, your scent has changed, Scarlett. Your wolf has matured. I can smell her on you now."

I stared at him blankly as I digested his words. Had my wolf finally reached maturity without me noticing? I searched my mind for a sign of my wolf's presence. I had been waiting for this moment since I hit puberty. Most of my peers had already matured, leaving me like an outsider when it came to the pack.

All shifters had to go through two stages of puberty: the natural human one and the beast underneath. It could happen at any time, but basically, it meant that the connection between human and wolf was fully formed. It wasn't until this happens that we were allowed to attend actual pack events. Most of my friends had already matured. I had been left in the group of late bloomers. Sometimes, it happened that a wolf never matured. These people were seen as Omegas. They were still a part of the pack, but they would never be considered true wolves.

I shifted back and forth on my feet, concentrating hard. "I don't feel any different."

Wyatt took a sip of his coffee. "You will trust me." He pulled the mug away from himself, peering down into the cup with a small look of disgust before setting it down. "But you know what this means?"

"What?" I questioned with a raised brow.

He met my gaze with a knowing look. "You don't have to wait in the car like the other pups during the meeting tonight. You're a true wolf now," he teased as he gave me a wolfish grin. I rolled my eyes at his comment, but on the inside, I felt a bubble of excitement.

* * *

I had only ever seen the pack house from the outside, having never been allowed to enter it before. I found myself getting anxious as I followed Wyatt down the dirt driveway and around the side of the house. In the back, there was another building, about the size of a guest house.

I could hear the sound of happy voices carried on the gentle evening breeze. My palms felt sweaty in the pockets of my sweatshirt as my nerves got the better of me. Wyatt gave me a grin as he opened the door. "So it begins."

I rolled my eyes at him as I walked past him into the large open room. The smells of other pack members overwhelmed me for a moment. My eyes scanned the crowd warily, looking for familiar faces. I found my gaze gravitating towards the front of the room where the stream of bodies seemed to be moving.

That was the first time I saw *him.*

He stood near the front, greeting people with a friendly smile. My heart hammered in my chest as I watched him from where I stood at the back of the room. I had no idea who he was, but I knew he was perfect. His dark hair was shaved close to his head as if it had been shaved bare at some point and was finally being allowed to grow out. My eyes followed the length of his body, taking in every part of him. He had a lean body that spoke of endurance-honed muscles.

Wyatt elbowed my side. "Don't just stand there, Scarlett. People are starting to look at us." He urged me to move forward. I had to force my feet to move from where I had been anchored. My whole world seemed to be shifting on its axis, and I couldn't be sure I was standing on solid ground anymore.

My heart was in my throat as I approached my mate—at least that was what my wolf was telling me. This perfect male specimen was our mate, the one that the Goddess had ordained for us at birth. But what if he hated me? What if I wasn't what he was expecting? Insecurities that I had never felt before began to flood my brain.

I dug my heels into the floor. "I can't do this. Let's go home."

Wyatt grabbed onto my elbow and led me on. "You're being ridiculous. We all had to go through this, Scarlett. Consider it your official initiation into the pack." I gritted my teeth as every step brought me closer to the finality of my situation.

The Alpha and his mate were standing together, greeting the other pack members as they filed into the room, grabbing seats for the meeting. I remembered them from the times they had visited my home when I was much younger, way back when my mother was still alive, and my father held a prominent position in the pack. They looked older and a little more worn down, but that had to be expected of people in their positions.

"Alpha Aaron," Wyatt spoke formally as he reached out a hand, a standard human greeting. I danced on the balls of my feet, wishing that I hadn't accepted Wyatt's offer to join him. I was still in my work uniform, smelling like grease and probably looking unkempt from the busy workday… not the way I wanted to make my first impression on the pack.

"Wyatt," he replied, shaking the hand that had been offered to him with a firm grip, "it is good to see you again."

Wyatt beamed at the acknowledgment, turning his eyes toward the female beside the Alpha, bowing his head. "Luna Victoria."

She gave him a kind smile. "Wyatt."

Alpha Aaron's dark gaze shifted in my direction, a smile still on his lips. "And who is this beauty?" he questioned, lifting a brow as he examined me further. My cheeks rushed with heat, and I felt the sudden urge to hide behind my cousin like I did back in my younger years where I would cling to my mother's leg.

Wyatt wrapped his arm around my shoulder, pulling me in protectively to his side, and that only made me feel more embarrassed. "This is my cousin, Scarlett."

Luna Victoria gave me a knowing glance as she leaned into her mate's side. "Sweetheart, it's Conrad and Elizabeth's daughter."

"Of course, she is," he replied as if he had already known. My lips twitched with the urge to smile when she looked at me with a playful eye roll at his expense. Alpha Aaron crossed his arms over his wide chest, leaning forward toward me. "I can see it now that I've gotten a closer look. You've got Conrad's eyes."

"And Elizabeth's beautiful face," Luna Victoria remarked. "If I recall correctly, your mother was a late bloomer as well." I felt my head sink a little lower at her comment.

"David..." Luna Victoria called, turning toward my mate with a smile, "come over here real fast."

She glanced back at me. "Conrad helped train David when he was a young boy. I'm sure he will be very interested in meeting you." I felt my nerves spike as he turned in our direction, and I realized that he wasn't an average member of the pack. This was *their* son, the next heir: an Alpha born male.

I wanted to run, but my feet kept me firmly rooted in place. I was afraid to look up from the ground. What would I see staring back at me? I swallowed hard, trying to prepare myself for what was about to happen.

His shoes came into view, and I felt my wolf stirring under my skin. Wyatt elbowed me in the side. "Scarlett..." he hissed under his breath in a warning tone. I lifted my face to meet his gaze with bated breath.

His dark eyes widened in surprise as we drank each other in. Something in my mind snapped. I could feel it all, everything everyone had tried to explain to me about having a wolf. Her emotions and thoughts surged through me as I watched the corners of his mouth lift upwards into a smile.. a heart-stopping smile that was meant for only me.

I felt my own lips begin to mimic his. There were nothing ¬ one else in the room for us at that moment. This is what it felt like to have a mate, and I knew he was feeling the same sensations by the look in his eyes.

The moment was broken when a tall dark-haired female placed a kiss on his cheek. "I'm sorry I'm late, David. My shift went into overtime. I had to help Doctor McCarthy deliver the Johnsons' twins. Those pups are going to be a handful. I can tell you that now." She finished with a soft chuckle of amusement.

I hadn't even seen her approach us I had been so lost in a different world. My smile faded quickly as my brows furrowed in confusion as I glanced between the two of them. He looked rather stiff as she grabbed hold of his hand with hers, turning her face in my direction.

"Hello. I don't think I've seen you before." She tilted her head to the side.

"That's because she's only just matured, Eva," Luna Victoria commented toward her, both of them sharing a look of understanding like two people who've already been through it.

"This must be very exciting for you then," she remarked with a bright smile, completely unaware of what had happened between me and the male she was holding onto as if he were hers. My wolf was growling possessively in my mind, struggling to free herself so that she could eliminate the competition.

"David, this is Scarlett," Luna Victoria introduced me. "Conrad's daughter," she supplied as if it were my own special title.

I felt like the rug had been pulled out from under my feet and I was falling without anyone to catch me. My stomach was in my throat, but I forced myself to speak. "Hi…" I replied in a tense voice, finding it hard to hold his gaze.

David pulled his hand free from Eva's grasp and took a step towards me. He lifted his hand slightly like he w   reach out to me, but he thought better of it, deciding to pocket of his slacks instead.

"It's nice to meet you, Scarlett." Goo flesh, and I watched his pupils dilate a bit as

"Your father was a great man. The pack lost a great warrior when he passed away. I lost a dear friend," he added, trying to keep things from getting strange in front of all the onlookers. None of them seemed to know what had transpired between the two of us.

I gave him a small smile that didn't reach my eyes. "Thank you." He looked like he wanted to say something more to me, his lips parted slightly. Alpha Aaron stepped forward, his dark eyes calculating as he glanced between myself and his son. I lowered my gaze to the ground, clenching my jaw tightly.

"Well, we should get this meeting going." He wrapped his arm around his mate and pulled her into his side. "It's wonderful to have another true wolf added to the pack."

Wyatt grabbed my elbow, and I tensed slightly at the touch. Now that I could connect to my wolf, the world seemed too overwhelming. Every sensation moved through me like an exploding bomb. I let him lead me away to some empty seats, but my mind was adrift as I looked around the room. I had matured and met my mate, only to find out that he already had someone at his side. How could I compete with her?

My gaze focused on the female in question, Eva. She was a fully matured female compared to myself, who was still growing into my body, which was mostly knees and elbows. She seemed kind, and she didn't waver under the gaze of all the people in the room. She looked like a queen. I certainly wasn't much compared to her. That was why she was the one standing on the stage, holding his hand.

I sunk down lower in my seat. I could hear Alpha Aaron's voice as he spoke to the group, but none of the words were able to pierce through my racing thoughts.

"We are happy to announce that the mating ceremony of Eva and David will be held at the end of next month," Alpha Aaron said with pride in his voice, clapping David on the back as he stood next to a smiling Eva, hand in hand. My heart dropped, and I sucked in a painful breath. This wasn't how things were supposed to go. I was his mate, not her.

I couldn't sit in that room for another moment and listen to any more words. I leaned over to Wyatt. "I need to go," I whispered. He looked over at me in confusion as I rose up out of my chair and hurried toward the exit. I didn't look back, but I felt David's eyes on me, my body heating up everywhere his gaze drifted to. It was getting hard to breathe as I pushed open the door and flung myself out into the night, letting the cool air wash over me.

I sucked in ragged breaths as I tried to overcome the ache in my chest. No one had warned me maturing would be so painful.

If you enjoyed this sample, look for
His to Claim
on Amazon.

CATCHING GENESIS

NICOLE RIDDLEY

CHAPTER I
Worst Birthday Ever

"Happy birthday!!!" They chorus as soon as I step into the kitchen.

Mom is beaming, carrying a stack of pancakes dripping with maple syrup to the breakfast table. A single candle is burning right on top of it. Dad is already sitting at the table, smiling wide.

"Hyaaaahhhh!!!" I hear my sister yells as she bounds down the stairs behind me.

I huff the candle out before she even reaches the bottom of the stairs.

"Genesis! Damn it!!!" she yells in frustration.

"Autumn Harmony Fairchild! Language!" Mom admonishes her.

I flash my sister a victorious grin before I turn back around and give mom and dad an angelic, innocent smile.

My sister Autumn is two years younger than I am. Last week was her birthday, and I blew out the candle on her special birthday pancakes. I knew she would try to seek revenge. Unfortunately for her, I came downstairs early today, and just like that, I've foiled her evil plan of revenge.

Mom disappears into the living room and I give my sister another mischievous grin. She takes her seat beside me at the breakfast table and scowls at me.

Not only are our birthdays close together, Autumn and I look almost the same. Sometimes people thought that we were twins. From our light hazel eyes to our red hair. The only difference is that Autumn's face is a little bit rounder than mine and my red hair is a darker red, closer to Auburn, while Autumn is more of a strawberry blond. I'm also a bit taller than she is. I'm 5'11" which is just a little over the average height of most she-wolves, and Autumn is 5'9".

"Happy Birthday, by the way," says Autumn "Are you excited yet?"

"Excited about going to school on my birthday?" I ask back, sharing my stack of pancakes with her. Mom gave me too much.

"No, silly! About possibly meeting your mate today!" she replies, looking at me as if I've lost my marbles.

"I don't know...I'd be more excited if I don't have to be stuck in school the whole day on my birthday." I am, but I'm not going to admit that to her.

Yeah, we're the regular werewolf family, and as werewolves, we get the gift to sense out our mate as soon as we turn eighteen. That means for me, sometime during lunchtime today, if my mate is already eighteen and he's living somewhere around here.

"I had to go to school on my birthday too," she reminds me. "I can't wait to turn 18 so I can meet my mate already." She sighs. "Oh, I bet he's so hot. Hotter than your mate. The hottest guy in the whole pack."

"My baby girl might be meeting her mate today!" mom exclaims as she comes back from the living room where she hid my birthday gift. She places my gift on the table and says, "You're excited, right?"

I'm going to be asked this question over and over again today, it seems.

"No, she's not. She's not going to let any boys near her until she's at least 40," announces dad.

I resist the urge to roll my eyes at both of them as I rip open the wrapper. I already knew what's inside. It's a new airbrush paint set and mediums. I'd been giving obvious hints about wanting it for months.

"Thanks, mom, dad! I can't wait to try it out." I give them both a hug.

Actually, I am very excited about meeting my mate. I can feel my wolf, Ezra, being restless and excited the whole night.

My Ezra is excited, which makes me even more excited. That's why I'm all dressed up today. Well okay, so I'm dressed the same way I always dressed for school every day. Jeans and t-shirt. Nothing special, but yeah, I am very excited about possibly meeting my mate today. Not that I would ever admit that to my parents. Goddess, no! That would be so embarrassing.

Autumn and I walk to school. It's just a 15-minute walk. The weather is mild and I always enjoy the short walk.

When we get to school, Autumn heads off to where her friends are waiting, while I stroll inside to where my friends usually hang out.

Penny, Reese, and River are hanging out by our lockers as usual. Reese and River are mates. Penny hasn't turned 18, so she hasn't found her mate yet.

"Happy birthday, girl!" yells Penny as soon as she spots me, drawing the attention of most other students loitering the hallway.

She pulls me into a hug and soon after, Reese and River do the same.

"You're going to have to wait until after school for your gift," says Reese excitedly.

"You're going to be 18! Finally. Are you excited?" asks Penny.

"I don't know. I think I'm a bit nervous," I admit.

"Yeah, I'd probably be nervous too, meeting our mates for the first time...but it's exciting too!" shrieks Penny, clapping her hands excitedly.

"Don't be nervous, Genesis. It'll be okay," soothes Reese.

"It's better than okay. It's the best thing that's ever happened to me," says River, wrapping his arms around Reese.

"Awww...isn't he sweet?" coos Reese with that look in her eyes as she stares up at River. "Anyway, we'll see you losers at lunch!" she says as River pulls her away.

"Later, bish!" says Penny. I just give them a little wave before I start digging my locker for my books.

"Boy, I wish we can mate with one of those hotties." she suddenly whispers as she stares dreamily over my shoulder.

I turn around to the sight of three male lycans walking down the hallway. They are so tall, about 6'5 or more.

You see, lycans are different than us regular werewolves. For one thing, they are known to be the direct descendants of the moon goddess, so they are treated like the nobility in the werewolf world. In fact, our king is a lycan.

Second, they are bigger, faster, fiercer, smarter, stronger and more powerful than any werewolves, even the alphas. They are like killing machines when provoked. You don't want to mess with them.

Third, in their human form, they are better looking and more attractive than us regular werewolves who are considered to be better looking than most humans...like way more. So, lycans are god-like smoking hot.

Fourth, they don't have to belong to a pack. They can travel anywhere alone and not be considered a rogue.

And fifth, they don't have mates chosen for them by the moon goddess like us regular werewolves. They get to choose their own mates, either another lycans, regular werewolves or even humans they're attracted to. They would form a bond, much like a werewolf's mate bond, or even stronger if they're both attracted to each other, to begin with. Once, I heard a story about a lycan who took an already mated she-wolf, leaving her mate broken since there's nothing anybody could do about it.

There are only three male and two female lycans in our school of over six hundred students. Only 10 percent out of those six hundred students are humans. All the teachers and the administration of this school are werewolves too.

The three lycans who are heading this way right now are Lazarus, Caspian, and Constantine. The female lycans who are not around right now are Serena and Milan. I haven't seen those two around for a few days now. They are, of course, drop-dead gorgeous.

I think Serena is mated to Lazarus, and Milan may or may not mated to Caspian. There are rumors that those three boys are closely related to our ruling king, but we don't know for sure. There's not much else that we know about the lycans in our school. Not even their last names. They keep to themselves and pay no attention to us mere werewolves and humans. That makes them so mysterious and much more attractive to the female population here.

So yeah, those three god-like looking Adonis are drop-dead gorgeous. Jaw dropping. Panty melting. And I so would be making a fool of myself if I don't stop drooling over them—like Penny— and all the other un-mated she-wolves around us right now.

I quickly turn back and start pulling books that I need from my locker. There's no way a lycan would be interested in an Omega like me. Lycans are attracted to strength, intelligence, and beauty. Besides, I might be meeting my mate today. Flutters of excitement start in my tummy at the thought. My wolf Ezra is getting excited. We've been waiting for this for years.

I grab Penny's hand and drag her along to get to our class before the bell rings. We share English lit class together.

"I can't wait to be out of this place soon. Thank goodness we only have a few months of school left." I inform Penny.

"Oh, I don't know...I don't mind school. There are lots of hot guys around, like those lycans." she says. " Or like those boys...too bad they're such jerks and man-whores," whispers Penny in my ear as we pass the popular group in our school.

Logan Carrington, our future Alpha is kissing or rather shoving his tongue down the throat of Mia Brown, the head cheerleader. They're together, but everybody knows they're seeing other people on the side. Zeke Walker, future Delta has his arms around Elle Johnson and Marie Jacobs, while talking to Hunter Stevens, the future Beta. I think Hunter isn't so bad. He doesn't seem like a player like the other two. He talked to me once or twice before and seems pretty nice.

"I wonder if he's digging for hidden treasure down her esophagus," I whisper back and Penny starts laughing.

Hunter turns to look at us, then his eyes shift to me, looking amused. I think his lips twitch a bit like he's trying not to laugh. Cuddly bunny and fuzzy slippers! He must have heard me.

I practically push Penny into our English lit class, while trying to hide my flaming face.

Yes, I do think that those boys are pretty hot. There's no way in hell would I admit it to anyone, though.

Logan and Zeke have this class with me and Penny. They enter the class ten minutes after the teacher started teaching. Not that she would say anything.

Logan slides into a seat in front of me and my wolf stirs. I stare at the back of his golden head for a bit. Logan is about 6'2", well-muscled; has high cheekbones and sharp features like a model; bright blue eyes and golden blond hair. When he smiles, wow. His straight white teeth and those adorable dimples are simply to die for. Well, maybe I have a bit of a crush on him. Just a little bit. I think a lot of the girls here do.

The rest of the classes went pretty well —boring and uneventful. Art is the only subject I look forward to. Did I mention that my mom is an artist? Well, she is, and I'm very proud of her.

Lavinia Fairchild is quite well known. Every werewolf household here has at least one or two of her prints or originals. My dream is to go to an art school and be as good as her.

We are sitting at our regular table during lunchtime when I suddenly smell that wonderful smell that I can't describe. Whatever it is, it smells awesome! Ezra, my wolf is fighting to be let out and take control. I guess I was born during lunch time. I stand up and start to follow my nose to identify where that smell comes from. I can't help it. I have to find it. I vaguely hear my friends calling my name, but I can't seem to focus on anything else but that smell.

My nose brings me to the popular group table. Oh no, I can't seem to bring my feet to stop. Ezra's taking control. Everybody stops talking. Logan Carrington? My mate is Logan Carrington? No no no no.

His beautiful blue eyes widen as he looks up at me. His eyes softened as they roam my face. I can see lust and hunger flitting across his face briefly as his eyes move up and down my body. But then he looks away quickly. His breathing ragged. My wolf howls with joy and my first instinct is to jump on him and stake my claim.

"Follow me," he says gruffly, and swiftly walks out the cafeteria through the back door.

I follow him across the lawn to an Oak tree. The tree provides us a bit of privacy from prying eyes.

"What's your name?" he finally asks. His beautiful eyes are not even looking at me. I can't seem to tear my eyes away from his perfect face. The sun is glinting in his golden hair. The shadows fall across the planes of his sharp features.

"Genesis... Genesis Fairchild," I finally answer.

"Fairchild? You're an Omega, aren't you?" he says. "I can't have an Omega as my mate. My pack needs a stronger luna, not someone weak like you. Besides, I love someone else. Mia makes a better Luna than you ever could." Each word is like a knife slicing through my chest. Ezra whimpers.

Oh no, suddenly I know what's going to happen. My heart starts to race, my breaths come out short and shallow. I don't know what's happening to me. All I know is that my heart is breaking.

"I, Logan Carrington, future Alpha of Shadow Geirolf pack, reject you, Genesis Fairchild, as my mate and future luna of my pack," he utters coldly, not looking at me once.

My wolf cries and howls in pain. She doesn't understand. Why is our mate hurting us so?

"Hey baby, what's going on?" says Mia, wrapping her arms around him. Where did she come from?

"Nothing to worry about, sweetheart," he answers.

She looks me over with disdain. She pointedly pulls Logan's head down and plants her lips on his for a claiming kiss. He wraps his arm around her waist, and then they turn and leave. I watch her whispers something in his ear and they both laugh.

I watch them laugh as I fall to the ground, clutching at my chest. Oh, goddess, it feels like he just plunged a knife deep into my chest and twisted it. Then he just keeps yanking the knife up and down, left and right over and over again until there's nothing left of my heart but a bloody, twisted ugly gash in my chest. Ezra curls up in pain then goes silent.

*   *   *

I'm lying on my bed now. Everything was a blur after I fell. I remember seeing my friends Penny, Reese, and River running to me, calling my name in panic. They were asking me what was wrong. River carried me to his car. Then I don't remember anything else. The three of them must've brought me home.

"Talk to me, honey. Tell me what happened," says mom gently, pushing my hair from my forehead.

"He rejected me, mom. My mate rejected me." My eyes are tearing up again. I still find it hard to believe that this is really happening to me. I was wishing that it was just a horrible nightmare.

There are a thousand different emotions chasing across mom's face. Disbelief, anger, pain, sadness....

All the pain comes back. I start twisting in my bed and mom wraps her arms around me. Even mom's comforting loving arms can't stop or ease the pain away.

"It hurts so bad. Make it stop...make it stop. Mom, please make it go away." I sob, clawing at my chest. "I'd do anything...just make it stop." Goddess, it hurts so much, I want to die.

"My baby. My poor baby girl," cries mom. Tears running down her face as she hugs me close, willing my pain to go away.

After what feels like hours, I calm down, or maybe I'm just too exhausted to even shed a tear. Only my chest is moving up and down. Sleep doesn't come easily. In the middle of the night, all alone in the darkness, tears leak out again, falling down my face silently. My wolf, Ezra, is completely silent now, but I can feel her crushing pain, as well as my own.

I had been looking forward to meeting my mate since I was four. Mom told me about it like it's the best thing to ever happen to a werewolf. I had been waiting for someone who would love me and protect me and be by my side no matter what.

All werewolves look forward to meeting their mates. It's very rare that a mate gets rejected, but it happened to me. What is wrong with me?

All werewolves know you only got one chance of having a mate. What now? Will I ever be loved and have a family? Will my wolf, Ezra, ever comes out and be the same again? A werewolf without his or her wolf is only an empty shell. Most would eventually die or go crazy after they lost their mates. Their wolves decide to disappear when the pain gets unbearable. Now I understand how very painful it is, and we're not even mated yet. Will I die or go crazy too? I hope Ezra is strong enough to stay.

How could the moon goddess do this to me? What did I do to deserve this? I didn't ask for an Alpha. She could've matched me to another lowly Omega and I'd still be happy. As long as I am loved, I'll be happy.

How did this day turn out so bad? Worst. Birthday. Ever.

If you enjoyed this sample, look for
Catching Genesis
on Amazon.

ACKNOWLEDGEMENTS

I want to acknowledge my amazing readers, my wonderful publishers and my many supporters.

AUTHOR'S NOTE

Thank you so much for reading *The Run*! I can't express how grateful I am for reading something that was once just a thought inside my head.

Please feel free to send me an email. Just know that my publisher filters these emails. Good news is always welcome.
amber_lee@awesomeauthors.org

I'd love to hear your thoughts on the book. Please leave a review on Amazon or Goodreads because I just love reading your comments and getting to know you!

Can't wait to hear from you!

Amber Lee

ABOUT THE AUTHOR

Amber Lee lives on the snowy plains of Minnesota with her son and endless amounts of books. She lives comfortably with the knowledge others can appreciate the sarcasm and odd thoughts that so many psychiatrists couldn't.